BECOMING
HIS
MONSTER

AMELIA HUTCHINS

BECOMING
HIS
MONSTER

Copyright ©January 1st 2019 Amelia Hutchins
ISBN: 978-0-9977201-2-9

Authored by: Amelia Hutchins
Cover Art Design:Tenaya Jayne
Copy Editor: Gina Tobin
Edited & Formatted by: E & F Indie Services

Published by: Amelia Hutchins
Published in (United States of America)
10 9 8 7 6 5 4 3 2 1

STOP!

Read the warning below before purchasing this book.

TRIGGER WARNING: This book includes scenes of graphic violence and sex does have scenes that might affect sensitive readers. Rape isn't a joke, nor is it used for titillation in this book. If you know someone or have been a victim of rape yourself, get help. Don't let this asshole get away with it because chances are, your attacker will do it to someone else. You're not alone in this. Thousands of people are raped daily; there are hundreds of people who go free after attacking their victim because the victim is afraid to report or discuss the crime for a variety of reasons. No means no. If you or someone you know has been a victim of rape, get help. **RAINN** is available in many countries, and is a free confidential hotline. It is free to call and available 24/7 call

1-800-656-HOPE

WARNING!

This book is **dark**. It's **sexy**, hot, and **intense**. The author is human, as you are as well. Is the book perfect? It's as perfect as I could make it. Are there mistakes? Probably, then again, even **New York Times top published** books have minimal mistakes because like me, they have **human editors**. There are words in this book that won't be found in the standard dictionary, because they were created to set the stage for a paranormal-urban fantasy world. Words such as 'sift', 'glamoured', and 'apparate' are common in paranormal books and give better description to the action in the story than can be found in standard dictionaries. They are intentional and not mistakes.

About the hero: chances are you may **not** fall instantly in **love** with him, that's because **I don't write men you instantly love**; you grow to love them. I don't believe in **instant-love**. I write flawed, raw, caveman-like **assholes** that eventually let you see their redeeming qualities. They are **aggressive**, **assholes**, one step above a caveman when we meet them. You may *not* even like him by the time you finish this book, but I promise you will **love** him by the end of this **series**.

About the heroine: There is a chance, that you might

think she's a bit naïve, or weak, but then again who starts out as a badass? Badasses are a product of growth and I am going to put her through **hell**, and you get to watch **her** come up **swinging** every time I knock her on her ass. That's just how I do things. How she reacts to the set of circumstances she is put through, may not be how you as the reader, or I as the author would react to that same situation. Everyone reacts differently to circumstances and how Magdalena responds to her challenges, is how I see her as a character and as a person.

I don't write love stories: I write fast paced, knock you on your ass, make you sit on the edge of your seat wondering what happens next books. If you're looking for cookie cutter romance, this isn't for you. If you can't handle the ride, *un-buckle your seatbelt and get out of the roller-coaster car now*. **If not, you've been warned.** If nothing outlined above bothers you, carry on and **enjoy the ride!**

DEDICATION

This one is for everyone just trying to make it through the week without stabbing someone in the eye with a fork. Because let's be honest, we all want to occasionally do it. Look at you, you badass, not stabbing anyone. That's a win! And to all my girls, you know who you are. You are my rock stars. To my group; you're my tribe. You get me.

ALSO BY AMELIA HUTCHINS

The Fae Chronicles

Fighting Destiny

Taunting Destiny

Escaping Destiny

Seducing Destiny

Unraveling Destiny

Unraveling Desstiny - *Coming Soon*

The Elite Guards

A Demon's Dark Embrace

Claiming the Dragon King

A Guardian's Diary

Darkest Before Dawn

Death Before Dawn

Midnight Rising *2018 (Final Book)*

MONSTERS SERIES

Playing With Monsters

Sleeping With Monsters

Becoming His Monster

Last Monster Book *TBA*

Upcoming Series

Wicked Knights

Oh, Holy Knight (Such Violent Delight Anthology)

A Crown of Ashes

TBA

If you're following the series for the Fae Chronicles, Elite Guards, and Monsters, reading order is as follows:

Fighting Destiny
Taunting Destiny
Escaping Destiny
Seducing Destiny
A Demon's Dark Embrace
Playing with Monsters
Unraveling Destiny
Sleeping with Monsters
Claiming the Dragon King
Oh, Holy Knight (Such Violent Delights Anthology)
Becoming his Monster

BECOMING
HIS
MONSTER

Death wasn't my ending. It was merely my beginning. Sometimes you had to break everything down to bare bones; you had to destroy everything you were to become what you were created to be. I'm me, only better.

Lena Fitz-Motherfucking-Gerald

CHAPTER
one

It seems to me, that love could be labeled poison and we'd drink it anyways. *~Atticus*

My eyes slowly slid from the storm brewing above us back to the charred remains of the club. Club Chaos was nothing more than a gutted-out shell of the once glorious nightclub. I'd watched Lucian set fire to it, his midnight eyes reflecting the flames that burned within his soul before he'd turned, walking away from it. They'd loaded the covens into waiting buses, moving them to Spokane, into the newly remodeled Guild.

It hurt, watching them mourn me as they assumed I was still buried in that nameless grave next to Joshua's. Lucian hadn't burned the club down because he'd had to; no, he'd burned it to the ground because he'd wanted to. They mourned who I had been, and I mourned her as well.

It didn't matter, though, because I wasn't that girl anymore. I mourned what I had once been, but I wasn't upset to let that girl go. She'd been weak, selfless, and unable to take the reins on her own life—but I could now.

I wasn't held back anymore; my emotions didn't hold sway over the choices I made anymore. It was freeing to not care, not having to consider others when I made a choice. But it didn't change the sadness I knew I should feel at watching them mourn me.

Mourning *her*. Not me.

"Do you feel that?" Joshua asked, interrupting my internally fucked-up thoughts. His eyes slowly settled on the rubble of the club and a slow whistle escaped his full lips. "That's eventful."

"I feel it, whatever it is, it's heading right towards us," I announced, turning away from the pile of bricks and debris that had once been the only thing standing between us and certain doom.

"Not towards us, Lenny. It's following the sweet scent of witchlings, right to the Guild," he corrected as he pushed a strand of hair that had fallen into my face away, tucking it behind my ear. My eyes darted behind him to where the others like us stood, silently awaiting orders. "This isn't our fight anymore."

"It may not be our fight, but it is our bloodline they seek to destroy. I'm not going to watch them feed on our coven, brother. You don't have to come," I said when a muffled sound of agreement erupted behind us. "I can handle it on my own."

"Of course I do," he shot back, irritable that I'd even consider leaving him out of the fight. His dead eyes held mine in silent rebuke as he shuffled his feet and slipped his hands into the pockets of the jeans he wore. "You and I, Lenny, we're in this shit together now, sis. Me and you against the world, right?"

"Yes, but it isn't their fight. They're not blood, and I'm pretty sure that whatever he is, he can kill pretty much anything. Maybe even us, which makes this high-risk and not their fight. I'm going with or without you, now. They're moving faster as if they scent blood in the air. The choice is theirs to make, but I'm leaving," I said, vanishing into thin air after one last look at the burnt-out remnants of Club Chaos.

I materialized on the side of an abandoned building in downtown Spokane. I slowly scanned the Guild, noting that even in the blackout of the entire Pacific Northwest, lights burned brightly from within. It was a beacon in the endless darkness that had consumed our area, a hope for those who weren't strong enough to stand against what was left of this world.

We remained far enough away to be undetected by the creatures that helped the covens depart the buses and navigate the street to the tall steps of the Guild. I waited in silence as I let my body become one with the shadows, allowing them to absorb a part of me as I watched the deadly beings that had now become a part of this world.

"You're not alone anymore," Joshua said, pulling me back from the edge of a building to where he and the others stood, awaiting orders. "Get your hood up. He won't let you go if he sees you, and no matter what you think, you're not ready for them to see you yet. You're not mentally ready to face him or our mother. Unless you're ready for them to know you're back from the grave. You died, remember?" he scoffed.

"I didn't really die," I shrugged as I watched Lucian's tall frame emerge from one of the buses. I swallowed hard, taking in his hard, muscled form with an ache that shouldn't even be there lodged in my throat. "I just ceased to be human."

"To them, Lenny, you did. Lucian raged for weeks,

and now you're about to pop up on his radar again. He's going to demand answers you cannot explain yet. He's going to expect you to be the same girl you were, and that version of you is dead. It's going to be like you felt when I told you who I was inside the cabin. He still sits beside your grave and silently stares at it, which means he's still grieving you. You wanted to know what he is; this is going to destroy you figuring it out without interfering in that."

"It isn't me he sits beside that grave visiting, it's her. It's always been her he wanted. I just happened to be her fucking shell. I'm pretty sure he may be shocked at my sudden return from the grave, but I also think it's what I house inside of me that he will crave. Not so much my flesh or that I am still here. And we have a plan, Joshua, stick to it. I want answers; they have them inside the Guild. Can you do that?"

"You know I can, Lenny. Do you think the runes will hold them long enough for us to save them?" he asked, changing the subject to the matter at hand.

"I think they will, but not for too long. You'll need to be gone when they fail because I doubt they'll fuck around long enough to see whose side of this war we are on. We need a distraction to be able to get close enough to them, but also to disturb the air enough to see the creatures when they get here. I can feel them, they're close."

"Music works, yeah?" Brandon drawled, his Southern accent thicker than normal. It tended to rise when fear etched into his youthful face. "I can find enough stereos to cause static and disrupt the air enough to see them fuckers. You reckon they'll give pause with the music long enough to let us get close enough to lay down the rune stones?" he asked.

"I think if they come at us, a certain little sister of

mine can give them pause. I don't fancy dancing with the devil that can end whatever we've become." Joshua watched me, testing my readiness to do what was needed if the situation called for it. The others didn't know I'd planned to get captured to ferret out answers, nor did they need to know.

"Whatever it takes," I uttered beneath my breath as I stared at the man who had once been my lover. Anger rushed through me as the carnal memories replayed in my mind. Joshua's words registered in my mind amongst the chaos, and I snorted. Whatever we'd become? No one really knew what or why we'd survived our deaths. Only that we no longer held mortal souls. We were soulless, and yet we had somehow clung to life without them. Joshua had recanted his own end, and I'd listened, more confused than I'd been, which had sent us searching for answers that weren't forthcoming. It had been why I'd known taking my life wouldn't be my ending.

Joshua had told me his own tale inside that cabin, and I'd left knowing that no matter what happened, I'd come back. That I would always come back. The issue was, I wasn't the same, and I felt it all the way to my bones.

"We're out of time," I announced as the air shifted and the creatures on the stairs leading into the Guild paused, sensing trouble brewing. Brandon vanished to start his tasks, and I waited, watching Synthia and Ryder as they directed the witches into the building that was heavily warded. Those wards pulsed and glowed against the sunset that rose and bathed the world in a pink and purple shade of beauty.

Lucian stepped away from the others. His expensive suit had been exchanged for jeans and a tight-fitting shirt that hugged his body like a lover's caress. Muscles bunched against it with every subtle move of his powerful frame. His black hair was tied behind his neck, and a touch of stubble covered his strong jawline. Black, unfathomable depths of midnight scanned the parking lot where the last of the buses had just pulled in to drop off the last of the witches. I swallowed hard as those midnight eyes moved in my direction, scanning the darkened shadows where we hid, and tugged at something I'd thought I'd managed to kill when I'd taken my life.

I pulled the cloak up tightly around my face, pulling the faceguard up as I did. My weapons lined my back, weapons I'd trained with until exhaustion claimed me night after night. From morning until night, I trained to learn what I had become, to test the limits of this new, improved body. And every night when the sun set behind the mountains, I lay in bed, dreaming of those midnight eyes and the secrets they held.

Betrayal stung, the memories of my death were foggy at best, but then I'd been leaking brain fluid as well as spinal fluid as I'd done what I had to do. Pieces of it were fragmented, lost to me. It didn't matter how many times I replayed it, or searched my mind for those memories, I couldn't grasp onto them. The only thing that stood out was him; speaking to the whore he'd loved. The woman who'd ruined my life and countless others in her never-ending need for revenge.

"Are you sure you're ready to do this? You can sit out; no one will blame you for doing so," Joshua assured me. I turned my gaze to the creatures who now pawed the earth, disturbing the ground they stood upon. "We're out of time." Red eyes stared at the helpless witches who slowly made the tireless trek from the buses to the stairs leading up to the Guild. They eyed their prey. "They can't sense them." His words hung in the air between us as I watched the hellish creatures inching closer as their prey lies in wait, unaware of the horror stalking them. Joshua spat on the ground in annoyance, and I patted my multitude of weapons one last time.

"Let's do this then, shall we?" I popped out of existence, landing atop the Guild as I stared down at the creatures who continually worked to get the witches inside. I tensed, waiting as the others formed a line around the staircase once the last witch had passed the bottom step. Once she had, I materialized beside Joshua, displacing time and air as noise erupted around us.

Imagine Dragons's *Whatever It Takes* exploded around us as Josh blinked away the distortion from moving with inhuman speed while I focused on the hellhound-looking creatures and their misshaped handlers. Yellow skin stretched over faces as if the skin they used had once belonged to someone or something else. Yellow eyes that resembled cats stared from within the borrowed skin as they slowly, clumsily proceeded to close the distance between us. All hell was about to break loose, and I smiled coldly, needing the pain that came with fighting.

CHAPTER
two

Change is to focus all of your energy, not on fighting the old, but on building the new. *~Socrates*

The air around us exploded with power; sizzling against my flesh as I turned, peering over my shoulder as Lucian and the others processed the scene unfolding before their eyes. The Fae moved in behind him and his men, moving dangerously close to us. They assessed the situation with cold, calculated gazes that sent a wave of worry washing through me. Idiots, all of them. They failed to see the real threat just beyond the veil that hunted them like moths to a flame. My eyes moved between the huge, looming beast that foamed at the mouth past giant, razor-sharp teeth and the creatures who I knew were just as deadly.

We slowly turned as one, our minds linked as we tossed the smooth, black stones towards the stairs. The wards ignited, runes melting into useless heaps of black fluid as it buzzed and locked them into its protective barrier. I watched Lucian closely, his luscious mouth curved into a deep frown as he stopped inches from the melted runes.

"You will die if you don't remove them this instant," he warned calmly, as if he didn't care one way or another. It sent a warning through me, knowing if anyone could get out of that barrier, it was him and his men. His tone was seductive, alluring, and the exact thing I'd spent the last few months craving and longing for. "I won't ask you again. Remove them or die."

I opened my eyes against that voice, turning away from him to calm the fluttering in my chest. My family was in there, inside that Guild and helpless against these monsters that hungered to consume them. I listened as he and his men, along with the others, started working to undo the wards and runes we'd placed.

"Let's do this," I said begrudgingly. My arms itched as the runes I'd painted on them ignited, sending more power into my body. I soothed my useless organs, maintaining the death that kept them unbreathing, the blood refusing to course through them as power erupted instead. My heart threatened to thunder against my chest as it tried to awaken. A swelling of pain crushed against it in a viselike grip as I ignored my past, and embraced my future. Monsters at my back and monsters in front of me swam in my vision as I gripped the dual swords behind my back and brought them forth, crouching in fight against the ones who wished to feed off the blood of the witches.

The monsters at my back could wait. I lifted my swords, pushing the faceguard down to be able to see the monsters in front of me. Chaos was about to break loose, and I didn't need my vision or orders disturbed. "They're coming!" It came out as a hiss of warning as the others moved closer, forming a line with us and the Guild at our backs. We waited as they slowly moved forward, their masters centered in their midst, issuing silent commands. They stood well over seven feet tall, giants with wolf-type creatures that easily reached their waists.

"There," Joshua called out and swung his blade as the first wolf lunged. He severed the head, sending it back towards its master, who screamed his displeasure. The body thundered to the ground, releasing black ooze that pooled around it onto the pavement. I heard the others behind us growl and hiss as what we were really doing registered. They were under attack by creatures who wanted what they were currently herding into the Guild: Witches. *Our fucking witches.*

My blades came up, lashing out as the air crackled with a beast that exploded forward. They moved as if they sifted, displacing air as they blinked in and out of existence, or more to the point, back into this plane. As if they could now cross the barrier between their world and ours with a mere order from their master. With every portal opening without warning, more and more creatures passed into our world effortlessly.

We'd searched for a way to close the portals but even standing guard to kill any creature brazen enough to cross over as we stood guard, it was an endless fight. There was also the issue that a lot of creatures had already crossed, and were here now. These ones, however, were mindless killing machines that tended to feed off the blood of witches. We'd hunted them for weeks, learning their strengths and weaknesses as they slaughtered coven after coven gluttonously.

It wasn't until we learned that they were being controlled that we started making headway. But as we did, they changed tactics. Their scent had changed as well, and with it, we'd lost them until now.

One of the masters closed the distance between us, his sluggish movements turning sharp and calculated as he moved to fight me. I smiled coldly at him, lifting my blades as I pulled more power to me.

I stepped closer, intending to remove its head from its shoulders when it toppled over without me making a move. I glared at the gushing black blood that pulsed from the severed neck. "That was my kill," I muttered at Joshua, who glared at me.

"Then focus," he snapped harshly as his head shook. "Get out of your fucking head and get into the fight."

"I'm here," I argued, already running at one of the creatures. I flipped mid-run, launching myself into the air as I landed smoothly on its shoulders on my knees, bending forward, shoving my blade through its chest as I finished flipping back onto my feet. I wiggled my brow at Joshua, who stared back at me with wide, horrified eyes.

I slipped one sword back into its sheath and touched my naked face, my own eyes rounded, and I turned to find midnight ones staring right back at me. Lucian's eyes narrowed as it registered who was standing in the middle of the chaos unfolding in the parking lot before him. Chaos raged around us as the world stopped as we stared at each other.

"Lenny, go now. It's too fucking soon," Joshua demanded, aborting the mission we'd agreed on. I didn't move, remaining rooted to the spot with my eyes locked into the endless zeniths of midnight. "Lenny!" he shouted over the raging battle, as swords clanked and met around us. His hands shook me, and I dispelled the panic that threatened to choke me.

We stood in the middle of the battle as blades sliced

around us, sending black blood oozing and splattering over us as I decided my next step.

"The wards and runes are down!" someone shouted, and I swallowed hard as I turned and stared at the spot Lucian had just been at. We moved, pushing through enemies and fighting our way to the back of the line, or so I thought we had.

"Go, get out of here," Joshua screamed, but it was guttural, wrong. I turned, staring at my brother and the monster that held him. I unleashed power, sensing the storm clouds that clapped thunderously above the battle that continued to unfold. Lucian held Joshua; I withdrew my blades, inching forward to save him.

"Creature," Lucian hissed from where he stood a few feet away. Joshua dangled helplessly in his grasp, hanging in his deadly grip. Anger laced with ice-cold fear as the knowledge of what he may or may not be able to do to him registered in my brain.

I pulled my mask up and over my head, dropping it onto the blood-covered street as I revealed the ugly scar that adorned my neck like a fine string of diamonds. His eyes flinched as if he'd been physically slapped in the face as he took in the damage. His body tensed as blue flames danced upon his fingertips.

"Port," I begged, but Joshua shook his head as a strangled noise escaped past his lips. I could see the fear dancing in his eyes as I tried to instruct him to leave, but he couldn't.

"He can't." Lucian's tone was lethal, malice dancing upon his face and features as he stared at me. I watched helplessly as Lucian tossed Joshua towards Spyder. Spyder watched me silently, his eyes taking in the scar with an emotion I couldn't place. His fingers erupted with flames, and Joshua cried out as it burned against his flesh. "Him for you," he said, his eyes slowly dropping to land on my midsection which was bared to his gaze. Slowly, ever so slowly his throat bobbed as his eyes lifted to hold mine once more. They locked with mine in silent battle.

"Sorry about your girlfriend, Lucian." I smiled, locking onto the tick that now moved in his jaw as he flinched and bared his flat, white teeth in warning.

"Lena wasn't my fucking girlfriend," he seethed coldly as those eerie blue flames grew brighter.

"Oh, ouch," I chuckled. "I wasn't talking about me. That would just be awkward, now wouldn't it? I meant Katarina. You know, the whole gone soul thing," I continued, buying time to figure out how to get Joshua out of this alive. I stepped backwards, watching as his massive frame mirrored my action, hunting his prey. I had a motive; if I could reach the others, maybe they'd trade Lucian for Joshua, and we could be on our way.

"Drop the fucking act, I know what you are, creature," he demanded.

"Do you?" I asked, stopping to tap my finger on my chin. "What am I?"

Hands grasped me from behind, and I dropped, rolling as my body vanished, only to reappear on top of the Guild. I stared down at them, watching as the Fae and others began moving closer towards the group of soulless beings. People blinked in and out as they sifted and materialized until the air became unbearable as power from both factions exploded around us. Raw electrical current sang in the evening air and floated on the breeze.

Lucian observed me, and I sensed him before he stood inches away from me, perched on the edge beside me. He was close enough that I could inhale his addictive scent.

"Let him go, tell Spyder to release my brother, and I will tell them to leave and you, you can have me, Lucian."

"And you'd come with me, just like that, when you know I mean to destroy you?" he laughed wickedly, the sound sliding down my body like a caress against my flesh.

"You've made me come a lot easier than that, Lucian," I smiled coyly as I closed my eyes against his intoxicating presence. I lifted my face to the heavy air, enjoying the thick scent of the impending storm as it lingered thickly around us.

"Stop pretending to be her, it's fucking pathetic," he snarled, the warning hanging heavy between us.

"Ouch," I laughed huskily, letting him hear what his proximity did to me. "That's harsh, even for you," I pointed out. "He either lets go of my brother, or we fight. Can you kill me, Lucian? Do you have it in you to take my head from my shoulders?" I asked, and disappeared.

I appeared next to Spyder, kicking him in the side as I pushed Joshua free. He staggered, righting himself as he spun to peer at me. Spyder's hands wrapped around my throat, yanking my body against his as I freed Joshua. The flame-covered digits singed my flesh as I groaned as pain erupted. I moaned, stifling the urge to scream as the wicked smile dropped from my lips. My eyes pleaded with Joshua as I struggled to smirk.

It was as we'd planned it. I was the only one caught, their only prisoner.

"Go." The word sprang from my lips as I urged him to see it through. The air thickened as Lucian appeared right beside Joshua, just as he disappeared. I stared at the space he'd once occupied and hoped to the Gods I wasn't wrong. I hoped I survived this. Midnight eyes held mine with a coldness that sent a shiver racing down my spine as his lips curved into a deadly smile.

"Now you die," he uttered as he stepped closer.

CHAPTER
three

The scariest monsters are the ones that lurk within the souls… *~Edgar Allen Poe*

I was thrown into a transparent dome that looked as if it was crafted of glass, but the moment my feet touched inside, colorful wards ignited and lit the glass up like a Christmas tree in the dark. Glyphs swarmed the wards as runes outside ignited, sealing me inside. *The fuck?* I turned, slowly eyeing Spyder who paced beside me as I inspected the dome and its weaknesses. He mirrored my movements, the predator in him showing to hunt its prey. I stopped, pausing to smirk at him.

"Missed you too, big boy," I said softly, not hiding the edge to my need that flowed through my tone. I stopped moving, letting him take an eyeful of me in. They'd stripped me out of my clothing, removed every weapon into an impressive pile that had Synthia nodding with appreciation.

I'd been redressed into a sundress that was white;

boring, but at least it was clean. Spaghetti straps adorned the shoulders while a soft length of lace covered the bodice. The skirt barely covered my backside, which I didn't even bother trying to hide as I started pacing again.

"Cut this shit, if you were my kitty, I'd feel you. I don't feel shit. Nothing other than the need to wrap my hands around that pretty neck and drain the life out of you," he sneered, and I frowned deeper as I stalled a moment to look into his endless depths of loathing.

"You're a big boy, Spyder. Let's see you fucking do it. And that bond you speak of? I have no beating heart. Not at the moment anyway, and the whole slit my throat to save people ended my life. You remember that, don't you? I'm pretty sure you were there to play witness to my dramatic downfall. I'm not one hundred percent sure, though; you see I was sort of leaking brain fluid everywhere and it all got hazy and started blending together. I know," I said clapping my hands as I smiled at him with bright eyes. "Why don't you tell me what happened before I woke up!"

"And how did you do that?" he purred thickly as icy blue eyes dipped to the cleavage which the dress barely managed to contain. Slowly, they traced up my body until they paused on the pesky scar that stood red against my flesh.

"Wouldn't you like to know? Why don't you come in here and I'll tell you," I laughed huskily, toying with him.

"In fact, I would like to fucking know," he countered as his head dipped and his eyes glowed brighter, deadlier.

"I'd like to know that one as well," Lucian butted in, his tone sliding through me as if it could cut me in half. I tore my gaze from Spyder's and watched as he moved from the shadows and stared at me coldly.

"Mm, you look good enough to fuck, Lucian," I purred thickly as I swallowed the heat that rose with his darkening stare. "Almost, but not quite…" I uttered hoarsely. My vision swam as heat made my lids grow heavy with need as they trailed down his powerful body. I missed that body slamming against mine, the sheer power of it as it dominated me until I submitted.

"Shut your fucking mouth," he ordered, his stare never leaving the ugly scar on my neck. "And the fucking question?"

"Make me, Blackstone," I challenged as I crossed my arms and stared at him, fully aware that he couldn't, not without opening the prison he'd tossed me into. That hadn't been in the plans. Chains I could get out of; rooms easy; but a dome warded, surrounded by runes with pulsing glyphs? Not something I'd imagined they would have here. My eyes moved to the people who crowded into the room behind him, and I frowned, creasing my brow as they swung back to him coldly. "An audience again, Lucian? So soon after the last time?" I swallowed hard as I refused to show an ounce of fear in his presence.

"They're here to help me take you down, to extract what is keeping you alive. Tell me what I want to know, and I'll finally end your pathetic life painlessly. There's no one left to feel that pain for you this time, creature," he continued, and I shook my head, smirking at him.

"Kinky, did you let it slip out that I like it rough?" I asked huskily, my voice escaping the thickness of my throat as I stared into his inky eyes. Black silk beckoned me forward, the silent promise of endless pleasure dangling just beyond my grasp.

Again, the tick hammered wildly against his jaw, indicating he wasn't as unaffected as he pretended to be by my sudden appearance. "I know, would you like to play a game with me?" I asked, clapping my hands together and sending a loud noise around the dome, which seemed to absorb it. "You can slit my fucking throat and rip out my heart… Oh, wait; we already played that game, didn't we? Yeah, my bad. *I* slit my throat to save *your* heart. Stop me if you remember this one, Lucian. Damn, it almost sounded fun," I shrugged as his nostrils flared in anger. I brought my finger up to drag it over the scar as my mind raced to find a way out of the room.

He flinched, but those midnight orbs that held the countless galaxies in their depths lifted and I momentarily forgot we were done and I didn't belong lost in their inky depths any longer. My teeth scraped across my bottom lip as I basked in their heated depths, momentarily adrift in them.

"Do it, let's see what you guys got," I snickered once I'd recaptured my composure. I forced myself to end the staring match, yanking my gaze away from his. "Got some tunes to go with the show? I think I missed my last chance to pick a theme song on my way out, but then there's always next time, right? Come on, you sexy bitch, get in here and cut me the fuck up. I know you want to, I won't even fight you."

"Magdalena?" My grandmother's voice floated to me, and I stiffened against it. I turned slowly, seeing her through my peripheral vision. I turned away from it, and her, unwilling to look at her yet.

"That's fucking low, even for you, and we all know how low you can go, don't we? How dirty you play and like to be played with?" I turned as more entered, and anger pushed to the fore as I watched the coven marching in right behind Kendra. My eyes lingered on her swollen belly and then dropped as her hands came up to cradle it. No matter how much I fought it, a pain snaked up through me and tears swam in my vision. My hand lifted to mine, feathering it where my child should have remained growing and then dropped to form a fist at my side. I spun away from her, staring at anything but her. I studied the glyphs as if they held interest, ignored her pleas to turn around and look at her. Anything to not look at her pregnant, swollen belly.

"Lena?" my mother screamed, her tears forming in her throat making it hard to understand her, and yet I had.

"Get them out of here," I demanded softly, hating the weakness that flowed from my eyes as I ignored their pleas.

"Why? Afraid those closest to the girl you're pretending to be will be able to spot the real you?" he asked.

"They didn't know me, Lucian. You did, though, didn't you? You knew all my dark and dirty needs and desires. You, above of all else, knew me inside and out. You knew my hopes because you crushed them. You knew my desires because you played me with them. You knew my wants, my needs as no other could or would ever know. You saw through my skin and exposed the flaws in my soul. You saw through the walls I'd erected and known I was as broken and shattered as the world around me, and somehow you glued me back together. And when I had finally risen, when I had finally found my feet and rose to stand on them, well, then you kicked them out from beneath me and sent my world crashing down around me. Who knew that the man who had built me up would be the one to tear me down?"

"Is that what you think, creature?" he asked sadly.

"I died because of you, because I had loved you. I *killed* our baby because it couldn't live with what *your* girlfriend had placed inside of me. Your fucking game destroyed my world, and now you want to call me a *creature*? I belonged to this world, you don't. He deserved more. *I* deserved more from you."

"You play her so beautifully, don't you, creature?" he mused.

"Unfortunately, it's not a part I'm playing. It's what you left of me. I'm stuck playing it because it's the only thing I know how to do. Survive. You did this to me," I chuckled indifferently with a shrug. "I am what I am, and if you're strong enough to kill me, I guess it won't matter either way, now will it?"

My fingers trailed softly over the glass barrier, dragging along the smooth surface as power rippled in warning. Spelled glass covered in ancient wards meant to keep monsters like me locked within sent electricity rushing through me in warning. I paused, finding a vulnerable point and digging into it with my magic. I pushed harder, sensing the one who'd placed them was close. A woman stepped from the group, putting her hands against the glass as she stared back into my soulless pits. She had a crown of red, unruly curls that framed her petite face and war glyphs tattooed into her flesh. She was beautiful in her own right, a warrior to the marrow in her very bones. I felt it as I peered deeper into her soul, yet the moment she touched the glass, I felt *her*. As if a part of her had become the wards that locked me into this cage and held me prisoner.

Interesting.

I filed the information into my mind for later and pushed more power against hers.

"Bloody hell," she groaned as she shucked her robes and pushed both palms flat against the glass. I watched her wards rise, stacking over one another as she struggled to redo what I undid easily. One weak point and I'd unraveled everything she could throw at it. She was efficient, quick, and layering powerful wards one after another. Wards so strong a normal creature wouldn't be able to untangle—but I saw them, through them, ready to capture the beginning before it was placed. I pulled my hand away, surveying the perspiration that beaded her flesh, slowly dripping from her hair as she sagged against the glass.

"You think they could hold me if I hadn't wanted to be here?" I asked, needing to see how she responded.

"Think I fucking care?" she snapped, and I laughed, slapping my palm against the glass and watching as her back bowed. I pushed more and more magic into bringing them down, so much that my power formed and shot through me. Darkness slithered over my flesh, caressing my arms until it filled the whites of my eyes, turning them pitch black, as if I'd been plucked from the TV screen of *American Horror Story* and placed into their endless, secure prison. I nibbled my lip, sucking it between my teeth as I toyed with her until she screamed and blood dripped from her nose.

"Keep going, you can do it," I encouraged with an evil laugh that even scared me a little. My magic slithered around hers, pulling her flush against the glass as I watched her struggle to get away from it. She screamed as Synthia stepped forward, pulling her as she struggled to undo my hold on the female.

I felt the rush to continue, to end her until she was nothing but a lifeless corpse, but I pulled back and watched as she sagged in relief as Synthia's electric blue eyes lifted to hold mine. She knew I'd released her, which I hadn't needed to, but that I had.

"You're pure fucking evil," the female uttered as she lifted her eyes to hold my lifeless ones. "I can feel it in your magic, your touch. You're evil incarnate. You don't belong here."

"Is that what they told you?" I laughed soundlessly. "I assure you this, druid: If I were evil, you'd be nothing more than a corpse right now. You laid those wards assuming I had no knowledge of them or their origin, but I did. I could have added mine into yours so that it drove back through you, ending your life. Rather fucking sloppy of you, really. Disappointing for someone with so much power running through her veins. You should be glad that I am not what they say I am, or you'd be very much dead right now. But then I guess the only thing I am good at killing is myself, isn't that so, guys?" I asked, tossing my hand around in a useless gesture. "Tough crowd," I smiled coldly, letting my magic fill the dome until it pulsed and strained with it.

"Magdalena," my mother's tone slithered through me like ice water on a hot day. I plastered on a fake smile and lifted my lifeless black eyes to hers. I watched her flinch and recoil from me, but then I didn't really blame her. I did resemble most horror movies nowadays with their invasion of demons and their wonky-as-fuck eye affliction. I'd recoiled myself as I stared at the monster I'd become in a mirror. Thick black veins ran through my flesh, pulsing with strong dark magic as I let it rush through me. I tilted my head, staring her down as I slowly closed the distance between us, giving her enough time to scamper away from me.

They all took a step away from the glass. Away from me.

Whatever.

I was what I was, and I'd become it to protect them. All of them. I'd saved one child because only one of us could have survived what Katarina had done to us. If I hadn't, she'd have buried both of her children. It also wasn't as if I'd wanted to play their game, but then the rest of us had been nothing more than collateral damage.

"Hello, Mommy," I purred coyly as the memory of her damning me to Hell came back. "Did you miss me?" I asked, hating myself for doing it. "Am I everything you wanted me to be and more?" I laughed coldly in a deadened tone. It filled the dome, but it was empty.

I wandered closer to Kendra and leaned my forehead against the soothing glass. I slowly, carefully tapped my nail on the glass, watching as her mouth formed a perfect O as she listened. She stepped closer, tapping back as she watched me. It was in our language, the one we'd perfected as children when we were in trouble, and only a wall separated us.

"It's you," she cried as she shook her head.

"It's not her." Lucian's voice pulled us back, forcing my eyes to swing to his wide frame, lingering on it. "It knows everything about her, all her secrets and everything else. It knows all of us, every single person she's ever encountered. That isn't her; it's the seal wearing her like a fucking suit."

I stepped back and forced my eyes to return to normal, matching hers identically. She caught it, but even now I could see the distrust forming and growing in her eyes. Good, it was time she started using that brain. "I'm glad you're doing better, that you're healthy and your daughter is not dead like my son is."

She shook her head as horror registered on her delicate features. "Magdalena…"

"I'm fine. I really am. I'm okay with what I have become," I muttered as I backed away from the glass, turning on my heel to move to where Lucian stood, glaring. "So what's it to be, then, Lucian? Lock me up, tie me up? Kill me? Dissect me for your perfect fucking seal? Whatever it is, get on with it already. You bore me, Blackstone. I have places to be, creatures to kill, and none of them have to deal with you or yours."

"I'm about to show you why you're mine," he chuckled. "I'm about to shove you back into that box and toss your ass into the first endless void I can find."

"And if it isn't inside of me?" I laughed coldly. "What then?"

"It's there, I can feel you. You forget, you're a part of me."

CHAPTER
four

Let your plans be dark and impenetrable as night, and when you move, fall like a thunderbolt. *~Sun Tzu*

My eyes slowly roamed over the men, who began removing their shirts. Power exuded from them; raw, untapped, uncut electrical current filled the dome before they'd even entered it. Brands slithered over flesh; muscles rippled as weapons were checked and placed into their holsters. The dome trembled, and for a minute, I couldn't rip my gaze off the male perfection being displayed to see what was happening inside it. I stared up as the dome's ceiling opened, revealing a glass ceiling above it, and through the glass the large full moon shone down, lighting up the room in its earthly glow.

My stomach rolled, dropping to my feet as I lowered my gaze to Lucian's. "Get them out of here, now. Please," I uttered thickly as my mind did the math and rushed with chaos at what was about to unfold. How the fuck had we forgotten *that?*

"Don't think you're in a position to be making requests, creature," he leered as his body rippled with power. Behind him, Ryder, Zahruk, and Spyder all tossed their shirts aside and stared at me as if I was enemy number one. They shed any resemblance of humanity in the process, and stretched their necks, rolling their shoulders as power moved through the rooms in the same motion.

I took an involuntary step back, putting more distance between us. They were fucking ripped, muscles coiled as brands pulsed with raw, live magic that wasn't from this realm. Runes danced upon their chests, covering the flesh. I exhaled slowly, letting the air in and out of my lungs as I struggled to calm the tension I felt, which coiled in every nerve ending at what was about to happen. Magic rushed through me as I considered what was happening, and reveled in the thought of a worthwhile fight. It had been a while since I'd had a challenge.

"Synthia," I said, staring at her until she pulled her eyes away from Ryder and stared back at me. "I didn't kill your druid, so you owe me. Get my family out of here. They don't need to watch this happen." She just glared at me, and I growled. "I'm about to fucking die, get them out of here!" Her eyes narrowed and yet she ignored me, settling her gaze back on Ryder with a frown.

She was afraid I'd hurt them? Her shoulders lowered, and those eyes came back, staring at me as if weighing her options and what she would do. Hope flared through me, only to be dashed as she gave me her back. I groaned and brought my wrist up to my teeth, letting the sharp fangs drop as I ripped through my flesh, biting an entire chunk loose before I stepped up to the glass and dipped my fingers into the blood. I brought them up and began painting.

Blood slid over glass as my fingers smudged over it, twirling as rune after rune was placed. It clashed with the ones they'd placed on the floor, but mine were older, more powerful. I held eyes with Lucian as I continued to paint in my blood, watching as the men sweat while waiting for the druid, who had begun working on the glass to allow them into the dome. It was taking longer than they'd anticipated, which worked out well for me. Everyone held their breath as I continually moved my fingers, painting the dead language over it.

"The fuck is she doing?" Zahruk demanded, his sapphire eyes finding mine as they glared in warning.

I broke eye contact and lifted my eyes to the moon, which hovered just barely out of sight of the hole in the ceiling.

"Healing runes maybe? I'm not sure. Whatever it is, they're fucking old. I think it's a dead language, or maybe one not from this world. How would she even know a dead language if she is as young as you said she is?" the druid said as she continued guessing out loud what I'd painted onto the glass.

"It's primitive," Lucian said, forcing all eyes onto him, and I grinned.

Primitive meant old as shit, which meant whatever I was, was too. It also said Lucian was old as well.

"Hurry the fuck up and get the wards done. She's almost done." The angry clip in Synthia's tone couldn't hide the worry and hesitancy from me. Her man was entering this dome with an unknown, and she wasn't, why? A hiss escaped her cherry-colored lips as I slapped my palm against the glass in a finishing touch and it briefly ignited before fizzling out.

"I don't think whatever it was worked," the druid stated absently as she paused and stopped removing the wards as she examined my work. Her eyes continually scanned the trail of blood before she once again began to remove the wards.

"I'm going in to keep her busy," Lucian announced and I smiled coldly. "Guard the fucking door, Spyder. Don't let this monster out." His tone was clipped, and hatred oozed from every word he'd ordered.

I watched him as I slowly backpedaled away from his entrance. I didn't look away from the deadly eyes that threatened to drown me again. They would be a perfect death, drowning in the obsidian depths that swallowed me whole. He waited, stretching his neck as the druid worked faster. Her fingers danced as the magic clung to them, weaving with her magical touch as she removed and rearranged them.

Once he was inside, he rushed at me, and I remained rooted to the spot, allowing it. My head slammed against the dome, and I laughed huskily against his ear. His hands moved, finding my throat and gripping it tightly as a moan exploded from between my lips. My breathing hitched as my eyelashes fluttered to dance upon my cheeks. My hands lifted, not needing the air he thought to keep from me, gripping his shirt before I ripped it open, sending the buttons sailing through the air to scatter across the floor. My legs wrapped around his waist, pulling his massive body against mine until a guttural growl filled the dome.

His forehead lowered, pressing against mine as he assumed I'd succumbed to his traitorous grasp around my throat. I inhaled, greedily indulging on his scent as my legs dropped to hang in the air. In one motion, I brought my hands up together and shoved him away from me, using magic to garner strength before I lifted my foot, kicking him backwards. It sent him sailing across the dome, crashing against the other side of it. I watched as his eyes widened in surprise, which he concealed almost immediately, but not fast enough.

"I didn't state how long I would let you abuse me, now did I?" I laughed and brought my hands up to my neck, trailing my fingers over the swollen flesh. "I think I'm wet?" I asked, letting my hand trail down to my body as his eyes changed, burning with blue flames. "Fuck yeah, but then you always had that effect on me, didn't you?"

"You're not my Lena," he snarled.

"No, I'm not. That Lena was weak, I'm not. She was easily broken, and I will never be broken again. So yes, your Lena is dead. I was just a casualty of your fucking game. I guess winning it came with some serious consequences, now didn't it?" I retorted as he paced on the other side of the room.

"You're not my Lena," he repeated.

"The fuck, Lucian," I said as I threw my hands in the air. "Did you go daft while I was being reborn?" I asked, finally placing my hands on my hips as I listened to the others joining us in the dome.

"I know what you are, creature. What you do when you think you have fooled the world, and what drives you. I know because you're my creation. My responsibility. You're not fucking tricking me again, ever. She had no soul, so how the fuck are you controlling her corpse?" he demanded.

"Oomph," I snorted. "I'm soulless, Lucian. I can't be controlled by you or anyone else. Or it, because it cannot latch onto anything inside of me," I explained and watched as his eyes narrowed. "So, gentlemen," I exclaimed as I turned to face the others, who'd entered silently. "How are we going to play this?"

"To the death," Lucian answered, but something in his tone had caught and hesitated.

"So be it then," I smirked.

All hell broke loose.

CHAPTER
five

My biggest fear is that eventually you will see me the way I see myself. *~Anonymous Author*

I paced the dome, watching the men as they mirrored my movements. I sensed them before they lunged, moving together as one powerful assault team. As if they'd done it a few times recently, which they probably had. I materialized on the other side, away from them and watched as they stopped, sensing my new location.

The moment power filled the small room; I disappeared as it groaned from the immense magic filling it. The room erupted into utter chaos as everyone moved at inhuman speeds, sifting and materializing as body collided with body. Growls and groans exploded, filling the place as they struggled to decipher who was who, and where I'd gone. The moment we all became corporeal again, I tensed. I took in the bloodied bodies and shirtless chests that were now covered in a fine sheen of sweat. I, of course, was dripping blood from where they'd caught me but hadn't been able to maintain it as I'd used my power to dissolve into mist. It wouldn't be that fucking easy for them to catch me, not anymore.

"She's not fucking normal," Zahruk shouted, his nose dripping blood from where I'd connected with it.

"No shit, Sherlock," he snapped. "She isn't even a she," Lucian grunted as he swiped blood from his lip with his thumb.

"Ouch, that hurts. You've been in it; shouldn't you out of everyone here know that I am female?" I laughed as he glared. The sound was as cold and empty as the space where my heart had once beat for him.

"You going to actually fucking hurt her or just keep letting her go?" Ryder seethed as the question uncurled from his tongue. Golden eyes locked with mine and I winked at him, fully aware he wasn't fucking around.

"If it was Syn?" Spyder injected. "Could you fucking kill it so easily then, fucker?"

"You're the assholes saying it isn't her, so what's the fucking issue?"

"It's wearing her face and her bloody, sexy scent," Spyder snapped back, pushing the hair away from his bloodied face.

"Let's finish this shit," Lucian snarled, moving faster than I could follow. I didn't see him until I slammed into motion, only to be knocked back as I collided with his massive chest. His body slammed against mine, knocking me to the ground. I kicked up, landing on my feet before I lifted a leg and kicked him directly in his chest, sending him sailing across the floor. He slammed against Spyder and snarled his irritation as he turned to look at where I'd stood, but I was already in motion again.

Another body slammed against mine, and I bounced

off the glass that kept me in. My face bounced, and I cried out, kicking back into the endless speed that sent us all moving around the dome's small interior.

Someone grabbed me, and I turned, finding Spyder's icy blue gaze locked with mine. Lucian closed in behind him, and I stood on my tiptoes, nipping Spyder's plump bottom lip before I vanished once more. Bodies collided with bodies, but at the speed we were moving at, you couldn't tell who was hitting who, or if they were friend or foe, except me.

Everyone was against me.

I guess it was what I got for saving the world. No good deed goes unpunished. The moon climbed higher, inching towards the center of the dome's glass ceiling, which meant this little workout was about to be cut short. I was running at a speed faster than they could match until something plucked me from midair, right out of motion and slammed me against the dome's unforgiving wall.

I stared up into midnight eyes as he slammed me back against the glass repeatedly. I shot forward, slamming against him as I moved us away from it, forcing us to the middle of the room, He grabbed my arms, slamming us against the ground as I wrapped my legs around him, intending to roll us until I was sitting in his lap, but others landed around us. My arms were yanked above my head, Ryder's liquid amber gaze locked with mine as he secured them. Zahruk and Spyder secured my legs as Lucian lifted, peering down at me. I remained in place, wondering what they thought they could do to me. Once they'd secured my legs, Spyder moved, grasping his hands around my throat as I moaned, catching him off guard with it. Laughter bubbled deep from within and his eyes heated to liquid pools of desire.

"Kinky, gentlemen, but I already played this game too. Turns out, it's just not my kind of thing after all. Sorry," I purred thickly before I vanished from their hold.

"How the fuck?" Zahruk demanded, his growl sending the hair on my nape up in awareness as the predator in him unleashed its claws. "How the fuck is she doing that? She isn't Fae, and she sure as fuck isn't anything I've smelled before. She smells like midnight, mixed with whiskey and magic and something darker, sweeter."

A dagger sailed in my direction, and I vanished, appearing next to where I had stood as I plucked the weapon from midair. The metal singed my flesh, and my power erupted, leaving nothing more than a melted piece of steel in my hand. I dropped it to the floor and smirked at the handsome male who watched me with a heated gaze, as if he wasn't sure if he wanted to fight or fuck me, or maybe he'd prefer we did both at the same time? Men.

I licked my lips, staring him down as the others panted as they caught their breath, controlling their breathing in the respite before we started up again. I was toying with them, playing with them. I hadn't even started yet.

"You're yummy, and apparently rather good with a blade. Tell me, creature, can you pierce flesh as well with your other blade?" My heated stare dropped to the one I questioned, leaving no room for error in my meaning. Once more I lifted them to hold his dark, sapphire stare. "Can you wield it as well as you do your toys?" I chuckled as his eyes widened at my brazen question. His brands started slithering, pulsing as a sexy smirk flirted on his lips. I felt it, the death-by-sex vibes he was aiming directly at me. I frowned, bringing my hand up to cover a yawn as he continued pushing power into his magic. "I have no soul. You cannot feed from me, which means your power has no pull against my mind. Not that you'd need it," I smirked with a mixture of heat and lust filling my gaze. "I bet you're a wild fucking ride, aren't you? I bet you crook your finger and the panties just melt off in their need to let you play. Tell me, Zahruk, do you want to play with me?" I chuckled and vanished as the others collided where I'd stood. I exhaled at the heap of male limbs and naked torsos that untangled. "I'm not going to be that easy to kill, gentlemen."

"This isn't working." Ryder's growl pulled my eyes to where he stood, glaring at me.

"You thinking lethal?" Zahruk asked, and Lucian nodded.

I watched Zahruk as he pulled out a wicked-looking blade. My gaze zeroed in on it, narrowing as I took in the craftsmanship of it. The blade buzzed with power, and when he threw it tip over end, sailing through the air directly at me, I smirked. I let it sink into my chest before I pulled it out, gazing down at the exquisite blade. Power exploded in the dome, and I peered up, staring at Ryder as his form exploded and his beast stood before me. I vanished, popping up behind them as they paused, turning slowly in my direction with their lethal stares trained onto the blade.

It was something strong. Something they feared.

Ryder's eyes shifted from gold to black, and his wings expanded. I tossed the dagger onto the ground at his feet, sensing it was what had forced the beast to join the fray. I moved again, but this time Lucian's fist collided with my face and sent me flying backwards. I bounced off the wall, crashing against something solid, something hard. Fire burned in my chest as I gasped, expelling air from my lungs as I peered down at the blade, which had pierced my chest. I slowly lifted my vision as it swam to the sapphire eyes that smoldered as he watched me react to the damage he'd just managed to do.

I blinked past the fire in my chest and smiled as blood dripped from my lips. I pushed my body further onto the blade as I touched his lips with mine. "Come on, baby, I want more. Give it to me, all of it. This bitch is starving, so feed me more of those long, sexy inches," I purred thickly as blood splattered his face as air bubbles exploded from my damaged lungs. My foot lifted, sending him and his blade sailing across the floor to land at Ryder's feet.

I ejected forward as my claws extended but stopped, mid-lunge as the moon bathed me in its eerie light. I stared up into the light and groaned.

Shit.

Fuck.

Not now.

I was winning…

My eyes glazed over and I watched the men slowly approach, surrounding me,

"The fuck is she doing?" Spyder asked.

"Take her head!" Ryder snapped, but it was too late.

My body slammed to the floor and flipped. I stared sightlessly at the moon as my head lifted, only to slam back against the floor. Thunder erupted in my ears, covering their noises, their voices.

Dying.

I was fucking dying in the middle of the best workout I'd had in a very long time.

One…Pain erupted. It exploded as it ripped through me as blood shot from my lips, covering my mouth.

Two… Pain met and warred with confusion. My ears rang with it, drowning out the screams and gasps from those around me who watched it unfold, silencing them.

Three...*Pop!*

Brain and spinal fluid leaked, spilling onto the floor from the crushed skull. I'd fought, I'd fought him, my hands grasped, never touching him. I screamed, everything hazy as I struggled to live, to continue breathing long enough to finish my task. I fought to live, almost able to hear their screams again, but not quite louder than a whispered breath in my ears. I rolled to my side and then she was there, and my body jerked as pain erupted. Horrifying pain burned through me as I shielded my head from the force of her anger. My midsection became her target, and I gave up guarding my damaged head to protect my child. My innocent unborn child. Another kick forced me to move, to turn my back on her assault as blood pooled from my face and head. It was everywhere, leaking from my nose, my mouth, ears, and the pressure became unbearable as I forced myself to rise, to get up and finish what I'd gone there to do. *To save them.*

My eyes locked with Lucian's, and I saw his panic, the knowledge of what was unfolding before his panic-stricken gaze. I swayed on my feet, unable to catch myself as I fell down, only to get back up, slowly as I stood before him, locking my eyes to his and the pain that continued to slice and tear me apart.

Screaming erupted from outside the dome, but I couldn't look away from him. I tried but failed. I could only wait for what had yet to come. The worst part still had to play out before life returned to ebbing and flowing, returning my body to what it had become.

White-hot pain ripped me apart, severing tissue and tendons against the flesh of my throat. It was bone-deep and visceral pain. I screamed, but no noise escaped the damage done to my throat. I dropped to the floor, hard, landing on my knees so hard that the bones snapped, shattering. My hands lifted to my throat as they had that day, trying to stop the blood that flowed from me, leaking into the ground. My body tumbled to the floor even though I still continued to tell him what I needed to.

Death was the price we paid for our sacrifice.
No good deed goes unpunished, ever…

I watched lifelessly as Lucian's feet, along with the others', left the room. They were at a loss for what had happened, or why he'd been forced to watch it happen again. After some time passed, someone else entered, and the wheels of a bed were moved past me, through my blood that was thickening in the pool around my head, my body. I'm picked up; the lifeless corpse I left behind is moved, gently placed onto the bed they'd wheeled in.

I screamed, but they don't hear me. They never did as I remained stuck in the vessel that death claimed. It's a silent echo, a scream that never escaped past my lips as Lucian waited for any sign that I'd come back to him. I'd been there, aware, and yet unable to make him see I was alive.

My arms are strapped into restraints, and I want to laugh at the uselessness of it. They exited the room, and I waited, I waited for them to come. The ones who always returned when the moon reached its zenith, full and reoccurring. The souls of the damned and lost who come to take mine from me. To take my world away from me, one I didn't know I could want as much as I did.

The dome was closed, sealed, and yet I could still feel his presence close to me, as I had when he'd remained beside my rotting corpse. We'd played out this scene before, him sitting beside it unable to know the horrors that played out beside him, inside my head. The runes ignited, locking us inside the dome.

They're coming.

I'm coming back.

Flames licked the glass, eating through the wards as if they're nothing more than a nuisance. They vanished as if they'd been placed by a child instead of a talented druid. Music exploded into the room, and I listened as Lucian growled, searching for the source. Breaking Benjamin's *The Dark of You* filled the room, and I wanted to laugh and tell him *I* am the source of that song; my heart played it over and over until it had become a piece of me.

"What the bloody fuck is happening?" Ryder's tone was sharp, worried. "What is she doing now?"

"Gods," Lucian gasped, the sound raw and haunted as if he had plucked it from the haunting melody that filled me where my soul should be. It would have hurt my heart if I'd had one still.

The leather restraints were undone, slowly releasing my wrist. My body floated from the bed, levitating in the air, and they appeared. My hair hung limp, floating below me as the grisly damage was exposed. Ghostly images of female perfection mixed with their grey images, their white, crisp gowns so contrasting different from my blood-soaked one. They moved me away from the bed, away from him. Caught in the powerful web of their unimaginable power, I floated weightlessly as they controlled me. Power rushed over my flesh, and I continually floated until I was between them, marched to a spot where they have enough room to take the world from me.

Once there, I'm stood upright, rooted in place, continually ensnared in their magical hold. My arms lifted, my fingers posed as if I was the world's most graceful dancer. They spun me around, slowly assessing the damage I'd done to save them, to save him from what they'd planned to force him to become. The music grew louder; matching the turmoil that plagued my mind at what was unfolding around me. At what they were about to take from me.

And then they began, undoing the damage to my body with their powerful magic. The pain eased, becoming comfortably numb as they continue to fix the wounds I'd endured.

My eyes were sightless up until they were healed, the subtle sheen of white removed and the film that covered them in death healed. Everything went dark, and I waited, I waited for them to do as they always did. I knew it was coming, it always occurred after the damage was healed, and my mind could focus on what they stole from me. My body floated to my knees, landing gently against the cold marble floor. They gathered around me, pushing me down until I'm flush against the strongest of them, her hands stroking my hair in a motion meant to comfort me. She touched me as if I am a promised gift, the world's most valued treasure.

The music thundered around us, growing ever louder to mirror my emotions. I looked around, taking in their ghastly images, their rune-covered arms and pristine dresses of purity. Everything I no longer held or would ever be again. They began securing me, holding my arms and legs down as one settled between my thighs. Gentle green eyes watched me knowingly. I started to fight, to struggle against what I knew they planned to do. My screams were silent but filled with enough pain that they knew I was in it, they knew the pain my silent horror held.

I didn't stop screaming, I never did. I bucked against their hold, fighting to keep what they intended to steal.

Her hand touched my flat belly, and my fight intensified, the struggles became a fight to the death against them. My voice exploded, filling the dome as her hand pushed through my stomach, digging into my womb. It was anguish mixed with the throes of pain and loss. The sound was deafening to my own ears, the loss so searing that if I'd had a soul, they'd have shattered it.

"No!" It ripped from my lungs, exploding into the room as it bounced off the walls around us, echoing through my ears. "No, *he's* mine! Don't do *this!*" Tears streamed down my face, hot and wet against the cold flesh I lived inside. My black tears fell, as black as the empty void of my soulless corpse. Devoid of life, filled with darkness and as my sightless eyes formed, becoming endless voids, they hissed. I screamed at them with sunken-in pits that had once held eyes that viewed the world differently. Now, now I had become a monster who wanted to destroy it.

Her hand pushed into my womb, and my spine arched, hating the searing red-hot pain that enveloped my mind. Pain exploded, enveloping everything as she dug around in my womb. A sob exploded from my lips as blood splattered against her ghostly flesh. Just as fast as it started, it ended. I struggled against the hold they had on me, on my corpse. I *needed* him. I screamed, allowing all the anguish and pain to bubble from my lungs and explode into the dome. It was pure anguish, mixed and filled with pain so raw and deep that even those who stood outside the dome cried with me.

Then they vanished, only to reappear in front of the one who now held my son. I pushed up from the floor, able- and full-bodied but empty. As cold as death itself. I rushed towards them, only for them to lift their hands and send me back, sailing against the dome's wall. Bones shattered only to re-fuse, stronger than before.

"No! Don't take him from me, he's mine! I love him. I can't do this, give him back, please!" My voice cracked and broke apart, echoing through the room. I moved forward, igniting my magic and everything I held inside of me as I prepared to fight them. The entire dome rattled with the intensity of the magic I wielded. "Let me see him, now!" I demanded. My screams turned into pain; they echoed through me. I rushed at them, and fire burned my flesh to the bone. The barrier they'd placed preventing me from reaching my son. *They* kept me from my *world*.

They'd all perish for their trespass against me.

I screamed as I hit the floor, my hands barren of flesh from pushing through the barrier to reach them. To reach him. Black curls atop a tiny head were all that was visible. I pulled myself back up, forcing myself to get back onto my feet. I had to see him, to know him. He was why I'd done this, why I'd let my death happen. I at least needed to see what he'd looked like!

I was thrown back again as the flesh began to melt from my body and they came towards me, slowly, cautiously. They were right to fear me. Once they reached me, I was again caught in their powerful magical web as they healed me anew, again.

I'd yet to stop screaming as I turned my dead, inhuman, sightless eyes at the one who cooed and calmed my son. Flesh healed, regrown as it melded against my bones. Black tears fell uselessly down my cheeks as I watched her cuddling my world. The world she'd just ripped from my womb.

"You're unclean now," she uttered over the top of his naked body, her chin brushing against the thick black curls, so akin to his fathers.

"He is not like you, you agreed to give him to us," they uttered together, their voices uniting as if they were one being. "Name him, and he will know it."

I stopped screaming my voice raw and inhuman as I leveled her with a deadly stare. "Harbinger," I laughed coldly. "Harbinger of Doom, the one who will kill this selfish world. He will rip it apart and swim in the blood of those who trespass upon us. He will find me, I am his *mother!*" A light flashed behind her, and they passed through where I could never go. My son's glowing soul grew brighter, bathing my face in blue light as he passed into heaven, which would never accept me.

I dropped to the floor, wailing until nothing more escaped from my lips. I rolled into the fetal position, lifeless as sobs exploded, silent and yet containing pain that never eased or lessened. I remained there until it happened...

Thump...thump...thump.

And just like that, my body was reborn again.

Slowly, I sat up and turned to stare into horrified midnight eyes, the shock on his face overriding the emotion that continued to ebb and flow through me. It took effort to rise to my feet, to rise from the pain that ached from the rawness of the loss all over again.

"Lena," he uttered thickly, aware of the truth they'd laid bare to him. His eyes lowered, taking in the glyphs and runes that had given them the right to do as they'd done. To take my world and protect him from what I had become.

He moved faster than my eyes could track and held

my body against his. I pushed away from him, but his hold was too much. Anger ripped me apart, and I screamed through my aching lungs as I finally managed to push him away from me. I surveyed the others, hating the wet eyes and tears that rolled down their faces from witnessing my fall.

"Did you enjoy the fucking show?" I asked, hating them for seeing my pain lay bare to their eyes. A sob bubbled up from my lungs, and I forced it back down. Synthia stared at me, her eyes wet with tears. "Open this fucking dome and let me out!" I demanded forcefully.

"Lena," Lucian said my name like a fucking prayer as it rolled off his tongue.

"Lena is no more! She died for you, for *him*! You did this to me. You and your whore gave me no choice!" I seethed as my hair floated as my power rose, raw and unchecked as hatred burned through me. I was a powder keg set to detonate.

"You're alive," Spyder said as he held his hand against his own heart.

"Let me *go!*" I snarled, uncaring that everyone was now calling their own power to them as mine rose dangerously high. Lucian stepped into my path, and I slapped him, hard. I continued even though he did nothing to prevent it. He could have easily blocked it, but yet he let me inflict the pain I'd felt and continued to feel on his face. I didn't want to harm him, but I needed him to feel the pain I felt, to know that I suffered.

"Open the fucking door," he urged, and I paused, setting my forehead against his chest, inhaling his scent deep into my lungs before I found the strength to push away from it. "Let her go," he mumbled as he stepped back, staring at me through eyes that swam with unshed tears.

I didn't stick around to see if they fell, or if he'd actually shed a tear for the child we'd lost. I vanished the moment the door was open and the wards were lowered.

The death echo ate at my soul, my core. It thrummed through me until it touched the empty womb that would never hold life again. I'd made the ultimate sacrifice to save them, to save him. Oh, I'd known I would be back. Heaven wouldn't take me, and Hell couldn't contain me, which left me adrift in my own hellish prison.

Just soulless beings that couldn't die.

Empty. Devoid of what we'd once been. Craving to be what we had been, but unable to ever feel or know life again.

I didn't love anything anymore. I didn't *hate* anything anymore. I didn't feel much of anything anymore either, other than an endless need to kill, slaughter and destroy anything that threatened the creatures who'd just held me prisoner. Ironic, since loving them was what had gotten me to this point in the first place. The only time I did feel anything was during the death echo as I relived my loss, over and over on an endless loop I couldn't escape.

"It happened again, didn't it?" Joshua asked as I materialized beside him. I nodded, and his arm looped through mine in comfort. "We were drawn to it, to you. Something is pulling us here as well, do you feel it?" he asked.

"I do, I can," I nodded. "We need to figure out what it is and eradicate it."

"And if it is our blood?"

"Then we kill them all."

CHAPTER
six

If this is a dream, let me slumber, let me never awaken to find her gone. She's fire, she's whiskey, and she's mine.
~Lucian Blackstone

I stared at her, the minutes turning into hours as I waited for her to vanish, for it to have been nothing more than a dream. I'd felt her heart as it had begun beating, linking the bond that connected us as if she'd never ceased to exist, and yet she'd fucking died in my arms.

The darkness inside of her was seductive, unreal, and yet she's something stronger than I could sense, feel. How she came back was a mystery, one I planned to unravel, and yet I didn't fucking care. She's here, and it was all that mattered.

Watching her death echo had almost brought me to my knees. The loss she felt as the reapers had taken the child from her womb had felt real, even to me, one who doesn't feel. Lena had suffered long after the air had left her lungs and her body had grown cold. Had I still been holding her as she'd been going through hell?

The runes she'd painted on her skin had burned into her flesh, trapping the seal into her corpse. She'd sacrificed herself and our child to save the world, a fucking martyr in her own right, and yet she'd known, she'd known death was only her beginning.

Her prick of a brother hadn't died either, and my mind raced to replay her actions after he'd taken her to the cabin in the woods. How had he known, and were they the same? She was stronger, faster, and more powerful than any of the others she seemed to run with now.

Untapped magic oozed from her pores, a reminder of how immortal she'd become. I wanted to grab her, tie her up, and force her to tell me what had happened, or how she'd known she would come back.

I'd felt her soul escaping her body—or Katarina's portion of it. The reminder that she was created by magic shivered through my mind as I watched her. Her body was new, beautiful, and the darkness inside her only made my dick hard to experience this new and more durable version of her.

There were differences in her, the black that filled her eyes until it swallowed up the whites of her retinas. The lines that pulsed with magic as her anger grew unchecked, and the way she fought. She fought like she fucked: fast, hard, and with no fucking mercy. My mother fucking match in every way and yet she didn't want me.

She'd taken us on, and she'd laughed at our efforts as if we were an inconvenience she didn't mind playing with. So what was she doing here? Protecting her family, or was there something more pulling her to this place?

Her back stiffened and she turned, throwing me a look that dared me to come play with her again. I wanted to play with her; I wanted to slam my mouth against that full, sexy fucking mouth that did such naughty things when it pleased. I wanted to feel her tremble around my cock as she demanded and took everything I gave her, and yet for the first time ever in my existence, I wanted to hold her against my body, listening to that heartbeat that mirrored the drums of war. To feel the warmth of her that screamed with life.

She'd come back to me, and I didn't care how or why she had, as long as she stayed. Spyder settled beside me, emerging from the shadows as he slinked into the spot next to me.

"How? How is this even fucking possible? I felt her die, and then I felt the emptiness she left when she killed herself," he snapped, his hair a mussed fucking mess of strands from running his fingers through it or ripping it out.

"Something brought her back," I uttered thickly, hating the weakness I felt but uncaring if he felt it. "Something powerful enough to take her from death without a mortal soul," I pondered. "She's…more. She smells like hellfire, mixed with enough power to light up the entire world."

"I don't care who brought my kitty back, only that she's back, Lucian. I felt like my world had been torn apart without her."

"You know she's mine, right? I don't envy fighting you for her, brother," I hissed.

"We'll see who she chooses, if she even wants anything to do with either of us. She deserves the fucking moon for what she endured alone. You created life with her, something neither of us had thought possible, and then she lost it. She loved him, your son. She sacrificed him and her life to protect you. Who the fuck does that? You're a fucking prick for not seeing her intentions."

"You think I don't know that? If I'd known she was going to play the fucking martyr, I'd have strapped her into chains and kept her in my room until the end of days. Neither of us deserves her, neither of us are worthy of that woman," I mused, watching as her spine straightened and then arched, seductive and intoxicating. That's what she was. She was all woman, all black lace and fire that I burned to touch and yet knew I couldn't, not yet.

The moment I'd seen her fighting my world tilted, the thought of the seal using her flesh to dole out its evil had burned through me as if my world was on fire. I'd been sure it was the seal, using her as a meat suit to create havoc, and yet she had laughed at us as if she'd found us lacking.

The moment her heart had begun to beat, I felt her. I felt all of her, the emotions that churned through her, the wrongness of what she had become, but most of all, I felt my Lena trapped in a cage that couldn't hold her.

She'd told me to let her go, but that was beyond what I could do. I didn't love anything, but Lena, Lena made me feel more than anything else in my world had ever come close to making me feel. Emotions were beyond me, beyond what I was.

I'd thought I'd loved Katarina in the early days, but it was lust I'd felt for her. The creaminess of her flesh as it had touched mine. Her body was addictive, and yet I'd thought it more. I'd thought it love, but her death…it only left me empty.

Lena's death had brought fucking tears to eyes that had never experienced them before. She'd taken my seed and created life with it, and just like that, it had been taken away from us. Her death had brought the creature that I am to its knees roaring in denial, and then I'd sat beside her lifeless body, scouring my mind, my world, for a way to bring a soulless body back from the grave, only to find nothing.

I'd buried her in a nameless grave, one I watched endlessly as pain had forced me to remain there. I'd thought I had loved Katarina, but Lena, Lena made me want to destroy the entire world I'd fought to protect. I'd wanted to bring down the stars and snuff every fucking one out of existence for shining without her.

Lena was the stars, and I her darkness. She shone brighter than anything this world had to offer me before her, and she exposed parts of my darkness that I'd never thought could be brought to light, but she was light to my darkness. She had been vibrant, full of life—and now, now where she'd been beautiful before, she was ethereal in immortality.

It made the lines of her face more defined, exposed the subtle curves of her flesh until even those who hadn't noticed them before itched to trace them intimately. Her hair was fuller, more vibrant in color, and her eyes, those beautiful blue eyes were lit from within with a fire that refused to be snuffed out.

"And if she is here to kill us?" he asked, interrupting my thoughts.

"Then I'll have fun playing with her," I announced. "I doubt she was brought back to kill me. If she was, and her purpose was such, she'd have done it already. No, someone brought her back for another reason, and we need to figure it out soon. I refuse to let her go a second time."

"You don't have her," he laughed soundlessly.

"I have her; I've always had her, Spyder. She just doesn't know it yet. Obviously, you don't realize it either.

I'll get her back because she's my moon and the stars that burn in my skies. She's mine, and nothing short of me dying will change that."

"You cannot be killed," he scoffed.

"Exactly, and even if I have to force her to remain hidden from the world to continue to exist in mine, I will do whatever it takes to keep her. Even exposing what we are," I warned and he tilted his head as he considered it.

"Katarina wasn't worth this mess, but Lena is worth the world. I'd help you destroy it to protect her, you know that. Our bond, it went deeper than it should have, so be warned, I want her too. I want to feel her shatter around me once before you claim her, Lucian. I'm owed that."

"If she wants you, she'd have had you. Her sexuality isn't something she hides or sheds for one man. Lena is everything sexual and sensual in this world. Her body was made to be fucked, but her mind, her mind is much more than just sex and chaos; it's a storm that burns with the fires of life and love. She's my fucking match, Spyder. My world," I growled. "If she wants you, you can join us. If not, it will be your loss."

"We'll see," he mused, turning his eyes to watch her as she stood guard over the Guild like a silent sentinel. The others followed her lead; whether they realized it or not, she was born to lead. They'd follow her wherever she took them, which was another indication that whoever had brought my Lena back, had known who and what she could become. "Deviant, Bane, and Devlin are currently closing down the other clubs; see that they do so without drawing unwanted attention to themselves."

"And Club Chaos? Will we fix it up again, so we have a fallback shelter? I don't imagine this Guild will withstand Lucifer when he finally emerges. I'm positive he isn't finished coming at us yet. He's somewhere licking the wounds of his loss, but he'll resurface when he is ready."

"Club Chaos already stands once more. Now that her ghost isn't haunting the halls, or everywhere I look, I rebuilt it. It's now able to withstand whatever comes at us. I'll protect her coven for as long as I can, but eventually, they will need more than we can give them. They feed off the mortals, unknowingly. But still, without the walls remaining up between worlds, their magic will falter. It's the curse I placed, the failsafe that ensures they don't win the game. It cannot be undone."

"And what of the others who have been surfacing in the chaos? What do we do about them?" he queried.

"They're here because Lucifer has been freed. If they intervene before we are ready, we'll end them without warning. That's another reason why we need to close the clubs and get them back to us. Our numbers are small now, even with the shadows we have trailing them, the hellhounds scenting out their trail, we need everyone back here for when shit hits the fan because this isn't over."

CHAPTER
seven

I wish I could show you when you are lonely or in darkness, the astonishing light of your own being. ~*Hafiz*

Lena

I felt his stare the entire night, eating away at the defenses I'd erected once the slithering, slimy fingers of the death echo released me. When day broke across the sky as the sun rose to replace the night with the first rays of the sun, the others vanished from the line. I didn't move, unable to leave this place as if held here by invisible hands. A cold hand gripped my heart as I considered what would be keeping me here. As if I'd been brought back to be his fucking lap dog and guard him.

"It's him," I muttered as anger pulsed through me. "I think we can't leave because of him."

"It may not be him," he offered as his blue eyes slowly took in my ash-colored face. "It may be the bloodline, our blood. They're inside that place too."

"I guess it could be," I agreed, even though I didn't think it was. I didn't want to have to end our own bloodline to escape the pull to this place. "It's worse today," I admitted. "Like I can't leave," I shivered as the words escaped. "Like I can't leave here even if I wanted to," I muttered breathlessly as panic filled my chest.

"We will figure it out," Joshua said as his eyes looked over my shoulder. "We will figure out why we slink back to this place, hiding in the shadows like fucking puppets. Lucian is coming, Lenny. You should try to leave before he captures you again."

"You should go, I can't," I growled. "Leave before he ends up catching us both."

I turned, not waiting to see if Joshua did as I bid him to. Lucian's approach was slow, calculated. His strides exuded power as he stopped right in front of me, peering down into my gaze. Had he waited for the others to leave before he'd approached me? Biding his time until we appeared weak and outnumbered? Maybe, but I got this feeling it was something else.

Not that it mattered, if I wanted to hurt him, I would.

I'd come back colder, emptier, and stronger than I'd ever been in my other form. I was no longer mortal, bound by their laws or rules. Not having a soul had benefits; for instance, when someone died right before me, I didn't care. I didn't flinch or bat an eyelash at the loss of the human, or whoever it was who perished. I envied them their death. I had felt nothing until he'd touched me, fighting him had made me *feel*. Before last night, the only thing I'd felt was the echo of my death as it played out every full moon. It was freeing, refreshing not to care what happened to people.

Before, I'd felt everything.

"We need to talk," he growled as he stared down into my empty eyes.

"I don't think we do," I returned aloofly. I shoved

my hair over my shoulder as I stared up into his obsidian depths, reveling at the galaxies that shone back at me. My heart raced, and I hated it. It was why I'd ripped it out of my chest last time I'd hidden in the shadows, watching him. He'd once been the hunter and I his prey, but no more.

"You're alive and I watched you fucking die," he snarled. "I held your fucking corpse in my arms for hours. Days, Lena," he muttered as he scrubbed his hand down his face with irritation.

"I wouldn't have become a corpse if you'd left me out of your fucked-up games. Maybe if you and your girlfriend had left me and mine alone, we wouldn't be at this point, now would we?" I asked.

He recoiled, his eyes burning with an intensity that left me trembling.

Lucian: 0. Lena: 1.

"You weren't supposed to be a part of it."

"I know, but I never even existed until she split an egg and filled it with poison. I was in it before I was even real, Lucian. But then you never cared before when innocent lives suffered for you and your game, so why would that change now? You destroy lives and leave chaos in your wake and yet still, you'd play it with her, wouldn't you?"

"You can either come with me, or Spyder and my men will destroy your friends," Lucian murmured, his tone cold and unforgiving. I looked past him to where his men stood, weapons at the ready to hunt down the others at his request. "Choose."

"Fine, you can have a few minutes of my eternity but no more. I'm not your plaything anymore, Blackstone. If that is even your real name," I seethed. "I can smell you, you know. That thick, earthy scent of burning brimstone and ashes; the death and despair that oozes from within you. What are you?" I asked breathlessly, stepping closer to him. "Let's talk about that, shall we?"

"You don't need to know what I am to fuck me," he replied smoothly.

"Oh, I think you have the wrong idea," I chuckled. "I'm not fucking you. Last time it ended rather badly for me, wouldn't you agree?" I asked pointedly, lifting a blonde brow at the question.

The tick in his jaw twitched, the only indication I'd struck a nerve. The sky opened up, sending a light drizzle of rain down through the ozone, dusting his thick black lashes with droplets. His hand lifted up, shoving a strand of hair away from his face before he lunged, catching my arm and bringing my body close against his.

"I never wanted that for you," he uttered as his tone hitched as if it hurt him to admit it. "It also wasn't just about fucking you, Lena. It was always about more, and the more of you I got, the harder it was to let you go."

"But that's what I got, wasn't it? One day to know I held your son in my womb, and then he was gone. My only choice as his mother was to let him go. To let him be free of the monster I now hold within me. *Your* monster," I whispered thickly for his ears alone. I closed my eyes and lifted my face to the rain, letting it wash away the pain I felt. I used it to hide the tears that streaked down my face, only it couldn't hide them. I knew what he would see, as if I'd painted my lashes thick with mascara; black streaks rushed from my eyes to race down my cheeks.

"Don't fight me, or they will hunt them down and destroy them all."

"Are you sure they'd win?" I asked as I stepped closer, placing my hands flat against his warm body. "Are you afraid of me, Lucian?" I asked as he swallowed hard.

"Not of you, sweet girl. I'm afraid I'll wake and you'll still be buried in that cold fucking earth where I watched them place your rotting corpse."

Ouch. Point for Lucian. "You should be afraid of me," I shrugged. "You'd deserve it if I disappeared. You deserved the pain you felt because it's nothing compared to what I endured as they took my son and left me alive."

"You think I wanted you to die?"

"I think it doesn't matter what either of us wanted, it's what happened. You can stronghold me into coming along with you, but you fail to see that no matter what you do, you'll never find that whimpering girl you lost. Your Lena is dead, she's in that dark fucking hole you so gently placed her into. Don't expect me to play her, not even for you. I won't, I am not weak and I will not fucking bow to you."

"You are her; I can feel the bond, Lena. Can't you? Spyder felt it as well the moment your heart started beating. I take it your brother assisted in hiding you from us again? Preventing me from feeling you when you returned to this world?" he demanded.

"I didn't do dick," Joshua snorted, his eyes wild with the need to defend me. I took in his flexed hands, aching to fight Lucian, itching for the fight he'd so relished at my death. Not for me, but because his anger demanded he avenge what I'd lost: his nephew. My head tilted, and I slowly brought my eyes to Lucian's dark gaze, and pushed Lucian away from my brother, hard.

Joshua's eyes snapped towards mine; the others let out low, rumbling growls of warning, and I smirked. Fucking hell, they wanted to compare dicks, and I was the only one lacking one to join in their little competition.

"Let's go, asshole," I snapped in frustration as I ground my teeth together. "We all know you have dicks, and some are bigger than others, but this isn't a dick situation other than you all acting like one."

I met midnight eyes that sparkled at me with the silent promise of retribution for my comment with bored contempt. I hadn't lied, I wasn't afraid of him. I was, however, afraid of what he could do to my brother. I followed him when he turned on his heels, heading towards the Guild silently. His massive strength and power oozed from his pores to sizzle across my flesh. It was something I'd once craved as a heroin junkie desired the prick of a needle against its flesh. My feet sloshed through the growing puddles mindlessly as I stared at his broad shoulders. I didn't even care that I was still dressed in the tiny sundress, which was now sheer and doing very little to hide my body through its flimsy material. My body reacted to the cold, and that gave me pause as I continued to follow Lucian past the stairs that led into the Guild.

My nipples hardened as I followed him and I frowned, wondering how it responded to it if I hadn't been bothered by it. I wasn't human anymore, which meant I wasn't bothered by shit like the cold or being uncomfortable. It ran like a well-oiled machine, working well to hide what we'd become, and yet it mimicked a human and the reactions they experienced well. Like it knew we had to pretend to be human or perish against the sea of monsters oozing into this realm daily.

Once inside, I paused, taking in the array of creatures that stood between us and the empty hall on the other side of them. Arms folded across chests, weapons sat at the ready for any sign of violence from me. Magic hummed around me, sensing me as if they could feel out whatever

I'd become. I laughed coldly as Lucian turned to stare at me.

"Did you bring me in here to kill me?" I asked softly, my eyes aglow with the irony I currently felt.

"I want to know what the fuck you are and how you're still alive, Lena. People without souls don't come back, they cease to exist. They sure as fuck don't experience death echoes. Ghost relive their death, no other creature has ever had to relive it. It's a punishment for not crossing into the next realm."

"But I am here, and I do experience it, and that bothers you, doesn't it?" I exhaled. "You don't like not knowing what I am, and yet you expect me to be fine with the fact that you are an unknown as well. Sucks, doesn't it?"

"Answer the fucking question." His tone was harsh, angry as his eyes searched mine as if he would see the truth in them.

"I don't know what I am, only that I am here. I also don't fucking care how it happened or why. We just came back, and when we did, we were alone or with those who knew we would rise. There was no one around to explain it or tell us what we'd become. Can I go now?" I asked, crossing my arms to mirror his angry stance. "I need to go find something to change into, something more…less sheer and flimsy as fuck."

"I have a room upstairs, you're joining me in it for a while," he said in a rough, grated tone that made my spine both straighten and curve with need at the same time.

"If there's a bed in it, I'd rather a torture device in a cell. I believe there's a rack down in the catacombs I passed before I took the grimoires from this place."

"That you somehow managed to retain even after you died." It was a statement, not a question. Lucian watched me as a smile lifted to play across my lips. "Dead things cannot play with magic, nor retain what they held in life. They don't retain grimoires, which are living things."

"And?" I asked crossly. "I don't owe you an explanation for anything. I gave you everything I had to give, which in case you forgot, included my life. I owe you nothing, Lucian. Yet here I am, so tick-tock, asshole. I have other shit to do."

"I need to know how you are reanimating the body, how you're able to control it," he snapped.

"It's my body, my mind, but I seem to have lost that pesky soul that made me give a fuck. Which means I literally have no fucks to give you. Not a damn one, big boy. You want to fuck? I can do that, but it may be a dead fuck, get it?" I wiggled my brows as his frown deepened. "You want to…" I blinked as something wet and icy splashed me in the face. "Did you fucking throw holy water in my face?" I asked as I sputtered and wiped my face off.

"She's not a demon," Ristan said, his silver eyes narrowing at me as if I'd grown a second head. "Her heart is, in fact, beating. Strangely, though… It's in tune to yours, Lucian. When it beats, it holds your rhythm. I don't feel anything but darkness and rage coming from her though, a lot of fucking rage." His eyes saddened, and he frowned as he stared at me. "There's an endless pain consuming her from within, pain she cannot control."

"Back the fuck up before I end you, demon," I growled low, meaning it.

"You're mortal-ish. I've never smelled or seen, let alone felt anything like her before. That black shit, though, that's worrisome. It smells of midnight, and yet only cursed things bleed black or owned things. Curious thing you've become, little one."

"That you know of; you see, there are not just a few worlds with gaping fucking holes in them, the doors are all open. The creatures we fought last night are not new to us, but they were to you. You didn't see them, which is why I'm standing here right now. Had you been able to sense or see them, I wouldn't have had to make my presence known yet. You are not aware of the monsters that hunt in this world now. I've fought shit that raised my hair, and I'm not easily scared lately. Those hounds we killed? They feed off the blood of witches, almost like a vampire but not quite. Before the hounds, it was demons, not from Hell, not from Faery. They didn't need a soul to enter this world, they only need the gate opened, and in they walked. Some vampires consume souls, not blood. Creatures I've never even heard about are now here, feeding off the humans and no one seems to care. Those vampires? They bled black, as I do. So as far as I am concerned, what I am is the least of our fucking worries right now. Make no mistake; even if we are no longer human, we are no longer at the top of the food chain. We are the food, ladies and gentlemen."

"How can you say that if you don't even know what the hell you are?" Synthia asked pointedly.

"Because there are creatures that I fought and I had to run from, Synthia. Creatures that easily took some of the others out," I countered. "We don't die, but we can be killed; which means we cannot stop them from doing what they came here to do. That is what we've been doing while you all hold up in your safe little haven pretending the world hasn't gone to shit."

"You've been alive for months, and yet you couldn't be bothered to end our pain?" Kendra's voice cut through the room, and I tensed. It hit me harder than a brick wall at a full run, knocking the air from my lungs as I turned to stare at her across the room.

"Your sister, the one you loved so much?" I asked, staring at her across the distance that kept her safe from the monster I'd become. "She isn't in here anymore. That light I once had burned out. That fight I had to live? Died with me. I don't eat, I don't sleep, and I love nothing. I am not her, I am a shell of what I was, and I do not want you to expect anything of me. I will let you down, and I will fucking enjoy it."

"You're my sister!" she snapped. "No matter what the fuck you are, bitch. We mourned you. *I* mourned you. You're my other half. We buried you in a nameless grave with only fucking initials that let the world know you ever existed. It damn near broke me! So who cares if you eat or sleep, and I don't need you to love me, Lena. I want my sister back. You're my sister. So whatever the fuck your issue is, get over it. Your heart beats. That means you live."

I smiled sadly at her as her eyes glistened with unshed tears. "I don't need my heart."

"Bullshit," she snapped angrily, her turquoise eyes alight with tears that flowed from them. "You're alive, I know you are. I can feel you, here," she cried as she touched her chest.

As she watched I let my claws extend. The serrated nails pushed into my chest, the sickening sound filling the room as I withdrew my still-beating heart. It beat, dripping black blood down my chest and onto the floor below as I pulled the useless organ out. I dropped it onto the ground and looked up, peering into her eyes.

"It beats when *they* decide to bring me back. I don't

need it to beat. I don't need you or him, or anyone. I don't miss you. I don't feel *anything*, Kendra. I only know hate and pain, two things I refused to feel in life, and now it's the only thing I can feel. The two emotions I refused to feel in life are now the only thing I know. You did bury me. I was in that coffin until I was removed from it, but I wasn't alive, and I'm still not. I didn't need air or food. I didn't waste away waiting for Joshua to come unbury me. I just existed in that cold box, unfeeling. He didn't have to rush because I'm not alive. Those days I spent in that cabin with him, he knew I would meet my death, and he would be the one to bring me back from it. He explained sacrifice and what I would be rewarded with if I had the strength to make it. I wasn't a saint as you're trying to make me out to be. I chose death to save you and my son, but I also knew I wouldn't die. I killed my child; I did it to protect him and you. But I also did it because I couldn't stand the thought of losing to those assholes. I won the fucking game, hands down. I ended it, and I'd do it again just to say I did."

"You did it to protect us," she argued.

"I did it because I didn't have a choice. It was you or me; one of us wasn't walking away, and you were too fucking weak to see it. I was already dead; the seal was inside of me. The only way to null it was to remove the souls and find something strong enough to hold it. I am, and I did. But now that it is over, so is she. Your sister is dead, deal with it. Push it to the back of your fucking mind, throw a fucking fit, do whatever the hell you need to do to accept it, I did." I knew it was a slap in the face, but she had to face it. Pain ached, burning my insides until I wanted to lean over and retch with it.

Pushing them away was the only way to protect them

from the monster I was becoming. I could feel myself evolving, growing as the others continually did. Some went missing and never returned, while others returned changed or worse than they'd been. Efficient killing machines couldn't be loved, nor should they be, and that was what I was becoming. I didn't want to watch them break apart again; they deserved better. I'd watched it, cold and detachedly as they'd fallen to pieces in the wake of my death. But I was changing into something cold who watched with a detachment of emotions, as if it was how I protected myself. My feelings were ice-cold, and anything else seemed foreign, wrong somehow.

"Lucian, tick-tock, you're wasting my time," I said, turning to him and flipping him off as his eyes took in the empty hole in my chest where my heart had been. "Eyes up here, big boy. You might make my panties wet if you keep eyeing my hole like that."

"You just ripped out your fucking heart," Ristan said, his eyes wide as shock shone from them. It marred his pretty face and made me want to mess his perfect hair up.

"It's an over-exaggerated organ," I shrugged. "It's not even close to the shape they said it was, and it only reminds me that I have to continue when my son is dead and gone. You want to know how I kept my presence from you. I ripped my fucking heart out the moment it began to stir after I was reborn." My flesh was already healing, the immortality speeding the process as I stood there, bickering for no other reason to give Joshua and the others time to flee. "I left it in that coffin for you, though. After all, that useless thing was what drew me to you in the first place, Lucian."

"Follow me," he snapped, his eyes still locked on the heart that beat upon the floor. "Spyder, collect her heart."

"Can I keep it?" Spyder asked as he mean-mugged Ristan, who licked his lips as he stared down at it. He bent down and retrieved it before he slipped it into a sack Ryder handed him.

"Oh, Spyder, you've always had a piece of my heart," I chuckled. I blew him a raspberry before I wiped the black blood from my hand onto the dress as my claws retracted. "Be careful, though, the last person who picked it up ended up buried in my coffin when I crawled out."

"Who is in your casket?" he asked.

"Someone who meddled where they shouldn't have," I shrugged indifferently.

CHAPTER eight

Once we accept our limits, we go beyond them. ~*Albert Einstein*

My gaze roamed over Lucian's wide shoulders, following him up the staircase and then down winding hallways until we lingered before a door. My mouth watered as my nose greedily sucked in his earthy, woodsy scent. Something about this creature made my emotions stir, ones I'd thought had been snuffed out with my life. My teeth ground, hands fisted at my sides as I waited for him to open the door he'd paused in front of.

Of all the shit to deal with, couldn't I get a break? Why did everything inside of me scream to push this man against the wall and devour him until I'd taken my fill? I wanted to rip him bare and ride him like a beast in heat that wouldn't stop until she'd soothed the ache he'd created.

He turned slowly, those sinful bedroom eyes slowly lowering to my clenched jaw and then my balled fists as if he sensed exactly what was running wild through my mind. I lifted a dainty brow as he mirrored it, so I flipped him off and then slowly crossed my arms.

"Is that an invitation, Lena?" he asked huskily.

"You wish," I grumbled. His eyes darkened as they slowly dropped to my mouth and then lower, flinching as they landed on the ugly scar on my throat. I'd somehow managed to sound uncaring, cold even. I didn't care what he thought, or if it turned him off. Caring took effort, and I didn't plan to waste my energy on him.

I hated that my body wanted him, and it had since the moment I saw him standing on the steps of this Guild. It had heated, which was new since I didn't radiate body heat unless I put effort into it, and yet it had. It was unnerving. The fact that I'd wanted to taste his lips, to feel the heat from his body as my fingers wrapped around his massive cock bothered me. His mouth was a drug, one that I wanted to taste. Worse than that, I wanted him to look me in the eye and tell me that I wasn't this emotionless animal I'd become.

But I was. I felt hate, despair, and emptiness as deep and wide as the darkest abyss of Hell that grew inside of me. No amount of touching or feeling him would erase that. His close proximity did, however, soothe the coldness I felt to my bones.

He paused as his hand touched the door, pushing it open as he stepped back, allowing me room to enter it. I strolled by him as though I wasn't affected by him at all. I surveyed the dark room, which was done in hues of black and red silk, with a large bed set in the center of it. Just fucking great. Two things I didn't need in my life at the moment: Lucian and a bed. The door closed behind me, and I turned to face him with my mask securely in place.

"Tell me what you feel right now, in this room," he ordered.

"Nothing," I muttered harshly as I swallowed hard against the need to have his hands on my flesh. Before last night, I hadn't felt much of anything, but the moment he'd touched me…that changed. I'd felt him, whereas, before him, I knew I *should* feel. The others touched me in practice as we'd fought, and yet their touch hadn't even alerted me to the fact that my skin had been grazed. Lucian's touch singed my flesh, stirring emotions I'd prayed were unattainable. I'd felt him right down into the empty space that should have housed my soul, and it ached. *I* fucking ached. I'd felt his warmth and craved more. I'd felt emotions so raw and intense that it had terrified me. Even while I fought him, I craved his kiss, that sexy, sinful mouth that could take away the pain.

We had some major issues that dying hadn't fixed.

"You don't hunger, and you don't sleep," he pointed out softly, his tone a silk caress over my flesh. "So how do you heal?" he asked, his obsidian gaze slowly moving over the ruined dress I wore. It singed my flesh in its heated wake, sending gooseflesh pebbling across it.

"I just heal," I admitted as I turned away from the heat banked in his depths. I was terrified he'd see through the cold façade I was showing him. It was how I shielded myself from what I knew could unravel the hard exterior that protected me now. Out of everyone in my life, he'd known me on a visceral level. He'd peeled away the layers, finding the broken girl who lay beneath them. If he tried, he'd start to bring down the walls faster than I could repair them, and I wasn't ready for that. I may not ever be prepared for what he could do to me again.

"Every creature has a way that they heal which is

unique to them and their breed. What's your body telling you right now? What does it crave to heal the damage you did to your chest, Lena?" he questioned, his tone soothing as he delved into the mystery I'd become.

I turned back to stare at him, finding him closer than I expected. His hand wrapped around my throat and I was pushed against the closest wall. I brought my hands up to his on reflex, staring into the dark, midnight eyes I'd craved as I lay awake inside my coffin. His mouth slammed against mine, and I moaned. His tongue pushed past my lips, devouring my tongue as it dueled against mine for dominance. I moaned, opening to his assault with a naked hunger I couldn't ignore. Time passed, and yet I didn't break his kiss, or pull away from him. His hand tightened, and I opened my eyes again, finding him watching me as he pulled away. He'd discovered a few things, like the fact that I didn't need air anymore, and I wasn't kissing him back. It wasn't because I hadn't wanted to kiss him back, it was because so many fucking emotions had slammed into me that tears had begun sliding from my eyes as the memories of our last kiss came rushing back.

"Don't touch me!" I screamed as I wrapped my arms around his back and yanked his hair, pulling his head away from mine. I dropped my weight, intending to attack him, but he backed up, his hands raised with their palms up as if he sensed my distress. He took in the black tears that leaked from my eyes, which had gone black as well. Gone was his beautiful Lena, and in her place was the darkness I'd become. The cold dead thing, the sunken eyes, and the monster that haunted my dreams stood before him.

"You feel me, Lena. My touch, my kiss," he murmured as he watched me for any sign of weakness.

"I don't want to feel anything!" I screamed, the sound

piercing my ears, shattering everything made of glass inside the room. Heavy footfalls raced down the hallway and then the door was ripped open. We ignored them, staring at one another. "I don't want to feel anything ever again, Blackstone." It came out on a hiss, a warning of breath as my chest rose and fell.

"Because then you'd have to face it, right? You'd have to feel everything at once, and you're afraid to do so. You're not fucking weak. You're the strongest, most stubborn woman I have met in my entire life—and I am eternal. You don't want to face your emotions because they'd be too much, wouldn't they?"

"I'm leaving," I muttered as I started towards the door, only to find Spyder standing there, blocking my exit as he held my heart in his hands. "Really, Spyder? Throw it away already," I sputtered.

"Not a chance, Kitty cat," he drawled thickly. "I feel it, everything you're trying not to feel. It's why you rip it out, isn't it? So much fucking pain," he said sadly.

"Why don't you tell me? You assholes seem to have it all figured out already. Why do you even need me here to answer questions?" I asked, and then something inside of me snapped to attention. My eyes moved to the wall as if I could sense trouble approaching. Everything inside of me snapped at once.

I tried to dissipate the wards to vanish, but they refused. Instead, they pulsed, screaming in warning that they'd been altered. I pushed past Spyder, racing down the hallway with urgency. I took the stairs three at a time, rushing past the heads that lifted as I raced towards the front doors of the Guild. I didn't pause, didn't wait for permission as I exploded through the doors and screamed.

"Incoming!" The scream turned every soulless pair

of eyes in the vicinity towards me as weapons were unsheathed. I skidded to a stop beside Joshua, patting myself for weapons only to find none. "Fuck!" I screamed as I watched the others wincing, worry covering their faces. The issue when we fought was this: We changed. We evolved, and we didn't know how or why we did, only that we did.

CHAPTER
nine

If you realize that all things change, there is nothing you will try to hold on to. If you are not afraid of dying, there's nothing you cannot achieve. ~*Lao Tzu*

The sky cracked loudly as thunder rumbled, lightning following close behind it, brightening the sky and the precarious clouds that threatened to let loose a heavy rain. It continued, growing stronger and louder as if some invisible being controlled it. Every bolt of lightning that exploded in the sky lit the silhouettes of monstrous beings that hovered just above the thick, darkening clouds. A monstrous horde of slithering, gyrating beings edged out of the shadows, encircling the Guild. We stood shoulder to shoulder, preparing to battle them. The taste and craving for battle ignited a fire inside our beings.

I ignored Lucian and his scent that clung heavily in the air, beckoning me like a lover's caress with the promise of release. He'd fucking kissed me, and so many emotions had exploded through that it terrified me, leaving me boneless with need. I'd felt more in those seconds as his mouth touched mine than I had since the day I'd slit my throat.

Another bolt of lightning crashed through the sky, lighting it up as winged creatures began their descent towards us. I once again reached for my swords and found only mere wisps of spaghetti straps. *Oomph*. I stepped backwards, rounding on my heels as I leveled Synthia with a cold, detached look of loathing.

"A little help, you took my clothes and my weapons."

"So I did," she shrugged as if it bothered her little, but my body was instantly covered in a tight leather suit that hugged every curve perfectly. I tested it, noting that it allowed me to still easily maneuver. My dual swords were back, or at least the equivalent to what I'd had before they'd taken them. I unsheathed them, palming the weight and testing it. I patted my waist, finding more blades as a smile curved my lips.

"You and I should be friends," I uttered as I took in the craftsmanship of the new blades. I turned on my heel, taking my place beside my brother as I sensed the immense power she radiated as she stepped next to me, withdrawing her own blades.

"We could be friends, but you need to work through your shit first. I'm a queen; you're…well, whatever the fuck you are now. When you figure it out, come see me. I can use some badass bitches around here. We can paint our nails and compare weapons." I eyed her titanium blades as she leveled a chilling gaze on the monsters that approached. "You have issues, Lena, but if you learn to use that anger for good, you'd level the fucking field with it."

"I didn't ask to have issues," I muttered beneath my breath.

"We never ask for issues," she smiled sadly, her tone gentle. "It's not about how you fall, Lena. It is how you get back up that defines you. Not that you didn't fall fucking spectacularly. I mean, that took strength, and I really don't care what the fuck you are. I'm glad you're back, however it happened. And it's not gone; it's just waiting for you to find it again."

"What the fuck are you talking about? I don't speak code, Synthia."

"Your light, asshole," she snorted. "It is there, inside of you. Nothing can smother your fucking light except for you. Light it up, Lena. Let the world see the fire that burns inside of you. If they try to smother it, smother them. If it's Lucian, use your tits and smother him. Works on Ryder all the time; you see, he can't very well argue if his face is in them, now can he?" she chuckled as my mouth dropped open. "You're pushing them away to protect them, but who is protecting you from being hurt?"

"I don't need to be protected anymore," I growled as the monsters moved forward, close enough to attack. They had multiple heads, red eyes, and pasty grey skin that clung to bones as if they'd been starved. It looked like someone had bred Cerberus with a hellhound, who had then mated with a fucking zombie. The stench of them was overpowering, roiling my stomach as I swallowed down the urge to throw up. Black-eyed demons stood behind them, smirking through yellowed teeth as they watched us prepare to battle their horde of monstrous three-headed dogs. I swung at the first dog's heads, plural, taking all three off in a single, efficient swing.

"Everyone needs someone, even if that someone is a dominating asshole who bosses you around," Synthia growled as she lunged for a hound that started towards me. She cut it in half, her swing graceful as she ended it in a skillful move that sent all three heads rolling onto the pavement as if she was a dancer who had practiced her craft to outdo any move I could make. I frowned, staring at her.

"The fuck is your issues, ladies?" Erie growled as she jumped on another beast, slamming the outside heads into the middle one as blood exploded from their mouths. She didn't bother with weapons as her hands glowed, her body a magical display as it slid through them as if she was fire and they were ice. She smiled at me as blood dripped from her clothing.

"Girl talk," Synthia said as if it explained everything.

"Bitch talk, really? Right now? Are we going to fuck them up or check out each other's nails? Mine are fucking broken because I'm fighting, as I should be. You?" she snapped, staring at Synthia, who lifted her hand and bared her nails.

"Happy Anniversary," Synthia said.

"It's not my anniversary for shit," Erie snapped and narrowed her eyes on me as if I'd know what the fuck Synthia was speaking of.

"It's the nail color, and if these fuckers mess them up, this Goddess is going to lose her shit. I'm on the last bottle of this color, and the factories are closed down because supply and demand is shit with the nearing apocalypse."

I rolled my eyes and exploded into the air, landing in the middle of the fray. I slashed and danced until my arms ached and burned as blood oozed down my face, lathering my hair in it. I was so engrossed in the battle that when I used my blades to scissor a demon's head from his shoulders, I almost took off Lucian's too as he watched me.

"I'm not done with you," he shouted over the sound of swords clanking and meeting in the street.

"Yes, you are," I shouted back, turning to attack the nearest demon and pausing as the red being stared at me. "What the fuck?"

"Don't kill the red one!" Ristan growled as he stared me down. "It's easier to fight in this form. I'm the only red one here," he shrugged as he pushed his hand through the chest of a pale creature and withdrew the heart, biting into it.

Eww.

"Fucking demons," I groaned as I turned around, only to end up nose to chest with Lucian. "Back the fuck off or fight me, asshole!" I demanded.

"I've been fighting you. I've been fighting you since the moment I fucking met you and kissed you outside of your house!" he shot back angrily, his midnight eyes burning with desire.

The sky erupted into balls of flames and heat enveloped us. I stared up; sensing something big was above us, just out of eyesight. It took effort not to hit the ground as leathery wings came into view, sending my hair rushing into the air as it landed feet away from where I stood, tearing into the demons. Huge teeth severed them in half, tossing body parts in the giant beast's wake.

"Oh fuck this shit, I'm out," I groaned as I threw my hands up in the air in frustration. "Who the fuck brings a dragon to a demon fight," I blanched as it turned to stare in my direction with glowing eyes as blood dripped from its talons.

"He's on our side," he explained, grabbing a demon who rushed at him and removing its head quickly with a bored expression on his face. I blinked and frowned as he turned back towards me, his eyes smiling with anticipation.

"You might want to fill the Fae in on that one, they don't look too pleased about his presence," I pointed out. The moment Lucian turned away to see what I'd meant, I bolted.

The fight was dying down, but no matter how many we took down, even as the last few fell beneath our blades, I couldn't shake the foreboding feeling that continually grew inside of me. I stood in the middle of the carnage and stared up at the thick clouds still gathering above us. Demons couldn't control the weather, or at least not any we'd faced in the last few months. They simply didn't house enough power to control elements.

"This isn't over yet," I shouted over the multitude of people talking as they cleaned their weapons.

I felt him, close enough that whatever was inside me that drew me to this place, to him, alerted as if alarm bells were sounding from within me. I spun around, slashing my weapons out to protect. Lucian spun out of the way at the last second as something with wings landed in front of him, claws aimed to end his life.

My heart boomed, coming back online as red-hot rage surged from within, My nose flared, smelling the putrid scent of burning earth, brimstone, and ashes as the taint of evil slithered over my flesh. Thick black wings with bones that protruded from the edges blocked my way, and I moved without thinking, without waiting to see what it did. I jumped on it, biting its face from behind as it let loose a pain-filled scream that cut through the air. It ripped at my hair, my face as it tried to dislodge me. My teeth extended, ripping and severing flesh as I screamed back, gurgling blood as I tore it apart.

"Run, Lucian!" I shouted, demanding he listen in case I lost the fight, but he didn't budge. Instead, he just stared at me. Burning blue flames lit him from within as he took me in, fighting to protect him from whatever the fuck this thing was. "Lucian, go!"

The creature dug its nails into my arm, and I screeched as pain burned. Black blood leaked down my severed flesh as I continued to stare at Lucian, fuming that he'd place his life in danger, which pissed me off since I shouldn't fucking care and yet here I was, fighting tooth and nail to protect him!

I saw red, my nails exploded into serrated claws, and I tore at the creature without thought, without care. I ripped it apart with teeth and nails that were as sharp as the finest blades. Blood exploded from its neck, and my hands ripped into where I'd torn it apart, removing the head from the spine as I flipped over, landing in a bloody heap in front of Lucian. My hands went to my back, digging against the pain that echoed through my body.

I ripped my flesh from my own body, screaming as earth-shattering pain threatened to consume me. I ripped at my spine, tearing through the suit I wore as my hands found the flesh that rippled and obstructed them. I freed them. I exhaled as something broke free, slicing through the air behind me. Black gossamer wings whipped the air behind me as I stood before Lucian in the ruined leather suit. I whimpered as pain mixed with pleasure and my spine arched to relieve the pressure.

"Gods," Lucian whispered as he stared at me, watching as I fumbled with the weight that now forced me to my knees. I rose to my feet, teetering on them as I tilted my head, staring at Lucian with a hunger that raged within me. I struggled to calm the panic that welled inside of me as the wings stretched.

"I don't think that is what she is," Synthia said as she brought her hand up and a short, backless shirt covered my naked breasts. I wanted to thank her, but words were elusive as the pain mingled and lessened as chills rushed down my spine.

One of the soulless stepped closer to Lucian, and everything inside of me turned cold. Her hand extended, touching his chest, and I moved, thoughtlessly, uncaring that she wasn't foe as I reached her, ripping her head from her body and then watching emotionlessly as she dropped to the ground, dead. I stared at Lucian who was splattered in her blood and smiled.

"He's mine," I uttered through the heaviness of my tongue.

I turned to Synthia who put her hands up in a motion of surrender and stepped away from Lucian's side. "Alpha bitch in the house, everyone back up. He's yours, we won't touch him, promise. You earned this one, Lucian. She's becoming your monster, enjoy it."

Black eyes met and held Lucian's as I slowly stepped closer. I smirked, feeling the need to mark him, to lay claim to him in the most primitive of ways. One step, then another, and the moment those dark, silky depths filled with heat, I turned, walking away from him. Catalina would regrow her head, but she'd been used to make a pretty important point. He was mine. He wanted to act like a caveman and bang his chest as he announced I was his? Well, I could play that game too.

"Lenny, what the fuck?" Joshua growled, and I turned to give him a pointed look as one delicate brow rose in question.

"What?" I snapped as my body readjusted to the new

burden. My vision swam as the ardor of the battle lessened. He pointed at Catalina, and I frowned. I swallowed a grunt as my eyes moved back to his and I smirked.

"She's on our side."

"My bad," I shrugged.

"No more killing our guys. Same side, same fucking team," he continued, and I smirked, lifting my blue eyes to his as they danced with laughter.

"She touched him," I pouted, or tried to.

"Oh boy, this should be fun," Synthia snorted as she clapped a hand against Lucian's shoulder and my eyes zeroed in on it. "Happily married, he's all yours."

CHAPTER
ten

You pierce my soul. I am half agony, half hope…I have
loved none but you. *~Jane Austen*

I stood in the middle of
the conference room, which was a vast antechamber that
held runes painted on the walls. It looked as if they'd
plucked it from the legends of Faery and dropped it right
into our world. Synthia stared at me, her tongue in her
cheek as her violet eyes perused what I'd changed into.
They changed, turning from electric blue to violet as she
continued to stare at me as if she was afraid I'd grow
horns next, which honestly scared me too. Ryder stood
behind her; his finger traced her bare shoulder blade as
she bounced those ever-changing orbs from me to the
book in front of her.

"Have you told them she is here and ready?" she
asked, and Layton answered. He was leaned against the
door with his blond man-bun firmly in place. His back
was against the wall, foot flat as he rested there, staring
at me.

I felt like I was on display, the ever-changing freak within their midst.

"They're witches, slower than a hooker strolling down her corner in winter waiting for a John." His eyes seemed to grow distant as he continued to watch me.

My own eyes lowered to Synthia again, staring at her as her finger pushed yet another page over as she pored through the pages of the book in front of her. It was a book of mythology, and ancient from the looks of it. Yellow pages creaked as she turned them, the scent musky and yet almost alive.

"Harpy?" Her head tilted as she stared up at me. "It fits; well, if you take out the fact they thought Harpies had the head of a woman and the body of a bird."

"Could be, she's faster than most creatures and fights like she is possessed by demons." Ryder's golden eyes seemed to look through me instead of at me.

"Teeth that grow, nails sharper than any blade, but the way her eyes turn and that black that seems to burn from within, it's almost like something is haunting her from within. Plus, she has no soul. Harpies have souls."

I stared at Synthia. "Does it even matter what I am?" I asked, seething that they seemed obsessed with discovering what I was. They'd been poring through books for the last few hours as Alden had gone to fetch my mother with Layton. Layton returned, but they hadn't. The hours on the clock continually ticked by as I stood in the room, uncomfortable with their scrutiny as they tried to figure out what I had become.

"Of course it does," she scoffed. "Lena, if you have a weakness, it's important to know it. If you can be killed, again, you need to know it so that you can protect yourself from it."

"Anything else we should know about you? Anything that you feel when your face changes," Zahruk asked, his sapphire eyes peering at me as he pushed the sizeable ancient tome in front of him away from where he sat. He rose, stepping closer towards me.

He was hot, as in *I'd ride that fucker for days and still want more* hot. But he wasn't Lucian, and I burned for him. I burned to feel his touch, to taste his anger as he fucked me. I wanted him and yet the emotions that he made me feel terrified me. Not that I'd let him fuck me either.

"I feel hatred, anger, and pain. It's red-hot, and when it comes, I ache to destroy; to kill things, to maim. I crave it so bad that I taste it." I examined my nails, dismissing their wide stares as the words tumbled out. Black blood marred the nailbeds; I was filthy and needed to shower, but they'd brought me here instead. They'd had me standing for the last few hours as they examined every change, every minute detail of my new body.

Ryder had touched me, searching my spine for where the wings had disappeared. It had sent a ripple through me as he took in the angry red flesh where my wings now hid in. I had wings. Real, mother fucking wings. It still blew me away as the others had yet to change or return to us with them. I had something no one else did.

It also screamed wrong and deadly to me. Being close to these creatures had once terrified me, and yet it didn't anymore. I felt like their equal now, as if I belonged among them. Whether it was because we were all mutually fucked-up in our differences or something else, it felt right. But that was a problem on its own; it bothered me to feel right with them.

"Are they coming or not?" I asked, my irritability

rising with every drawn-out moment they watched me. "I need to shower and wash off the battle."

"They may be a while," Synthia frowned as she spoke softly. "I had clean clothing sent to Lucian's room for you. He agreed to let you shower there. If you prefer a room of your own, it should be ready by this evening. It's a work in progress getting this place up and running. I'm still shorthanded. If you prefer, I can find someone else's room for you to use."

"His room is fine; he's out, correct?" I asked, turning to look at Layton who nodded. I nodded thanks before I turned and exited the room. With one last look over my shoulder as they stared back down into the pages of the old books, I left in search of a warm bath and solitude.

Inside Lucian's room I snooped, exploring the items he'd left out on the dressers. I lay on his bed, holding the blankets to my nose before mentally slapping myself and peeling myself off of it. I felt his presence in the room, his essence. It made my body react; my mind whirled with what had happened when I'd killed myself. How he'd reacted. It made me think of the child I'd sacrificed to save it, and that hurt me more than I wanted to admit. I didn't want to feel it, to mourn him.

Emptiness was soothing; pain consumed and destroyed.

I stripped naked, tossing the ruined clothing back into the room haphazardly as I eyed the clawfoot tub longingly. I spun around, taking in the huge four-poster bed with black silk wrapped around the banisters, to the thick, soft carpets that my toes dug into. The place was beautiful, opulent, and if every room looked like this one, it was no wonder it took them forever to make one ready. I inched deeper into the bathroom, letting the cool air soothe my flesh as I pulled down a wrapped ball and smirked. I slowly unwrapped it, dropping it into the tub.

The soothing, exotic scent of honeysuckles and spring filled the bathroom. It smelled inviting, and the water steamed from the tub as I waited for it to fill enough to climb in and soothe my aches. Once inside, I pushed the ball around the smooth tub's bottom, watching the tiny air bubbles as they percolated up, releasing the sweet scent. Once I'd washed away the black blood and grime of the fighting, I stood, bending at the waist until the tub had fully drained. I reached for another bath bomb of the same fragrance and dropped into the empty tub before sitting and replacing the dirty water with fresh, clean water. Leaning against the tub, I closed my eyes.

"Lucian," I uttered as I sensed him in the room with me. I opened my eyes, peering up into his midnight gaze. My teeth skimmed my bottom lip as heat smoldered in his eyes. He didn't speak; instead, he just continued to stare at me.

He swallowed hard before he backed up, grabbing the clean clothes that had been placed on the counter before he marched out of the bathroom. I looked around for a towel and noted there wasn't one. Brilliant. I groaned as I sank beneath the water and remained there until my skin pruned. I finished washing off and then stood from the tub, uncaring as the water cascaded down my body. I stepped out of it, slinking my naked ass into the room.

My eyes took in the vacant room with a glare and then landed on the dark figure who watched me from the corner. My hair dripped endlessly as I swayed my hips, letting him see the damage I'd done to retain his fucking seal in my flesh. Runes danced over my skin, pulsing with a sacred beat only a few could hear. Candles ignited, and

I paused, staring at him as he held up a towel.

"You stole my clothes," I accused. "I need them." My heart, that traitorous organ that had grown back, began to beat wildly against my chest wall as I stared at him.

"So I did—come and take them back," he challenged as he stood, as his power rippled in the room, making it feel much smaller than it had without him in it.

I didn't back down from his challenge. I wasn't about to let him flaunt his massive amount of power or control to feed that ego of his. But I also didn't want him to touch me, because the dam would break and with it the emotions I kept at bay would flow over.

Standing firm, I watched him slowly walk to where I stood, towering over me. My teeth scraped over my lip as I peered up into the endless depths that seemed to always see through me. His hand released the towel which fell to the floor as they wrapped around my waist, hoisting me closer to his intense heat. I allowed it, tipping my head back further as his mouth lowered to mine.

Heated breath fanned my mouth, his lips trailing gently over mine as his intoxicating scent assaulted me. The subtle scent of scotch and citrus made my nostrils flare with awareness and memories. It was like coming home as his lips touched against mine, sending fire burning through me. Emotions ebbed and flowed, and I struggled to ignore them, to push them away as he touched me.

His tongue pushed past my lips, finding mine as I continued to stand still, letting him drive us until his hands released me, gripping my hair as he yanked my head back to devour my mouth as if he was starving and I was the most erotic delicacy he'd ever tasted. A moan ripped from my throat as he continued kissing me until he pulled away and I nibbled on his lip, sucking it between my teeth as he growled. I tasted his blood as he struggled to calm his reaction to it, to me. Those large hands hoisted my body, lifting me as he moved us towards the bed.

Tears rushed down my face, leaking out memories, and emotions flowed through them. He set me down, leaning over as his thumbs wiped them away.

"I'm afraid to sleep and awake to find you only a fucking dream," he admitted, and the thickness in his voice sent more tears flowing as I gazed up into the galaxy that stared from within him. He placed his forehead against mine as he rested his knees on the floor, staring up at me. "I've dreamt of this every fucking night since…since you chose to leave me."

"I didn't choose, Lucian. It was the only way to save him from what they planned. Our son was to be the Harbinger of Doom, the one created to house a seal that would destroy this world and countless others. I felt it inside of me, and then him. It was evil, pure evil that wanted to rip this world apart. I was his mother; it was my job to protect him even at the cost of his life. I did it for him."

"We could have found a way around it," he seethed as he stood up, pacing in front of the bed.

"No, no we couldn't have. Don't you think if I thought there was some way to save us all that I wouldn't have tried? I was going to die no matter what. I had no soul. If they had succeeded and taken back the soul, Kendra would have been eradicated. If I survived and lived to carry our child, his life would have been forfeited by the monster that had attached to his soul. He'd have been hunted to be used against this world. You chose my fate. You and Katarina brought me into your game, and I was nothing more than collateral damage. I chose how I went out and who I took with me. I'm sorry she can't come back to play with you, ever. But you should have thought about everyone else who you dragged into this game and sacrificed as you played it."

"You think I care that she's gone? You died, Lena. *You. Died.* I watched you slit your fucking throat, and there wasn't anything I could do to save you. I need to know how you bound the seal to your body without a soul being in it. If it is ever able to be freed..." He let the threat linger between us.

"I am scarred with the runes and wards that hold it inside of me. I will never possess a soul for it to use, nor do I want one. I like this me better. Not needing anything works for me. That list includes you, Lucian. Whatever I had for you died when you and your crazy ex-girlfriend decided to place me into your game. Me, I might have been able to accept, but the price I paid to protect you and this world, it was too much. So as long as the runes cover this shell, it cannot escape nor act."

"And you can harness its powers," he replied, turning to stare at me.

"Clothes? I'd rather be dressed for this conversation," I muttered as I lifted from the bed to a sitting position, not bothering with propriety as my legs spread and I enjoyed the hitch in his breathing as he lowered his gaze to my naked flesh.

"You think I'm going to let you go? Never. You're mine, no matter how fucking lost you think you are, no matter what you have become, Lena. You are mine, and that didn't change for a moment. You want to play chase? I hope you like running because I will hunt you down and claim you every fucking time you run from me. I crave you, I crave you more than I crave the cage that holds me.

You don't get to walk away from me, ever. In a million worlds, you would be the one I chased."

"To the grave?" I chuckled as the tick in his jaw began hammering at the reminder. "I'm not going to be that easy to chase this time, Lucian. I literally died last time. You did try to warn me, though, didn't you?"

"You were never an easy catch," he murmured. "Elusive, hard to control, and reckless, but never easy." He strolled closer, kneeling between my legs as his heated kiss landed on one inner thigh and then the other. I watched his dark head as he lifted his face to gaze into my eyes. "I like the fucking hunt, so if you plan to run, you better run fast because I promise you this. I will be faster. I will catch you. And when I do catch you, I will never let you go. You're immortal now; whatever you are, I can sense your lifespan is endless like mine, and that pleases me. Yes, you died, and I'm sure it sucked, but all living things die. I'm not sorry that you're immortal, nor am I sorry that when I fuck you, I'll not have to hold back. When you're finished throwing your little tantrum, I'll show you what it is like to be fucked so hard you feel me for an eternity because, Lena, you will."

"Give me my clothes," I uttered thickly.

"You have no idea what I am, but you will soon. I can feel you, which means we are connected now. Whatever you are, you're strong, but I assure you, little girl; I'm still fucking stronger. And there's a thread connecting you to me, and them to me. Whatever you are, you're mine still, not because I demand it, which I assure you, I do, but because whoever brought you and the others back made it so. You feel me, Lena. You stand outside this place protecting something inside. Whether it's the seal connecting you to me, or the fact that someone high up brought you back is to be determined. It doesn't change us one fucking bit. I held your lifeless corpse in my arms and had to let them take you from me. I will never let anything or anyone take you from me again."

"I'm not yours. That weak being who gave you those doe-eyed stares? She's dead."

"Good, because you're unbreakable now," he chuckled. "You're sexier, colder, and pissed the fuck off, just the way I like my women."

CHAPTER eleven

No great mind has ever existed without a touch of madness. ~*Aristotle*

I stewed at his words, hating that no matter how much I ignored them, it replayed in my head on repeat. Was he the reason we remained here, stuck to this place unwillingly? I'd assumed it was our family, which it could be, but the others who served Joshua seemed unwilling to leave it either.

It ruffled my feathers, and as I marched into the huge conference room, it didn't help that his smug ass was there to greet me. As if he hadn't just floored me with words or knocked me on my ass with them, only to walk out and leave me with my mouth doing a fish out of water impression. *Asshole.*

Taking the seat beside him, I turned, staring at my mother and Kendra, who eyed me warily. I shut down the emotion and turmoil that stewed inside of me and allowed the darkness and its calming effect it had on me to slowly rise. It wasn't until Joshua joined us that I stiffened. I glared at him, wondering what the hell he was doing here as well.

My grandmother stared at me, her matching blue eyes trying to see past the shield I'd slipped into place. Lucian being so close had butterflies I'd thought I'd ripped the wings off of soaring inside of me. Joshua sitting on the other side had a hurricane of anger mixed with pain that we had come to this place and time, and now had to explain how we'd gotten to it.

"Benjamin," my grandmother whispered thickly, choking on emotions.

"I am not Benjamin," he declared gently as he folded his scarred hands in front of him. "I'm Joshua, you buried Benjamin."

"Impossible, we did the spell to be sure of who we'd buried," she argued as power rippled through the room, a warning of her own turbulent emotions flaring.

"We were exactly the same. The spell used to create us, and the soul we shared, was Katarina's first attempt to close a twin with a fractured soul in it."

"Then she'd have died when you separated and it fractured," she said pointedly.

"Had it been her own soul she had used, yes. She hadn't talked Drake into it yet and had to be sure it worked first. She was able to pierce the veil and met him long ago, and once she'd sunk her claws into him with the promise of untold power, he did whatever she asked of him, including murdering the seer in the woods. Or more to the point, the woman you thought was a seer. He'd set up everything, done all the legwork and spells as she'd told him to, and the results of it were Benjamin and me being born from one soul, split into two.

"When he found me, I was in Afghanistan. My unit

was assigned to join with another on a mission outside a town. Imagine my surprise when he was the leader of the second unit I was to find and help. He explained where he was from, who he was, and what you had done. He told me we were meant to be one person, and that the only way to manage it was for me to die. The next day we were supposed to be in the center of Kandahar, so I used runes to paint my flesh before we set out. I was prepared to die, but not ready to allow it to happen. So when he lured me to the bomb someone had set in the middle of town in the heavily visited shopping area, I murdered him. Unlike Lena, I do not have a fractured soul because I was the light. The spell they used to create us was to balance Yin and Yang, to eventually become one. My soul was stronger than his, so when I left my tour, or his tour, after they'd sent you back his body instead of mine, I became him. I reported back to my father that it had worked, that all his effort and time hadn't been for nothing. When he'd gone to tell the soul of his lover the truth, I waited. When Drake returned, I murdered him and for all intent became Benjamin. You had already buried me by the time I'd returned. Lena had left town, and even though I watched her, I had to wait to see what would happen. Drake had told me his plans, how Lena and Kendra were carrying the dormant soul. The moment I returned, it began to unravel."

"You met him?" my mother whispered through eyes shining with unshed tears. "Was he, was he evil?"

"No, misled, but not evil. He did what he had been told to do, and while I don't think he would have hesitated to end my life to finish his goals, he wasn't evil. He told me about his father, and I told him about his mother. I told him of the sisters he'd never meet, and how much the coven needed him but Drake had beaten him, snuffed out any humanity he could have had. I am dark, mother. I was the moment his soul met and dissolved into mine. His magic became my magic, and his secrets became my truths. I knew his past, his horrors, and everything he'd been told. It was how I knew that if Lena ended her life, she would come back.

"The plan was to break the spell Katarina had placed on Lucian by making him fall for the darkness in Magdalena. Making him care for her before the solar eclipse was crucial. Lucifer had used his abilities to ensure she was fertile, that her womb would take his seed. They planned everything, right down to you sending her to that club outside of Portland. That was where he allowed his barbs to plant the potion into her womb. Then he allowed them to escape, to rush back here where he knew Lucian would be waiting. The only thing they didn't plan on was how far a mother would go to protect her own child. I'd told Lena what to use to ward her womb, to protect her child. I told her what she held inside of her and what it could do to her son if it lived. How it wouldn't ever be a child but rather a monster, the true Harbinger of Doom. They'd wanted to force Lucian to murder his own child, and the only way he could save this world would have been to do just that. They wanted to hurt him, for what I'm not sure. That part was never told to Benjamin. But Lena would have lived under the control of the monster inside of her, had she lived. Once she gave birth, she would have ceased to exist. Just an empty, soulless corpse, but the man who came to me promised she'd live if she did as he instructed us to."

"Who was the man?" Lucian growled thickly with his question.

"I don't know who or what he was, only that he promised me Lenny wouldn't die for having ended up in the middle of a game she hadn't agreed to play in. The others were with him, the soulless as we call them, informed me of his truths, and I asked him to show me. To show me what she would become. And so he did, and I became first. Everything he said would happen played out, and no matter what we did, it didn't change the path Lena dove headfirst into. So I told her the truth. I told her if she was strong enough to do it, I'd save her."

"You knew you wouldn't die?" Kendra snapped heatedly.

"No, we didn't know for sure," I answered harshly. "I knew you would live. When I met Lucifer at the house, I knew I would die, and that you would go on. I knew one of us had to die to fracture the soul. My son was cursed; he held pure evil within him. My first and only decision as his mother was to take his life with mine. To free him from the monster they'd intended him to be, and to give his soul back to Hecate so that he may be reborn again. By taking my life, I saved yours. One of us was not living through that night, and you weren't the one with the cracked skull. You ended up in Hell because of me, because of my choices and who I had been with. You didn't deserve it, nor can I ever make up for it, but I could sacrifice myself to save you. To protect the world from what my son would become. I knew I'd come back; I'm not sure how or why I trusted the word of a man who wouldn't even show us his face, but I did. I felt it. So I took my life, ending my mortal one for whatever I have become. I do not regret it. This world doesn't need more heroes; it needs monsters that can do what is needed when needed without having to worry about the hindrance of a soul that stands in the way.

"You see, I knew dying wasn't the end because, without a soul, heaven wouldn't take me and Hell couldn't hold me. I just existed now. I don't run based off what my heart tells me to do, something else controls me now. I don't know what it is, or why we are drawn to this place where you and these creatures dwell, but neither do I care as long as I can kill. I'm not your daughter, I'm so much more. I think I love you still, but I no longer care if I do or if I don't. That should scare you because it also means that I do not care if you live or die, but I think I should, so I protect you. I am not bound to the coven, nor do I use your magic. I use something greater, stronger than your coven could ever offer me or us. We are evolving into what remains a mystery to even us. The man who created us, he has not returned, nor does he beckon us to him."

"And if he told you to kill us?" Kendra asked.

"You'd die," I said without hesitation.

CHAPTER
twelve

We're all a little fucked, but otherwise still standing.
~*Lena*

Time held no meaning, and since we'd left the meeting where they'd drilled us for hours, I'd stewed. I'd ran my answers through my mind a thousand times since I'd walked out, leaving them to determine if they'd ask us to leave or stay. If I were them, I'd tell us to go or fight us. We were dark, deadly, called by the night and the endless blackness that bathed the skies above the Guild. We were an unknown threat no matter how you chose to look at it.

"You shouldn't have told her that," Joshua said from where he stood beside me.

"It's the truth," I argued. "Should I have pretended otherwise? I do not want them dead. I fear him coming back and using us for whatever purpose he created us for. Do you not?"

"I don't think he created us to kill our coven, nor those we love, Lenny. I think he created us to protect something, maybe even Lucian. You said he felt a thread; I felt it in that room with him. We need to figure out what he is so that we can figure out why the fuck you grew wings and what we are," he muttered as he scrubbed his palm over his face and shook his head.

I shrugged. "What does it matter what we are? We're not dead, and that's exactly what I would be if he hadn't told you how to save me. Everyone here has sacrificed something to be here, even you. You had to give your life to be sure mine wouldn't end. You trusted him enough to do that, so who cares who he is?"

"You're not seeing the bigger picture. What if he made us kill this world?"

"Don't go there," I frowned, rubbing the crease between my eyes. "I have yet to feel a pull to anything but this place, and yeah, maybe Lucian but that could be because I'd thought I loved him."

"And now?" he scoffed as the question came out guarded.

"Loving him ended my life; it ended my son's life. I cannot go back there, or ever be the girl I was before this happened. Life isn't black and white; it's muted in the undertone colors of what forges you into what you become after it's fucked you. I was filled with color, hope. I thought if I loved enough, if I sacrificed enough, I'd save the coven and everyone. I was wrong. I don't know about you, Josh, but this second chance is more than I expected when I slit my fucking throat. I'm with you, the brother I buried, and yeah, there's a huge piece of me in that coffin with Benjamin. Or the old me. I don't feel the weight I used to carry on my shoulders. We're stronger now, able to protect the coven more than we ever could have managed before."

"But we don't care if they live, and there lies the problem."

"I'm still me," I muttered. "I'm still one of them, and I know you feel it too. I don't carry the obligation, but I love them enough to know I'd die for them still. Dying didn't change that for me. It didn't change it for you either, we just don't love them the same. It's like an echo in my mind, telling me that I do, even as the darkness says to let them go. You?"

"I wouldn't watch them fucking die, I'd fight for them. You just told them otherwise."

"I told them the truth, and yeah, the truth fucking sucks, but if the man who created us told us to, we could very well slaughter them. That scares the fuck out of me, so yes; I wanted them to fear us. If they fear us, they will take precaution around us, and they will ward themselves against us. Better they let go and fear us than cling to the hope that we are what they lost because let's face it: we're not fluffy fucking bunnies anymore. We're created to kill, whatever we are, we aren't something they should want to hold close. Fearing us might just keep them alive."

"I'm going to go on patrol," he mumbled as he stepped out of line and another fell into it beside me.

My head ached from the endless questions along with Lucian's touch. Mid-explanation his hand had gripped my leg, slowly pushing the skirt I'd chosen to wear up until he'd grazed my sex. It had taken everything I had not to moan or rip his clothes off and ride him until I fucked that man out of my system. That man was the bane of my existence, and now we had forever to play cat and mouse, which just pissed me off.

"I'll patrol the back of the Guild, see if we can find any fuckers willing to dance," he informed me before nodding at something over my shoulder. "He isn't going to let you stay out here. He's about to come fetch you, Lenny," he laughed, and I growled.

I turned to look over my shoulder, frowning as anger shot through me. Fetch me, would he? I felt a ripple of power that shot through me without warning. Feathers exploded into the air, slowly floating down as I turned left, and then right…slowly. A frown tugged at my lips as I winced at what I'd done.

"Jesus H. Christ, Lenny," Joshua groaned.

I'd impaled both soulless beings on either side of me, right through the temple. I swallowed hard as I started to turn, dragging bodies on my wings. "Oops, my bad," I winced as I shook my wings, hearing the dull thump as the bodies slid from the razor-sharp bones of my wings. "Those are lethal."

"You need to figure out how to control that," he warned, and I eyed Lucian who stood on the stairs amidst the others who'd all sat on them, watching our silent vigil into the midnight sky. Synthia covered her mouth, but the way her eyes shone and crinkled told me she was laughing. Ryder beside her was shaking his head and chuckling at me openly and Ristan, the silver-eyed demon, well, he just wiggled his brows and muttered something to Olivia who he had finally brought out of hiding.

Probably not a smart move considering we were hanging around unwillingly. I pointed to my spot line, and another person moved in, taking my place with a worried glance as the others had yet to fill the vacant spots beside me for fear I'd impale them as well.

Like I'd tried to do it…

I had zero control over what these fucking wings did and no idea of how to even begin to control them. I felt them ripple at my back as the wind ruffled the feathers. I strode towards Lucian, wondering if my wings would work on him, but they vanished on the trek to him.

"You control them," Ryder laughed, and I tossed an irritated glare in his direction. "They do as you want them to, or react to your mood."

"I have no idea how I even did that, let alone how to control what they do. I just thought of how I'd like to impale Lucian and ended up sticking them into Lar and Kaden's fucking skulls. *Yay me.* We need to talk," I said pointedly at Lucian.

"Talking isn't what I want to do to you, little witch."

"I'm not a witch anymore, asshole. Inside, please," I said impatiently, tapping my foot on the pavement.

"Fine, we'll go inside where we can speak in… private," he mused, his eyes flashing liquid flames as if he no longer cared if anyone knew what he was.

"If you think it means something else, you're wrong. I need to pick your brain, and either we can do it here in front of everyone, or alone. You tend to like to keep your secrets. The choice is entirely yours to make, Lucian."

"Inside," he growled, his hand snaking out and slipping his fingers through mine, and my body jerked in reaction. My wings unfurled as my eyes slowly rose to hold his. "They don't scare me, little *witch*."

I turned back to the others, nodding before I winced at the two dead bodies I'd accidentally created and then back to Lucian, only for the air to thicken with danger around us. Everyone braced to fight as shadows swirled around us, bathing the Guild in a thick, dark mist.

"Hello, Lucian," a deep, disembodied voice said silkily. "I see you found my gift."

CHAPTER
thirteen

O, teach me how I should forget to think! ~*Shakespeare*.

Every soulless being present except me dropped to their knees. The crunching sent a chill racing down my spine as I turned my gaze back to the bodiless voice. I knew that voice, on a physical level. I swallowed hard, as my heart erupted as chaos slithered through my mind, racing down my spine. From the midst that surrounded us outside the Guild stepped a man with black hair and violet eyes that smiled as he held his arm out, extending it to a small, petite midnight-haired beauty. I stared into the purple-blue depths and expelled a shaky breath because I knew those eyes, knew them with carnal knowledge. Full lips tipped into a beautiful smile, telling me he knew me as well; memories flowed between us and I trembled as images flashed in my mind.

I'd watched those eyes lock with mine as his wicked tongue had tasted me, forcing orgasm after orgasm to shake me to the core. He was in that room, the one

I thought had been no more than a dream. It felt like a lifetime ago, but it hadn't been.

He'd done things to me, bad things. But he'd also been the one to save me. Hades had removed Lucifer from the fight, giving me time to finish the job. If he hadn't been there that day, I'd be a lifeless vessel, carrying the Harbinger until he was ready to be born to destroy the world. The silence passed between us, him reading my face as I replayed his part in the epic finale of my life. And had he just said I was a gift? My eyes dropped from his, turning to the others who still bowed before him as if he was some sort of God to them.

"Hades," Lucian said in a clipped tone, pulling my horrified eyes back to him. "Persephone," his tone gentled, and I glared at the dark-haired female who stepped from the safety to Lucian's side, swishing her hips as she strode towards him.

The hair on my nape rose as my power unfurled, rage growing with every step her dainty feet took her closer to Lucian. I moved, getting closer as I closed the distance between Lucian and me. Once I was close enough, I turned, drawing my blades as I stared at her, blocking her path to Lucian. The warning was there, shining from within my black eyes. If she stepped closer, I'd end her.

"Stand down, Magdalena," Hades ordered, and my fingers released the blades which clattered to the pavement deafeningly. I brought my empty hands up as I stared at them, swallowing hard as my gaze darted to his in shock.

"How did you do this?" Lucian demanded, his tone carrying a silent warning.

"You were about to lose them both, so I saved the one I could," he said with a shrug, as if it mattered little to him. "You'd lost enough, and given enough to a cause you never asked to protect. It was the least I could do."

"What the fuck *is* she?" Lucian growled, his nostrils flaring as his hands tucked beneath his arms, which almost looked as if he'd relaxed. His thumbs were up, which he only did if he was trying to appear unthreatening.

"Special," he chuckled as his eyes slowly roved over me before settling on the scar on my throat. "Figuring out what she is should be half the fun, friend."

"Explain what the fuck you did to bring her back as she is. She's fucking heartless, literally," he warned with his tone barely above a whisper that carried on the wind.

I swallowed hard, my traitorous useless heart thundering in my chest as the Goddess of the Underworld and her husband stared at me. Persephone moved towards me, tucking in a stray strand of hair that had fallen into my face. Her mouth lowered to hover over mine, and heat singed my flesh as she inhaled deeply, touching my cheek with the tips of her fingers. After what felt like hours, she pulled away and stared into my eyes with something dark and familiar in her ice-colored depths.

"Beautiful," she murmured as she kissed my cheek and then turned, sidling next to Hades where she stood, keeping the barest hint of distance from him.

"I asked for help, something you couldn't be bothered to fucking do. You think you have to do everything alone, but you don't. So I did what you fucking couldn't do." Violet eyes clashed with midnight ones, glowing as his hair rose as power thrummed in the air, biting my flesh as if I was being shocked a multitude of times. The mist darkened until I felt smothered by it, which terrified me since I literally didn't need air to live. "I had no idea what he would do to her, but I did know she would die. That she would die as you watched it unfold. I did what I had to do to prevent an all-out fucking war, and that is exactly what is coming. Her little stunt, and taking away your ex set Lucifer off; he's started something we cannot stop."

I couldn't move, couldn't blink. The others had remained on their knees, heads bowed as he spoke. I could feel the power in the area growing out of control. Sweat trickled down my spine, between my breasts, and the entire time, Persephone watched me with inhuman eyes that noted the discomfort. There was something gentle in the way she looked at me, an understanding that I wasn't sure I wanted to see. I was Hades's bitch! My body trembled as panic started to take hold, and then something comforted me, soothing magic that eased my nerves and bathed my body in a chilled embrace. I thanked her without saying a word, moving my lips as she continued to calm my response.

"I didn't ask you to save her!"

"You'd have let her fucking die?" Hades shouted right back at him. The earth trembled around us, lightning rocked through the sky followed by loud claps of thunder.

"She'd have come back!" Lucian raged, and the wind picked up, whipping my hair against my face. His hands exploded into blue flames as souls danced and slithered around him, forming armor as he continued to scream. It was getting fucking freaky. My senses were overwhelmed, my nerves fried to the point that even Persephone and her magic couldn't soothe the panic building inside of me. "Now when she dies, there's nothing to save!"

"She never existed outside of magic," Hades said softly as his magic seemed to dissipate from the air around us. "She would have been gone forever had I not fed her the sliver of a soul from the River Styx. Had Nyx not added the night into her and brought her back at my request, she'd have simply ceased to exist or became a mindless body controlled by the seal she carried within her. Lena was created of no more than magic mixed with a sliver of Katarina's soul. Everything that you admired or loved of Katarina was eradicated to become her, to lure you to your death. Once Katarina had melded her soul together, Lena would have been a vacant creature who had no mind of her own. She wouldn't have even known who you were anymore, Lucian. They intended to keep her that way until your child was born. Unleashing it upon the world, which by the way, she fucking prevented by no small miracle. I had no idea they were aware of my part, and if she hadn't had the strength she did, she'd have died in vain. Nyx was watching that night, aware of the favor I'd asked of her and found your little witchling worthy. So she stands before you on her own merit. She earned the respect of a Goddess who respects no one, on her own. That is a feat unheard of in this day and age, all things considered."

"If you'd broken the wards, she wouldn't have had to die in the first place."

"Yes, she did. Your son was the Harbinger. I let you see her death echo, the one she is cursed to relive every full moon, the price she pays to come back to you. She said his name correctly. He'd have been that and worse if he'd been born to her. He wouldn't have stood a chance. You think Lucifer hadn't told half of Hell what he was planning to do with your unborn son? He made sure you'd have to kill him or watch him die. One of the twins wasn't leaving that circle alive, he'd thrown that around enough that I knew which one he'd take out to hurt you the most. Once I knew Katarina was part of his plan, the one you'd bred with seemed more like the one destined to die. I told you to find something soulless to love so that we didn't have to watch you hurt again and again, and so I took it upon myself to make it so. Now Lena has an army at her back, one she will control and fight with *beside* you, unlike Katarina who was always *against* you. I have Cerberus at my gates, and now you have Lena and her army guarding yours."

"How did you create her?" he demanded, his fists clenching and unclenching at his sides.

"I tasted her, pushing a sliver of a lost soul into hers. Not enough to be controlled by the evil she houses, not unless she decides to let it. Your woman is stronger than most, brother. She is fierce, even though she be little. Nyx did the rest. There's something else you should know. Lucifer is aware she is alive, and he is free now. He will be hunting her as soon as he is back on his feet and able to do so, which brings us to this next pickle. There's a way to bring her back, but she'd have to choose to do it freely, she'd have to want it enough to follow through with it, and it would bind her to him as much as she is now bound to you."

"How?" he asked, the one word a thunderous boom in the night as everyone else held their breath.

"She would have to take the soul her sister grows inside her womb. She'd have to kill it the moment it took its first breath, murdering it for its life source. She'd be human again, whole. But she would be part of him until she took her dying breath."

"No, never," I uttered as anger bubbled up. "I'd rather die than be attached to that monster."

"And you're not one now?" Lucian seethed.

I flinched and recovered before I laughed softly. "Afraid of me, Lucian, or are you afraid that I am immune to you now, like this?"

"I'm not afraid of you, but darkness only grows. Eventually, you will not be Lena; you'll be whatever the fuck they created you to be."

"I created her to be yours," a soothing voice whispered through the night, as inky and beautiful as the woman who seemed to appear out of thin air. "She will always know you, and what she once was. She is revenge, chaos, and beautiful disaster. The night in her veins is pure, and yes, it occasionally comes out of her eyes as memories. She is not evil, but she is not of the light as she once was, either. Does that bother you, Lucian?"

"Nyx," he uttered as he took a step closer towards her and then stopped. "You did this to her."

"I did, and I am not sorry for it. She is a warrior and the rage she felt was beautiful and intoxicating. Her sacrifice was heartfelt and pure. Who else would be better to guard you than someone willing to end her own existence to save you from pain?" She stopped in front of me, touching my cheek with her hand, and emotion stirred to life vividly, as if the world had been bathed in a kaleidoscope of beautifully-woven colors that started and ended with her.

"Mother," I whispered even though I hadn't wanted to. I felt her in my bones, in the darkened mist within me, I felt her. As if she was a part of me, my creator.

"Ignore him; he gets pissy when he hasn't eaten enough souls, love. You're utterly perfect in your imperfect way as he once said you were before. She is, isn't she, Luc?" she laughed, and the hair on my nape rose as the name slipped out. "Oh, calm your tits. He was Luc first, before Lucy's dad ever even lay on that whore of a mother he sinned with," she said with a frown as my mouth dropped into an even deeper frown. "Don't look at me like that; your God was a sinner before he was a saint, but then aren't we all? Did you really think angels just came to be? He lay down in that Garden of Eden and created life with a serpent. Imperfect life, and then grew bored of them and created humans." She shrugged. "And so your world was created. And now you know how the humans were created and in whose image. No, sweetling, we are not his. You're giving it away here," she said as she tapped her head. "We're connected so that I know if you are ever in trouble."

"Get the fuck outta my head!" I shouted, scaring even me as my mouth worked to speak, finally.

"You'll get used to it," she retorted. "Anywho, you're welcome," her words were pointed at Lucian. "Hades was correct, I did find her worthy. The war is brewing ever so closely, and we needed what Lena would become on our side, what with your unwillingness to join us in it. Now that she will be forced to wage it beside me, so too will you. Those who kneel are hers now, her army. One created with an iron will for revenge and hatred. If she chooses to take the unborn soul of Lucifer's child into her body, she can choose to free them of her control. If not, she will lead them. She is your gift from me, for what you have sacrificed to prevent this war, but it is coming. The only hope we have to win is keeping the last gate from opening. Enjoy, brother mine."

"You're a God?" I asked, turning to stare at Lucian.

"No, I'm not."

"Then what are you?" I snapped. "What am *I*?"

"You, my dear, are a primordial being now," she chirped as she strolled towards Synthia and sniffed. "You're new, newly born."

"I am daughter of Danu," she said stiffly. "And not for dinner, but I do love the brands you wear."

"They're not brands; they are strands of the night woven into my soul. Much like Lena has, but where I can control mine, she has yet to learn and so it shows from where her soul used to shine. She will master it quickly, as she has learned to harness her powers and sprout her wings."

"She's a harpy," Synthia countered.

"I am Nyx; I do not create Harpies. I am Destiny's mother. I am the mother of darkness and death, not women who resemble nightmarish chickens. Now, have fun my little Furies and don't kill too many creatures."

"Furies?" I uttered through clenched teeth.

"You're created for revenge, chaos, and that is what it will take to close the gates that have opened. Unless, of course, you prefer the chaos of this new world?"

"I'm a Fury, like the mythical creature?"

"You are," she chuckled as the night enveloped her and she vanished. "And you're his now, forever. Be gentle to him, for he has been through hell without you."

"I'm not his," I growled, but the mist cleared, and the midnight sky hovered above once more. I stared up at the multitude of stars that blinked and burned out, sailing across the sky in a vibrant display as they fell. Her throaty laughter was the only indication she'd even heard my refusal.

CHAPTER
fourteen

Rule your mind or it will rule you. ~*Horace*

A Fury!

I was created from chaos and darkness. Just what I never wanted to be, and yet it felt right. It felt *good*, and I was the leader of an army? I felt like I should be miffed or upset, but I wasn't. Instead, I felt as if I was where I was supposed to be.

"Follow me," Lucian ordered, and I turned on him with a mocking grin marring my lips. I put my tongue in my cheek as I watched his eyes narrow on mine. "You're not that fucking badass, little girl. You want to go toe-to-toe with me? I fucking dare you to try it."

"You think I wouldn't?" I asked, and I tried to attack him. Nothing fucking happened. I was literally unable to do anything. Before, I'd been able to hurt him, but I hadn't felt the burning need to obliterate him, either. Just to make him feel my pain.

"Bound to me means you cannot hurt me," he laughed

coldly.

"The fuck! What the fuck, Hades?" I demanded, swinging my eyes to his.

"Sorry, but he's right. You cannot hurt him, not with the intent to really harm him. Other things, though…I didn't take away everything, sweet one. Just the inability to actually hurt or harm him," he chuckled as he watched me.

I frowned, and stared down at my hand and then back towards Lucian who watched me with a burning need bathed in his midnight depths. This was crap! I wanted to fucking murder him, and yet I couldn't touch him as the anger radiated through me.

"Don't encourage him, husband," Persephone warned. "She has suffered enough at the hands of others; she should at least be able to hurt him back. She lost a child, something we have to know the loss of," she uttered as her hand slipped to her slim belly.

"You'd have to fuck me to have a child, *wife*," he snapped coldly.

"Oomph," I snorted. "I'm sorry."

"For what, dear?" she asked. "I chose not to have a child with him who would be stuck in that miserable Underworld for eternity. The Gods would never have let him come with me when I left for the time I'm allowed. I wouldn't leave my child there so he could corrupt it."

"You think I'd corrupt him any more than you and your family would?" Hades asked, his eyes glowing with his anger.

"Okay…we're going now," I said, turning to grab Lucian's hand as I rushed us towards the Guild, pulling him with me. That wasn't something I intended to process, let alone get in the middle of.

"Now you're in a hurry to get me alone?" he chuckled.

"Fuck off," I retorted as I continued to move us towards the entrance of the Guild. I wanted away from the arguing Gods, away from their massive power that sent chills racing through my body.

"How about we do this?" he asked. One minute I'd been pulling him behind me, and the next I was in the room with him alone.

"How did you do that?" I asked as I swayed on my feet as I struggled to maintain an upright position. My body thrummed with his power, unable to catch up with the way he'd moved us through the Guild.

"Magic," he replied as he tilted his head, staring at me with a hungry gaze. He stepped closer, stalking me until my back skimmed the wall, and his hands trapped me there. I stared up as his mouth touched my cheek and then pulled away to smile down at me with a predatory, hungry gaze.

"Stop it," I ordered as his mouth lowered, brushing against mine without kissing me.

"Stop what?"

"Stop looking at me like I'm a freak! I heard you, you know. I get that you don't like me like this, but I won't bind myself to that monster. I won't do what he said just to get out of this."

"You mean take the life of a child," he amended. "I'm willing to do it for you."

"Just because she's his daughter doesn't mean she's evil," I answered as my forehead creased and my eyes closed. "Lucian, what the hell is going on? What the hell are you that Gods intervened and saved me from death?"

"You aren't ready for that, even after everything you've been through, you're not ready to accept what I am yet," he disclosed as he lifted his hand, and I ended up flying through the air without warning, only for him to reappear in front of me, shoving me to the bed as if I was weak. "When you're ready to accept me, I'll tell you what I am and why they chose to save you."

"But you don't trust them or why they did this to me, do you?" I asked as I stared up, cupping his cheek with my palm as I watched him. His heat undid me, sending a shock that registered in my core, unraveling me without warning.

"Gods do nothing for free, Lena, ever." His mouth lowered to mine, brushing the flesh as heat rippled through them. I rolled away, noting he'd let me create distance between us. I couldn't think with his mouth that close to mine, and his body, that fucking body still did things to me that the simplest of touches sent fireworks exploding through my system.

"It's not going to be that easy," I muttered as I pulled my legs to my chest and leaned against the wide, cloth-covered headboard of the bed. "You got me killed."

"I warned you plenty of times to stay away from me. You should have listened. Not that it would have saved you from me."

"I tried to stay away from you, I couldn't," I argued as I stared into the turbulent storm brewing in his nighttime depths. "I was like a moth to the flame and I ended up charred, didn't I? You thought you could protect me, silly boy, but you're the one who ended my life as surely as if you'd wielded that blade. I was dead the moment you kissed me and just too stupid to realize it."

"You were put in this game by Katarina and Lucifer, never by me. I've never used an innocent life to lure her to me. You were as much a surprise to me as I was to you.

You were something I couldn't stay away from, and even when I tried, I couldn't stay away from you. If you think I'm letting you go again, I assure you, I will not. Losing you once was enough, Lena."

"You chose her! I remember it, you calling her to you. You didn't want me, you wanted her." Tears slipped free, running down my cheeks as I scrubbed my face, hiding the memories.

"I called out to her to protect you and the child you carried, yes! I'd have told her anything she wanted to hear. I'd have left with her too if it meant for one fucking second that you would have lived. I begged her to come to me, to *save* you. I had no idea you would go to them, nor could I break through the wards to get to you. I didn't even know I had a son because you decided to keep him from me. And why didn't you tell me? Afraid I wouldn't accept him, or were you just planning to hide him from me?"

"So you wouldn't hurt as I had to," I answered as I closed my eyes and leaned my head back against the softness of the bed frame. I swallowed hard as I felt his eyes burning my flesh. "I knew he was doomed, and that my only choice as his mother would be to end his life. You didn't deserve to know of him. I asked if you wanted children, and you said you couldn't have them and dismissed me. I told you I loved you and what did you do? Do you remember?"

"I left, because loving me is a death sentence and look at how well that worked out for you." He grabbed my legs, pulling me to him until I was forced to fight or curl into the heat of his body. "I pushed you away because it was the only fucking way I knew to protect you from this happening. I didn't want this for you, even if I had to let you go to prevent it. You should have come to me, told me what was happening. I'd have destroyed worlds to save you. To save him," he uttered thickly.

"And I would have lost my sister, and you'd have been forced to kill our son to protect me and everyone else from the monster he would have become," I whispered tightly. "I was going to lose the fight and I knew it, but I wasn't letting her have you either."

"Kiss me, Lena, kiss me right now before I do something we will both regret," he urged, and I turned over, staring up at him.

"No, no, you want me? Earn it."

His mouth crushed against mine and I moaned against his sinfully delicious mouth. I felt too many emotions as he held me there, kissing me softly until he slowly pulled away from my mouth to stare down at me. I rolled him over, straddling him as I stared into his endless eyes. My hand lifted, and I slapped him, hard, tears streaming down my cheeks as I watched him take it. Over and over, I hit him until a sob ripped from my lips.

"I know," he growled as he rolled us, pinning my arms against the softness of the bed. "I failed you, I know. You shouldn't have been the one to die, but then you seemed hell-bent on ending your own life. You were reckless and had you come to me, we could be in a very different place right now. I would have done whatever it took to protect you from this. Whatever it took," he uttered as he stared into my eyes, his meaning crisp and clear. "We'd be together, all three of us."

"In a world you destroyed? Do you think I could have lived in it? My family is safe because I had the balls to do what I had to do to save them. You think he wouldn't have come after them? I was the bait to his trap; he'd have killed us all to get to you. You and I both know that once you'd unleashed whatever the hell you're hiding from us, this world wouldn't exist anymore. You may have gone on, and you may have saved me, but what about everyone else? What about my family and my friends."

The tick in his jaw moved, and I didn't need him to tell me or answer me. It didn't take a soul to know he'd have wiped out a world to protect someone he cared about. Whatever he was, he was powerful enough that Gods had brought me back to keep him happy. Not that I wasn't thankful, but I had a feeling they weren't done messing with my life.

"I should go," I informed him softly, hesitantly, but he didn't let me move or get up. Instead, he just hovered there, close enough that he was inhaling my scent, and I wondered if he was relearning me. Learning how to track me by scent alone? I lifted up, claiming his mouth without warning. My arms wrapped around him as I took from him. My tongue pushed deeper, finding his and dueling against until he growled thickly. The need was brutal, sending a wavering ache deep in my belly. I moaned against his heated kiss as I slowly pulled back, staring into the liquid pools of desire that watched me.

"You kiss me like that again, and I swear to everything within me, I won't let you leave this room unscathed."

"I'm sure it's hard for you," I mused as he rolled from me and sat up, placing his head in his hands as he rubbed his temples in frustration. "Discovering your ex is back from the grave. We've gone through too much together," I mumbled as I stood, fixing my clothes. "But I meant it, Lucian. You want me; you have to prove you deserve me. I went to hell and back, and I sacrificed our child. So no, I'm not ready for this, for whatever it is. Whether you just want to fuck me or fuck with me, I'm not ready to go there. I can't," I said as I moved to the door.

"It was never like that and you fucking know it," he snapped, moving to the door to slam it shut. "You…"

"I what, Lucian? I poured out my fucking feelings and gave you everything I had, and you threw it away? You made me feel as if I didn't matter. Like what I said to you had no fucking meaning, and then you left me in that room to cry alone. Tell me I'm wrong," I whispered thickly as emotions swirled to life inside of me. His fiery glare made my stomach ache; my body tightened, and yet it wouldn't be that easy this time. I had shit I was trying to deal with, and his issues weren't my problem.

CHAPTER
fifteen

It's easy for people to joke about scars if they've never been cut. ~*Shakespeare*.

I surveyed Synthia, watching her endlessly as she ran the Guild with quick, efficient tasks that had people milling about as they set up perimeters and checkpoints around the city. Alden listened and offered advice when she stumbled, as if they'd done this a million times before. Creatures walked about, accepting orders and rushing to do as she bid them to. She was a natural-born leader, one crafted to rule this Guild. I hoped that one day, when the world wasn't collapsing around me, I could be as she was now: strong, fierce, and a total badass. These creatures worked together towards one goal: to protect those who weren't strong enough to protect themselves. As I sighed, Ristan turned from where he stood across the room and slowly made his way to the stairs, sitting beside me.

"You think you don't fit in here, but you do," he stated offhandedly as I turned my heavy stare towards him. "You see the girl with red hair? The one who placed the wards against you in the dome? That is Erie; she's not here of her own free will, more here to hide from the thing which is hunting her. She's forced to choose between hiding here or being used to save an entire race."

"And yet she chooses to be here, why?" I countered as I took in the warrior who turned her bright blue eyes in my direction and then tossed red curls over her shoulder, dismissing me.

"Choices are tricky. Her race and the one that depends on her did that to her face, a warning to any who thought to love her or mate with her. Druids do not birth females, and yet she is one. Magic is what created her. Same as you," he said softly as he smiled, and Olivia blushed across from us as she placed a hand on her swollen belly.

"She is close to her time," I said sadly. I took in the couples that worked together like one well-oiled machine. Ciara and Blane bent over a map as Synthia pointed out things to them. Ryder stood behind her, his eyes surveying as he listened. They'd been through hell, and yet they'd come out stronger for it, because of it. I'd listened to Synthia as she gave me a quick rundown of what had happened to her and it only made me respect her more.

Maybe there was hope for me after all? Maybe.

"You're lost inside that head of yours again," Ristan said as his silver eyes held mine with sadness. "Change is hard; changing who you are is a lot harder. It doesn't mean you're not you, though, Lena. It just means you evolved, and that makes you stronger. Most people would have given into the darkness, welcoming it to take away that pain. You didn't, and Nyx is right: there's a war coming to this world, and we can use someone like you on our side. You were given a second chance, it's more than a lot of people get. Don't throw it away. Use that pain to harness it, to redirect it after those who think to hurt you or anyone you care about."

"I'm like this because of what he is," I said with a subtle nod in Lucian's direction. "I'm here because he is something big, something deadly. They brought me back to keep him from destroying this world, doesn't that bother you?"

"If he wanted this world destroyed, it would be. If he wanted us dead, he'd be against us, not helping us track down those who opened the gates. He's trying to undo what has begun. We can't push everything that escaped them back through. All we can do is close the gates and hunt down those that are here, feeding off the human race."

"That's pretty optimistic, all things considered," I scoffed angrily. I'd seen the monsters that had crawled out of those open gates, and they weren't feeding on the humans, they were slaughtering them.

"The sky is always falling around here, and yet the world continues to turn. The sun continues to rise. I learned long ago that we make our own choices, and most of the time they're fucking wrong. Some so wrong that you end up scarred for life because of it. How you decide to wear those scars, though, that is up to you. My own father brutalized me for what I was, for a choice he'd made. He claimed my mother as a concubine and then hated what they created together. He spent my entire life trying to destroy what he'd created: me. My sister, she was tortured as well. He cut and broke her ribs until she learned to take his torture in complete silence. When he took her ribs, bending them from her chest, she didn't utter one single cry from her lips. Yet in our own way, we loved him. We killed him, but yet his scars didn't define who we would become. He didn't shape us into what we are. You lost something, and you're still trying to learn how to live without it. It's your scar, Lena. Wear it proudly; know that you cared enough to shield others from carrying your burden. You're a fucking badass in your own right. You got a nod from a Goddess for your valor. Most creatures never even know they still exist and you had two willing to move mountains to bring you back from the grave before you'd even placed one foot into it."

"Isn't Synthia a Goddess?" I asked as she lifted turbulent blue eyes to mine, smiling before she bent her head back over the map she was studying.

"She doesn't count, she's new," he chuckled. "My point is, death wasn't your fucking end; it's your beginning. You decide what happens from here on out. Don't waste it pining away on what could have been, and if you shove people away enough, they'll eventually stay away."

"They're safer without me," I acknowledged, holding up a hand to staunch off any retort he may have had. "If the Gods told me to murder them, I would. Hades had full control over me, Ristan. He could have told me to take my own head, and I would have. It wouldn't be something I could ignore if he ordered me to do it. He told me to drop my weapons, and even though I didn't want to, I did. I know you're trying to help and that you mean well, but that's my family. They're my bloodline. They're safer from me if they fear what I have become. If they die, then what am I fighting to protect? No, Ristan, fear keeps people sharp, it keeps them alive; it forces them to prepare, to take steps against what can happen. They've warded against me, which makes them safer than before, when they thought I was just the girl they'd lost. Now they know I'm not her, and they're safer for believing that. Let them fear what I have become. They won't make a mistake and think I'm the girl they buried in that empty grave."

"You're trying to scare everyone with what you've become, but Spyder seems unaffected by it," he snorted, and my eyes followed his to where Spyder had bent down, whispering in Lucian's ear. I tilted my head, watching him as he stood erect, moving directly towards my location with a stereo carried at his side. My eyes dropped to his waist, noting the sack that had dried, black from my blood. My heart continued to beat inside the sack, and I frowned.

"He is off his fucking rocker," I muttered as I stood, watching him approach, wondering why my heart, the old one, was in the sack he'd tied to his waistband. Which he continually carried around like a trophy.

My gaze followed him as he sat the stereo down and smiled at up at me as I narrowed my eyes on him. "I see you, Lena. I *see* you."

"What the hell does that even mean?" I snapped as I crossed my arms to give him a blank look.

"I see you, Kitty, and this little façade you're playing, showing everyone the dark side of you, it ends now." His tone was hard, but the seriousness in his eyes played with my heartstrings. Was my mash that cracked? His finger pushed against the play button and I stared at the old boom box he'd pilfered from somewhere as Rick Springfield's *Jessie's Girl* started to play. He stood to his impressive height and wiggled his brows as he watched my face contort into utter horror.

The look in his eyes made my hackles rise as everything said to run away, quickly. My eyes slowly took in the people who now all stared in our direction, fully aware of the spectacle he was making of this. The music was loud, grating against my inhuman senses as I watched him.

"Are we fighting?" I asked, doing my best to ignore the fact that everyone was watching us. His lips started moving as he sang with the vocals. Loudly and off-tune in a deep baritone that sounded out of place. My eyes grew large, rounded as his body started moving, his hands clapping as he found the beat and just went with it. It was like a train wreck that I couldn't look away from. Spyder dancing was almost as scary as Spyder fighting back in that sex club in Portland. His feet moved, his hips rocked as he stared at me, serenading me in front of the entire Guild with no fear of being laughed at. He actually looked…hot…

"Oh, we're dancing." My tone was filled with awkwardness as I watched his massive body moving, hips gyrating as his neck moved to the beat.

He got closer, mouthing the words as his body continued and he started moving around me in a circle. I looked between him and Lucian, and then back to the dancing maniac who was watching me like I was about to be eaten whole. His eyes darkened as he got to the part about it being mute. I swallowed hard as he near-shouted the words, holding deathly still until that part of the song had passed. Then once again, as if he hadn't just professed his love through the lyrics, he started dancing faster as if he couldn't help it.

Spyder grabbed my hand, pulling me closer before he threw up his hands as he found the beat again. I lost the fight. I threw my head back and laughed, the sound foreign to my ears. I couldn't stop laughing. I laughed so hard that I held my stomach as it hurt from laughing so hard as I landed on my knees on the floor, continuing to laugh uncontrollably.

Tears streamed down my face, unchecked as the laughter rippled through me. He dropped down in front of me, settling on his knees as his dark eyes held mine.

"There she is," he uttered breathlessly. "There's my pretty kitty. I see you. You're in there, still you. I want you back."

"You're insane."

"If dancing like a fucking idiot to a song that makes total sense to me about you gets you to laugh, I'll do it a thousand times a day just to see you smile."

"Fine, but you have to get rid of that," I said, pointing at the bag still tied to his jeans.

"No fucking way. I've been fighting Ristan off tooth and nail because he eats hearts. This one is mine; it's the only piece of you I can get away with having."

I turned, staring at all the eyes that watched us, and groaned the moment I caught the heavy, heated narrow midnight gaze across the room. I leaned over, kissing Spyder gently against his lips chastely. "You and I will always have Portland," I murmured before I pulled away from him, standing back up to my feet.

"What happened in Portland?" Ristan asked as he popped another kernel of popcorn into his mouth and crunched it. "Oh, come on, this is better than Demon-On-Demand and Fae-Per-View together! It's like an actual drama without the commercials or waiting for the next episode!"

"Ristan," Spyder growled.

"Good job, big guy. You made her smile. I almost like you now. I'd like you a lot more if you gave me that heart," he chuckled, and I rolled my eyes as I headed towards the door, dismissing them both for their crazy antics.

CHAPTER
sixteen

This trouble you're in isn't punishment, its training.
~Hebrews 12:7

Grueling pain mingled with aches as hour after hour of testing our skills went by. The sun had risen and was just beginning to set as the twinge of being watched sent a shiver up my spine. They'd poured out of the Guild to watch as we'd honed and tested our skills. We'd done this vigorously as we'd trained without knowing what we were, and while we knew what we were now, it still didn't let us know our limits. Sweat dripped and pooled between my breasts until I slipped the jacket from my shoulders.

I fought to forget. To endlessly hone my skills while forgetting the pain even for a few moments. It felt as if it weighed me down, a vise grip around my throat that never released, never lessened its hold. It felt as if I was slowly drowning and no matter how much I fought, I sunk deeper into the watery depths.

Music started, Imagine Dragons's *Natural* erupted,

filling the evening in the beat and I turned, staring at Spyder who smirked back, the stereo held high above his head as if he'd stepped out of the screen from *Say Anything*. It was official; he was my favorite monster, but clinically insane or high on acid. It was really fifty-fifty there. I stood there, dumbfounded as I watched his smirk turn into a smile that sorta scared and excited me. He wasn't right in the head; that much was clear. I shook off the laughter that threatened to bubble up and looked back to Joshua who glared over my shoulder, at Spyder.

Today my heart beat; it beat endlessly as my arms burned with each massive swing of the blades I wielded. My body ached with a need only one man or being could fix; which was an entirely different problem I had no desire to settle anytime soon. Not until that fucker earned it, not after what his actions and plans had done to me. That wasn't something I could just forget or sweep under the rug. Not when our child had paid for it with his tiny life.

Our child.

The innocent being who I'd sacrificed to protect from evil that he'd housed. That burned me the most; the need for revenge was a constant thing on my mind. It was almost like it fueled the hatred inside of me. I knew one creature that would pay for what had been done to us, one who would be ripped apart the moment I had the chance.

"Damn you, Lenny. Focus!" Joshua snarled as I drew blood with my blade. I paused, watching the black droplets that leaked from the wound.

"I am!"

"No, you're not, or I wouldn't be bleeding, now would I? You're lost inside your fucking head again," he accused as he dropped the tip of the blade to the street and started at me.

"So what if I am? I'm still kicking your ass," I pointed out flippantly.

My sword cut through the air, swiping and defending as he brought his up to counter each blow easily. Blow after blow crashed against metal, but my arms were weakening, and every swing grew harder as the burn ate through me. I ended it, sending his blades crashing to the ground, and watched as he lifted his hands in surrender.

"Are you tiring?" he asked and shook his head as his eyes rounded with surprise.

"I don't tire," I lied, and he puckered his lips and then whistled low as his eyes adjusted from black to blue, staring at me with worry.

"What up, Lenny?" he demanded.

"Nothing," I lied, rolling my shoulders. "They're getting better," I acknowledged and stared up at the blistering sun. It was fall, and hot as hell. The weather was wonky. But then the whole world was in the shitter. "You're keeping the new ones on track?"

"They're still adjusting, but worth keeping."

"I'm not sure we can send them away," I frowned as I rolled my left shoulder, noting the strange pain in it.

"What the hell is going on, Lenny?"

"I don't know," I replied honestly. "I ache like my body needs nutrients, and yet we don't hunger. I'm afraid to even ask if we eat and what the hell it would be. We have not eaten in months and we're fine, so why would I feel like this?"

I listened around us as the weapons stopped meeting and turned around to find the others staring at me. I swallowed as my eyes narrowed on them, zeroing in on the weapons they still held. I watched Catalina move, her eyes never leaving mine.

"Get back in line and train," I demanded.

"Make me," she hissed as she watched me closely, as if she planned to attack. My hackles rose as I stared at her.

It wasn't her who approached, closing the gap between us. It was Philip. He drew his swords, approaching with swift, precise moves that forced me to lift mine to defend or be decapitated. His lips curled into a sneer as his eyes turned as black as the sky that turned to midnight above our heads. My brow creased as I stared at him, watching as he lifted his swords and leered coldly.

"You want to lead us? Prove you are worthy. Prove to us you're strong enough to lead," he challenged, and I swallowed hard as our swords slammed together. "Your pain is a weakness, one that holds you down. You're weak, Magdalena. So fucking weak, pathetic, and broken that you're not fit to lead us into battle," he snarled as he continued sending blow after blow against the weapons I held.

"What is your fucking problem?" I demanded.

"You will never lead us," Catalina quipped, her own weapons flying in my direction as I cried out as the others started towards me as well. "Fight us!"

"Rules?" I offered as sweat dripped down my neck; my arms burned, a fire rushing through me as the adrenaline spiked, and I waited for them to state their rules. Typically, it was nothing fatal. Adrenaline was seductive, like Lucian's cock when it was pounding into my body. I couldn't get enough, and I never wanted it to stop once he'd started.

"To the death," she snickered.

"Then die, bitch," I snapped as my swords crisscrossed, sending her head sailing across the vacant street we stood on. I spun around as Philip's blades cut through the air, whistling a warning as they rushed for my neck. Seconds, seconds are what it took for my blades to block his, sending one blade into tiny pieces as the metal exploded as power ignited into mine.

My swords hummed with it, lighting to an iridescent blue as I moved in a blur of speed and feathers. Blood splattered against my face as I severed his arms, and then cut his body into two pieces as I bent sideways to escape another attack.

"Next," I uttered through clenched teeth as I turned to face the others, sensing the array of magic as it was directed at me. They swarmed me, encircling the space I stood in, and I smiled coldly, wondering if I should point out the stupidity of that idea. No, I'd let them learn it the hard way.

I sent my swords in a wide circle, pushing magic through me into the weapons as I took the first few who'd been stupid enough to stand that close to my blades. I stepped over the remains, moving towards the larger males who slowly backed up, thinking to lure me towards the largest to become victim to the others who stood back, hoping I fell for the ploy. I didn't, I'd had a damn good teacher. I watched as one moved, sending his blade out, towards my midsection. I flipped mid-run, twirling through the air with my blades like a boat propeller, landing in front of the largest as I tossed one blade into the air, using my wings to pin him into place before I brought my blade down hard, cutting him into two separate pieces. My left hand reached, grasping the other sword as it came back down, and sent my blades between my arms, backwards. Grunts erupted, and I turned, peering over my shoulder with a saucy smile curving my lips.

It was endless; they came against me in pairs or more until their bodies littered the street like discarded trash. Blood ran from the street in a river, following it down until it hit the sewer drain. A coppery tang filled my mouth from taking a few elbows to the face, and yet no blade had touched me. I exhaled as I took in the carnage, hating that it was my people that lay in severed, bloody pieces on the street.

I turned to face the last one, and my sword tips skidded to the ground, scraping across the road as I stared into midnight eyes that had filled with hatred. I watched as he bent to retrieve the blades he'd lost earlier in practice before everything had gone to hell.

"No, Joshua," I snapped, but he didn't listen, as if something else was controlling him. My chest ached as I watched him slowly approach me. My gaze swung to the Guild, and the people who watched us in silence. "Don't make me do this, I beg of you!" I pleaded. Lucian was arguing with Synthia, his hands fisted at his sides while the others watched us, silently taking in our moves, studying us. Nobody was planning on intervening and stopping this from happening. No help was coming to prevent this fight that I would give anything not to be a part of. "Please!"

"Fight me, Lenny," he chuckled, the sound eerie and causing my hair to rise with the wrongness of it. His blades crashed down, and I brought mine up, but not fast enough to defend the blow that cut through my arm. I screamed as I swung out, sending his blades away from my body. I didn't want to do this; I'd had to watch his death echo, which to me, was the worst one.

I had watched it for the first two full moons, and then I'd been unable to stomach seeing it again. I'd observed him standing in an open field with a dark shadow; that shadow had explained his deal, explained what would happen to him upon accepting it. I'd stood there, frozen as he'd explained that it was for me, because of me, but Joshua hadn't blinked, hadn't hesitated. I'd had no idea it was Hades, or that he was trying to help us, to help me, which now made sense, but the pain of watching it was unbearable. Joshua had died to save me, to be sure I'd come back; he'd gone first. He'd died and become this monster because Hades had found him and explained what would happen once he entered our world again. It was why Joshua had never come home after he'd killed Benjamin. Because he'd lived. He'd survived until my life had been placed on the line. And now I was fighting him, my hero. My world.

"I'll drop them," I warned, knowing if it were Joshua in control, he'd yield to me. He didn't, and I fought the tears that rolled down my cheeks as my eyes burned with anger. "Fuck you! Fuck you to Hell!" I screamed as anger thrummed through me, making my hair rise with the power that exploded from my pores. I brought my arms up and fought with vigor, watching as his blades clattered to the ground as I landed blow after blow against his body. Once he was teetering on his feet, his body a sliced up mess, I expelled the scream that had built in my lungs. "Enough! It's enough! Please…"

It wasn't. He reached down, his body a mangled mess as he retrieved the swords and turned around, slowly, his balance as much of a mess as the tattered remains of his torso. Blood oozed from his wounds and yet he continued to come at me. Over and over, he swung his blades, and I easily deflected them with his clumsy movements. Anger rippled red-hot through me, and I knew, I knew it wouldn't be enough until he lay in pieces with the others. My wings unfurled, and I stared at him, waiting for him to swing once more, and then I lunged, severing my brother in half.

"I can't do this!" I screamed until I was hoarse, my voice little more than a rasp that escaped my dry throat. I shouted at whoever had forced this fight, forced my hand. I dropped to my knees and waited there, waiting for them to come back. To be put back together again, whole. They didn't, and after hours passed, people on the stairs departed as night fell on the macabre scene. The sun came and went, flies swarmed the bodies as the blood dried and the stench of death lingered in the sun's heat.

I put them back together, finding the part to the body and placing it close to it. Panic began to swallow me whole as the knowledge of them being really gone started to eat at my mind. Hopelessness began to consumed me, the never-ending dread that I'd slaughtered them all, along with my brother, raged inside of me. I screamed, I shouted, I begged, boy, did I fucking beg them to bring them back to me. I cursed the Gods, and in the next breath, I begged them to just give them back to me whole.

I stood, staring at Lucian as I dropped an arm next to a body. I was covered in dried blood that felt like it would never wash off. It was sticky, coating my flesh and clothing as I inhaled the sharp, nasty scent of decaying corpses. They were bloating, disintegrating around me where I stood, lost without them. I'd done this to them. I'd killed my army and my own brother. Panic began to choke me, and then the music started to play softly.

That song.

My eyes rose to the sunlit sky, feeling the heat of it against my flesh as I stared into the beauty of it. There was no full moon tonight, no phase that should bring about my echo of death. I dropped my eyes to the gore and heard it.

My son's beautiful wail; his cries that haunted my every wakeful moment. My throat tightened and my hands fisted against my sides. It wasn't real. I exhaled deeply, lifting my eyes to the stairs, and frowning as I found Lucian watching something behind me.

He started forward as if he was haunted, and then his actions slowed and uncertainty played across his rugged features. Then Nyx was there, appearing beside him as she pushed him back as she shook her head. They argued, and he pushed her away, and I watched as she landed on the ground, lifting her dark eyes up at him before she was rising, moving towards him with a warning in her eyes.

"It's her fight, not yours or mine. Only she can decide what happens here, Lucian. You cannot choose for her, and neither can I. It's her pain, her weakness to overcome, and she alone has to choose which she is willing to sacrifice to remain strong, to remain here with you."

"She already did! This is fucking torture, Nyx. You know it, and I know it. Do you have no fucking heart, woman?" he demanded coldly.

"No, I don't. I've never pretended to have one either. I refuse to be weak," she hissed. "That loss is holding her back from what she must become. Furies are born of rage, vengeance, and anger. Lena is dying because there's so much fucking pain that she cannot grow into what she must to survive. She has to find a balance and quickly. Right now the only thing keeping her alive is the pain, but every moment she feeds from it, it takes more and more of her until it will consume her. This isn't something you can choose for her, or take away from her. One option holds the future, the other is certain death. She knows what she will choose because she can feel it. She deserves so much more than you or what she has been given. To find a woman like her with so much strength is rare these days, but to find one who does as she has, well, you are aware of how rare a breed she is. This place seems to be a beckon for them, though…" She paused, eyeing the women who stood shoulder to shoulder, staring at her through narrowed gazes. "I would enjoy finding my Furies here, would I not?"

"They're not interested, Nyx. Let it go," he snarled as he placed his hands at his sides in balled-up fists. I watched them flex as if he was fighting to hold what I knew was behind me. His son, the unborn child we'd created together. I'd thought I was releasing an unborn child, but he hadn't come out as a fetus. Instead, he'd been fully formed and aware of what I'd done. They'd pulled him fully formed from my womb, and I'd felt it. I'd known it the moment they'd removed him that he was aware.

I turned, staring at the woman who held him covered in a blanket. His little arms stretched, jerking as if he sensed I was near. I wanted to scream at her to hold him tighter, to stop his struggles and fears, but I couldn't. I walked towards them, my heart filling my throat as I started past the endless body parts that rotted at my feet. I paused as I reached out for him, watching as she lifted my son to me.

Everything inside of me screamed to take him; to hold him one fucking time before I released him. Tears slid down my cheeks, and I wailed; something inside of me broke to pieces, and I screamed in frustration because I knew, I knew I wouldn't ever touch my son. I would never know the feel of him against my arms, or cradle and soothe him. My outstretched hands turned into fists as I dropped them at my sides. I swayed on my feet, emotions warring with my need to touch him once, but once would kill us both. His cries lessened, and he stilled, and his fist went to his mouth as a tiny noise started. The blanket fell away, and I stared into midnight eyes, as he sucked his tiny fingers as he stared at me.

"I love you." A sob escaped my throat to bubble up as I shook my head. "I love you so much, but I can't choose you." It escaped as a broken sob, and pain lanced through me, shattering what little heart I had left. "I'll always love you, my little Harbinger. Always and always, until I am no more; until I turn to night, and I'm given to the earth," I reassured him as he watched me through innocent eyes. I turned away from him, staring at Joshua's corpse. He still hadn't risen, nor had the others. My head swung back to where my child had been, finding the spot vacant and empty. He'd had midnight curls of hair, and matching eyes just like his father's. Endless depths of midnight darkness had watched me. His flesh had held the runes which matched mine, placed there to protect him and mark my sacrifice. Runes to protect him in his next life, to show the world that he would rule it. He would have been beautiful, had he not been cursed to be born as my child.

"Get up!" I demanded as something inside of me slipped into place. I screamed at them, baring my loss of the son I'd lost all over again. Everything inside of me turned to rage, abandoning the pain that had once eaten at me. The buildings around me trembled as my power shook them, threatening to level the entire place if my warriors didn't heed my call. I screamed again, letting my newly found rage ride through me to reach them. I screamed until my voice cracked like thunder through the sky as I released the last of my anguish and embraced the growing rage. It bubbled up like a shaken can of soda, shooting through me until the ground vibrated and whined against the pressure I released. I dropped to my knees in the middle of the corpses and slammed my hands flat on the ground as I sent my power searching for them. Power rippled around me, and I felt its deadly cold as the day turned to night and thunder snapped and rumbled above us. "Rise!" Lightning flashed across the sky, followed directly by thunder.

"Shit, that's unfortunate," Nyx exclaimed as my eyes lifted to hers over the dead that littered the streets. In the next instant, she was beside me, placing a calming hand on my shoulder. "Pull it back, little one. Lucian, she needs to be trained. She's more powerful than I imagined she would be," she hissed as her hand tightened against my shoulder. "I suggest you use your normal methods on her. If you choose not to, Styx will be my next choice. You and I both know he'd love her unblemished flesh."

"Train her how?" he demanded.

"She has to learn to control the rage, or she will level more than a few city blocks. I've underestimated her. She is not a Fury, she is the Furies. She is three in one, Lucian. It's unheard of, but she took all three into her body when I created her. I'd assumed others would take pieces of them from her, but she prevailed and seems to have contained them all. To me, it doesn't matter if she learns to control them, but to her, it does. If she cannot control them, she will end up killing others, and I'm certain she still cares for the weak mortals she loved. They're weak, useless, but she cares for them." She flicked an invisible piece of lint from her dress as she rose to tower above me. "Styx is waiting, salivating for a chance to teach her if you're unwilling."

"You're a fucking sadist," he snapped.

"You are one too, and I know she enjoyed the pain

you inflicted on her. Did you think we wouldn't watch to see who won this last game? We were always watching you. That little shack didn't have thick enough walls, and you knew it. You enjoyed us watching you fuck her flesh, claiming her so that we all knew she was marked. There's also the fact that bringing her back meant I had to sit through every fucking boring and not so boring parts of her life. I had to relive them all, every fucking mundane emotion she'd ever experienced. Do you have any idea how tedious it is to go through them with them unaware that you're beside them, reliving their life?" she frowned as she eyed me. "It's why I have not created new Furies in centuries. But then it wasn't really my choice, either. Choose."

"I'll do it," he growled. "If Lena agrees," he hissed as his midnight eyes dropped to hold mine with a warning in their seductive depths.

"Lena, it wasn't a question that takes thought. Styx is a fucking monster, he enjoys taking pretty things apart," she hissed as she knelt down, staring into my eyes. Her platinum eyes stared into mine, glimpsing the indecision playing in them. Her smile turned dark, her lips pulled back, exposing serrated teeth that looked like lethal blades. "Torture or pleasure, pick your poison. One will only break you, the other will fucking devour you. You will not enjoy Styx's brand of pleasure; that much I promise you."

"Lucian," I uttered through clenched teeth. "I choose Lucian."

"I thought you would, smart girl. Have fun, and pay attention to what he shows you. I can't have you focusing on pain if you murder what little of your family members remain. Your army is now yours to lead; the pain is no more standing between you and them. The cries that torture you will cease now, and he will be reborn. Had you chosen him, he would have killed you. He was your death. He is not of this world, nor will he ever be. When he is reborn, this world will tremble with fear. He's been chosen for a reason. If he wants to, he will find you again when he chooses to. If we survive the war that is coming," she uttered softly, her eyes gentling as she watched me.

"How do you know that?"

"Because death is never the end to our kind, only the beginning," she frowned and then dropped her eyes with a faraway, haunted look in them. "Unlike you and the others I brought back, of course. Your deaths meant something, something bigger than you will ever understand. How you can hold three Furies inside of you is impressive, which makes you one of a kind, Lena. Don't fuck it up. None who held them before you ever retained their memories of who they were, and yet you do it beautifully. You're one of a kind, rare, very rare indeed. Don't break her, Lucian. I have big plans for this one. Big plans indeed," she chuckled right before she vanished.

I stared into midnight eyes who watched me with a heat banked in their depths, and anticipation etched on his face.

"I may enjoy this a lot more than you will," he growled with blue flames burning in his eyes.

"It doesn't mean I'm going to continue after we've finished training, Lucian. I told you before, earn it. You didn't just fuck me over or screw me. You placed my life in the middle of a fucking war with your crazy ex, and she was only crazy because you continually fucking murdered her over and over again. I can almost understand her trust issues and her motives. You're enough to drive any sane woman insane."

"I told you a million times before, Lena. I'm not your fucking prince charming, I'm your nightmare. Now follow me."

I glared at his back and then I winked at Spyder, who watched us. I knew he hurt, and I knew he out of everyone here knew I was still me, but I refused to let them see it. He saw me, inside of me; through the darkness and ugly bits, he saw that I was still me, just that I'd buried myself so fucking deep into the darkness I wasn't sure I'd ever come back out.

CHAPTER
seventeen

Some men play with your head; others rip your soul out and consume it. ~*Lena*

I followed Lucian's stiff back as we made our way down the vacant hallway towards his suite. Synthia had offered us a more private location and neutral ground for what was sure to be a mind-fuck of a lay. I'd almost agreed, but something in Lucian's demeanor had stopped me cold. His dark, sinful gaze had warned me to remain silent, and so I had. Not because I'd felt threatened, but because I wanted to use his bathtub to wash off the filth of the battle that had just gone down outside.

"Bathe; the only blood I want to see upon your flesh is the blood I put there," he growled as he shook out of his suit jacket, folding it before he carefully set it on top of the large dresser. My eyes remained locked on his large hands, so adept and skilled. He loosened the tie he wore, placing it atop the jacket. Next, he rolled the sleeves up past his elbow and then paused, staring back at me.

"Do you plan to torture me, then?" I asked, locking gazes as I waited for his answer.

"Nothing you can't handle, witch."

"I'm no longer a witch, Lucian. That part of me died with my soul. I am no longer human, nor do I crave anything. Including you," I warned as my lips drooped into a frown that marred my mouth. I expelled a shaky breath, knowing it wasn't true.

I craved him more than I craved anything. As if he was an extension of my soul and through him, I held onto some form of myself. It was why I'd wanted to let him go, to not feel that urge or tug of humanity that had once held me down.

"Bathe, use the salt in the cabinet," he uttered. "It's going to be a long night for you."

"They didn't say sex, they said you needed to train me. To teach me control," I offered, extending a way out of this.

"Do you know what the body's most basic need is?" he asked, as he watched me through cold, detached eyes.

"No."

"Pleasure, and the need to succumb to it," he explained. "When you first experience it, it feels wrong because it's new. It's exciting, and everything in this world tells you how wrong it is. Once you've tasted it, once you've admitted that it's normal, it becomes the one thing you need. The hardest thing you can do after that is deny it when it's right there, offered so freely. I'm going to bring you to the edge of pleasure, and you're going to deny the urge to jump off that cliff. You won't come unless I allow it, because once you can force pleasure away, you can control everything else easily. Your wings are under your control, ruled by emotions. When you're pissed, they extend, right?" he waited for me to nod and then continued. "Yet you can't prevent them from unfurling. Once you can control your most basic need, they will easily be controlled. So yes, Lena, I'm going to fuck you. We're going to have sex because there's no fucking way in hell I can do this without being with you. I'm going to teach you to control your basic needs, to be in control of how you react, and that means fucking you. I could do it without entering your body, but I've yet to touch another woman since you entered my life, and I'm positive that no matter who I fucked, she'd be lacking and she sure as fuck wouldn't be you."

"Tell me how it works, how you teach me to control my body's response." I lifted the blood-soaked shirt over my head, tossing it aside as I slipped out of the shoes that had pruned my feet, sloshing blood onto the floor. His eyes lowered, taking in the splatter of it where I walked towards the tub. "Well?"

"I'm going to dominate you."

"And you think you can?" I chuckled, the taunt lying heavily between us. I smell it then, the atavistically acute scent that is exclusively his. It's something ancient, something forgotten, and yet it unravels me to my baser needs, the most basic thing inside of me that is unquestionably woman.

Lucian is a temptation; one that doesn't just sneak up on you and slowly removes your inhibition. No, there's no subtlety about him. He weighs on you, the scent, the midnight eyes that consume and devour. He stares at me like I'm some precious fucking gift, and yet he fucks me like a savage. Lucian is everything dark, and yet the moment he touches me, it's not the darkness I fear, but rather the flame that threatens to destroy and consume me.

He's a fucking monster, and I'm about to show him his match. The tit to his tat, his motherfucking downfall, I'm about to show him the monster within.

I slipped out of the jeans, tossing them aside as I turned to throw an angry glare in his direction, but I didn't make it that far. I was slammed against the wall on my stomach, his touch burning me as pain shot up through me. I growled low in my chest, letting the noise build up and then escape from between my lips.

Lips touched the back of my neck, softly before his teeth grazed the delicate flesh as his naked, smooth chest pushed against my spine. He wasn't afraid of the deadly wings that had razor-sharp edges, but then I was sure not much terrified this man. His mouth sent heat pooling low in my belly, my sex tightened with anticipation as his hot breath fanned my ear.

"I think you want to be dominated by me," he uttered as his nose ran down the flesh behind my ear. "I think that one man and one man alone can dominate you. Not because you're weak, but because I'm the only man you'd ever allow to dominate you. You're fierce, Lena, a fucking beautiful, chaotic storm that cannot be contained, and shouldn't. This world underestimated you, hell, even I did. I won't do it twice." He pushed away from me, his heat still sliding against my flesh as I turned to glare up at him. "Now bathe, because I'm about to show you what real control looks like."

"Are you planning to watch me bathe?" I murmured as I reached for the bath salts, knowing his eyes watched the curvature of my spine as my hips flared. I knew he scented the arousal he'd created, but the thing was, he thought he could so easily dominate me. That I was going to bend to his will, but it wouldn't be that easy.

"I'll give you some privacy," he said softly, and yet he remained there, staring at me as I set the scented salt aside and stepped into the tub, turning on the water to rinse the first coat of blood off my flesh. Once it wasn't as thick, I used the soap, purposely covering my body in a thick lather before I rinsed that off as well.

After I'd ensured the bathwater wouldn't be blood red, I dropped some of the salt into the freshly-run bathwater and slowly sat down, feeling the heated weight of his gaze.

"If you're going to stand there, you can help me wash," I offered, unable to stop the smirk that lifted my lips as he growled, warning me he wasn't enjoying having to wait for me to finish my bath. He deserved it.

Once I finished, I towel-dried my hair and then braided it neatly before wrapping the towel around my body and moving to lean against the doorframe, staring into the dark room beyond. Lucian's shadow was there, lit only from a single candle whose flame danced in the room.

"Setting the mood, are we? The mood is pissed off, and slightly over this shit," I informed as I stepped deeper in the abyss, hating that my body grew heated, ready for this creature. I hated it for betraying me; I mean, couldn't it understand what had happened? The events that made it into what it was were huge, cataclysmic shit that had literally left me without a soul. Okay, so I had a fucking sliver of one. Wasn't that what Hades had mentioned? Someone else's soul resided inside my body to retain some semblance of my mind.

"Is that so?" he chuckled; his deep baritone voice slithering over my heated flesh, unfurling need to the pit of my being. "Kneel," he ordered.

"I'm not a sub, and you're not a Dom," I growled

as I stood clothed only in a towel in the middle of the bedroom. "I will not kneel to you," I warned.

"You'll kneel," he replied huskily as he stepped out of the shadows wearing only a pair of faded jeans that hung loosely from his hips. I swallowed hard, hating the fire that burned from deep in my belly as every nerve ending came alive with the sheer magnitude of perfection that was Lucian Blackstone. "Not because I demand it, but because in order to train you to contain what you are, I have to tear you down to nothing but a blank canvas. You will yield so that I don't have to murder Styx after I've just managed to forgive him for his last trespass."

"He may be safer for this, you know, self-preservation and all that jazz," I argued beneath my breath.

"He enjoys breaking pretty things," he warned as his hand snaked out, stealing the towel I'd used as a shield against him. I swallowed the scream that threatened to bubble up and escape the pout I wore on my lips. "He'd ruin you, and I assure you, sweet girl, you wouldn't enjoy his touch. You know you enjoy mine, no matter how much you want it to be otherwise."

"Still not kneeling to you," I warned. "I will never bow before you."

"Is that a challenge?" he laughed huskily as he knelt on the floor, staring up at me with his midnight, heated gaze. His lips moved, hovering against the inside of my thigh as his tongue snaked out, licking before his teeth grazed the flesh. My body almost buckled from the subtle motion alone, threatening to not support my weight.

"If I challenged you, you'd know it," I admitted as I threaded my fingers through his silken hair, grabbing a handful before I pulled his head back as I lowered to my knees in front of him. He allowed it, watching me as I let my mouth hover just inches from his. "You want control, fucking take it from me. That is a direct challenge…" I was pushed down with my hands held in a viselike grip above my head; my wings unfurled, and yet he slammed me hard against the floor, rendering them useless. I grunted as his knees trapped my legs as his other hand circled my throat, closing it off to the useless oxygen I no longer needed.

"No matter what you've become, I'm still stronger," he growled against my ear as his teeth pulled the delicate flesh, nipping at it until it released it. His hungry lips moved to my shoulder, kissing the scar from his claim that had forged a bond that had followed me, even in death. "You're mine, you've always been mine, and you will always be mine. Not even death could take you from me, Lena. I'm glad you're stronger, harder to break now. It means I no longer have to hold back. I don't have to fear breaking this pretty little neck of yours. You will kneel, and you'll beg me to fuck you. Those things are certain, because I know what your body craves, and I enjoy watching you struggle."

I couldn't speak, not because I lacked the oxygen to do so; more because he was crushing my throat. I bucked my hips as his teeth sank into my flesh, mirroring the exact scar he'd given me on my inner thigh. My body responded in a blaze of fire that ignited in my belly and unfurled until I was dripping with sweat and the anticipation of what it promised.

His hand left my throat, sliding between our bodies until they danced on my pussy, gliding through the sleek mess that his touch created. They trailed through it, his thumb stalling against the peaked flesh to roll over it as my hips lifted, the moan exploding from my lips before I could prevent it from escaping.

"That's right," he laughed huskily against my ear. "You feel me; your body needs what I can give it. So you will kneel, and I'll fuck this tight flesh so you can reach your most basic fucking need." He rolled from the floor, standing up to stare down at the mess he'd left laying on it. I trembled from the loss of his touch, but I didn't beg. Instead, I replaced his hand with my own as his darkened gaze watched me.

I felt nothing. Nada. My fingers pushed through my flesh, and I swallowed hard as I sat up, peering up at him as worry sank into my mind. "The fuck," I exclaimed as I tried again as the panic turned into a vise around my newly regrown heart.

I rose from the floor, moving towards him and grabbing his hand, pushing against my sex and moaning as the sensation came rushing back.

"Motherfucker!" I seethed as I backed away from him as if he was the vilest, uncouth fucking creature I'd ever encountered. "What did you do to me?"

"Lena, what is happening?" he demanded.

"I can't feel it," I admitted as I reached for his dress shirt, pushing my arms through the sleeves as he stared at me in confusion.

"Can't feel what?" he asked carefully, his eyes darkening as they slowly lowered to where my hand was stroking my flesh as my heart raced against my chest. Slowly, they lifted to hold mine as I raged.

"My fucking hand! It's like it doesn't even register that I'm touching me!" I moved to the door, throwing it open as I raced down the hallway, ignoring the sound of his bare feet as they followed me. I rushed into the main room of the Guild, sliding on the smooth floor as

I searched through the heads that turned at my sudden entrance. "Motherfucking bitch," I fumed as I didn't see Spyder, but then he was there, moving across the floor as he took in my disheveled appearance.

"Problem?" he asked, and I swallowed hard as I took in his heated gaze that slowly traveled down my body to where the shirt covered me past my thighs. "Kitty, you seem to be in a compromising position here. Something we can help you with?" he asked.

"Touch me," I demanded and his eyes lifted to mine, then briefly moved to Lucian who stood directly behind me. "Spyder, I'm not asking!" I hissed when he continued to stand mere feet away from me.

I felt Lucian's nod more than I saw it and watched as Spyder stepped closer, his hands slowly moving to my waist, holding me. I gripped one, peeling it off my hip to press it against my breast, feeling the heat of his palm but nothing else. A terrified groan left my lips as I stepped on tiptoes, pulling his mouth down to mine. My tongue darted in, claiming his and then tears begin to fall in earnest. I was fucking broken.

I released him and watched the heat pool in his glacier stare that could have melted the icebergs in the Bering Sea. I shook my head, confusion marring my mind and face as I turned to stare at Lucian as it hit me.

"Motherfucker, Hades!" I seethed, the scream turning into a growl as it exploded from my lungs. "This is fucked up, even for you!"

"Is there a problem?" Synthia asked as she and Ryder started across the floor to stand close to us.

"A problem? Yes, a huge fucking problem," I seethed as it exploded from my lips, dripping in sarcasm. "I can't feel pleasure unless Lucian is giving it to me. I'd call that a huge fucking problem!" I swung around, glaring at Lucian, whose eyes seemed to burn with the newly found knowledge that we'd just learned.

"Awkward," she uttered with a frown tipping her lips as she stared at me, helpless to offer anything that would take away the panic growing inside of me. "I mean, you liked being with him before, so this isn't so bad, right? You can still…"

"Not the fucking point!" I argued. "I can't orgasm unless he is touching me; it's a massive fucking problem. I can't even get myself off! I'm broken."

"You're not broken, Lena. You're adjusting. Maybe it's something that just needs time," she offered.

"No, she was his gift. There's only a few men she can touch and feel, the others didn't need to be able to give her pleasure," Hades said as he appeared from thin air and leaned against the stone column. He shrugged when I gave him a seething glare. "You have a sliver of a soul, Magdalena. Beggars can't be choosy. I did what I could, and I put everything I could into retaining who you were, and your mind. You had enough left for three lovers. You can choose me, Lucian, or Lucifer, but I'm hoping you don't go for the latter one. I didn't bring you back to leave him, or to run to the arms of your enemy. You can, however, feel others if he is touching you, or he allows it." He shrugged again as if he didn't care which I choose.

"I get Lucian being on the list, but why are you on it?"

"I tasted that pussy once," he smirked as his violet eyes glowed and power erupted around us, slithering over my flesh. "My wife doesn't respond to my touch, but you did. If things don't work out, I left you only one option."

"Because you don't think I'd go to Lucifer?"

"He did bash your fucking head in, and I protected

you. Don't get me wrong, Lena, we wouldn't be in it for love. We'd fuck. But that's only if Lucian relinquishes you. I don't think he is quite ready to do that yet."

"You'll never have her, Hades. She is mine."

"She always has been, even before you knew it. She was, after all, created to lure you in and distract you. Now that the bitch is out of play, thanks to this one," he said hiking a thumb in my direction, "you can have her. I'm leaving, but you should know that Lucifer is closing in on her, drawn by her scent. He's aware of what she is and who she is with."

"He can come, I'm ready for him."

"The next time you shout my name, you better be fighting something you can't handle, or need me for other…things."

CHAPTER
eighteen

I will not bow to any man, nor will I cave to this inner need that demands I do so. I am the monster they will fear, the one who has come back to seek revenge. I am Lena.

The world was chaotic, a broken place that teetered on the edge of a massive overhaul it hadn't asked for. My world, on the other hand, was fucked. I was fucked. Lucian didn't seem to mind or be bothered at the news that I'd been brought back and my body only responded to his. Or maybe he did care but preferred it this way. Back inside the room, I hesitated in stripping myself bare, unable and unwilling to face what was now my new reality.

"Strip," he ordered and produced a cane as he paced around me. His eyes flashed with darkness, the promise of pleasure lacing every word that dripped off his tongue in a silken caress.

When I continued to just stare at him with a glare that bordered on murder and loathing, he smirked. It tugged up at the corners of his generous mouth, dripping off that tongue like a silken caress. The cane shot through the air, slapping my naked ass, and I growled.

"I'm going to take that from you and shove it so far up your ass that you'll need twenty-four nurses, thirteen doctors, and a fucking midget to get it out!" I snapped, the warning reverberating through the room.

"You feel pain, but not pleasure."

I rubbed my ass as I stared daggers at him. "I felt it."

I watched him set the cane down as he turned to stare at me where I stood on pins and needles from the new discovery of my limitations. Of course, I could feel pain and not pleasure, why not? Everything else was turning into a shit show, why not add this to the mix?

Muscles rippled as he stared at me; dark, muscled, sleek utter perfection is what Lucian Blackstone was. His runes and tattoos danced in his flesh, even in the candlelight, they beckoned me to touch them. To drag my fingertips over the sinewy hard flesh that would send a ripple of electrical current through me, aimed right at the broken vagina I'd been reborn with.

I ripped his shirt off of my frame, letting the clean cotton dress shirt pool to the floor at my feet. I was sleek, hard-muscled, and jagged edges. I was no longer the soft girl I'd been when he'd first fucked me. I had no confusion on what he would do to me. He'd wreck me, it was a given. Fact. Fact: Lucian Blackstone wrecked things, bent your will, destroyed any sense of self-preservation you may have thought you had, and he did it fucking well.

I could have been an asshole, I could have attacked him and went to war with his body, but I was curious to know how it felt to be controlled by something like him. To bend the will that wanted to rip his hair back and devour his mouth. I wanted to hurt him as I hurt now, but I also wanted what he could achieve: Mindless, leg-shaking, earth-shattering pleasure that would take away the pain.

I kicked his shirt away and knelt before him, my hands folded in my lap as I lowered my eyes in a demure strangeness that forced me to give up control. His hiss was enticing, the air escaping between his teeth as he took in my fake surrender, because I wasn't stupid and neither was he. I'd make the world's worse submissive.

"You kneel now?" he questioned and my eyes lifted to his, the rage I felt at giving myself to him without him earning it burning bright in my stare. I opened my mouth to speak and yet slammed it shut as my teeth snapped together loudly. "Get on the bed," he ordered, and I stood, doing as he said.

Once there, I watched him as he collected a few things from the dresser, moving to stand at the side of where I now lay, awaiting his next command. He bent over, kneeling beside me as his mouth lowered to the needy flesh between my legs. His tongue snaked out, trailing from my wet flesh to my inner thigh. He pushed something against my clit, and then he laughed gutturally as he pumped it.

My hips shot off the bed as pleasure shot through me. I lifted my head, staring down at the pump he'd placed on my clitoris. "What the hell are you doing?" I asked, and then my back arched as he pushed his finger inside as he added yet another pump to the thing attached to my pussy.

"It's a clitoris pump," he chuckled as he rubbed his fingers around it. My back arched into his touch and my body flooded with a multitude of heat and sensations as he watched me. "It's going to make it harder for you to ignore your body's needs." I stared into his dark, hypnotic gaze as goosebumps covered my flesh. He squeezed it again, and I moaned, unable to suppress it. I could feel the flesh swelling beneath the contraption he'd connected to it. His eyes slowly took in what he'd done, and I lifted, staring down where the tube had sucked my clit, making the pink flesh red as it swelled into the tube. "In order to control your power, you have to gain focus and control of it. You can control your response to the anger like you would your pleasure. You decide when to let it out. Once you can control your own orgasms, you can master your response to anything," he explained, his fingers drifting to run his scarred knuckles over the wet flesh between my legs. "Your body runs off your emotions now, once you cease to control it, it controls you.

"I'm going to teach you to be in control of how you respond to it. Anger is much akin to pleasure, both can control you easily. You crave the emotions they bring as they ebb and flow through you. You'll be your own Dom, Lena. You will control it as if your powers are the submissive, and you the master of them. For now, I'm the Dom, and you're my submissive. You only come when I allow it, or you will be punished for it."

"Are you high?" I asked as I sucked my bottom lip between my teeth before releasing it. "I don't have a submissive bone in my entire body. I don't like to be told what to do, or did you forget that part?"

"You think I'd forget anything about you?" he snorted as he moved from the bed, shucking his pants as his cock bounced free from the jeans he'd worn. My eyes feasted on the flesh, staring at the massive cock that stood proudly against his navel. I swallowed hard as he settled back on the bed, staring down at me as if I was his favorite meal, one he intended to savor slowly. "You are not a submissive, and you wouldn't be one normally. This isn't a normal situation, and if it weren't a matter of life and death, we wouldn't be here naked, together. You'd still be holding me at arm's length, but you and I both know what is at stake here, *who* is at stake. If it weren't important, you'd have ignored Nyx. You can still try to do this yourself, or you can let me help you. You decide your own fate, my little Fury."

"Fine, tell me what to do, and I'll do it," I uttered.

"Scoot to the edge of the bed," he ordered huskily.

Once I had done it, his mouth found my flesh as he pushed my legs up against my chest. A scream built inside of me, bubbling in my lungs as it slowly built up until I was shaking, trembling, coming undone.

"Lucian," I cried out as the orgasm teetered on the verge of the precipice. Dark eyes held mine as he continued to stop until I was almost too close to prevent it from unraveling and exploding from inside of me. I needed to come, and the bastard knew it. He enjoyed torturing me. That much was certain.

"Green means you're safe, not close to coming. Yellow means you're close and on the verge, and red, red means you're coming for me. Remember that because I'll ask it often in the coming days."

"Days?" I asked, sitting up on my elbows to stare at him from between my legs.

"This isn't going to be a quick fix," he offered. "You're a new creature, something you and I both have no idea how to control. I'm not going to lie and say it doesn't excite me that I get to bring you into my world, Lena. Because the idea of teaching you control is a fucking turn-on, but knowing that I'm one of three you can actually fuck? That makes the primitive being inside this flesh hungry to devour you."

"I can still fuck, Lucian. I just can't get off, but that

doesn't mean I won't try," I warned and before I knew his intentions, I was slammed against the bed with his nose pressed against mine. His smile was wicked and deadly as those silken midnight eyes stared into mine.

"I will destroy anyone who thinks to touch you."

"Jealous?" I taunted as I stared into his eyes. He smiled, and it wasn't friendly. It was all teeth, the warning there in the pits of his midnight gaze as he remained unmoving, watching me for any sign of weakness. Once he was sure I wouldn't smart off, he moved.

My tongue licked over my lips as I watched his cock bounce with every step he took, moving around the room until he was once again before me. His legs spread wide apart as he stared down at my naked, swollen flesh.

"You're wet," he mused as his fingers pushed into my needy flesh and I moaned as he slowly began working my flesh. His other hand moved to the side of my hip, pulling one nipple clamp up as he easily maneuvered it onto my nipple. His mouth lowered, clamping down hard as his teeth grazed the peaked flesh. He followed it to the other, placing the second one before he pulled it into his heated mouth, suckling the flesh before he lifted his hard head. His fingers continued to work magic into my aching core, and I purred for him. "Good girl," he urged as he withdrew his fingers to the tip, only to surge it into my body harder. "So fucking wet. You're the most beautiful creature I've ever seen, Magdalena. Fire and ice, whiskey and flames," he growled through a thick tone, laced with desire.

"Red," I replied huskily as I rode his fingers, needing the release they dangled right out of reach.

His hand moved to the pump, squeezing it as a scream rose from my lungs, and I gyrated against him, uncaring if this was training or not. I wanted him, I wanted him to throw caution to the wind and fuck me like our lives depended on it.

"I won't fuck you if you don't want me to," he uttered, and the pain in his eyes burned my insides. "I'll make you come, and leave you untouched. I'll earn it," he offered even though I could see the pain it took to offer me such a thing. As I decided on what to do, he pushed something into my body, and I swallowed hard.

"Lucian," I uttered as I stared at the ceiling. "It isn't about fucking, it's about what happened. It's not that I don't want to; it's that you have to earn me back. You want me; you have to show me you do. You have to show me that my sacrifice wasn't for nothing. I'm not saying I did it just for you, but I wouldn't have to have chosen what I did if I didn't feel the way I did."

His hand slid up the inside of my thigh, and the bullet ignited, right on my pleasure spot, directly on the fucking G-spot. Why couldn't he be like other men who wouldn't know what it was if it came with a map? I moaned, rocking my hips as he watched it unfold from between my legs.

His hand lowered and the sound of flesh being rubbed only sent my body spiraling towards the edge faster. "Yellow!" I screamed as I gritted my teeth as he watched me. The bullet turned off, and he removed his hand and my body instantly stalled out.

"Bloody hell," he groaned as he stared at the wet mess he'd made between my legs. He swallowed hard as he rubbed his hand down his face and covered his mouth. His hand touched my leg as he added another squeeze and the device sucked on my clit, pulling it further into the pump. I whimpered and lifted my head, staring down at it and then up at him. "Almost there," he groaned as he pulled the bullet out and stared down at me. "Tell me to use a toy, tell me you don't want me, and I'll do it."

"I don't want a toy," I whispered through dry lips. "I want you. But I need you to know that it's not a thing we can just keep doing. I don't care if I can't find pleasure without you. I'm not ready to forgive you."

He swallowed and nodded and pushed his cock against my opening. His cock was life. I screamed as he stretched my flesh, my muscles clenching against his intrusion. It burned and ached, but *I* fucking liked *it*. I rocked my hips, adjusting to take him and then I was screaming. "Red!" I trembled as the orgasm teetered on the edge.

He withdrew and stared down at me with sweat dripping from his forehead. "You're a fucking virgin."

"Is that going to stop you *now*?" I asked as I ground my teeth together as I stared at him in disbelief.

"I'm your first," he smirked as he leaned over, sucking the tip of a nipple before nipping it between his teeth, letting them scrape across the flesh.

"Lucian, you were always my first even if I did it with someone else. No one else ever made me feel anything like you did."

He slid in, and there was no waiting, no training. Bare fucking bones. I screamed as he stretched my body and I struggled to adapt to his sheer size. He knew it and slowed, holding still as I whimpered as pain mingled with a hint of promised pleasure. His mouth lifted, finding mine and claiming it as his hand released the device's hold on my clitoris and he removed it.

I moaned as it was released, only to be replaced with his fingers. My legs wrapped around him as he lifted and I slid down further on his cock.

"Jesus," I hissed as I rolled my eyes to the back of my

head and just felt the sheer magnitude that was Lucian Blackstone. His hands gripped my hips as he sat me on the edge of the bed.

"Don't come yet," he ordered as he pulled out and slammed back into my body that clamped down hard around him, as if it wanted more. "Bloody hell, you feel so fucking alive," he whispered as he kissed my forehead and the soft column of my neck before his mouth trailed over my collarbone. His mouth was searing my flesh, undoing the walls I'd placed around myself as he slowly rocked his hips, giving me time to accept him again. "I dreamt of this every fucking night since you died. Every moment I begged the Gods to return you and every day you were still buried in that cold fucking ground. Only you weren't there, were you?" he growled, and his body started to move harder, faster. Every thrust took me closer to the end, and I mumbled *red*, warning him as he shoved me down, staring at me. "You could have fucking made it known you were alive."

"This isn't the time," I muttered as my body trembled around him. "Red," I warned, and he pulled out, stalking away from me as I watched his naked ass move. It was a really nice ass, but it was tense. His shoulders strained as he walked away from me. "I wasn't ready for you."

"I don't give a fuck if you were ready! I fucking lost you, and you let me think you were gone. I sat beside your fucking corpse! Were you alive then? Did you think it fucking hilarious that I sat with you and you were what... sleeping?"

"Dead, Lucian. It takes almost a month to come back. You sat beside my corpse as I lost our son. You want to be mad? Too fucking bad. You don't get to be mad at me." I sat up, hating the itch that indicated my wings were about to make themselves known. "I died; fact! I lost my life and what little bit of my world I'd created. I lost everything for you! Protecting you and everyone else, and you think you're pissed? I'm fucking furious!" My wings exploded from my back, and I was marching on him, intending to rip him apart, but the moment I lunged, I was thrown backwards. "Ahh! I hate this. I hate that I can't hurt you and yet you can hurt me. I hate you!"

"Good, because it will make this so much fucking easier," he snarled as he walked towards me with purpose and I smiled. Bring it, big boy. The moment he got close enough I slapped him hard, not intending harm, but intending to get his attention. He slapped me back, but it wasn't hard. I turned my face back towards him and jumped into his arms, grabbing his hair as he used my hips to push my body down onto his.

I exploded without warning, and then he sank his teeth into my shoulder, and I howled, screaming as the orgasm ripped me apart. My wings flapped, as if they were as turned on as I was and then my eyes closed, and I let him take us soaring past the clouds as his hips rocked with every thrust of his cock until it shattered me again. His mouth was hard when it found mine, pouring all his frustration and pain into the kiss. My toes curled as my body reacted to his, taking everything he gave back tenfold.

It wasn't until he hissed and captured my face between his hands as he moaned and found his release inside of me that I opened my eyes and stared at the floor behind his head.

"Lena, don't…" We fell to the floor, and I screamed as we landed hard without anything to break our fall.

"The hell! Why didn't you tell me you could levitate?"

I demanded.

"That wasn't me," he laughed, and I turned to give him a scathing look. "You can *fly*."

"Awesome." Not. Like I needed another thing to learn how to control. With my luck, I'd probably end up in the engine of a plane and splattered across the entire country. I struggled to gather my wits, which I was pretty sure he'd just fucked out of me.

"I'll earn you back, Lena," he said as he leaned up and rolled onto his stomach, slowly removing the clamps before kissing each nipple. "I'll teach you to control your body and powers too. But you're mine, you're something I cannot fucking walk away from. I need you to understand that, because I'd kill whatever stands in my way of getting to you, anything and anyone. I lost you once, but I won't again. I will destroy the Gods if they fucking try to hurt or do anything to you."

"Nyx is more than a God," I murmured as I traced my hand over his shoulder before I turned and reached for his shirt. I needed a shower and somewhere to think. I ended up in the chair, slipping into his shirt as I watched him dress.

"I will do as I said, Lena. I assure you, I can destroy her and Hades, or at least send them somewhere they won't be found. You sleep with me tonight."

"You're not going to start that caveman bullshit already," I argued.

"One fucking night," he growled. "One night to hold you and know you're alive. And don't worry, I don't sleep either."

"Bullshit, I have slept with you before," I frowned. "You snored."

"I learned to adapt, but I assure you that I was never

asleep when you were in my bed."

"Really? Because I'm pretty sure you did…" Hadn't he? "Either way, I'm not repeating what we just did again anytime tonight."

"Careful, you've been gone for months, and I've been celibate." He watched me absorb that tidbit, and I nodded. "I'll get you clothes so you can tell the others where you will sleep tonight."

"Fine, but don't think I'm letting you fuck me again."

"Fine."

"Jerk," I mumbled as I waited for clothes he'd promised to let the others know what the plan was. I still didn't know what he was, but what I did know was this, Lucifer was coming, I could feel it.

CHAPTER nineteen

The prince of darkness is a gentleman. ~*Shakespeare*

The putrid scent of death clung to the world. The noxious odor of brimstone, mingled with newly lit fires that danced like living things. The flames leapt around, orange and blue as they burned hot and out of control. Flames licked buildings, logs, and anything else they could reach as it oozed from the depths of Hell, pooling smoke into the air that choked those not strong enough to survive its acrid poisonous scent. I eyed one of the patches of fire, the flames licking the air, warming the area I stood in. Pushing through the thick smoke, I eyed the decaying corpses who'd fallen to the cadaverous new world order which twisted and rose from the ground, taking form as I slowly approached its ruler.

Lucifer watched me, smoke billowing around his form like steam as he stared back with an intensity that shook through my core, my body. This creature was bathed in sin, created to lure the pure into impurity. Sex oozed from his pores as he pulled the lit cigar from his lips and smirked as small circles of smoke escaped from his lungs, filling the sky as he exhaled. His bare arms were covered in tattoos; fine sinewy muscle clenched and unclenched as he tossed the lit cigar onto the ground, uncaring that it lit yet another fire into this world.

Power radiated from him, leaking from his body to tingle and graze my flesh as I made my way towards him, lazily, uncaring that he watched the sway of my hips or the fullness of my breasts as I did so. His eyes were reflecting the fires and my image as I stopped inches from where he stood. His tempting lips opened, the smile all sensual and alluring as I watched him through my lashes, unwilling to let him see the effect he had on me or my senses.

"Do you like what I did with the place?" he asked, his blue depths pooling into liquid heat as he lifted them, holding my stare. His arms stretched as he indicated the new world, the chaos he'd brought to it, and the death that clung to it.

His hair was shorter, cut and styled, which was alluring on him. It framed the sharp lines of his jaw, defining them and the utter perfection he'd been carved into. His power shook the world as he released it, letting me feel the magnitude of it as he watched my reaction and smiled coldly as a tremor slid through me. His wings unfurled, significantly increased in size now that he'd been freed from his prison.

"I think you could do better," I said aloofly as I watched him bend down as he picked up a human skull, lifting it in his hands as he placed it on the wall of skulls behind him. It stretched out as far as my eye could see—a never-ending wall of human skulls from the victims he'd sacrificed as he forged his new empire. It was impressive, the lengths he'd gone to just to show me his strength, his unworldliness. He smirked wolfishly at my words as he sat on the wall, crossing his tattooed arms over his chest as he stared. "You do know that you will fail, you always do. We will stop this from happening."

"You and what army, my sweet little hellcat?" he scoffed as he rose, slowly approaching me as his hand trailed over the curve of my hip. I didn't take my eyes from his as he continued to touch me, to tease me with the pleasure he so freely offered. "You want this. I can feel your need, so fucking dark and delicious that it makes my cock ache to fill you. To show you what a creature such as you've become can feel with something like me, Lena. Tell me you didn't enjoy my touch, my sex fucking that sweet pussy. It clenched around my cock so fucking tightly. You're so much more…appealing than your sister. You didn't fear me; instead, you welcomed me. You welcomed the horde of the damned watching your body being ravished, just as you did when Lucian finger-fucked you in front of his club. You wanted me, even if you thought I was Lucian, you still wanted me when you figured out that I wasn't him. I felt it, and if I'd contained the extension of myself, you'd have let me finish in that tight pussy. Tell me you wouldn't have?" His eyes devoured mine, demanding I answer him, and when I didn't, he laughed huskily. "Keep your secrets if it helps you sleep at night, but I am the prince of darkness, and you will be my queen. He can't keep you, nor does he see the evil churning inside of you. I see you, my queen, all of you. You're beautiful chaos, mixed with the throes of sin and delight who begs to be taken, fucked in ways that man cannot even begin to comprehend. You were never meant to be mortal or to be held down by their laws. Let me have you. Let me show you what you can become with the right man beside you. Help me set the world on fire, and dance with me as it burns to nothing but the ashes of these insignificant humans."

"Why would I help you?" I asked, not moving from his touch as he stroked my flesh, his fingers dancing over my cheek as he slowly, seductively caressed me. I let the darkness I'd been holding in come out, watching as his eyes slowly studied the change in my features, the sharpness of the Fury as I let it out for him to gaze upon.

His lips skimmed over mine, unafraid of the darkness that filled my vision as it oozed out from where I'd held it in. His mouth sent a ripple of exquisite pleasure racing through me, rushing towards my apex, which caused his nostrils to flare as he scented my arousal.

"Help me end this world, or I will come for her. I'll come for your sister, and take what is rightfully mine. That child is mine, Lena. She holds the purest blood in her tiny form, the darkest evil in her precious mind. She is my daughter by right. I will come for her, but I am willing to settle for you in her place."

"And if I don't want to be yours?" I uttered as his tongue snaked out, tracing my bottom lip before he sucked it between his teeth and I moaned loudly as his teeth pulled, teasing the fatty tissue before he released it and studied my face.

"You want honesty?" he whispered before he pulled me closer, ripping the shirt from my body as he stared down at my breasts. Heat licked my flesh, creating an ache in my nipples that hummed and begged to be touched. His hands cupped them, testing their weight as his thumbs brushed over the pebbled peaks. "I want you, I've wanted you since the moment I tasted the chaos and fire that blossomed and burns inside of you. Help me take over the world, Lena. Become my queen, and I'll show you what real love is. Do you know why I was kicked out of heaven? I wanted to know what made mortals so weak, and yet they were special. I questioned why they could love and yet it was forbidden to us. Why they got to taste sin and we were forbidden for touching, fucking. I wanted to be them, to know what it was that made Eve lie down in that garden and ride Adam's cock. And she did, she fucking took him with vigor, riding him until she glowed with pleasure and I fucking wanted that too. So I was cast from heaven into Hell for wanting what he allowed them to taste. How fucking fair is that? Could you imagine never knowing what it felt like? Never feeling pleasure as someone experienced these perfect lips." His finger traced my mouth, pushing between them until I closed them, sucking his thumb deeper as his eyes darkened with lust. He hissed as his eyes heated with need, raw, palpable need that shot through me. He withdrew his thumb and pressed his mouth against mine, pushing his tongue deep into my depths as a groan escaped his lungs. He was skilled, created for luring women to their doom. His tongue dueled against mine, fucking me with nothing more than it as he made my knees grow weak, and yet he held me as if I was the most precious thing in this world. He pulled away, raining kisses down my neck as his fingers pinched my nipples, stealing a moan of pleasure that rushed from my lungs as my head rolled back. I inhaled the brimstone and death, sucking it deep into my lungs as I let his lips devour my will, my body a tool for his pleasure, to be used as he wanted. I cried out as his mouth touched my breast, sucking one nipple between his lips before his teeth scraped over the sensitive flesh. He rose, cradling the back of my head as his mouth devoured mine.

"Rule with me, darkness. I can feel it pooling inside of you, begging to be freed from that tight hold you have on it. It wants what I can offer it, what you crave, I can give you. You think I'm evil, that my intent is to destroy, but it isn't. I want freedom, I want to be here with you and the other immortals that walk these streets and feast in the flesh, in the open freely. I'm sick of punishing souls, exhausted from being punished for wanting to taste the pleasure others took so freely. I'm not the bad guy here, have I hurt you? Yes, but only because you were his and I craved you. Imagine my surprise when I learned you survived, that you had come back stronger, darker than any woman before you had. Katarina was beautiful, but you, you are so much more than she could have ever hoped to be. He took from me, he took everything. He took the one woman I loved and murdered her, and I was supposed to just accept it. I'm not a weak prince; I'm the fucking prince of the Underworld, the fucking devil. And you? You're the queen of darkness, the one female who could rule at my side and devour anyone who stood in our way. Rule with me, at my side. You can make him feel what he forced you to endure; you can show him what it feels like to lose everything as you have. Help me show him what it is like to lose everything he loves. Show him what it feels like to be betrayed as he has done to both of us."

"And what do I get in return? You think I care about revenge?" I scoffed as my fingers threaded through his newly shortened hair as I leaned in, claiming his lips, letting him feel what I had to offer. It cut off his words, forcing him to taste the pleasure I had to give, the fire he so wanted that burned from within. I felt the growl as it rose from deep in his chest as I pulled from the kiss, scraping my teeth over his full bottom lip. "What can you offer me that he cannot?"

The world burned around us as we stood amidst the fire, the inferno that raged as the desire that burned through us. His face glowed from the eerie light of the dancing flames as he peered into my eyes, searching my face for the answer he thought I wanted. His mouth crushed against mine, his intent to take me to the ground and fuck me explicit, but I wasn't that naïve or easy to obtain. My hands threaded through his hair, yanking his mouth away from mine as I demanded he answer me.

"The world," he smirked as he framed my face with his hands. His voice was a silken caress that slithered over my flesh and consumed my mind as I stared into his beautiful blue eyes that danced with possession, as if he thought he already had me. My body tightened as my spine arched, spreading in invitation. "They've had their time. They're destroying this world, a gift from the Gods and yet they spit on it. They murder each other, tearing this world apart as if it belongs to them alone. We can take it back, we can bathe in their blood as it boils, Lena. He will never destroy a world for you, but I will. I will tear down the walls that hold the other monsters at bay and let them in, to join us. I will rip this place apart, piece by fucking piece for you, and you will reign at my side. Say yes, say yes, and I will come for you. I will walk right up the steps of that Guild, and I will claim my queen where the world can see it unfold." Lucifer's eyes watched me, studying me as I considered his words. His heady stare caressed me as if it was fingers stroking chords inside my body, his fingers slowly touching my cheeks as he watched me, waiting, letting me decide my fate.

"If I do agree, you will leave my sister and her child alone," I stipulated. "I will not share you, and you will prove to me that you want me more than them. I'm a selfish bitch, and I'm a starving one. I will never share you with another, nor will you seek another's pleasure. You will be mine, and I will be yours. Do you understand me?"

"Deal, but only if you let me fuck you in front of him to prove to him that you are mine," he smirked as his arms wrapped around me, tightening against me as he pulled me into the warmth of his body. "I want him to hurt, and I will use you as he watches us together. I want him to know what betrayal feels like, what it tastes like."

"Deal," I said, smiling against his lips before he sealed it with a heated kiss.

"Deals with the devil aren't that bad, now are they, my sweet queen?"

"We will see if you hold up your end of the bargain. They'll be expecting you, Luc," I uttered as I slid my lips across his, enjoying the taste of him before I stepped back, staring at his chest which led into an impressive V that disappeared into his jeans. "Don't keep me waiting, I get bored easily." He stepped back into the fires that burned among the rotting corpses of the victims he'd taken pleasure in slaughtering.

The world was already hell, what would it matter if we added more corpses to it? I pushed from the dream, righting my body as I peered up into angry midnight eyes. He inhaled, his nostrils flaring as he scented Luc upon my flesh.

"You smell like Lucifer," he snapped.

"And?" I asked softly as I leaned over, kissing him

with Lucifer's taste still on my lips. I pushed my tongue deep into his mouth, forcing his tongue to play with mine before I slid over him, staring down into his eyes as I devoured his mouth like it was my own playground. I let the darkness behind my eyes glow, bathing him in its alluring scent as he growled against my kiss. The need to do as Lucifer had said was seductive, exhilarating as it exploded inside my mind. The queen of the new world sounded pretty fucking good to me.

CHAPTER
twenty

Be careful who you trust, the devil was once an angel.
~Zaid K. Abdelnour

"You're playing with fire," Lucian warned as he gazed up at me, rolling me beneath him as his body dwarfed mine, his scent a heady mix of wood and spices. He was all male, right down to wherever the fuck he was. He pushed his heavy cock against my naked sex and watched me, studying or memorizing every fine detail of my face. "You'll get burned if you try to fuck me over, and I won't have mercy."

"You think I care? I like pissing you off, the angry sex, the fucking like we're going to war? And you must think I'm afraid of the flames that dance in those endless depths. No, Lucian, I'm not afraid of being burned, and I think the odds are in my favor," I murmured as he dropped his mouth, kissing me until I groaned and uttered his name against them.

"Tell me what he did when you went under, when you went to him," he demanded as he pulled back, gazing down at me.

"Jealousy doesn't suit you, Lucian. Afraid I'll switch sides on you? I muttered as I peered up into his burning stare. He'd known I'd met up with Lucifer, but then even I smelled Luc's scent on my flesh. His eyes burned with anger as he watched me, curious to see what I'd do next, or maybe deciding if he should strangle me? I didn't care either way. He had no idea of the betrayal coming, no indication that of what I was planning, which was fine since he tended to leave me in the dark more often than not. He didn't even trust me with his secrets, so tit for fucking tat. He deserved to feel betrayal, to know what it felt like, the sting that sucker-punched you in the gut without warning. He also had some cosmic karma coming for what he'd allowed to happen to me. I was waking up, and the devil was in the fine print.

I rolled us again, staring down into his inky heat-filled gaze as we silently warred with each other. My head bowed as I brushed my lips over his, letting him feel the molten heat that built in me that he created. My body rubbed against his, and I felt his growing erection as he growled from deep in his chest, letting it built as he watched me slowly rubbing my heat against it. My teeth scraped over his lip, capturing it between my teeth and drawing blood as I sucked it into my mouth. His growl turned guttural, dangerous before he slammed me backwards, knocking the air from my lungs as his hand wrapped around my throat tightly before his mouth crushed against mine.

He entered my body hard, no mercy given as he violently took me to the throes only he could send me sailing to. The man was built to fuck; it was as simple as that. Pain mingled with pleasure, sending my senses dancing on the line as he forced me to accept what he gave. He stared into my eyes, watching as the orgasm tore through me, sending me into a trembling mess as I whispered his name like he was my fucking salvation. I rode the storm of emotions, the endless orgasms as he rocked his hips, noting every fucking time I cried out or grew closer until he gained control of me, my pleasure, gauging my needs as no other could. He didn't care if it hurt and neither did I, he was a storm, and I danced in him until we went over the edge together. The only thing that mattered was him, climbing that motherfucking cliff together over and over until we both were a tangle of limbs and sweat.

"He'll never fucking touch you again. He'll never have you, Lena. I would raze the world and be damned for eternity gladly before I let him have you," he growled thickly as if his mouth had become swollen. His penetrating gaze consumed mine as I stared into his darkened depths.

The building rumbled, and Lucian's dark head lifted, searching the wall as if he could sense what was currently setting off the wards. I swallowed hard as I rolled away from him, leaving his cock sleek and hard with my arousal as I left him. I smiled as I swayed to the bathroom, putting on the black sundress and thin black panties.

It was a new day, a new dawn, and I'd be damned if I was planning on being on the wrong side when shit went sideways. I hadn't chosen this life, but I sure as fuck wasn't letting myself end up dead again, if it was even possible.

Lucian dressed as I waited, leaning against the wall as I gazed at his utter masculine perfection. Footsteps sounded outside the door, rushing towards our room. I lifted my head, listening before I peered back at the man who'd made me into this monster and took a long, leisurely look before I stepped from the wall, swallowing hard as the person outside began pounding. Lucian gazed at me as if he perceived exactly what awaited us outside. The warning in his eyes was deadly, and just that, a warning to not fuck him over. As if he sensed I was about to.

I slowly followed him from the room, a skip to my step as we walked to the main room of the Guild, staring at the utter chaos that was unfolding. The walls cracked as energy bombs exploded against them from Lucifer, who was doing exactly as he said he would: knocking on the door.

"It's Lucifer." Ryder's tone was tense, angry and a hint of disbelief flickered in his golden eyes. I smirked as I considered my next move, my decision unwavering as I followed them to the glass that held Lucifer outside.

Smoke billowed around the buildings on the far side of the block, fire bathing his image as he stared directly at me. I smiled back at him, turning to watch Lucian from my peripheral view before I stepped back.

"Let's go fucking welcome him, shall we?" Lucian growled, the hatred burning so deep that his voice made me tremble.

Too little, way too late.

I followed them out of the doors, smirking when the song began to play loudly around us. It was that song, the one he'd played as I'd fallen prey to him in his club. Marilyn Manson's rendition of Sweet Dreams filled the night. I watched them all, staring at him as they realized the Furies had placed stones around the stairs, along with added runes and wards to hold them here, to keep them prisoner.

I exploded past them, materializing outside the wards, safely away from them. I turned, staring back at Lucian who glared at me, his eyes screaming murder as he slowly put it together. I'd summoned Luc here. I'd called him to us from *his* bed. I tilted my head, staring at him before I slowly moved to stand mere feet away from Lucifer, where his demons converged around him, protecting his back as he let that hypnotic gaze slowly take in my new form.

His hair was darker here than it had been in the dream walk we'd shared earlier, his tattoos hidden by the leather jacket he wore. His eyes though, they swirled with an inner fire that pulled me in, calling to me. He was the epitome of a fallen angel. He lured souls to their doom, his beauty pulling them in without warning, the monster within stealing what they treasured most before they had any clue it had been taken. He was the perfect thief, the ideal creature to reign in Hell. As I gazed upon him, I realized why God had forced his fall, forced him to Hell where he could do what God himself hadn't wanted to do: Punish us for our sins. He was his perfect warrior, all beauty but lethal, deadly, and created to reign. His eyes danced with victory as I held my hands out, palms up in surrender as I took the last few steps to him.

"You're even more beautiful than I thought possible, Magdalena," he uttered as he pulled out his own blades, dropping them to the side as he stepped forward, pulling me against his body as his mouth touched, skimming against mine. He pulled me closer, turning me in his embrace as he faced Lucian. I leaned against his heat, allowing him to spread my arms wide and then place them behind me until it looked as if I was on display. I held his neck as I stared up at Lucian, feeling his rage and anger as he watched me through a murderous glare. Lucifer's mouth lowered to my ear, sucking the lobe between his lips before he slowly kissed his way down my throat, nipping where my shoulder met my neck. His hands ripped open the dress, shredding it easily as he exposed me to their angry stares that watched us in disbelief and horror.

"You fucking traitorous bitch," Lucian growled thickly as Lucifer laughed huskily, sending a shiver down my spine as it vibrated against me. "You were always a part of this, a part of his fucking game. And I fell right into it, didn't I?" he demanded.

"Of course she was, she's my queen," Luc sneered as he turned me around, kissing me until I was moaning against him, holding on to his neck for life as he drove me over the edge with lust. I was unable to deny the pleasure I felt as he rubbed my body with his hands. He stirred to life an inferno to match the one that blazed around us; the one which consumed the world as we created our own.

He lifted me, ripping the panties from my body as he settled me above him. His cock still hidden within the jeans he wore, but then I didn't need it out to come. I groaned against his mouth as he smiled his victory right there for the taking. All he had to do was push that throbbing cock into my core, and our deal would be locked, sealed. I opened my mouth to his kiss, the blistering heat of it making my air hitch in my lungs as I pulled away, drawing my hooded stare to Lucian's. Lucian watched us, his own stare a murderous threat as he paced in front of the wards.

The music hit a crescendo, and my fingers trailed through Luc's hair, holding him down as my mouth fucked his. He lowered our bodies to the ground, his wings expanding as we lowered until I was above him, rocking my body against his with need. I held his head down, fucking him with my mouth as he struggled to free his thick cock, sensing the moment he released it. I stared down as it pushed against my sex, the electrical sensation of lust shooting through me.

He pushed against my opening, and my hands lifted his head as my mouth lowered, and then I slammed him down, hard. Once, twice, *pop*. The sound echoed around us as I smiled down at the murderous prick who'd taken motherhood away from me. Blood exploded into my eyes, bathing my face and my mouth as I continued to pound his head against the unforgiving concrete. I stared down with a smirk that was all serial killer and no pretty as I admired the bloody heap that had been utter perfection seconds ago. Too bad it wouldn't end his miserable fucking life.

I stood, naked, bathed only in his blood that coated my body as if it was paint. I wiped my face, licking my fingers clean as I peered down at the prince of darkness. He gurgled, already healing from what I'd done to him. The mangled mess seized, making grotesque noises as his demons gawked, unsure what to do as they stared at the mess he'd become. He turned to his side, stumbling to his feet before he turned his ruined face towards me. His wings began to move, and I turned my head to the side, studying him and every weakness he had. My own wings expanded, and I spun as he charged, severing his head, which bounced and then stopped right on the stairs, right at Lucian's feet.

"That was for my son," I uttered thickly, reveling in the revenge that slithered through me, the intoxicating taste of it so strong that my eyes closed and I stood there, basking in it. I rolled my head, letting loose the muscles as the magic and power rushed through me as I opened my eyes to stare at the demons who were now comprehending what had played out.

Lighting crashed close by, and then it struck

everywhere. The entire night turned into day as bolt after lethal bold crashed down, slaughtering the demons who'd come to protect their prince. The night was scented in electrical current as I stood there in all my naked glory, watching as they perished, sent back to whatever dark pit they'd crawled out of. The Furies slipped into the wards, into the protection it offered, chancing the anger of those they'd earlier trapped inside them.

Once they were within, I let my Fury out. Every bit of anger, loss, and hatred let loose at once. The smell of burned flesh permuted into the night as bodies that had held the demons melted under the bolts of lightning.

Everything came out.

Everything I'd kept inside of me, power, anger, rage, and the pain. Oh, the pain was intense as it exploded from me, and punished those outside the protective barrier. I let it all go so that I didn't have to feel it, live with it.

The world trembled as the scream ripped through my lungs, echoing with the power I unleashed. It rode the bolts down with the demons, slamming into them with the force of my emotions as I held nothing back. My hair rose as my flesh glowed with the runes painted upon my flesh. One after another, the demons popped, sizzled and then melted into nothing. The bodies of the humans they'd stolen turned to ashes, floating in the air around me. It looked like a blizzard, ashes rained around me, floating with the wind and breeze as I turned, staring at Lucian. Once the last demon had popped and exploded as my mortal head had done that fateful day I walked towards the wards.

And Lucifer thought I'd be his fucking queen? Please. I was the fucking reigning queen. The queen of the dead, the undead, and the pissed the fuck off.

Once I was inches from him, I lifted a dainty brow and glared at him. "Bitch?" I snapped.

"You…" he stopped, letting his gaze drift down my naked body which was painted in our enemy's blood. "I was wrong."

"You're damn right you were," I growled back. "If you think I'd so easily slip and land on his dick after what he did to our child, you're not ready for me. He killed my son, so I did what I had to do to get revenge. He may not be dead, but he knows I'm willing to fight him to get to that point of our relationship."

"He cannot be killed, not without offsetting the balance."

"Fuck the balance. Everything can be killed. And I don't really want him dead; I want him to suffer for the rest of his miserable fucking life."

"And you didn't tell me your plan, why?" he demanded.

"Now you know how I felt when you begged Katarina to let you in. Betrayal stings and you now know exactly how I felt before I slit my fucking throat. I thought you wanted her, and yet I sacrificed my life to protect you and everyone else. So the next time you think you're doing me a favor? Don't. Or I'll make you feel it tenfold."

"You're fucking hot when you're evil," Spyder drawled from beside Lucian. "She's like your evil fucking twin, but with a nice rack."

Synthia snorted and then I was dressed, even though the blood was still crusted against my flesh. I stared at Lucian pointedly, watching as his eyes crinkled in the corners as a smile played across his lips.

"Lesson learned," he agreed. "Let's get inside; you have Lucifer in your hair still."

"I may not shower for a week," I muttered. "I enjoyed being covered in him."

He growled, and I wiggled my eyebrows, sauntering past him as I followed the others into the Guild.

"You'll shower, because I won't smell him as I fuck you, Lena. Next time, warn me so that I don't have to punish you."

"Punish me?" I smirked, watching him as he stopped me, pulling me back as the others moved inside.

"I almost took those wards down tonight. If I had, everyone else would have died. I can get through your wards, the runes? They won't fucking hold me now. Not being able to get you before? I made fucking sure I'd never have to go through it again, but the cost is anyone else in the general vicinity will die. Don't do it again. You get me? Because I won't lose you, not even if you switch sides. I'll hunt you down and tie that tight ass up to my bed for eternity just to keep you. I can't and won't lose you again. Whatever the fuck you make me feel? I want to keep feeling it. So careful, because I don't play by rules that you understand, and I don't care who I take out if it ends with you living, or staying with me."

"You know, they have a word for that, it's called sociopath," I muttered as I lifted up on my tiptoes and tried to kiss him. His hand came up to block it.

"You are not kissing me with Luc on your lips, and he is. He's everywhere," he growled as he indicated my entire face and then smirked. "You were a fucking sight to behold tonight, but I mean it. No more secrets where he is concerned." He pushed me towards the Guild's door, and I allowed it, even as I smelled the brimstone as Lucifer healed. He'd be back, and pissed.

CHAPTER
twenty-one

By the pricking of my thumbs, something wicked this way comes. ~*Shakespeare*

Inside the club the men paced, every once in a while tossing me a dirty or disapproving look. I got it, I'd walked Lucifer right up to their front door, but he had been coming here no matter what I'd done. My gaze moved between Lucian and Ryder; both men refused to stop pacing, and I was getting tired of the looks they kept throwing my way. I shrugged at them when they did, somehow managing to not show how rattled I was at what I'd just accomplished and how it felt.

I'd smashed Lucifer's head into the ground until it had popped, just as mine had done when he'd sealed my death in a pretty bow. Chewing my lip, I peeked at the coven from beneath my lashes, watching them as they stared between them and me as if they feared I'd be punished. They were terrified, and they should be. Lucifer was coming to claim his daughter one way or another, he would take her.

"You do realize that you brought the fucking devil to the one place we have brought people to be safe, right?" Synthia groaned softly. Her hair hung down her shoulders in gentle waves of platinum as she stared me down. Her hands lifted, rubbing her temples as the stress oozed from her into the men around her.

I nodded as I slowly took in her stiff demeanor. She had changed from her fighting leathers into a soft, cool baby blue camisole that hugged her full chest snugly. A tight pair of jeans hugged her shapely legs, showing off the well-muscled physique of her lithe frame. Weapons were holstered, and yet I didn't miss the fact that while they seemed relaxed, they were very much ready and on edge because of what had happened outside. They were ready to defend this place with their lives if the need arose.

"He was coming here anyway, and nothing could have stopped him if he wanted in. I needed to know why he'd sought me out, and once I had, I used it to get him to me. He is coming for his daughter; one way or another, he will make a try for her. We thought he wanted eyes on the ground since he was trapped in Hell, and once he was released, he'd forget she existed or was soon to exist, but that's not the case. He wants her still," I admitted. I shrugged when she continued to stare at me. "I also needed to get revenge, to show him that I am not the weak mortal who he almost beat to death that day. I needed to show him I was ready for him to buy Kendra time."

"You could have mentioned you had a direct fucking line to him. Instead, you acted like it was no big deal and that it had been nothing. You smelled of brimstone, reeked of it, actually. You didn't even give us a fucking clue as to what you planned to do, which could have ended badly or been a fucking disaster, Lena," Lucian snarled, the room shaking with his anger as he let it out. Midnight eyes locked with mine as he glared murderously, inches away from me. I shrugged, smirking as his eyes darkened with his anger. I owed him nothing. "You could have given us an indication of what you'd planned, or that he was on his way instead of leaving us yanking our dicks in the dark as we stumbled to figure it out. All that little show you just did for him? It's only going to piss him off more than he already is. It didn't even buy us time, which it could have. We thought you actually made a fucking deal with him, so you're very lucky it didn't cost you that pretty little head of yours." He rubbed his eyes with his knuckles before dropping them to reveal the unearthly blue glow as whatever lived inside of him peered out at me. "Instead, you forced me to watch you as you rubbed yourself all over his cock, knowing he intended to fuck you right in front of me as I was forced to watch it happen!"

"And? Am I supposed to feel bad for you?" I frowned at him as I shook my head, pushing my hair back from my face. "If I had told you, you wouldn't have reacted as you did. You wouldn't have responded at all or enough that he believed it. You'd have given it all away, so yes, I left you in the dark, but I'm not stupid, asshole. You never stumble. I wanted to see how brash and cocky the prick could be, and we now know that he isn't afraid of us, why? Why isn't he afraid of you and everyone else? What's changed since he ran from you last time? Something has, and we need to know what. We also needed to know he was close, which he is. He isn't leaving this area until he gets what he wants, and that isn't something we can just hand over to him, now is it? No. He is here because his child is here, which means we judged him wrong. He cares about his daughter, his flesh and blood. So if you not knowing which side I was on hurt your feelings, suck it up, buttercup. I don't have time to worry about your feelings right now. I released Lucifer from Hell, and now he is after my family, my blood. So I'm sorry that watching me seduce the devil hurt your feelings or bothered you, but we no longer need the witches to scry for him because I've tasted his blood. He cannot hide from me any longer. That's a win, Lucian. No matter what you think, it's a win, and we fucking needed one."

"And if it had gone wrong, what then? If he'd suspected you would betray him, he could have fucking killed you!"

"I'm already dead!" I shouted back crossly. "He already helped kill me, and it wasn't what he wanted to do. He wants to do whatever brings you the most pain. Not me. Killing me doesn't work anymore because he's already done it. He may want, now that I smashed his head into the pavement, but this has never been about me. It's about you. I'm already on borrowed time, and I no longer fear death. I can't, it doesn't help us get anywhere. I'm tired of losing, aren't you? I want to end this war before he succeeds in bringing down the doors between the worlds, before the veil falls and monsters we cannot possibly hope to win against come to this one. We can't close the doors without knowing his plans first, and even if we do manage to close them, there are still thousands of creatures who have escaped their worlds into this one. I'm tired of fucking losing. We're losing right now, and no matter what we are trying to accomplish, we have to start now. Monsters are feeding off the human race, devouring them to sustain life, and they need our help. I'm sick of smelling the coppery tang of blood in the air and the noxious odor of brimstone. We're immortal, standing in a Guild that was erected to protect humans. It's time we start doing it, and we give them no mercy. No option to return home, we slaughter anything that doesn't belong here."

"That's a beautiful fucking speech, but we don't know how to close the gates or stop them from pouring into this world," Ryder injected, growling as he stared me down as if I'd just insulted them.

"The girl, Erie, she can ward the gates long enough for us to figure out how to close them. It should buy us time."

"She's gone," he admitted. "She's been on the run for weeks, and when she does stop here, it's only long enough to place new wards and get a hot meal and shower. There's no telling when or if she will show up again."

"Call her," I growled back at him.

"She's in hiding, and it's not like she left us a number to dial her up on," Synthia interrupted. "She's got her own problems going on. We will find another way to close the gates."

"We need something now," I pointed out, my eyes twitching as I considered just how many monsters were flowing out of those gaping holes in the world with every passing moment. More and more bodies were piling up as we stood around, waiting, wondering, and searching for a way to close the holes.

"No shit, but there's no easy way to close a portal," Synthia said in frustration.

"The only way to close them would be to destroy them," Lucian pointed out. "The portal is a door, destroy the door, and destroy the portal."

"And what's to stop another one from opening?" I

asked. "There's multiple entryways from Hell into this world, so how would we be able to destroy them all?"

"Hell isn't the same as the other worlds," he stated.

"Hell is the most dangerous of them all, isn't it?" I countered with a glare. Lucifer was coming for Kendra, and I felt it to the center of my being. I sensed his intention, and it scared me that she was a target. "He will come for his daughter."

"Kendra has agreed to hand her over," my grandmother injected, and my blood turned to ice as I swung my eyes to her.

"The fuck she will," I snapped coldly.

"He will never stop, and as far as we've learned, he cannot be destroyed without offsetting the balance. As much as I hate to admit it, Lucifer is needed in this world. He and the angels alike have created a natural balance. If we destroy him, we ruin that balance. He will never stop reaching for the child, and she is a Nephilim. Which means she is not ours to keep," she said softly, tears swimming in her eyes as she watched me.

"That's bullshit," I growled. "He doesn't get his child. He took away the chance of me having mine, and that babe isn't evil. She needs to be protected."

"She is a harbinger, the antichrist so to say. Nephilims aren't meant for this world."

I glared at my grandmother and turned to stare at Olivia. "Olivia is a Nephilim. She isn't the antichrist."

"She isn't of Lucifer's seed," Ristan pointed out as his hands rested on Olivia's protruding belly. "His child is and will always be considered something of a troubling matter."

"We're talking of an innocent child who didn't ask to be born. One who was created because he thought Kendra was me, and now you want to just hand her over to that monster? No, absolutely not. No one is born evil. Evil is created, and if we hand her over to him, she will be made into a vile monster like her father, by her father. No, that's insane and not happening. If Kendra fears what she carries, we will deal with it. We will find her a mother who wants her, but we do not hand our bloodline over to the fucking devil!"

"And who will protect her?"

"I will!" I shouted, my blood rising as I stared at my grandmother, who frowned as she shook her greying head.

"There's another problem which we came across as well. Mothers who birth Nephilims seldom survive the birthing process. Kendra's life is endangered with every moment she approaches this birth, Lena. She is weakening, as if it is slowly sucking the life from her to grow."

"What?" I whispered as I fought the sickness that clenched in my stomach. This wasn't happening. I hadn't made the sacrifices I had to lose her in the end, it wasn't happening.

"She grows weaker with every day, and no amount of magic seems to stop the process or whatever is happening to her. I have tried magic, vampire blood, and many other things but none of them stop the problems she is experiencing. Her bones are brittle, her hair is lackluster, and whatever she carries is feeding from her, as if it is slowly consuming her as it grows."

"Olivia, your mother, she lived?" I asked, dismissing my grandmother as I was unable to accept her words. I'd seen Kendra, and she looked fine; tired, but she hadn't looked like she was being consumed. Or had I not wanted to see it?

"My mother didn't survive my birth, no." Her head

bowed, and she frowned. "I'm sorry; I know it wasn't the answer you wanted. She died giving birth to me, and I was left outside a Guild, as most of our kind is."

I swallowed hard past the thick lump in my throat. "Other angels? Are there any who we can ask? Can *you* ask them?"

"I speak to my father, but they're rather busy with the current situation of the world and the sudden overwhelming numbers of souls entering heaven. I do know that carrying a Nephilim can oftentimes kill a mortal, and sometimes what they birth is barely human. I can tell you that it isn't rare for them to feed from their parents, or for them to kill a mother when they're born into this world. Angels aren't meant to be carried by humans, which is why heaven forbid them from mating with them. There's a handful of Nephilim births recorded, which means our information is limited. I'm sorry, Lena, but even if I could manage to call my father here, he wouldn't have much to tell you, and I think he'd be more inclined to murder the babe before she was born."

"I'm sure he would," I grumbled as I rubbed my temples. "She cannot die," I uttered as I turned to stare at Lucian. "She cannot die, do you hear me? I didn't lose our child just to watch her do the same fucking thing. Lucifer isn't touching her daughter, not as long as I draw air into my lungs. I'd rather fuck the balance than hand him my niece or watch my sister die because he mistook her for me. I suggest you figure out what we have to do to prevent both things from occurring."

"And you think I can fix it?" he scowled as his hands rested on his hips, eyes feasting on me in challenge.

"I think you better figure out how we prevent it from happening. You are the one he wanted to hurt, and we've paid enough for whatever game or slight you two have. Lucifer wants to hurt you, fix it. Now tell me how we destroy the portals because I really need a win right now. So tell me, how the fuck can he hurt you? What would he do to strike you where it hurts?"

"You're my only weakness, Lena. I don't care about anything else, never have, never will. I have been trying to save this selfish world so long that I don't even wince at the idea of it being gone anymore. They're so fucking hell-bent on destroying themselves that even their Gods have abandoned them."

CHAPTER
twenty-two

Hell is empty and all the devils are here. ~*Shakespeare*

Lucian

Fucking Lena and her flawed logic! I'd watched her through the night, scenting the brimstone that clung to her flesh as we'd fucked, and bloody hell had we fucked. She no longer feared what our bodies did, she didn't hold back.

And yet I'd smelled his putrid calling card, and I'd ignored it, even when her eyes had closed, and she'd appeared to sleep. I knew she couldn't sleep, she was like me now. Sleep wasn't needed, nor was feeding per se, even though if I had to pick a meal, her flesh would be it and I'd eat, often. Her smile when she'd awaken from her dream walk had punched me in the gut, and I'd let her control the situation, or I had until she straddled me.

Magdalena was a fucking beast in bed, and she wouldn't take an inch if it were given, she'd take it all. But the fact that I'd been stupid enough to even consider her switching sides…that was on me and I knew it.

I knew her, I knew her faults, her strengths and every

fucking weakness she had, and yet I'd thought her a part of Katarina's and Lucifer's diabolic plan for revenge and wouldn't she have been the sweetest icing on the cake? Watching her mouth on his had awakened the monster within; the darkness had risen its head and peered out, demanding we eradicate the entire world to show her what monster she'd fucked over, and then he'd touched what was mine in the most primal way possible.

Her sweet smile for him had ached, man, had it fucking ached, as if it had torn through the shields and barriers of what I am and ripped it to shreds in her wake. Her body against his had every soul inside of me screaming for retribution, to judge her and execute the threat, and then she'd smashed his fucking head.

Glorious in her naked perfection as she bathed in his blood, uncaring that it made her a horrifying monster as she smiled, finding pride in the bloody heap of tissue and bone she'd created. Her hair painted red from his blood, body painted in the stickiness of it as she'd stood, staring down with a darkness that was more ancient, more primordial than any other creature in existence at that moment.

I'd fought the urge to go to her, to lay her down in the middle of the chaos and fuck her to show her how turned on I was, how hard my dick was from watching my girl tear the devil to pieces with nothing more than her bare hands. She'd been beautiful. The most beautiful thing I'd ever seen from the moment I'd been created.

My motherfucking monster.

Then those cold, beautiful blue eyes had turned in my direction, and she'd smiled, she'd fucking smiled with blood dripping from her hair, from her body which had remained naked, right before she'd took his head for our son.

This wisp of a mortal, the girl who had told me to go have pretty babies had become a killing machine, and the pain she'd released, the anger, I'd tasted it. I'd stood there, feeling every pain, every loss, every moment of her life that she released in rage as she turned night to day with it, demons to ashes that filled the sky as she alone took on an army of them, uncaring of the odds, or the danger.

Lena had come back darker, yes. But she'd come back as a force of nature that even the Gods themselves would kneel to. Naked, she'd slaughtered a horde of demons naked, flesh painted in their leader's blood and she hadn't even once tried to cover it, rather she reveled in it. Her eyes had been wild with hatred as she took from them as they'd taken from her. No, Lena wasn't the sweet girl who blushed when I had told her what I wanted to do to her sweet, innocent body.

She was my fucking monster, and monsters didn't fear anything. They moved on, moved forward, and she was. Gods help Lucifer because she was hell-bent on destroying him. When we finished here, I'd take her away from this place, show her another world where she could let that darkness out to play, to let down those walls and just be who she was without fear of the coven rejecting her.

I'd take her home, to the one place I could release my own power without fear of it destroying all those she loved because no matter what she tried to tell the world or show them, Lena loved her people, all of them, and she still fought for them.

She had never needed Lucifer to become the queen; she was already one in her own right. She fought for the humans when no other thought them worthy, for the witches who the world judged and found lacking; she was the queen of the unwanted, the unloved, and the fucking underdog. And she was mine.

"You plan to crawl out of that fucking head sometime today?" Spyder asked as he escaped from the shadows, staring me down as if he could see the same image I was, Lena bathed in blood, naked.

"Kallum is back?" I asked, staring him down as I watched him shrug the words off.

"He's been back, he's no longer needed to watch Lucifer since he's here now," he admitted, and I grunted.

"You pulled him out?"

"I figured you'd be okay with it since we have our hands full here and figuring out how to close the portals without cutting Lena open to remove the seal isn't an ideal task."

"It's dormant, sleeping inside her womb," I expelled as I exhaled and turned to face him. "What the fuck is up with the dancing bullshit? It's unlike you."

"She needed a laugh, and I felt it. That need to know she's still her, no matter what she has become. Open your fucking eyes and look at her, Lucian. She's strong, but she is fucking broken inside. What she did for them, for you, it cost her everything. She may look healed, but she's still that scared little girl who walked into that circle and died. She's layered now, you need to peel them back, see what is waiting for you inside. She may just fucking surprise you."

"You don't think she hasn't? She took Lucifer to the ground with the promise of her sweet flesh and bashed his fucking brains in. Naked. Naked and uncaring that the entire world watched as she took on the devil in her birthday suit, with her bare hands," I mused softly, considering exactly what she'd done. "She showed him who she was, and how much damage she can do alone to him, but she also went bare bones to do it, making sure the world knew what lay in those layers beneath that pretty smile. She's not just one of the Furies; she's more, which may spell trouble, considering she does still hold the seal within her. If it ever awakens and figures out just how strong she has become, we could end up with us all on the losing end of this war."

"You saw the runes she used to seal it into her flesh," he muttered as his hand rubbed down his face as his sapphire eyes held mine. "Those were older than the Fae inside this Guild. The grimoires she still contains weren't just from this coven, they're of Hecate herself. Lena is a walking fucking killing machine, one who could set this world on fire alone. She cannot remain here once this is over. The Gods will never allow it."

"I'm aware, but they'll never make a move against her so long as she remains at my side. They won't chance me unleashing myself on this world or any other."

"Let's hope you're right. The portals are open, and heaven is teetering on chaos, which I'm sure you are already aware of. If heaven opens up, the angels will fall."

"They seem to be staying out of it for the most part. Those pristine fucks wouldn't care if the world ended; their father would, but they have been itching to fight for millennia against the children He created. Seal the Gates of the Gods; leave the rest alone for now. Let's see who slithers out to help and who runs. Hades has enough to deal with; we don't need more Gods coming here to move pieces onto the playing field."

"On it, but they won't be too happy if they figure out we locked them up for this fight," he pointed out.

His eyes lifted to the top of the Guild as if he was seeing her, where she prepared for bed. "She was something to witness today, even if she toed a line she shouldn't have. Not many can say they've gone toe-to-toe with the devil and left him a bloody, lifeless mess of shit on their shoes."

"She was something else, but do me a favor and stop picturing her naked. Half the fucking Fae are already doing so. There's also the fact that we need to sever that bond between you and her, now that it's unneeded."

"There's only one way to reverse it, and I'm not so sure I want to go there. That's a line I don't want to cross, and neither does she, not really."

"It's not a line I want you to cross either, but I need you focused and feeling you with me every time I fuck her cannot continue. No offense, Spyder, but I want you out of her head when I fuck her, and out of mine."

CHAPTER
twenty-three

The weak can never forgive. Forgiveness is the attribute of the strong. ~*Mahatma Gandhi*

Lena

Silently, I sat on the bed

lost in the turmoil of my thoughts as I processed everything that had happened today. I'd gone toe-to-toe with the devil without anything to protect me, without anything between us to show him just who had come back from the dead, and I hadn't flinched. That wasn't something the old me could have accomplished, and yet I'd enjoyed it. I'd enjoyed the feel of his blood as it bathed my flesh, painting it red as if it was war paint. I'd risen from his corpse stronger, weightless of the guilt from luring him to me. I'd wanted to scream and rage in that dream walk. I'd wanted to rip him apart, but the darkness inside of me had craved revenge more.

I exhaled and frowned as I stared at the door of the bedroom I now shared with Lucian, not because he'd asked me to stay here, but because I didn't care if he liked it or not. I needed him; some part of me needed him to be okay. Maybe it was the bond we shared, or maybe it was something of the old me holding on to what it could still grasp on to without destroying it. He was durable, unbreakable, which was more than I could say about Kendra.

I'd watched her tonight for hours after Lucian had left with his men to check out the damage along with the width of the portals to other dimensions that now were opening. Dominos, it was like fucking dominos, and once one world opened, another began the process.

My mind replayed Kendra, how she looked, the way she cradled her stomach as if she carried some gift from God himself instead of Lucifer. A Nephilim, they'd called it: Half-angel, half mortal, and death to the poor girl carrying it. She and Olivia had both taken to walking the halls for exercise, and I'd felt a flare of jealousy that I wasn't with them. That I'd lost my chance to be one of them cradling their protruding bellies as they discussed pregnancy together. I'd wanted to be the one who laughed with her, talked to her about the joys of it, and yet I'd never know that joy that spread on their faces as the child moved or kicked. No, I'd sacrificed mine because a monster had grown in his tiny, innocent soul.

The thought of Kendra dying flared anger into my mind, licking against it red-hot and it also terrified me. I knew I shouldn't feel it, and yet I did. I felt what was coming; the knowledge that Olivia's mother had also died in childbirth didn't help me. It was how she'd ended up in the Guild, and little to nothing was known about her actual death. I lay back against the soft pillows as I closed my eyes, forcing the turbulence of my mind to calm, the ache in my chest to cease throbbing as I considered how much longer she had before her time would be here.

Wasn't living with a soul supposed to stop the pain?

Wasn't I supposed to be free of the burden of feeling this sense of loss? Yet I felt it, right down to my black soulless core. I felt the loss as if it had already unfolded.

"You're in my bed, woman," a thick voice purred, and then a shadow filled my line of sight as I pried my eyes open to peer up at him. I gazed longingly into the dark exquisiteness of endless desire that offered infinite salvation, an escape from the debilitating pain of my thoughts.

"So I am," I uttered softly as I continually watched him, unwilling to close my eyes for a moment as he stared back. Slowly, he began to undo the cuffs of his suit jacket, his darkened stare daring me to argue as he began to strip bare.

Only Lucian Blackstone would wear a suit in the middle of an honest-to-Gods fucking apocalypse. He looked as if he'd just stepped right out of the pages of a *GQ Magazine* and right into the shithole of a mess we called home. He turned, dismissing me as he folded his jacket onto a vacant chair before he turned back, leaning against the wall as if he was trying to figure out how to handle me, or how to proceed.

"Your people are out tonight, scouring the streets and yet here you are, in my bed sulking. Not that I don't mind you waiting in my bed, but you don't seem like the wait-around type, little lady," he chuckled softly, his eyes turning into liquid pools of heat. His fingers lifted, slowly undoing the buttons on his crisp white shirt as he continued to stare at me.

"I'm not sulking, and I wasn't waiting for you either," I lied. I was waiting, not that I'd ever admit it. He didn't need me to boost his ego or add to the cockiness he already had in spades. Not that he hadn't earned the right to be cocky, or use that ego, I mean, he did. But I wasn't building onto it tonight.

"You're sulking, and you are waiting for me, in my bed." He slipped the shirt from his body, and my gaze slid down the coils of tense muscles that were covered in delicious tattoos and runes. I licked my lips and let my eyes drift to the V of his body that dipped below the suit pants he wore. He knew what I needed, what I'd come here for, and yet he didn't demand shit as he watched me with heat banked in those darkened depths.

"I can't lose her, Lucian. Not now, not after everything we've been through."

"And if you can't save her? Because it's not something I can stop from happening. Humans are not meant to bear Nephilims, Lena. Not even I can stop death when he reaches for a human; witch or not, she's his if he comes for her."

"I told you to prove it to me, to earn me back. I'm asking you to save her, to use whatever you are to save her life!"

"And I'm telling you that I cannot," he muttered as he placed the guns on the sideboard and sat beside me, his leg brushing against mine with his close proximity. "I can destroy worlds for you, slaughter millions, but I cannot save her. If it were that easy, she'd be safe from the cold grasp of death, and you'd have never died. I can't fight the natural order, no one can. If you are planning on me saving her, we're fucked."

"Then how do I save her?" I demanded as I stood up, putting distance between us.

"Come with me," he said, offering me his hand.

I stared at it as if it would bite me, and then slowly, very slowly, I placed my hand into his and let him tug my body closer to his. He started out of the room, and I followed him, allowing him to lead me towards wherever it was he was taking me.

We passed several doorways in silence. The sound of couples laughing or otherwise engaged met my ears as we moved towards a winding staircase that led upwards at the end of the hall. I followed him up the stairs; silence seemed to follow us as if those in the rooms had paused to listen as we moved higher into the Guild.

Eventually, we met with a guard, a giant Fae with burning green eyes that skimmed over Lucian before letting that eerie gaze land on my face.

"Yum," he said with such intensity that I swallowed audibly.

"She's mine."

"I wasn't interested in her, just her pain," he elaborated as those eyes seemed to see beyond me to what burned in my center: Pain and anguish that almost buckled my knees.

"Asrian," Lucian acknowledged softly with a nod of his dark head towards the door.

"It's not pretty," the Fae said, his eyes still focused on me, as a new sensation started around us. "I can take it from you. But only if you want me to."

"Take what?" I asked hesitantly.

"The pain, you have so much of it. Too much for someone so young, but you do wear it so beautifully if I may be so bold to say."

I stared into his multicolored eyes and winced, knowing he was taking it from me already. I felt the subtle pull of it, the offer for oblivion he could give me and yet I pulled it back to me, like armor. He was almost seven feet in height; his copper red hair was striking against his pale complexion. Eyes the color of lime surrounded by a darker grass green watched me, beckoning me to let him feed from my pain until the weightless oblivion of it took over.

"I need it still," I informed him coolly, as if it didn't debilitate and obliterate me from inside as surely as if it was a wrecking ball slamming into my heart over and over again. "Maybe another time, Asrian," I offered.

"I look forward to it, creature," he smirked as he reached for the door, pulling it open to let us pass through.

Outside was bathed in nothing, no lights covered the city. It was bathed in darkness, minus a few fires that burned here or there. A few blocks away from us, smoke billowed up through a building, which if I wasn't mistaken was where I'd once met a girl who had helped me. I wondered if she had gotten out of here, or if she was among the dead.

There were a lot of people I'd once worried about when the world had first begun to unravel, and even now, I hadn't figured out what had befallen them.

Across town the lights burned at Nightshade, a bar I now knew Vlad ran, which was currently doubling as a hold-up for those who needed sanctuary but weren't allowed to be around the humans whom the Guild housed.

"That is our reality right now," he pointed out as he stood behind me.

"I get it," I stated, not turning to look at him. I could feel his heat, soothing the chill in my bones that the sight created. "But she's my sister."

"And that means what in the larger picture?" he asked, his breath fanning against my ear as I stared out of the darkened city. "She may survive it; she's stronger than you think. When everyone else broke apart at your funeral, she rose. She remained brave even though she was breaking apart just like everyone else. Yet Kendra kept them together. You're a lot more alike than I thought you were. I couldn't stand to look at her, and yet I watched her hold the coven together, stepping in to keep them heading towards the larger picture. She knew what having this child would cost her, and yet she soldiered onward. She's been aware that she is growing weaker, and never once has she asked anyone for help. She intends to hand her child to Lucifer because she fears what it could become, and she is right to."

"Children are not born evil," I said, turning my head to glare at him over my shoulder. "Evil isn't born, it's learned. You choose to become evil even as you choose to be good. Life isn't black or white; it's lived in the grey areas. You make choices, and those choices decide what you will become, but *you* make them."

"Did you see him?" he asked, and I didn't need to ask who the he was that he asked about.

"Yes," I whispered as a shiver rushed up my spine. "He had midnight eyes and black hair. He looked like his father."

"I'm sorry," he said, placing a soft kiss against the back of my head.

"I know. I know you are. So am I," I admitted as I turned, staring into his dark gaze. "I need you to teach me how to control my urges, because I have to be able to be close to her in case… In case her time comes, and it's her end."

"I'll teach you control, but more than that, I'll teach you how to take over the world, Lena. How to make it tremble at your feet so that we can close the portals between ours and theirs," he said as he kissed my forehead. "I'll show you everything."

CHAPTER
twenty-four

He is sin, mixed with fire and I crave the burn only he can give me. ~Lena

The room was utterly silent; only his eyes spoke as he slowly pulled the silk that wrapped around the post of the bed down. I didn't need words to hear what he was asking of me. I wanted this from him. For him to teach me what only he could, to learn to control my emotions around Kendra, to harness the monster I'd become in her presence. Lucian was my teacher, but more than that, he was a monster who was unafraid of what I'd become.

"I will not stop once I begin, so you need to decide if you really want this from me. After watching you with him, I need to punish you, but more than that, I need to know you're really mine," he growled, the vibration of it sliding through me with the force of his words.

"I want this," I admitted as I stared into the heat that lingered in his darkened gaze. I swallowed hard, staring at him as I forced the words out through the thickness of my throat. "I want what you can give me, what you can teach me. So no, I won't ask you to stop. Not tonight, and I need this too. I need you to erase him from my flesh, from my mouth."

"Strip, slowly," he ordered as he wrapped the silk fabric around his hands, sitting in the chair that was mere inches away from the bed. I faced him as I slowly lifted my shirt over my head, discarding it on the floor as I stared at him. I hooked my fingers through the skirt, slowly preparing to remove it when his growl forced me to hesitate. "Leave that on, but remove your panties and hand them to me. Then I want you to turn around and show me what belongs to me. Make me need it, Lena."

"It isn't yours, yet. You have not earned it." My words were an open challenge; the fire that lit in his eyes only encouraged me to push it further, taunting this monster to take what he wanted. "This is just another lesson." That reminder seemed to darken those inky depths as he shook his head with a wolfish grin flitting onto his sensual mouth.

"Careful, that sounded like a challenge," he uttered with a guttural tone as lust pooled in his stare. That tone hit every nerve ending, firing neurons that triggered my body's response to him. Heat pooled in my apex, and the ache began to throb where I needed him the most. I hooked my fingers through the thin lace thong I wore and turned, bending at the waist as I pushed them to my ankles, stepping out of them before I brought my hand back up, testing the wetness that his heady stare created in my pussy. Once I'd teased him purposely, I deposited my wet panties in his hand and waited. "Are you wet?" he asked, already knowing I was from what I'd just shown him. The liquid pool of midnight that stared back at me made my knees weak, threatening to leave me at his feet, on my knees.

"You know I am," I replied hoarsely, my voice escaping my lips like the most skilled siren as she called to her prey from the depths of their grave. My back arched, hips flaring to spread for his viewing pleasure. "Why don't you touch me and see for yourself what you do to me?" I asked, needing his hands to explore my needy sex. I turned to face the bed, giving him my back as I placed my palms flat against the floor, showing him my needy pussy as I clenched with need for him. My legs spread apart, and I waited there, anticipation spiking as his heated stare greedily took in my flesh.

I wanted him, needed him, even if I wasn't ready to forgive him. I still wanted him to prove he wanted me, to prove he felt something for the loss of our child, instead of the coldness that seemed to enter his gaze when I spoke of our son. I should deny him this, the pleasure of my body and yet I also had my own selfish needs. The need to figure out how to control my emotions around Kendra, the deadliness of the wings that seemed to flare when my emotions ran high scared and terrified me around her. She had little time left, and I needed to be there when her time came without fearing what I may do to her.

The silence stretched in the room, and I tensed as I waited for him. I began to wonder if he'd just leave me there, standing exposed before his heated stare. I could feel the need of my sex pulsing, clenching with the urgency he awoke in my body, which was wet, dripping with anticipation for the man who drove me mindless with pleasure. This creature could send me to the highest peak, and then send me to the darkest, deepest depths with words alone, but his touch? His ability to control and wring out every single ounce of pleasure my body experienced was unmatched. I wanted what he could give me, no matter how bipolar it made me feel or sound.

His heated kiss touched my flesh, and I jumped as a scream bubbled up from my throat, escaping before I could contain it. His hands gripped my hips, holding me there as his tongue pushed through the folds of my sex, sending pleasure ripping me apart as he tasted what I'd so freely offered to him. My knees wobbled, and if he hadn't held me, I'd have taken an ungraceful swan-dive into the floor.

"You taste like heaven," he mumbled, the vibration of his words graced my flesh, and I rocked my ass against his face as throaty laughter purred from his chest. I whined as the heat of his mouth left my pussy, his body rising to stand behind me. "Such a greedy little thing, aren't you?" he asked as his hand slapped against my ass, biting into the flesh as pain replaced need, and then his fingers pushed through the slickened heat of my pussy, replacing it.

His other hand dug into my hair, pulling me up until I was leaning against his naked chest. My nipples hardened, needing his mouth to taste them. His subtle act of dominance turned me on, it made my body react violently with such subtle acts that I felt heat flushing my cheeks as I swallowed back the need to beg him to fuck me. He tugged my hair, aware of the reaction I had to it; his other hand left the wetness he created as they slowly trailed up my spine. I felt the stirring of my wings, the overwhelming panic that they'd hurt him took control of my mind, and I started to pull away from him, from the harm they could render to his person if I lost control as I was.

"They won't hurt me, Lena. You won't let them," he

promised as if he trusted me enough to think I held some control over my wings, which I didn't. I felt my eyes watering at his words. The calmness they created was soothing. "You control them, they don't control you."

They unfurled, and I swallowed hard as I felt him release my hair as he dragged a finger over the tip of one wing. The sensation was intense, erotic. His touch upon them was pleasurable on a level I hadn't expected, and a moan ripped from my lungs, pushing past my lips as he leisurely explored them without fear.

"They're beautiful, just like the woman they belong to. But I don't want to play with them right now; I want to play with you. Put them away, force them to retreat," he ordered thickly, and I winced, unsure how to accomplish it.

"Normally they go away when they want to," I admitted sheepishly. "I've yet to master how to force them to go. They tend to leave when they want to."

"They're ruled by emotions and the need to protect you. They react when you are overwhelmed, so send the emotions away, and they will go with it. You don't need them, make them feel it. Make them sense that you're safe, protected," he explained huskily, yet he didn't slow or stop his fingers as they danced on the extended wings. My body trembled from his touch, what he was doing to them as they shivered against the pleasure he created.

My mind slowly replayed what he had just told me; his explanation made sense. He repeated it, and I listened to the order in his tone, his cool control which seemed to ring in my ears. Nothing happened. I turned, facing him. Holding his inky stare as he smiled softly, the tips of his mouth the only indication he wasn't upset with my inability to control this extension of myself. Hell, I was frustrated by lack of my control over them, and he seemed immune to my faults.

"Kiss me," he ordered, his tone a mixture of lust and command. He didn't wait for me to agree or disagree. Instead, his hand cupped the back of my neck as his mouth crushed against mine. His tongue delved into my heat, twirling in an ageless dance of time as he took control until I was helpless to anything but hold onto him as he turned my bones to liquid. His hand slid down my back, and I gasped as I pulled away to stare at him in wonder. He pressed his forehead against mine, struggling to reel in his breathing even though I was pretty sure he didn't need air to live. Once I could think, I pulled away, sucking my lip between my teeth.

"How?"

"You were in control of your emotions the moment my mouth touched yours. Your body sensed your needs, your wants. As I said, you're in control of what your body does. They're reactive to what you want, need, and crave." He backed away from me, staring at my perky breasts before he bent down to retrieve the silk he'd dropped when my wings had expanded. He straightened, staring down at my body which was bare minus the short, mini skirt of black ruffles I still wore. He flicked a finger, and candles leapt to life around us, bathing the room and me in a soft glow. "Get on your knees, and submit," he demanded. "From this moment on, I am Master or sir, and you do nothing unless I tell you or you ask permission for it. Do you understand?"

"You and I both know there isn't a submissive bone in my entire body." Pointing it out didn't seem to get the point across as he stared at me, demanding I follow his command.

"I know what you are, Lena. I also know every bone in that tight little body and what it craves. That's not what this is about. This is about learning to control it, to become immune to the emotions that draw those beautiful wings to you. You're going to submit so that I can teach you how physical and emotional responses stimulate them. If you can control your body's response to pleasure and need, you will control them easily. The most basic need you have it to react to pleasure, or pain. I'm going to use both to push you to your limits, and I'm also going to force you to ignore them. I can only do it if you submit and let me teach you."

Slowly, I dropped to my knees at his feet and bowed my head, and the silk curtain of it spread to skim my flesh as I folded my hands in front of me, on my legs. I sat there, exposed and at his mercy. I listened as he slowly walked around me, his heated gaze singing my flesh as he took in my pose of submission.

The sound of fabric being removed told me he was taking off his clothes, or what he'd yet to remove before I'd stripped down to nothing for him. I imagined the taste of his flesh, the way it felt against my mouth as I'd leisurely tasted every inch of it. I craved the tang of his cock, the heaviness of it as it pushed into my mouth. Fuck, I craved everything about him.

"What are you imagining right now, sweet girl?" he queried thickly as his fingers traced the puckered flesh of one nipple, and then the other before it pinched the sensitive flesh, forcing a small cry of pleasure to escape my lips.

"Your cock," I admitted and then cried out louder as his fingers tightened, pinching me harder than he had been.

"Try that again," he offered.

"Your cock, sir," I purred huskily. I lifted my eyes to his, showing him the fire that pooled in mine, the match to the inferno burning in his. I watched as the eerie blue glow ignited. His mouth curved into a wicked grin as the last word slipped before between my lips, off my tongue. "The taste of your flesh against my lips, Master," I smiled demurely. "The feel of you as you invade my throat."

"You're going to cut this fucking thread I'm hanging by, but then you know that, don't you?" he growled as he stood, slowly unbuttoning the jeans he wore. "You're a bad girl, aren't you?"

"I'm your bad girl, sir," I uttered hoarsely, the huskiness in my tone as rough as his. I lowered my eyes to the floor, willing to play his game to learn some semblance of control again. I hated feeling out of control, and while I'd discovered my wings could be used to kill, and well, honestly I liked them, they were still new and being unable to control them was a problem.

"Stand up, grab the canopy of the bed, and don't let go."

Standing slowly, I turned towards the bed, doing as he'd instructed. My hands barely reached the wooden frame of the bed, but I forced my body to reach it as I stood perched on my tiptoes. I swallowed hard as his hands covered mine, slowly wrapping the silk around them and then tying them to the bed frame. Once he'd finished with them, he pushed my legs apart and gripped my hips. It forced me to hang there awkwardly. I had no control over my body. The only thing I could do was lean against the silk that held my arms suspended as he lifted my hips, parting my legs.

"I can't move," I uttered. His hand slapped against my

ass, and I cried out, turning my head to stare back at him. I watched in stupefied silence as that hand landed against my ass once more before it rubbed and soothed the ache it had created.

"You can't move, *what*?"

"Anything," I grumbled only to cry out again as his hand landed twice more, turning the pink flesh red where he punished me. "Anything, sir!"

He laughed, the sound a husky mix of possession and lust. His fingers trailed through my pussy, slowly pushing through the heat and wetness he was creating. His finger pushed into my pussy, and I moaned at the fullness he created, riding them as he used his other hand to hold my shoulder and control the rhythm.

"Your body is hungry for me," he rasped, the sound sending my already heightened senses over the edge as my body clenched around him. "You're close, aren't you?" he asked, and I nodded. "Words, Lena. Tell me what you need from me."

"I need you to fuck me, sir," I groaned as he added another, forcing my body to yield to his thrusts as he stretched it and readied me for his entry. My body was an inferno. The need to let go and feel overwhelmed me to the point that I was seconds away from succumbing to the orgasm that promised to let it all go, but he pulled away. I whimpered as the ache increased. Turning my head, I followed his back with my heavy glare as he pulled open a drawer and withdrew something.

"Face forward, Lena. Close your eyes, and spread your hips."

I did as he instructed and then cried out as he pushed something hard and thick into my pussy. It clenched, tightening around it as he slowly pulled it out and then pushed it in deeper. His mouth skimmed over the globe of my ass as his other hand slowly began to work my clit with sure, strong strokes that fueled the fire.

"That's it," he encouraged. "Don't come, not until I say you can."

"Please?" I begged, only to feel his fingers leave my flesh and slap against it in an exquisite mixture of pain and pleasure. "Lucian," I continued, and then the slap was harder, and everything inside of me began to uncoil. The moment I thought he'd send me over the edge, he stopped touching me, and all sensation stopped.

I blinked at the abruptness of it. My body ceased to feel pleasure or the mixture his touch allowed me to feel. I struggled to reign in the emotions but before I could, the wings unfurled, and I shook with the anger that it caused. *Everything* had changed. *I'd* changed into something *I* no longer recognized.

"Calm down," he instructed and I struggled against the silk that held my hands as the need to run took hold. "Lena," he urged as his hands slowly stroked my back, trailing down my spine between the wings. "Breathe, you're safe."

"I'm a monster," I cried as I ceased struggling. His touch calmed, it soothed the ache in the center of my being that told me the protruding things that currently flapped behind me were evil, vile things.

"So am I," he crooned as he kissed my spine. His mouth sent the fire pooling in my core, and I closed my eyes, just feeling the sheer magic of his mouth and what it did to me. "Put them away," he urged.

I shook my head as my body trembled. "I'm done, I've had enough for tonight," I whispered and felt him rising, leaning over my body to release the restraints that held me. He didn't push it, didn't question the need I had to end this right now, to stop everything because it was just too much.

Once I was free, I turned and stared at him. I could let myself feel with him, or I could walk away and not have to feel anything. I moved without thought, rushing him as he allowed it. I jumped before I slammed into him, feeling the power he projected as he caught me, slamming me down against the bed without me noting he'd teleported us.

His hands parted my legs, and his cock pressed against my opening. I rocked my hips in a needy motion as I waited for him to enter me, but he didn't. I gazed up into his eyes, eyes that asked permission, and I blinked.

Lucian didn't ask, he took; he conquered and destroyed and yet here he was, asking permission. "I need you," I whispered through swollen lips as tears filled my eyes. He didn't hesitate a moment longer. His body slammed against mine, and I screamed out as pain ripped through me. I dropped my head against the softness of the bed and met his body thrust for thrust with everything I had in me.

"Open your eyes," he demanded. "You and me, we exist in a place that others don't understand. You and me, we don't live in their world. You exist in places of my mind that no one else has ever explored, or been allowed to see. Do you understand me?"

"Just move!" I ordered, not needing his words or possessing a mind to know what he said, let alone comprehending the meaning. The man needed to stop speaking in codes. I felt him thrust; rocking his hips as he took me to that place that one could or ever would. My body exploded in blinding light as pleasure shot through me. My wings expended, and I rolled us as I took what I needed without thought, or care.

I rode him as if the hounds of Hell had set after me and he was my salvation. His grunts and moans encouraged and then I lowered my head, nipping against his piercing as my tongue flicked against it, pulling it as an inhuman growl escaped from my throat. I kissed his chest until I found his shoulder, and then I claimed him. I bit into flesh, tasting blood as it pooled against my flesh. I drank, sucking against the flesh until he was writhing and whispering my name as his orgasm tore through him.

Mine followed his, a never-ending wave of pleasure that washed through me and into him until we were both screaming and holding on to each other for an anchor. I uttered his name as I lifted my head, and stared down into inhuman eyes that seemed endless, ageless. Souls stared back at me, and I didn't flinch or back away.

"Mine," I said in a guttural tone, only it wasn't human. It was Fury. It was what I'd become, and as I pulled back from him, I saw the cuts from my nails, the gouge in his flesh from my teeth and I felt my stomach drop as I lifted my worried gaze to his, and found him smiling up at me. "I…Lucian, are you okay?"

"You're my monster," he chuckled. "You can't hurt me," he said softly. "I'm not human, nor am I something that can sustain pain, Lena. You think you're a monster? You have no idea what has laid claim to you. I promise you this, though, you will. And once you know, you may try to run from me, but this much you do know already. If you run, I will follow. There's no world where you aren't mine, do you understand? I would crush them, one by one to find you. Whatever this is that we share, it's more than I've ever felt before. It's more than I want to, but I'm not willing to walk away from you either. Do you understand me?"

"I understand," I lied. I didn't grasp anything other than the blood that oozed from the cuts my nails had created. I'd been oblivious to the pain, and never once had he alerted me to the discomfort he'd had to feel at my hands. I swallowed hard, staring down at my blunt nails and then back to the wounds.

I had to get away from this place, from him. I had to get away from my family because losing control wasn't bad, it was gonna be a fucking catastrophe.

"Don't you even think it," he snapped.

"I hurt you," I whispered horrified.

"Because I let you," he growled as he sat up, wrapping his arms around my waist. "If I was human, yes, you would have hurt me. I'm not, and I won't let you hurt them. Even if it means separating you from them, or forcing you to back down if you lose control. Let me help you. Let me teach you. Because either you let me or I'll chain you up and force you to let me."

"If I kill them, I will never come back from it."

"I know, which is why I would never let it happen."

"You can't always be there to stop me."

"Between me and my men, we got you. I got you, Lena. You're my monster, my Fury. I promise to not let you hurt them, to keep you grounded and protected," he said as he kissed the side of my face and my forehead. "Pretend to sleep with me," he chuckled, and a smile tugged at my lips.

"Fine," I uttered as I let him tug me down beside his naked body. "Someday you'll tell me what you are, right?" I said after a few moments in silence had passed.

"Someday you'll know what I am, Lena. Pray to the Gods that you can accept it when it happens, because I'm not strong enough to let you go."

CHAPTER
twenty-five

Mastering others is strength; mastering yourself is true power. *~Lao Tzu*

I stood outside, perched on the roof of the Guild. This spot was quickly becoming my favorite place to think or ponder the world around us. I escaped to it when the tension or foreboding sensation grew too much to handle, and the world seemed to tighten the hold it had on my throat a little more every time something else seemed to go wrong. Everything was going wrong, as if the deck was stacked against us and we were running out of cards to play. I had begun to open myself to Kendra, while still holding certain pieces and aspects of what I had become away from her. Those feelings, those pieces of my old self she craved, they didn't exist anymore, which she was slowly figuring out. I'd changed more than I could explain; choices I'd made had carved me into someone else, something else.

Lucian trained my body at night, and I craved those lessons like a drug user wanted a fix. I didn't let him reach the pieces of me that weren't healed, the broken parts that had yet to mend back together from the loss of our child; I wasn't ready for him to see them. I wasn't sure if I would ever be prepared for that. He either wasn't processing the loss, or dealing with it in his own way, which I understood and respected, but some emotion would have been welcomed.

"You rang?" Hades's deep baritone filled the air around me before a cloud of smoke filled the air, which he stepped out of as if he some way to literally step from the Underworld, into ours. I swallowed hard as I stared at him, peering into the bluish-purple depths that new my pain intimately.

"I need you to save my sister, make her into one of us," I uttered without bothering to hide the pain that laced each word.

Snowflakes began to blanket the world as the air grew colder around me. I turned away from him, staring out at the multitude of fires that burned through the city. Some built by humans who had yet to seek sanctuary in the Guild, fighting to stave off the cold of winter. I'd remembered how cold the world was, and didn't fault them for seeking warmth in the new world they'd found themselves trapped in. Besides, this was the Pacific Northwest, known for arctic cold fronts and unforgiving winters. Even though the cold no longer bothered me, I remembered what it felt like in the dead of winter.

"You want me to fight Death for her?" he asked, stepping up beside me as he hiked a dark eyebrow at my nod of confirmation. I felt him studying my face as I refused to turn away from the chaos of the city, or the billowing smoke of the fires that burned like my emotions.

"Name your price, and I will gladly pay it," I assured

him, knowing it wouldn't be cheap. I finally glanced away from the fires to face him. His skin was utter perfection, bronzed as if he'd spent months sunbathing in the Caribbean's sun.

"She cannot be saved, Lena." It was a statement, unwavering as he watched me ever so slightly taking in the darkness that seemed to escape my hold as I processed his words. "If she is to die, she will die. She may survive it, but it is doubtful. But if Death has pulled her card, it cannot be placed back into the deck."

"You saved me, why not her?" I argued.

"You weren't one of them," he admitted. "You were and are different than she is. She was the one born of your parents' unions; you were created with magic that Katarina wielded. You were just an empty shell that was forged to be used for another purpose. Magic created you, and that made it easy to save you since you held no purpose. The others…they were harder, and yet they made a sacrifice and willingly released their souls. Kendra will not do that, and you already know it. You never really existed, Lena. The same goes for Joshua. He was the first they created, and therefore able to shape into a Fury because for you, he was willing to change. We didn't fight Death for you; we just created you from what was left of you. The others, they were much akin to what you are, and it wasn't Death who plucked their cards, it was Nyx. It wasn't their time to die, and their selfless sacrifice awoke something in her to pull her to them. It made a simple task to intervene and send their souls below while keeping their minds in tacked. Kendra hasn't made some grand gesture of a sacrifice, nor will she. It isn't who she is. You know that. You're mad, but they'll all die on you. One day or another, they'll be gone, and you will be here without them. It's as simple as that. I told you that when I helped Nyx bring you back, I warned you that you'd watch them age and die and that no one would be able to prevent it from happening. Besides, your sister welcomes the end and therefore isn't worthy of being immortal. She isn't created like you, to know you were meant for something bigger than yourself. Hell, Lena, you stood up to the devil himself knowing your life was being forfeited and yet you didn't flinch away from it. You are worthy of being immortal."

"So I'm just supposed to accept that she may die?" I growled as my mind fought against the idea of a world that she no longer existed in. One where my family was gone, and I had to continue pushing through, moving forward. "I don't accept that. You're a God, Hades! Fight Death with me, we can win. Do nothing, and we all lose. No, no, you're a God, and you can win this. We can win this."

"It's not black and white, Magdalena. Nothing is as simple as that. Death doesn't lose, and you think he isn't here already if her time is near? He is the one thing that not even the Gods will fight against. He will not lose her if it is her time. If he's here, she's already dead, and you're just going to have to watch it unfold as we have done since the dawn of time." I tried to ease the frown that creased my brows as he continued to crush any and all hope I had left with his words. "No one escapes their time, not even if the Gods intervene and beg it to be otherwise. Death is certain for mortals. He is everywhere and nowhere at all, and when it comes for them, nothing stands between it and him. You can try other things, but if he has plucked that card, she's doomed. Nothing short of God himself intervening will stop it from happening. Pray the angels heed those prayers you continually send to the heavens, girl, because only her God can save her, and He doesn't seem to care lately."

"Go," I stated coldly, my hate and anger burning brighter than the fires of Hell that lit the streets before us. It ignited as violent as Hell itself as it burned the world around us to ashes. The fallen cities of this world hadn't asked for this war, and yet mortals paid the price with their lives as the Gods did nothing, as God did nothing to end their suffering. Why wasn't anyone helping us? Where were they in this fight? I remained there long after Hades had turned to smoke and disappeared from my side. I stared out over the remnants that had once been a bustling city that was now a wasteland of those strong enough to survive this new world.

My eyes settled on Shadowlands, and I blinked as Lucian's words replayed in my head. A sad smile played across my lips, and I shoved my hands into the pockets of the jeans I wore. I could ask Vlad to save Kendra, but I already knew her answer. She'd lived, and she wouldn't accept immortality. Not at the cost of her soul. They were right, and it hurt, it hurt like something was being ripped out of me, as if my own soul had been pushed back into a body it no longer fit, only to be shredded as it left.

The air beside me rumbled with raw power, and I wiped away the tears as I fought the thickness of my throat as hopelessness and despair choked me until I feared I'd literally fucking die from the pain. What kind of world was this fucking cruel?

"He didn't give you the answer you sought?" Lucian said as he stepped from the shadows and strode slowly to where I watched his approaching form.

"We need a win," I stated hesitantly, dismissing him as I stared up into the thousands of snowflakes that continually dropped. "I need a win."

"We found a gate that is weakening," he announced, stopping when he stood close enough that his heated breath tingled across the flesh of my ear. I stepped back, allowing his body to heat mine.

"And can it be closed? Or is it just another useless thing that we'll fail at?" I asked softly, dropping my hands until they brushed against his. The barest touch of flesh sent a shiver of desire racing through my system.

"We aren't sure, but I figured you would want to be with me when we tried to close it," he uttered as his nose traced the curvature of my ear. I shivered from the subtle contact, the heat of his flesh pressed against mine and I slowly turned, peering up at him from beneath my lashes.

"It's creating an unbalance in the world," I informed, knowing he knew it already but needing to know that I wasn't the only one who felt the disturbance. "We cannot lose," I murmured before I lifted on my toes, pushing my mouth against his.

Lucian was a distraction, a balm for the pain that filled the place where my soul had once sat. I was darkness, but he, he was the light at the end of the tunnel. Without him, there were no stars in this endless darkness. If I was the stars, he was the darkness that let me shine in its endless silken embrace.

His mouth crushed against mine fiercely as his hand snaked up through my hair, holding me in place as he pillaged and ravished. The taste of aged scotch undid me, throwing all caution to the wind as I started undoing his shirt.

Throaty laughter filled the air around us as his hands captured mine, stilling them. His midnight gaze watched me as I struggled to reel in the roaring fire that had ignited inside of me. He rested his forehead against mine as he spoke slowly and clearly.

"The men are waiting for us below," he informed in a husky timbre that slid over my flesh, heating the inferno within. "Afterwards, if you want to continue this…" he let the offer hang in the air between us. "You're hurting, but no matter what we do, no matter how much I distract you, it won't prevent what is coming."

"Just shut up," I growled as I pulled away, wrapping my arms around my stomach as I fought to hide the pain I felt. I'd tried to ask for help from them, and yet no one could save Kendra. But maybe the one who had put her into this position could spare her?

"Don't even fucking think it," he snapped as if he'd read my mind.

"He might have a way to save her," I uttered thickly as my teeth worried my bottom lip.

"He doesn't care about her, or the child."

"And yet he wants his daughter, Lucian. If he can save her, I'd do anything he wanted in exchange for her life, *anything*."

"He'd want you in exchange for her," he growled thickly, his eyes raking over my face before his hand pushed through his hair. "I will see what can be done to prevent her death, but not even Lucifer can stave off Death once he's plucked a card from his deck."

CHAPTER
twenty-six

If they stand behind you, protect them. If they stand beside you, respect them. If they stand against you, defeat them. *~Anonymous Author*

Death and despair loomed all around us, and sulfur reeked as it hung heavy in the air. Putrid and thicker near the gate, stronger with every step we took that led us closer to it. Corpses were littered between us and it, the rip of this world into Hell. It wasn't a Hell Gate that we stared into, but an actual rip in the fabric of the world that led directly into Hell. The ground was bathed in crimson, blood for the human corpses that looked as if something wild had used their bones to create art that had then been discarded like yesterday's trash. It felt wrong the closer we got, the stronger a sense of foreboding grew in the group who stared into the abysmal world beyond it. I studied the tear between worlds, the disturbance it created as magic mingled around us. It slithered from the hole, escaping to lure mortals to their doom. It made more sense why they're corpses were scattered about, as if they'd stepped inside only to be spit back out; soulless corpses, rejected by Hell.

"Do you hear that?" Synthia asked, tilting her head as we all heard it, the music and feminine voice that sung from within the other world before us.

The sound of the voice sent a thrill of excitement and fear snaking up through my mind, and I closed my eyes, listening to her sensual promise of seduction if I only stepped through the hole to join her. It was the song of the sirens, a promise of pleasure, and numbness from the pain and chaos that had filled this world.

"Jesus, it's a siren," she uttered thickly as she peered down at the corpses. "They're men, all of them."

"She is luring them to her, promising to end their pain," Lucian explained, his eyes slowly studying Synthia's face before it swung to me. It dropped as he took in the mutilated corpses and frowned deeper before he gazed up at the hole before us. "She sings to them, but once they enter the tear, she slaughters them and then sends them back out into their own world. She's not happy with her sleep being disturbed. Sirens do not come onto land unless they're forced, which means someone or something dragged her into Hell against her wishes."

"But it's more than that, isn't it?" Synthia asked as she tossed a femur bone down and rose. "Hell itself is calling them here."

"Like it's a living, breathing place?" I asked. I hated the mystery and bullshit that went with their fucked-up worlds. Faery was a living breathing thing that, more often than not, killed anyone stupid enough to enter it without the Fae inviting them in, and even those sorry bastards could end up dead. "It calls mortals to it, then what, spits them back out?" I continued carefully, not wanting to sound stupid or naïve even if I was.

"It is, but not what you're thinking. Hell needs souls to house, like a machine that needs coal added to continue burning. Souls feed the flames, and without them, Hell ceases to exist. Without the flames it would not hold the ones it had claimed, the evil that it contains would essentially be released into this world. They'd be free to roam the world again, with only a need for a vessel to continue their purpose."

"And wouldn't that just be fucking dandy," I grumbled as I studied him and then let my magic out to slither against Hell's, testing it and then smiling as it recoiled from mine. It fucking recoiled as if it couldn't stand the feel or touch of mine; as if I was the wrongness in this scenario and it wanted nothing to do with me. I pushed at it, poked it until something else pushed back from within the rip.

"Enough," Spyder warned as his gaze moved between me and the hole, and then he stepped closer. His finger trailed down my cheek, his penetrating gaze looking into the pain I felt at everything unfolding around us. "If you continue to challenge it, it may decide to become something else, something bigger to stand a chance against you, kitty."

"How do we close it if we can't even touch it?" I asked, lifting my heated gaze to hold Spyder's before swinging them towards Lucian, who watched us closely. His eyes missed nothing, including the connection I shared with them both. It was endless, this need to reach out for it, to touch it to make sure he was still somehow tethered to me.

"We find something holy and convince it to close it. Maybe if enough of them begin to tear into this world, they'd pull their head out of the fucking mud and man the fuck up. We need…a fucking angel," he said, moving his sapphire gaze from mine to Synthia and Ryder, who hovered just beyond the circle of Lucian's crew who'd joined us for this excursion. "We need an angel to poke it, and if we have one on tap…"

"I think they're already here," Lucian grumbled as he crossed his arms and stared at something behind me.

I felt it, the smothering power that rippled through the air around us. It felt pure, right, addicting as it slithered around me, sliding through me until I opened my mouth to speak and it slipped inside. I spit it out, the wrongness of it as it tried to sense what I was. My mind felt something slam against it, and I pushed back, hating the invasion that tried to see past my barriers. It lessened into a caress, a subtle coaxing to lower my walls, to let it into my mind to see what I was. I spun around slowly, searching the area around me for whatever had just tried to get into my mind, my body. My wings uncurled from spinning, sensing the need to protect me from whatever it was trying to blast into my being.

Blinding white light exploded around us. Streetlights exploded, raining glass and sparks down onto the streets around us. I brought my arms up to cover my eyes as it grew to a painful fluorescent explosion of blinding light around us. The scent of freshly fallen snow emitted, luring me to lower my arm as it slithered against my flesh, burning it at the same time. Once I felt it had dimmed enough, I dropped my arm and blinked against the utterly perfect creatures who stared directly at me. Beautiful, ethereal creatures stood before us, all gazing at me as if I was somehow wrong, and shouldn't exist.

I felt it, knew it without them saying it. I was wrong, evil. I felt it to the very fiber of my being as they gazed at me, pushing magic into my system, searching for a way past the walls of my mind to seek out what my intent was, to know what I was. I knew what they were as I pushed back, touching the minds of the beings before me who tilted their head, aware that I struck them hard and fast to know who and what was assaulting me.

"You don't belong here," one snapped, his green eyes reminding me of freshly cut lawns in summer. It stared back, an archangel from heaven that viewed me as something foul, something wrong. As if I'd been forged in the cauldrons of Hell and brought back solely to destroy Gods creation. "You're wrong."

"This world has gone to hell, and you're more worried about me? No wonder we are losing," I growled with an edge to each word, making sure he heard the underlying blame I was tossing at him. "Look around, we're the only ones here trying to close the gaping hole of Hell, and you want to come out and say I'm wrong? I'm not here to hurt this world, no. I'm here to mend it, to repair it and help the humans remain where they belong instead of pushing daisies up from Hell."

"And you think they belong anywhere else? They've brought this on to themselves with their treachery and killing of each other." He spat into the grass as if that settled it. His dark-skinned hand pushed his hair back from his face as he stared at me. Power radiated from him, his body a weapon forged by God himself when He'd created these beings.

"I don't think they deserve to end up dead," I shrugged. "I was mortal not too long ago, and I didn't deserve my fate. They deserve better; not all humans are evil. Not all humans kill or murder others. Besides, I've always been one for an underdog."

"They're vile creatures who seek and crave destruction. They enjoy chaos and ruining what was created to be cherished, loved."

"They're flawed, I'll give you that. But then, that isn't something new. They were created to be flawed, so you tell me if God would want His children slaughtered by Lucifer. I'm guessing He doesn't want them all bathing in their own blood at Lucifer's feet."

"Enough, creature," he growled, and then his eyes widened as he stared at me. "Fury," he uttered as his gaze slid down my frame and then back up to take in the wings behind me. He walked past me, his wings brushing against mine to send a sizzle of awareness pushing down my spine until I clenched my teeth against the power that burned through me.

Lucian and Spyder stepped up to protect me, their arms brushing mine as we watched the angel pushing his hand through the hole, watching as it disappeared into the void. The world around us trembled like the aftershock of an earthquake as he pulled it out, and then pushed it in further, pulling out a skeletal figure that he smiled down at before it began to sing, as if it could lull him to her side. My breathing hitched as he shook his head, confidence unshakable as he grabbed her head as she opened her mouth to scream. It was deafening, the noise that escaped her decaying mouth, and then her head was removed, hanging in his hand while the other released its hold on her body.

More archangels stepped past us, amassing in front of the hole as they spoke low, guarded against those of us who perked up to hear what they said. We all watched them in silence as they pulled and examined the hole, more and more angels seeming to converge on the location as they worked. A female archangel stepped behind the first one, turning cerulean blue eyes in my direction before she dismissed me.

Their light seemed to grow, and grow until I had to lower my eyes as they continued to work to do whatever it was that they were doing to close the hole in the world.

"How did you know where it was?" I asked, wondering if Lucian had felt the wrongness as I now did, or if he had another way to sense a disturbance in the world.

"It's not of this world. Anything that doesn't belong here calls to us. We've chosen to ignore it until Raphael called us to him," a female voice answered, and I turned, staring into the beautiful face of an angel. "Furies are only released when the end is upon us. So how are you here, how are you possible, little one?" she questioned as she stared me down, her power pushing against my mind, but her push was a question. She sought an invitation from me, without trying to force her way in, so I let her. I showed her my life, my world, and watched as she flinched at my choices. She exhaled with a gentle nod, staring at me as if I was some mythical beast she wanted to commit to memory.

"I tried to end this from happening before it had gotten this far. I sacrificed my life to save the world," I admitted out loud, knowing the other angels were listening. Her eyes softened as she nodded again, her wings expanding from her back into golden things of beauty that were mere outlines against the night sky.

"You sacrificed your life and the one you'd created to save the world, Magdalena Fitzgerald. A noble sacrifice and yet something unheard of for someone so young," she whispered softly, her blue eyes taking me in as she frowned deeper.

"And yet heaven wouldn't take me," I scoffed.

"Heaven can only hold a soul, which you didn't have.

Hell, on the other hand, can only punish a soul. Tricky things; souls make a human...well, human. That was why when the archangels were forged in heaven; He left them out of us. He may have welcomed you, but not once you allowed the darkness inside. Had you come to Him before Nyx had found you, you could have been made, as I was," she said.

"I was made as I was promised to be," I returned softly, not wanting to get on her bad side. "I do not care to be of heaven or Hell, I wasn't done fighting yet."

"And you think we do not fight in this war?" she asked as her mouth lowered into a frown.

"I think thousands are dead, and millions more will die before this ends. You could have helped us before we got to this point, the moment Lucifer entered this fight, you could have helped us and yet you chose not. Why?"

"Because we have rules," she said.

"Fuck rules," I growled. "Rules are meant to be broken. You let innocent blood fill the streets, and that's unacceptable."

"Lena, they can't fight unless rules have been broken. It's forbidden," Lucian explained.

"By who?" I demanded.

"God," she chuckled as she watched the anger drain out of me.

"Wouldn't God want us to win? Wouldn't He want to spare the lives of those who died needlessly?"

"There are always needless deaths on this plane. Hitler is a good example. Do you think He didn't sense what was happening? Humans are His favorite creation, but they're a very young race. They learn from their mistakes, and even He cannot prevent the big ones they make. He gave your people life, and He gave you choice. What you do with it is up to you. Not Him. He doesn't interfere unless it is something else He created that threatens this world. Hence why the archangels are now here, released to help close the holes in this realm that lead into Hell," she hissed.

"And what about the other ones?" I countered.

"Those are not something we can close, or help with. They're not of His making, and though we can help if you need, we cannot close the gates you opened by walking into Hell, Magdalena. Those were created by a choice. Lucifer knew those would remain open, and while he is of His creation, He will not interfere with him or fight against him. You let him out; you can put him back in."

"Tell us how to and we will," I said.

"You'll figure it out," the male said.

I turned to look at him as something exploded, the world trembled, and we were thrown backwards, away from the inevitable blast that burst from the hole in the world. I tasted blood in my mouth as something soft, yet hard moved beneath me. Lucian stared down at me, and then back towards the gaping hole in the world. My ears rang with pain as I swallowed blood and struggled to get back up. The world heaved in pain, and as I righted myself, lifting to my feet, I stared at the outlines of wings that covered the ground, where the lesser angels had stood seconds before.

"What the fuck was that?" I demanded, but as we got to our feet, we were left alone with no angels to answer us. Some of the archangels hadn't survived either, because the headless angels were there, no winged outline…just… dead? "They…died?"

"They only left the bodies that had housed them. Or at least the archangels did, the others, they are finished,"

Lucian muttered as he stared at me, dropping his gaze as he took in my disheveled appearance. He reached up, wiping away what looked like ash from his face, and I looked around the ground we stood on, noting there was in fact ashes everywhere.

"But it killed them? Closing that void killed the lesser angels and forced the others out of their host bodies, which means we're fucked," I mumbled as I let him search me for injuries as Ryder was doing with Synthia. Ristan seemed uncertain whether or not they'd actually closed the hole and continually searched the area around us for any sign it had been moved or something else.

"It's more likely they used a dead body to hold their light, and then used their grace to project their image from it. Angels are vain creatures, created in the image of purity and beauty. They hate mirroring *His* lesser beings that He created, even for a moment in time." Lucian finally released me once he was sure I hadn't been hurt by the blast.

"They think I'm wrong, that I'm bad."

"Furies are creatures who the Gods call to seek vengeance and retribution. They don't create you to host tea parties and galas, kitty cat."

"No shit?" I smiled as Spyder smirked at the sarcasm dripping from my lips.

"No shit, but I'm guessing you still fuck like you're going to war, and I'm owed," he pointed out with a heat-filled gaze that sent a ripple through me.

"Spyder, enough," Lucian growled as he pulled me closer to him as Ristan shook his dark head.

"It's gone. But something is wrong with the ground where it was," he murmured as he knelt down, examining the blackened earth. "I don't think they meant to explode with it."

"Lucifer has gotten smarter since the last time he came here," Lucian growled.

"Well…shit," I said as I felt the wrongness in the air around us. "I think they opened the fucking world up to the creatures Hell housed."

"I think you're right," he replied. "I think Luc knew they'd come, and they did exactly as he wanted them to. He alone didn't have enough power to open the realm, but with theirs, he would."

"So what you're saying is, Hell is wide open, and we're fucked in a not good way that leads to absolutely zero pleasure."

"Exactly," Lucian confirmed, and the ground began to creak, as if something was cracking below where we stood. "We should go, now," he snapped as he grabbed me as the others began sifting out.

CHAPTER
twenty-seven

There's a lesson to be learned in defeat. It's never about losing; it is about changing who you were to who you need to become to rise from the ashes of who you used to be. ~*Lena*

It took less than an hour

for Hell to rise up and claim the city as a whole. Screams tore through the night, and no matter how fast we moved to save the humans, they died continually before we could even reach them. We moved through the night, long past the rising sun of dawn, and deep into the next rising moon as we fought to save those we could. We made quite the fighting force, tearing through the streets as one, ending any creature who had decided to feast upon the blood of those we sought to protect. It didn't matter how many we saved, as long as we saved those we could reach before the monsters of Hell devoured them. I'd thought the acrid scent and taste of sulfur was bad before, but it was nothing compared to the taste of it now as it mingled with the coppery scent of innocent blood that had been spilled as Hell had risen up, into our world, fully freed.

Hell was here, a part of our world now. There was no

barrier standing between the creatures of it and ours; only us. Hours passed, and yet it felt like days as we fought to save those who had yet to be slaughtered. Side by side we fought to save the people of the city until fewer and fewer heartbeats sounded around us.

"We can't keep going like this," Synthia said as she removed a head from a demon and stared down the blood-soaked street at the corpses that littered it, dead before we could reach them. Bodies were strewn as far as my inhuman sight could reach. Some had been torn apart, others lay sightless as if they had just sat down and given up. Looks of horror covered their faces in death, as if they'd stared down the purest form of evil before meeting their end.

"We can't stop," Joshua snarled as he tore through a demon's chest, ripping the human soul from it as the body sagged and fell upon the ground to join the other corpses. Rivers of blood flowed down the streets, all draining into the sewers as we watched it, like a horror show playing out right before our eyes. "They're dying. It's our fucking job to save them."

"Everyone is dead," I whispered as I wiped my mouth with the back of my hand, choking on bile that pushed through my throat and threatened to spill into the river of blood and entrails. I took in several husked-out humans, as if something had literally sucked the life out of them, leaving only a dried up version in the bloody mud that lined the streets and alleyways. "Something else besides demons are feeding now, those are not normal corpses." None of this was normal.

Husks had been shed like something had lived in them and then discarded the humans' form like a snake shed its skin. As if it was wearing humans like flesh suits, but where the demons used them to walk on earth, these had been sucked dry and left behind. I bent down, touching one, and watched as it crumbled the moment I did. Its essence had been sucked dry, and then the creature had moved on to the next. The other bodies which had been similarly crushed into ashes the moment they were touched, blowing away in the wind as if they'd returned to the world as they'd come to it, in ashes.

"What the fuck does that?" I demanded as I fought the need to spew what little substance I'd kept down on our trek into the hellish world we now lived in. As far as I could see with my new senses, husked corpses filled the darkened alleyways.

"Something bad," Lucian offered.

We'd lost.

We'd thought the angels appearing would be a win, but instead we'd fallen right into the trap Lucifer had placed for them and us. Now, everywhere you looked was littered with human corpses, or what was left of them. Fires lit the night; Hell itself had risen and replaced this one classical town of rich history and trading post. Now, now all that was left was shelled out buildings and the dead.

"Welcome to the new world," Spyder hissed as he pushed his bloody fingers through his hair and stared down at the pile of ashes. "Hell housed thousands of monsters that other worlds couldn't contain. Hades houses the souls once they'd been punished, but Hell housed the worst of the worst."

"And what the fuck houses the larger ones?" I asked.

"Tartarus, and if it is opened, we will die. All of us."

"How do we know if it opens?" I asked.

"We'll know," Lucian said in a guttural growl as he

239

followed something in the shadows around us. "We got company," he informed as Spyder became a mixture of shadows as he disappeared into the real ones. Screams ripped through the night as I watched shadows hit one large one, and then pink mist exploded everywhere, bathing us in what was left of the creatures. No one said anything as Spyder's form solidified and he smirked at me as he walked towards where I stood.

"We should retire for the night," he said softly. "There are no more heartbeats near or around us. We need to regroup and get a fucking plan going before this entire shit-show leaves us wading in it."

"And we're not already?" I asked. My heart buried in my throat as the reality of what he said hit me. There were no more humans left in this town, not alive. "They're… we lost."

"We got played, kitty," he stated and frowned. "He won't get that lucky again."

"What does it matter if everyone is dead? What's the point of fighting if he won?"

"Because he took the town, he didn't take the world yet. We fight to survive. We fight until the last heartbeat is extinguished and there is no one left to help. We fight because we are the only things standing between him and his untimely reign of this world. He won this fight, he hasn't won the war, kitty cat. That is not something we will allow to happen, ever."

We sifted back to the Guild, and even though there were now thousands of humans we'd saved below, I preferred to be out on the roof, a sentinel guarding the Guild as I viewed the damage around us.

Earlier only scattered fires burned around the city. Now, the entire city was ablaze as building after building caught fire and eventually tumbled to the ground in a blazing pile of embers. How did you come back from this? Could they even rebuild it? It seemed as if we were fighting a losing battle, and those who needed us were now strewn over the pavement, nothing more than husks and empty corpses.

I felt them before I saw them, Layton, Bane, Spyder, and Lucian. They seemed to emerge from the shadows moments before the Fae sifted in, all coming to stand shoulder to shoulder at the edge of the Guild.

"Jesus," Synthia murmured as tears streamed from her eyes as she surveyed what I had been staring at. "New Orleans just fell."

"The City of Saints has fallen?" I countered as my stomach churned.

"The Guild…or what was left of it. They'd been gathering as many people as they could to protect, and couldn't distinguish the difference between the demons and humans. They sent a warning to the remaining Guilds to close their doors, and wait this out."

"They can't do that! They're supposed to stand against creatures who feed off the human race."

"That's not the same as demons, Lena. We were trained to fight Fae, to fight monsters we could see or feel, and they cannot sense them. New Orleans let humans in, and demons walked right through their doors and slaughtered what little of their numbers remained. We are fighting an enemy who has never been here before. Not these demons, Mages I can handle, Fae we can face and come out on top, but Lucifer? The fucking devil? They're unequipped. We are unequipped to fight him, and we are Gods, Horde Fae, Dark Fae, Furies, and whatever the fuck he is," she flicked her hand in Lucian's direction as her hair tumbled over her shoulders as they slumped. "Do you think if I knew what to do I'd sit here and watch *my* city burn?"

"I'm sorry," I uttered thickly as tears burned my eyes. "It's hard to watch it happen," I admitted as I felt Lucian stepping closer against me. "I gave my life to stop this from happening. Now, now I have to watch it happen and know that I gave everything I had and it didn't matter in the end."

"You stopped the seal from escaping, from using you to do so much worse than Lucifer can ever dream of doing to this world," Lucian whispered against my ear as he pulled me back against his warmth and I allowed it. I rested my head against his chest as I stared up at the starless night.

"Even the stars refuse to shine tonight," I uttered.

"What if we release the seal, and send it after Lucifer?" Synthia asked, and I swallowed hard as I turned to stare at her, not removing my head from Lucian where his heart had begun to thunder in his chest.

"You have no idea what you ask for," Spyder answered before anyone else could.

"What do we have to lose?" she asked.

"Everything," Lucian replied. "The seal wasn't even fully released, and yet it opened worlds the moment Lena stepped into Hell. Can you imagine the chaos it would bring down upon us if it was allowed to awaken? It's done what it hasn't ever been able to accomplish while it slumbered, if it is allowed to come out and play, not even your Gods will be able to stop it."

"But you can," I pointed out as I stared up at the starless sky once more. "You are its keeper, its holder. You alone can stop it if we unleash it."

"To release it, you'd have to give it control. In your new body, it would be unstoppable, it's not fucking happening."

"You'd need to kill me," I said softly as I turned in his arms. "But you could, couldn't you? Whatever you are, you can kill me."

"We're not exchanging the world for you, Lena. I won't allow it. I'd destroy it first. I'd snuff out every life in this realm and take you to mine. Do you hear me? I'd rip this world apart to protect you."

"So that's a no?" Ristan asked as he watched us from where he stood beside Ryder. Zahruk's sapphire eyes held mine before they moved back to the burning city.

"If the seal is released, every world will open into this one. You think Hell is bad? Imagine the outer realms joining this one. It would open to worlds twice as large as Faery with monsters this world wouldn't sustain holding. It would be like opening this one up to become one large feeding ground."

"That's a no," I stated as I watched another building crumble to the ground as embers shot into the night. "Nightshade," I uttered as it beckoned me. The bar remained untouched, wards so thickly built that they glowed like an earthy beacon of hope on the burning city was where the humans were running for. "We have to help them, now!"

The Fae sifted, and Lucian held me as we moved through space and time and appeared at the doors of the club, but within, only silence was heard.

"Vlad," Synthia whispered as she pushed the doors open as humans pushed and forced their way past us into the safety of the club.

Inside the coppery tang of blood was thick in the air,

and rancid. I pushed my elbow up against my nose as we entered it, finding bodies of immortals and humans in pieces littered on the floor. Silver eyes flashed in my mind; the gentle being that had always encouraged me and pushed me to be stronger, better, was lying on the bar with an iron rod protruding from his chest.

"No," I uttered brokenly. "No, it can't be."

CHAPTER
twenty-eight

Never fear bitches, I'm here! ~*Erie*

Ryder's approach to the bar was unnervingly slow, as if his feet dragged to the gruesome task of discovering Vlad's corpse laid out on the bar, with an iron bar pierced through his heart. I swallowed one, then twice as bile pushed heavily against the back of my throat as tears threatened to fall from my eyes. One foot in front of the other, he passed through the mutilated corpses that had been scattered onto the floor, left in tattered pieces by those who had desecrated the one place immortals and mortals had been safe to mingle. His hands gripped, turning the corpse over to reveal the face and then expelled a shuddered breath as his shoulders slumped and the body was set back down. His voice was thick as he plucked the note from the corpse, and read it before letting it drifted to the bloodied floor.

My eyes stared down at the bloodied note which read two words. *You Lose.*

"It's not him, thank the Goddess it isn't Vlad," he said thickly, his voice filled with the same emotion we'd felt seconds ago when we'd believed it was Vlad's corpse on display.

I started to collapse in relief, but Lucian caught me as Synthia released the soft cry of relief that splintered through her. I watched her in disbelief as she began to search for someone else among the littered bodies of immortals that covered the floor, face down in the river of blood that seemed endless inside the club.

It took hours of sorting through them to discover who had died, and who had been able to get away before this place had fallen to Lucifer. Hours passed as we helped her, piecing body after body together as the Fae began sifting corpses in and out of the club and back to Faery for their final burial. Fae sifted in and out, one after another until the bar was empty of death and then we began slowly cleaning it, as if for our own benefit it would help our mental state.

Hours later, humans began lining up at the doors, demanding entrance into the one place they could be assured safety from the new world, and one by one, they were sifted to the Guild where we were sure they'd be safe. It stung, knowing that this place had been a beacon of hope in a world rife with chaos and debauchery, and yet they flooded to it, even though it had fallen. Instead of running to the Guild as they should have, they came here.

"I didn't think he'd be in danger. The club has always been protected, always safe," Synthia whispered as she dusted off her hands on her pants. Her top was covered in blood, as the rest of her was, the rest of us. Blood smeared her sharp cheekbones, and then all at once, as if I'd imagined it, she was clean. "It's always been warded against anyone seeking to cause harm entering it. How the hell could they bring it down?" she demanded as Ryder pulled her close, kissing the top of her head as he comforted her.

"I'm guessing the wards we crossed outside removed the ones inside. Someone turned the new ones that Erie placed against us. They countered it, meaning Lucifer has a powerful fucking Mage or being on his side, working to undo what we did," Ryder answered, and I shook my head.

"Witches," I corrected. "He used witches. They're not strong wards, they're smart wards. They used wards that turned your wards into a weapon against those inside the club. So once the ones inside the club became entangled with the others, they nulled the beings in the club, rendering them all but mortal. It worked long enough to allow those in the club to be slaughtered, and then his wards once again became the dominant ones. Witches are taught to outthink our enemies, to not work harder, but to work smarter. This was a smart move, for them, not for us. It's not something those in here would have seen coming, and the moment they tried to fight back, the wards saw them as the threat to the club. They used your wards to kill your people. It's smart, and yet fits the monsters we are fighting. It was dark witches, judging by the taint of dark magic still heavy in the air."

"They were placed by Fae and a very talented druid. They wouldn't fall to mere witches, it had to be something stronger, much stronger," Zahruk snapped, his sapphire gaze alight with rage brewing in their endless depths.

"I didn't say any witch, Zahruk. They're dark ancient witches. Meaning they've sustained life for a very long time to gain an unbalanced footing of knowledge. If I'm right, they've spent a large portion of that time learning your people. The scent is old, musky and mixed with death. They're over a thousand years old if my senses are correct. They are searching for chaos and souls. That means they've found a use for them, some way to devour them…" I paused, inhaling deeply as the grimoires inside me reacted to the magic in the air, the decay that the witch's magic had left lingering. Admitting magic to these creatures still felt wrong, like a part of me still lingered in the past. "I can feel their darkness, which is the same as the magic in my head."

"The grimoires…they're still alive inside of you?" Synthia asked as her hands fisted at her sides. "They're old, but not that old. The Guild wasn't built that many years ago, and the elders have not lived that long. Even the older ones, the ancient Guild didn't have magic that old."

"No, but the grimoires were compiled of witches and bloodlines, meaning they kept their magic throughout the years, and the taint of it is in them. The spells that linger inside of me are very old, some light and some dark," I admitted softly as I explained what I felt in my own head from the grimoires that remained closed in my mind. "Spells are passed down through generations. These wards that took down the clubs are old, ancient ones shared through blood that calls to the grimoires inside of me. I'm guessing whoever Lucifer is using; it's from one of the bloodlines Katarina was born into. As with light magic, dark magic is also passed down through lines, only it is hidden between the pages where only those who sought out darkness would dare to look. In our coven, yarn was used to find the darkness in a line, to search their grimoires for the spells. If found, the purity ceremony would be used to bind any temptation to use it," I elaborated as they listened, their eyes narrowing as I laid it out for them. "I house both dark and light magic, even though I no longer house a soul. The magic of the grimoires is still inside of me, as is the seal."

"Who is it?" Lucian asked, his dark gaze demanding I answer him and yet he already knew.

"You know who did this," I said softly, staring at him.

"That's impossible; they'd be dust by now." His tone damned my words and yet his eyes seemed to sadden.

"Unless they found a way to feed off of souls of immortals?" I offered, and he frowned deeper as he stared at me.

"Who the fuck is it?" Synthia demanded.

"If she's right, it's an entire coven of dark witches. Dark, immortal witches now. They're evil, almost as evil as Lucifer himself, hungry for a power that they can't contain because they lack the vessel to use it. They'd crave blood, and souls to retain their immortality if they do still exist. I cursed them to contain the souls of the damned eons ago for trying to take something from me. Magdalena is right, though, this is something they could do, and they'd be powerful enough to turn our own wards against us."

"And they have Vlad now? Adrian?" she demanded crossly.

"Pray to your Gods that they don't, or they are already dead."

"Vlad isn't that easy to kill, he could be a vessel," I offered. "He'd fight against them, he's strong."

"He'd fight them, but they would win. They wield iron claws and teeth to weaken their Fae prey. They drain their strength and then feed on them for however long they can.

They suck them dry, leaving a husk of their victims in their wake."

"They are what were released from Hell today, aren't they?" I asked, utterly horrified.

"They and countless other monsters that have not fed in centuries and are starving," he nodded as I swallowed hard. "Unless they were already here, helping him; it would explain how he hid Katarina's soul in two vessels. I had wondered how he had done it, but if he had their help to remove and create a perfect replica, it would make sense how you are alive, and how you came to be a clone."

Ouch. I'd been a clone, not even a real person.

"Where would they go? Where would they take them to finish feeding off of them?" Ryder asked, his eyes glowing as he feared for Vlad and what would become of him.

"I don't know, if I did we'd already be there retrieving him," he supplied crossly as he stared at the empty side of the bar.

"That is my family they took!" Ryder snarled as his wings and beast exploded in front of us.

"Calm your tits," a silken voice groaned as people moved through the halls. Weapons were brandished as we stared down the hallway. The hair on my neck rose as they emerged. I uttered groan as dark shadows began slowly exiting the hall, to enter the club.

I expelled a soft cry as I watched Vlad, Adrian and countless others pour from the hallway to where we stood. "I wouldn't be that easy to catch. Give me some credit," he said in a guttural tone as he hugged Synthia and limped towards the bar.

I slowly walked to the bar and stared at the bloody mess of his body, noting he'd given them a fight before he'd retreated. He turned as he poured himself and countless other cups with top shelf bourbon before his eyes lifted, and the bottle crashed to the floor.

"Lena?" he whispered thickly before he was over the bar examining me. His hands cupped my cheeks as he stared into my eyes. "Gods, tell me it's really you?"

"It's me."

"How? I fed you my blood, and yet I felt nothing from you. You are…different. You smell different." His eyes smiled and yet it faded as he took in the tattered state of his club.

"It wasn't your blood or from lack of trying," I whispered hoarsely. "I came back because Nyx brought me back as a Fury," I admitted, and his forehead rested against mine as he chuckled.

"Of course you did," he said as he pulled back and stared openly at me. "I don't care how it happened, but I'm glad you're alive. I'm glad you survived. I'm not even sure why I am surprised anymore when you females come back from the grave. You crazy bitches pop right back up like daisies."

"What happened here?" Ryder asked as he downed a glass of the expensive liquor and then another.

"Lucifer fucking happened," Adrian injected, straddling a seat on the bar as he pushed guts off another to allow Synthia a clean spot to sit. "Lucifer and a group of haggled witches, who were surprisingly powerful considering they looked old, sickly and stunk of death and decay," he shrugged as if he didn't know what else to say or how to explain it.

"Fucking Lucifer used the world trembling as a diversion to bring down the wards. He brought in a group of witches, old ones. They looked young at first, but I could see past the glamour and the veil of magic they wielded. They were husks of flesh and magic, as if they hadn't fed in centuries, and then they opened their fucking mouths and began feeding on the partygoers inside the club, immortals and human alike were consumed like they were nothing. Child's play to the likes of them," Vlad growled as a shiver shook his large, muscular frame. "I barely got Adrian before I felt the tug on my magic. I felt it pulling me towards them, but a Fae got a shot of magic off, killing one of the witches, and then all hell broke loose. We had just enough time to get to the hidden rooms before the screaming started in earnest," he said as he pushed his hands through his midnight hair and frowned. "I saved who I could, but it wasn't much. It wasn't enough."

"You did what you could, cousin," Ryder stated, and I frowned as I took them all in.

They were a family, one who was smack dab in a war they hadn't signed up for. I turned my eyes to Lucian, wondering if my life could end this. I'd done it once, and even if it did open the gates to the other realms, wouldn't these beings be able to prevent those monsters from entering it? They were the legends of the Fae realm, all wrapped into one family who'd go to war to protect each other. They could work together to save this world after I'd unleashed the seal to slaughter Lucifer.

"No, they can't," Lucian snapped as he watched me. "We are not sacrificing your life, period."

"Lena?" Vlad asked, his silver eyes swirling as he read my emotions. "No, no sweetheart. Your life is precious to us, and you're a part of this family now. You all are whether you want to be or not. Releasing one monster to kill another one isn't the answer. We can face Lucifer together, all of us or none of us at all. There is no I in team, nor is there one of us that would allow you to die to save any one of us. We stand together, now drink. Because I'm assuming shit is about to hit the fan and all we have is right now, together."

"We can't beat him if we don't know where or what he is planning. We almost lost you tonight, and we didn't even sense you were in danger because he killed angels!"

"He tried," a deep voice snarled behind us, and we turned as one to watch the same archangels swagger into the club. "It's personal now," he snapped as his cerulean gaze met mine.

"The gloves are off, now pour a few rounds, because it's about to get apocalyptic really fast. Heaven just fell," he uttered thickly.

"Heaven cannot fall," I whispered in a horrified tone.

"Earth wasn't his goal, it never has been. He wanted the seal to open heaven to the world so that he could waltz right in and destroy it. Earth had to fall before he could bring heaven to its knees."

"So heaven and Hell are now in this world?" I asked.

"They always have been, but the gates were closed to mankind," he elaborated slowly, as if I wouldn't understand him. "You can't see them unless you're heading into one. That's why every once in a while, a soul will sneak back into this world. What you call spirits or ghost are just souls who slipped back out of the gates and came back, drawn to loved ones. The ones who wreak horror on humans are the ones who escaped Hell. They just have to catch the gate open or a crack in the walls to come back to what they know. Either way, no walls separate this realm from heaven or Hell, or more walls are cracking as we speak. Now, about that drink?" he asked as the shadow of wings stretched behind his back.

"An angel, a demon, a Fae, and a few monsters walked into a bar…" a feminine voice purred behind us.

"And?" Synthia asked as she turned to stare at Erie.

"And my fucking fantasies came true," she chuckled. "Bitches, have you seen outside? It's a fucking shithole. I just got accosted by demons trying to give me mouth to mouth. I need something to sanitize the taste and wash their blood off my hands. Oh, and I blew up a few Paladin to make this night even funnier."

"You killed Callaghan again?" Ristan asked as he tapped Vlad on the shoulder and helped him pour more drinks to the people piling into the bar.

"Just a little," she chuckled with a smirk that told me she'd enjoyed it.

"Who is Callaghan?" I asked.

"The male who thinks I'm his salvation. I'm his doom; he just hasn't figured that out yet." I stared at her with my mouth open as I tried to form a question and failed. "He thinks my vagina is going to save our races, but it won't. I mean, the entire world just literally went to hell, and he's still chasing me."

"You're a female druid," the archangel pointed out.

"And you are?" she countered.

"Raphael," he said as lightning lit the room and the shadow of wings covered the wall behind him.

"Uh, fucking hell," she smiled as she slapped him on the back and downed her drink in one swallow. "An archangel, we're so fucking fucked right now."

And that was the Gods' honest truth.

"Female, watch your language," he urged, and she shook her head.

"Oh hell, you ain't heard anything yet," she snorted as she tapped the bar for another drink and then peered around the room at the walls and the bodies strewn around the floor. "Jesus, did someone forget to clean up their dinner?" she asked.

"Lucifer was here," Synthia said softly as her hand rested on Vlad's.

"So these…these were your friends," she said in a whispered voice that spoke of understanding. "I'm sorry, Vlad. I didn't notice them in the excitement."

"The wards came down." Vlad looked at her pointedly.

"No, no they wouldn't come down," she said as she turned to focus on the walls. "They were voided out by something powerful. Or many powerful things," she amended. "The wards outside, they're not yours?" she queried.

"No, they were placed mere seconds before the bar fell to Lucifer."

"Dark witches?" she asked, and then whistled as turned back around. "The Guild," she whispered. "Bloody hell, the Guild has the same wards as we have here!"

People began sifting, and Lucian grabbed my arm, yanking me with him. I didn't fight it, didn't struggle as my stomach dropped and tears burned my eyes. My family was there, unprotected while we'd sat here, drinking…

CHAPTER
twenty-nine

I don't know, I don't care, and it doesn't make any difference! ~*Albert Einstein*

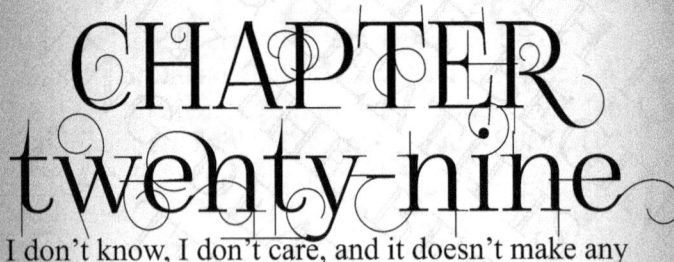 The Guild was silent as we approached, and yet it seemed calm. On the outside, we couldn't hear any screaming, no noise at all. We'd only been able to sift or materialize outside since Erie had placed some very powerful wards inside. I looked around; noting the fires that seemed to burn as far as the eye could see had yet to be extinguished. The sky behind it was foreboding, lit from the blazes and curling smoke that basked the night in an orange haze. I sent my magic slamming into the Guild, pushing past the wards as I sought out Kendra and the others and then relaxed as I found them still inside.

"Something was trying to get inside," Ryder growled thickly, his mouth a multitude of sharp teeth as his beast surveyed the bloody corpses that had piled outside the wards. Creatures had tried to gain entrance and died from their actions.

I followed them up the stairs and glanced inside where the witches were scattered in the main room, sweat pooling and beading upon their brows. They'd fought off whatever those creatures were outside, and won.

My gaze moved to Kendra who held her swollen stomach as she stared back at me. Her hair clung to her face; sweat dampened it and her clothes as she took a step closer to where I'd entered, and then hesitated. Slowly, I made my way to where she stood, and once I was at a safe distance from her, I paused, taking in her form for any sign of injury as she did the same to mine.

"You're okay?" I asked softly, my hands fisted at my side as I forced them to remain there instead of pulling her into an embrace as I itched to do so. I wanted to hug her and promise her that she'd be okay, but I knew I couldn't do that. I wasn't able to touch her without the chance of killing her with the multitude of weapons I now held. Wings that unfurled without warning, claws that shredded flesh, and magic that could kill without meaning to, and she had enough issues without my problems adding to it.

"I'm good," she said as her own hands dropped to her sides, staring at me with turbulence in her matching gaze.

"That's good."

"How is it, out there?" she asked.

"Bad, really bad," I replied honestly, hiding the sheer terror I felt at what lay outside of the sanctuary she was hidden in. I felt wards being placed, ancient ones that pulled on my magic without warning. I turned, eyeing the walls that screamed as ward-after-ward were placed into them. "You're safe, though, inside. Stay inside this Guild, do you hear me?" I demanded, and when she nodded, I nodded even though the churning in my stomach told me that even inside, she wouldn't be safe.

"I know what will happen when I give her life," she mumbled and I fought to keep my eyes from widening, or my face from giving away the horror I felt at her words. "I know my time is coming, but you'll protect her. You'll protect her from the monster that sired her."

"With my life," I agreed as I extended my hand towards her and then dropped it as the claws shot from my fingertips. I backed away from her as if she was a fire, burning me. "I need to go," I informed as I spun around on my heel, rushing away.

"Lena," she called to me, and I ignored her as if her pleas fell on deaf ears.

I stalked towards Lucian, knowing my time for learning was growing shorter as her pregnancy neared the end. I had to be able to help her through it, and if she expected me to protect a child, I had to contain the monster I'd become and quickly.

Ignoring Joshua's concern look and frown as he followed my path back to where Kendra stood, I shook my head knowing he'd go to her. He was able to comfort, whereas I wasn't. I ignored my mother's judging gaze as I stopped short of plowing into Lucian who simply pulled me closer. He felt my worry, and I didn't care how or why he could, only that he was my security in the storm of my world and the dangers I created by being here, being close to my bloodline.

"Get me out of here," I uttered hoarsely as he lowered his gaze to lock with mine. His fingers curled around mine, and yet we didn't move. He waited, watching as Erie continually added wards until she sagged in exhaustion. Once she'd finished, he and Ryder stepped forward, testing them until the wards screeched loudly, forcing those who had remained in the room to clap their hands over their ears or chance losing their hearing.

Bile swirled through my stomach as my mouth grew wet as I forced it to remain down. It was intense, the magic of them combined filled the room like a living thing, pushing through us as we swayed on our feet and yet the wards didn't buckle or give an inch.

"They'll hold for the night," Ryder stated, turning to stare at his wife, who nodded her agreement. "The others will settle the humans into the catacombs, and those who need sleep should seek it now. Dawn will come faster than we would like it to."

At his words, people started moving, and yet the majority lingered in the Guild's main room. I watched them as Vlad stepped closer to Ryder, pulling him into a hug that turned into heavy grunts as they exhaled the relief of finding him unharmed. Ristan and his mate stood to the side, speaking to the angels who had joined us. Adam sat with Alden, speaking in hushed tones to Erie who agreed or disagreed with what someone said.

A cup was pushed into my hand, and I looked up into sapphire eyes which watched me as I lifted the strong liquor to my lips and threw the entire drink back in one large gulp before holding it out for more.

"You think you can do it again?" Zahruk asked, ignoring Lucian's warning growl.

"Do what?" I asked, making certain I knew where his mind was.

"Get Lucifer to the door so that we can trap him, and get what info we need out of him one way or another," he snapped, tipping the bottle back as he drank deeply straight from the source. I tipped a second glass back and let him fill it to the rim again.

The heat from the alcohol surged to life inside my

belly, warming my flesh that had felt frozen with the shit that had gone down tonight. I handed him back the glass and nodded. I could get him back here, but he'd know it was a trap.

"I can get him back, but he'd know it's a trap. No, we'd have to make him think he was coming here by his own choice. He's the fucking devil, not an idiot. Besides, once we got him here, we couldn't hold him. We'd need something that can trap him here...a devil's trap?" I asked, turning to peer up at Lucian, who smirked.

"That would hold him, but not long enough to interrogate him. You'd need something more powerful, which I'm sure our new friends could help us with," he stated as he started us towards the angels who were staring at Kendra. It sent a chill down my spine as we approached their seats.

"You forgot to tell us something?" Raphael snapped as he stood, uncurling from the seat to stand nose to nose with Lucian. "You think she may have something to do with the fact that end of the world is nearing?"

"Her child is half-angel, isn't it?" he countered.

"She's pregnant with the fucking antichrist," he hissed low, not wanting anyone else to hear his words. The hair on my neck rose as a shiver raced down my spine.

"Is that a problem?" I asked, sucking my bottom lip with my teeth as the words left my tongue. Of course, it was a problem. It was Lucifer's child, and as far as we knew, not many Nephilims graced the earth because mating with an angel and being fully human was unheard of. Olivia was proof that it happened, but then her mother had died in childbirth.

"We will address this at another time when the world isn't burning outside the doors. But I'd say it's a problem, a very big problem."

I stared down the archangels who seemed to stare right through me as they began to peel their angry gazes from the unborn child my sister carried. I watched them as they focused on Lucian and then stepped back as if they feared him.

"You want something to trap Lucifer?" Raphael asked, staring at him as if he'd overheard us across the room. "We cannot help you with it, but there's a warehouse on Mission which just happens to have supplies we once used long ago to trap another archangel. I can't tell you what it is, or how to use it. We cannot interfere with that aspect. But if you were to say, trap him, we could hold him with what is inside the warehouse, if it even still stands."

"So you're saying that we have to sort through an entire warehouse to figure out what it is that will trap the devil because you can't say it out loud?" I snorted as I stared at them. "Can't we just use Pictionary to figure it out and then go get it?" I offered.

"Pictionary?" Hades snorted behind me, forcing my head to rubberneck in his direction. "If you're playing with archangels, I'm filming it for YouTube," he chuckled as he sat back in the armchair, folding his ankles together as he stretched out. "I'm guessing you assholes played right into Lucifer's trap and touched the hole that led into Hell?" he asked crossly.

"You knew it was a trap?" Lucian snapped angrily, his eyes lighting with those unnatural blue flames that seemed to explode when he was angry or really turned on. It wasn't the time or place, but those flames seemed to have a direct line to my core, which seemed to pool with molten heat that wasn't missed as all the men close to me turned and looked at me irritably.

"Really, woman," Hades chuckled as his eyes heated and seemed to look right through the leathers I wore. "You smell…good. Really good," he noted before he turned back to Lucian. "Turn off the lights, before she goes into heat. You forget, her emotions are now tied to yours in more ways than one. As much as I'd enjoy watching you with her, this isn't the time or place. Raincheck," he said, waving his hand dismissively. "Of course I knew, but I was busy securing other items to be used to close them when you went and fell in it. I mean, you should have known he'd lay traps for his feathery brethren to fall into."

"A fucking heads-up would have been nice," Lucian replied sharply, his eyes turned to hold mine before his nostrils flared with my scent wafting to him. I knew he sensed it because I did. My body was lit up from within like a fucking glowworm. "Lena?" he asked.

"I need to speak to you…alone," I admitted. "In private."

CHAPTER
thirty

I would challenge you to a battle of wits, but I see you are unarmed. *~Shakespeare*

Once we entered the room, I spun to him, grabbing his shirt to rip it open as I struggled to force the emotions to sink beneath the ebb and flow of lust that threatened to drown me. My lips drifted to his, and a moan stole from them as a throaty growl escaped from deep in his chest. He claimed my mouth as if it was the salvation we needed, fucking destroying me with the gentleness I didn't want or need. His kiss was the kind that made you feel drunk, dazed as he lay claimed to me on an entirely different level of seduction.

One moment I was kissing him as if he was the air I needed to breathe, and the next he pushed me away and smirked down at me with a fire banked in his midnight gaze. He shook his head as if he was dispelling the lustful haze my lips had created.

"Strip," he demanded, his tone even and clear as I swallowed the urge to slap the composure off his face.

"You're not getting off easy this time, and you're not allowed to surrender or demand shit. You want my dick? Earn it."

I paused, glaring at him as he fed my words back to me. "Excuse me?"

"You want my cock, you'll do as I say and as I instruct. If you're good, and you listen, you can come when I give you permission to. Not before or after, or you will be punished. Do you understand?" he asked as he watched me shimmy out of the leather to expose the black lace panties and bra Syn had crafted from glamour for me to wear. Something I really wish I had the ability to do.

"I understand," I agreed, knowing from the heat that flooded his eyes as I removed the bra that it wouldn't take him long to demand I ride his cock. I flung the bra aside, swishing my hips as I moved to the bed, crawling across the silk sheets until I was fully on the bed. I turned around only to be slammed down as his body hit mine, sending a shock of pain rushing through my body.

His hands moved to my throat, applying enough pressure that I gasped as his nose slid over my cheek. "Naughty girl," he laughed huskily. He released my throat, capturing my hands before I could touch him. He gripped them painfully as he pushed them above my head, using a length of silk to bind them. I lifted my head, staring at the thin wisp of fabric that now held them trapped above my head.

Lucian's mouth lowered to my exposed neck, trailing his tongue over the spot where my pulse raced and throbbed as he slowly sucked the flesh between his teeth, biting it gently. Heat pooled between my thighs, marking the proof of how turned on I was as he slowly let his fingers dance down my flesh to draw little circles around my nipples.

He pinched the hardened flesh, and I yelped as pain mixed with pleasure as he continued to slowly trail his down the heated path his fingers danced. Right as his hot breath fanned my peaked nipple tip, he sat back on his haunches, slowly taking in the sight of my naked breasts and thin, black lace panties that were drenched with my arousal.

"You want me inside you, don't you?" he asked, his hands lifting to remove the tie he still wore, because it didn't matter how fucked we were, or how balls-deep into apocalyptic-land bullshit we were in, he still wore it. I nodded, and he shook his head, releasing the grip he held on his tie to slap the inside of my thigh. "Say it, I want to hear you admit it. I don't want to see your fucking head moving. Tell me how much you want this dick, Lena."

"I want it," I admitted through heated cheeks that flooded with color as he made me admit it out loud. "I want you."

"Good, remember that," he chuckled as he moved from the bed and stood, stripping his body bare before he neatly folded the suit up and stalked from the room. I heard the water running and tilted my head, staring where the light was now glowing from the bathroom. Candles leapt to life in the bedroom, bathing me in a seductive light. "Is that pussy still wet?" he asked, calling from the other room.

"It misses you," I replied playfully as I listened to the water splashing against the porcelain tub. "Are you showering?"

"I am, don't you wish you were in here with me? Maybe up against the wall with me buried in that pretty pussy of yours?" he called back, and my body heated as

I glared at the flame of the candle as it danced on the dresser. "House rules, Lena. I tell you what to do; you say, 'Yes, sir.'"

"And what else does this little game of yours include?" I asked, watching his shadow as he moved from the bathroom into the bedroom, naked minus the towel that clung to his hips.

"You being helpless, at my fucking mercy," he purred thickly as his eyes raked over my body as he entered the room further, not in a hurry to fix the ache between my legs.

My gaze followed him as he moved to the large chest in the room, withdrawing several items from it before he slowly walked towards the bed, setting them beside me. He knelt over and placed his mouth against my nipple, nipping the soft flesh until it hardened against the grazing of his teeth as a growl resonated from deep in his chest to hiss over my skin. He knelt on the bed, removing the towel to expose his cock, which was already hard and ready to be used.

I wanted to climb him like a child at a theme park clamoring for the rides as they stood in line. I rocked my hips, letting him know I was ready for it, for him, but his only reply was to smirk, a wolfish grin that sent a shiver up my spine as I lay there, tied to the bed.

"Too easy," he uttered before he reached behind him, pulling out a length of dark cloth which he used to wrap around one ankle before securing it to the post of the bed, only to do the same with the other as I watched him. Next, he tied a smaller length of the sheer fabric around my head, blinding me to what he'd do next. "What do you feel?" he asked as his fingers traced a line from my cheek to my covered flesh.

"Helpless," I replied huskily, wondering why it turned me on so much to be at his mercy. Shouldn't I want to be in somewhat control of this situation? "Lucian…"

"You want to learn how to control those powers; you have to first know what having no control is like, and then how to push the needs away. You're about to learn what it is like to be denied your most basic needs, wants, and desires."

His fingers pushed beneath the panties I still wore, running through the wet folds. He pushed his thumb in a circular pattern as he worked my sex until I was meeting him with increased vigor, my body reacting on a primal level with the need to find what he so freely offered, and yet the moment the orgasm danced through my system with the first hint of building, he pulled away.

I felt the bed moving, felt his massive frame settling between my legs moments before his lips traced the inside of my thigh down one leg, stopping just above the knee before he followed it with his fingers, only to change sides and mirror the action.

"If you're planning to drive me insane, I think it's working," I uttered thickly and then yelped as his hand slapped against my pussy. My back arched into that slap, craving it as my mind became a red haze of need.

His throaty laughter was the only indication that he'd heard the whispered words. He pushed my legs apart, and then the sound of my panties being shredded filled the room. Heat fanned my naked flesh, his tongue snaked out, and I cried out as pleasure tore through me. His fingers bit into my flesh as his tongue traced a pattern through my sleek flesh; dancing over it as it flicked the one spot I needed him most.

And just like that, he was gone. I felt the bed move

and then tensed as something pressed against my ass. My entire body felt like a guitar string that had been pulled too taut, in danger of snapping.

"Lift your ass," he ordered, and I swallowed hard, but I did as he instructed. "You look so pretty tied to my bed, so utterly helpless and wanton," he crooned as he pushed something soft against my ass, and then I cried out as I felt the plug filling me. My body trembled against the intrusion, and yet this time there wasn't pain but only a fullness that danced with pleasure.

He played with it, watching my body, react as it heated me from within. My body tightened, growing flushed against his heated gaze even though I couldn't see it; I felt it. As if an invisible thread had connected us on a deeper level, and told me exactly where he looked, grazing my flesh in a scorching trail as it moved over it.

His finger pushed into my body, and I arched into it, using it to gain what I needed from him and yet the moment the orgasm began to grow, he ceased his touch, leaving me there to writhe in need.

"You're being a good girl, Lena," he murmured as his teeth skimmed the sensitive flesh inside my leg, his tongue trailing behind them as I fought against the urge to let my wings unfurl, to end this and take what I wanted from him. But in doing so, I'd lose what little thread I held on my control. "You want me to fuck you, don't you?"

"Yes," I cried only to buck as his hand slapped my pussy hard. "Yes…sir," I amended.

"Better," he growled as his fingers danced on the sore flesh. I felt him moving between my legs, pushing the tip of his cock into my welcoming heat, but he only gave me the tip before he pulled back, tracing it through my slick folds. "When you're a quivering, sweat-covered, swollen mess, I'll fuck you. Hell, I may even remove that toy and replace it with my cock and let you come from pain and shock as I take no mercy on your unused ass," he uttered hoarsely, and then he pushed into my body, and I screamed.

The fullness was unsettling; the ache it created was intoxicating and unexpected. My body clenched against him, holding him to me as the first ebb and flow of the orgasm began to build. He was hard, fast as he used me and then exited, leaving my body bereft and mourning the loss of his. His fingers replaced it, and then something else was there, pushing into my body. The buzzing started, and then pleasure burned and warred with a need too basic and animalistic that I had to fight it off, along with the wings that itched to explode from my spine. My body curled and struggled to get away from it.

There was too much pleasure at once. The fullness mixed with the plug as his mouth lowered to clamp over my soft nub as both began to hum inside my body. I twisted, turning away from it as if I could escape the pressure and orgasm that built white-hot through my body. He sensed it, but instead of helping me prevent it, he used it against me. He worked one as his thumb pushed against the other, holding it there, in place. His mouth was hot, scorching flesh as his tongue worked circles over my clit until I was screaming with sweat running down my neck.

I fought it. I fought my body on a level that terrified me as I fought against the urge to accept the orgasm, to let the wings out to hold him where I needed him, the claws that pushed through my fingers, and it was too fucking much. I begged him to stop, to let me breathe, and yet he pushed, he used the toy to fuck me hard and fast, and I had to fight him for control.

His hungry laughter filled my ears, my senses were sharpened as my vision was blocked and yet I was winning…until I wasn't. It ripped through me with a force of a hurricane, and I screamed, I screamed until he was there, covering my mouth with his hand as the world teetered around me. The toy was withdrawn, and then his cock was in me, fucking me until nothing else mattered or ever would.

"Naughty girl," he growled against my ear, and yet he didn't stop fucking me until I was exploding around him again as tremors tore through me, the sound of wood splintering filling the room. Then my legs were pushed up more, giving him further access to my needy core until his hands bit into my shoulders, using my hips to rip me from the bed to slam my body down on his cock over and over. The only sounds in the room were our labored breathing and our flesh meeting in an endless dance as old as time.

I was too full, too sensitive, and yet I somehow managed to keep my wings locked into my spine; my nails didn't graze his flesh, and his hands pulled at my hair, giving him access to my throat as he pounded into my body without mercy—and I didn't want any either. I wanted bare bones, I wanted him and the monster he was to fuck the monster I'd become. His monster, I'd become his monster.

He tensed, his guttural moan igniting something animalistic inside of me and I slammed him down against the bed, ripping the blindfold off as I stared down into the blue flames that danced in his eyes. I smiled down at him, staring at the others who watched me from within his eyes and purred as my mouth lowered to his.

"You're mine, monster. All mine," I whispered before I began rocking anew on his cock, feeling him already growing hard inside me again. "I warned you that I was not submissive," I laughed huskily, staring into his eyes as I leaned my forehead against his.

"You contained them, even though every instinct called for you to release them, to take control. You controlled them tonight, Lena. Good girl," he uttered as he kissed me with a fervor I matched, uncaring that laughter sounded outside the door.

"You're a good teacher," I replied. "I enjoy being taught by you."

"Good, because you're not leaving this bed until I finish with you."

"Is that a threat?" I asked, sitting up as I stared down at him, tracing my fingers down his hard, muscled chest.

"No, I don't make threats. I make promises, and I promise you won't escape this room no matter how much you want to until I've had my fill of you, and that won't be for hours, days maybe."

"Days? And here I had begun to see my eternity as a benefit."

"I'll never finish with you, ever. When this world turns to ashes, and the moon becomes dust, you will still be mine, little witch."

CHAPTER
thirty-one

And we're losing. Losing sanity, losing the fight, but we won't lose the war. The world is watching, holding its breath to see who comes out on top. Humanity is flawed, but the most beautiful things often are. *~Lena*

The warehouse loomed, vacant and abandoned before us. The entire thing seemed off, wrong, and yet the closer we got to it, the more those unsettling feelings turned into curiosity that drew us in, wrapping us in a dark embrace that made us *need* to see what was inside. It alone sat untouched by the fires that blazed all around it. As if similar wards to the Guild protected it. Since the angels had told us about it, I was guessing it was protected by strong magic. The sky above us was an eerie orange haze filled with smoke and sulfur that threatened to choke us, rendering us useless and yet still, we remained in place.

"Something is wrong, do you feel that?" I asked, turning in a circle as I peered up and around us, wondering if they felt the lure to run inside with everything inside of them. It called to me, beckoning me closer, forward, and yet something in my head screamed against it. It slithered over my flesh, the wrongness of this place. My flesh pebbled, sending goosebumps over my skin with every step I took that brought me closer towards the large abandoned warehouse.

"I feel it," Ristan muttered as he paused, hesitating as we stared towards the building that seemed to call to us, luring us towards it.

I stared at the large three-story building, an abandoned warehouse that looked as if no one had been inside it in a very long time. The lower portion of the warehouse had been tagged by graffiti that looked worn and muted now, as if time had taken away from the art they'd placed onto it. The ground around us was littered with debris from the homeless who sought places like this to stave off the cold of the winter. Yet no fires burned, no tents or other signs of the homeless had remained next this building. I stared at the garbage that also looked aged, long forgotten and left to decay around the building. The lower windows had been shattered, and yet the higher-up windows were made of thicker glass, probably to protect it from birds or other flying creatures from breaking them. I swallowed as my eyes climbed higher, taking in the different levels that seemed to change as I watched it.

On the highest level, there were grates outside windows yet no way into them from that height, and yet it looked as if they'd been recently placed. Scaffold seemed to surround the top, yet I knew that wasn't something humans would do, since they usually didn't go up that high without some semblance of safety measures, and yet there it was. Perched on the edge of the scaffolding were creatures or stones that had been chiseled and carved to look like gargoyles, watching us as we stared up into the thick smoke that clung to them.

I narrowed my eyes, fixing my gaze on them as I wondered why they'd be here of all places. This was an abandoned factory on the Spokane River, next to Gonzaga College, which had been one of the highest ranking colleges in the region. It all seemed wrong, horribly so.

"Those things aren't just for looks, I'm guessing?" I asked, dropping my gaze to find Ryder studying them as I had been moments before.

"They're part of the wards," Erie answered, her fire-red hair a mess of curls that she pushed out of her face. "Some asshole sent us here to die, horribly."

"What do you mean?" Ryder asked, his growl resonating from deep in his chest as I shivered at the fierceness of the sounds he made.

"If the wards are tampered with in any way, those beings awaken and rain down hell upon whoever touched them. They're tied into the wards, a backup spell if you would. An added security to take out any threat to whatever they've hidden in this building," she explained as her fingers moved in a slow pattern, as if she was testing the wards.

I swallowed hard as one of the gargoyles turned its solid head, tilting it as it stared down at us, luckily remaining on the perch it had been placed. I stepped closer to Zahruk, who snorted but stepped in front of me, as if I was something deserving of being protected.

"You scream a lot, woman," he whispered thickly as he watched me turn and eyeing him carefully. "You ever tire of him, come see me. I'll show you what it is like to be manhandled, and consumed by a desire hotter than the fires he was forged in."

"That's a nice offer, but you seem to forget that even if I wanted you, I couldn't feel you," I pointed out as I let the heat of his body sizzle against mine as I considered what he'd said, and Lucian's absence today.

"You think we wouldn't have ways around that?" he chuckled as his weapons withdrew from holsters, my own following his as if he'd perceived something I hadn't.

"I'm not sure I can remove them," Erie said, and then all hell broke loose as the wards pulsed in warning and those things on the top started to wake from their slumber. "Run!" she hissed, but it was too late.

Swords against creatures that weren't of this world did little to no damage as they attacked us. Ryder's clothes shredded as his beast emerged, towering over us with an impressive wingspan that both protected and blocked us from the first airborne assault.

We tried to sift out; or rather they tried and failed as explosions rocked the warehouses around our location. Something was off, wrong about us being here. I spun in a circle, staring at the Fae who seemed to put it together at the same time.

"It's a distraction," I uttered and ran from the fight, uncaring that they called for me as I moved at an inhuman speed away from the barrier that prevented me from teleporting. I materialized at the Guild at the same time as the Fae began to pop in.

The Guild's doors stood ajar, hanging from the hinges as if something had exploded from inside it. My feet were heavy as I peered around, swallowing the nausea that threatened to spill from my lips as I stepped over the body of my mother. Tears burned in my eyes, obstructing my gaze as I moved deeper into the Guild's now-charred main room.

"Where is she?" I demanded as Joshua turned and stared at me. His shoulders drooped as he shook his head.

My wings unfurled as anger rushed through me. "Where is my sister?"

"They waited for you to leave, and then they set off a device," he answered thickly, his own emotions rolling through him as fire burned in his eyes. "The angels took her, saying her child couldn't be born into this world or any other."

"They sent us to the warehouse to die," I growled. "And they attacked us from within."

My stomach sank; tears blocked my words as I shook my head. This wasn't fucking happening. Not my sister, not now, after everything we'd been through, after everything we'd come through.

"Count the dead, tally the numbers, and bring in the healers," Synthia uttered from the door where they'd entered behind me. "Your mother…"

I swallowed tears as I spun around, staring at Zahruk, who cradled her crumbled form in his arms as if she was a treasure he'd discovered. I dropped to my knees as I swallowed scream after scream and then stopped holding them back.

I stood, staring at her as I searched for my grandmother. "Grandma?" I asked Joshua who shook his dark head again.

"All the witches are dead or missing, as if they vanished when the angels took Kendra," he admitted. "I searched the dead, but I didn't find her among them."

"It's possible they went after them," I mumbled as I surveyed the dead or dying in the midst of what was supposed to be a sanctuary. "How could they do this?"

"It was spelled from those intending harm, or to enter to do harm. And something removed the wards to prevent fighting," Erie admitted without her usual candor entering her tone. "Someone fucked us. They removed the wards, and yet they twisted them as well. They work against anyone who casts or cast spells inside here. You need to not cast or use magic until I fix them," she said, turning her eyes to my mother's lifeless body. "I'm sorry about your mother."

"My mother…" I swallowed hard as I felt for the pain, and yet nothing. I felt nothing, as if something was holding the pain back from me. I swallowed again as I shook my head. I shook my head; denial clung to my tongue as I continued shaking my head. This wasn't happening. Not now, not when we'd been doing everything we could to prevent this from happening, to save the world! "No. No, this isn't real." I stared at her, waiting for the pain to rip me asunder, to tear me apart and yet there was only a cold detachment and denial in the place where it should have been. "They sent us away, and then they did this. What kind of angel would send people to their deaths and then murder innocent people?"

"The kind who think they're right. They think they're saving the world, so in their heads, we're the bad guys," Ryder expelled on a sigh. "Zahruk, catch their scent and get the hounds out covering every inch of this town searching for Kendra. Her time is near, and I fear they may not care or wait for her to have the child before they remove it. Zealots who fear what they cannot understand don't need a reason to murder innocent people."

"On it," he said as he moved to the table and placed my mother onto it.

Joshua stepped closer, closing her eyes as he turned to look at me. "I'm going with."

"Go," I said softly as I stared at my mother, the woman who had given me life. "Where's Alden?" I asked, knowing he wouldn't have left my mother unprotected.

"No," Synthia growled as her head snapped up at my words. Her violet eyes moved me to my mother, and then out the door. "Find him, now!" she demanded and blinked back black tears as I stepped to the corpse and pushed her blonde hair back from her face.

There wasn't a single mark on her that I could identify or find, and yet her heart wasn't beating. She looked peaceful in death, as if she was sleeping. I touched her cheek, lowering my mouth to her forehead as I placed a gentle kiss against the cold flesh.

"I'll fucking slaughter them all," I promised. "I will avenge you, mother. I promise you that," I sobbed as I shook my head, stepping back and feeling his presence before he even materialized behind me.

"Why are the wards down?" Lucian demanded and then his midnight depths settled on my mother's unmoving body, and he expelled a breath before he pulled me against him. "What the fuck happened? How did they get in?"

"We let them in," I uttered through rage and despair. "We let them in, and they killed her, and have my sister. They're going to murder her and her unborn child."

"No, they won't," he growled. "Spyder, find them, and the moment you do, fucking destroy them all."

"My pleasure," he chuckled as he stepped closer, running his finger down my cheek before leaning over and kissing it. "I will bring you their heads, kitty. I'll make sure they die screaming."

"They have Alden and Sarah, we need them back too," Synthia added as she helped a man sit up, his head a mass of cuts and bruises. "I want them brought back alive; they need to suffer for what they did."

"They're archangels, Pet. They aren't easily killed. If they are to die, it will need to be done swiftly, before they sense it coming. I'm going with him, to see if I can help them."

"You can't become shadows, I can. I can also kill angels whereas you cannot. You'll only hinder me."

Ryder stared at Spyder, and I hissed. "You can compare dicks later, find my sister!"

They vanished, and I stared at the blood that covered the floors and then Synthia's gaze as she did the same. Someone had fought hard...

I didn't wait to see if they followed as I rushed through the room, following the blood until we were down in the catacombs. I came to a stop as a bloody heap came into view.

"Oh, Alden," I murmured as I dropped to my knees beside him. Ristan was there instantly, his hands pulling the man closer, onto his side.

"Get Vlad, now!" he shouted as Synthia watched with wide eyes, horror shining in them. "He'll live."

"How did he get down here?" I asked, searching the shadows around us.

"Who cares?" Synthia snapped.

"Something dragged him down here and then left him. It was feeding off of him!" I shouted back, watching as the others lifted their eyes and then stared down at the bite marks in Alden's legs.

"We're not safe here," she uttered. She grabbed Alden's hand and then stared into the shadows, and then they shone with light. She lit the shadows up until there was no place to hide, nowhere for the monsters to go. I didn't move, didn't need to as she let loose a scream that misted the monster's into ashes, her own anger a palpable thing as she let go of the hold she held on it. "Nobody comes into my sanctuary and fucks with my people!"

"They left it open to be attacked," I swallowed as

Ristan's frown confirmed it. "I could almost understand their need to stop the child of Lucifer from being born, but to leave the Guild open to attack after sending us out to die, that I can't understand."

"War doesn't make sense, ever. Don't try to understand their logic, or why they did something evil. Evil doesn't make sense, it just happens, and you deal with it after it does," Synthia said as we watched Vlad sift in, his silver eyes taking in the damage done to Alden, along with the blood loss.

"I can't," Vlad whispered. "I can only try to save him, but Alden doesn't want immortality."

"I don't care what he wants, he doesn't get to leave me," she snapped. "Fix him, or turn him. I will not lose any more people today." She paused, turning to stare at me as tears filled her eyes. "We seriously need a win, people. We need the wards down, replaced, and then we need to get the wounded to Faery where they will be safe. After that, we need a fucking plan that gets us closer to ending this war because I'm sick of hiding and licking our wounds as they throw punches."

"Then let's do this," I uttered as I stepped closer to her, watching as Vlad pushed a needle into Alden's vein and started the transfusion. "He will need to heal mentally."

"He's the strongest man I know," she stated.

"He just lost the love of his life," I mumbled. "My mother…is dead." Tears slid from my face as I turned to find Lucian watching me from where he leaned against the wall, staring. "Find her, Lucian. Before it's too late," I begged, uncaring that it exposed my weakness, or that it was a plea. She was my sister, my twin. I sent my emotions and senses searching for the bond but felt nothing, only an emptiness where it had once been, severed in death.

CHAPTER
thirty-two

The storm is temporary but the love is forever.
~Anonymous Author

Day turned into night as we waited; every minute seemed like an endless vigil of hopelessness as we prayed to any God listening to bring them back alive. I struggled through emotions, the basic need to mourn my mother, and yet the coldness inside my body seemed at odds with what it took or needed. I'd felt the tears slip over an hour ago and yet they seemed to come and go, as if I felt it, and yet…didn't fully accept it? It was a war that seemed to be waging in my mind. I knew she was gone, I felt it. I felt the stab of pain that every once in a while would creep up and seem to strangle me out of the blue, but then just as quickly as it had come, it vanished, and I was empty again.

Joshua sat beside me, silent as he stared at the funeral pyres we'd erected for our mother and coven which seemed to spread out further than the eye could see. Over fifty bodies lay bathed, wrapped and ready to receive their final rites. Our entire coven was gone, missing, or dead. It seemed like a nightmare I wouldn't awake from, and yet in the place where my heart ached, it ceased to beat. As if it was protecting myself from the pain it knew I held.

Lucian placed his hand on my knee, and I stared at it, the warmth it spread through me was comforting and yet unneeded. I was missing a part of me, that part that should be screaming hysterically, bawling my eyes out because I'd lost my mother.

"Lena, how are you feeling?" Lucian pried, his eyes seeming to burn with the question as he stared at my side profile since I refused to look at either him or Joshua.

Alden was being given vampire blood, recuperating from being dinner to some unknown monster that had entered the Guild to feed. My mother was dead, and my family missing, and he wanted to know how I felt? I didn't even know how I felt.

"Empty," I admitted as I swallowed past the lump in my throat. "I feel…numb. I'm hollow, like I'm missing a part of me. I know I should be screaming, or crying, or shit, anything but this cold unfeelingness that I feel, right?" I reached for Joshua's hand, curling my fingers around it as I shook my head. "I feel pissed, like I need to kill things, anything. I can't just sit here doing nothing, it's too much."

"You're in shock. I saw a lot of it in Afghanistan. You don't sense what happened, you just keep moving. Not feeling it or giving into the pain of the loss you witnessed seemed to work, until you're alone and it's the only thing you do know. I think I'm in shock too because I'm just… numbed to what I should feel," he stated as his fingers tightened around mine.

"We should be screaming or crying," I uttered through

a heavy tongue. "So why aren't we?"

No, the truth was I couldn't feel her loss, not fully. I couldn't feel shit right now, as if all my emotions had gone mute other than rage and anger. Sure, it felt like something was squeezing my heart, or tearing it out, but not the debilitating pain I'd felt at losing Joshua, which is what I should feel, right? I wanted to burn down the world, to dance in the blood of the archangels as I bathed in their entrails. It was all wrong.

"I want to feel their organs as they turn to dust in my hands," I amended. "I want to drink their blood, and paint my flesh with their blood."

"That's…that's one way to cope with it," he said as he scratched his head, staring at me. "I feel sad, and lost. I feel like I lost my mother," he admitted, and I turned empty eyes to him, watching as a black tear slid down his cheek. "We lost our mother, and yet we have not even considered bringing her back. She's our mother."

"She is gone," I stated firmly. "She wouldn't have wanted to be like we are, or be immortal. She made it clear when shit started happening at home that if her time came, we let her go. I promised her."

"You did what? You knew immortals existed and that vampires were real and you promised to let her go?" he cried angrily, his hand dropping away from mine as he stared at me.

"I promised to honor her wish to go when her time was here, and so it has come," I said gently as I frowned. "I know you want to bring her back, but look at us. Look at how wrong we are, we're not even processing her death; instead, we are sitting here staring at her corpse as we prepare to burn it."

"You're not thinking of bringing her back, but I am,

so who is the wrong one?"

"I am what I was created to be, what you brought me back to be, Joshua. I cannot change that. I know if I had a soul, I'd feel her loss so fucking completely that I'd be shattered, but I don't. You got to retain a part of yours, but mine is gone. The sliver I have never loved her, I'm not sure it ever loved anyone. Maybe that is why I feel this weirdness in my being? You want me to scream and cry with you? I'll do it, but I won't feel it. I loved my mother, in life, I loved her so fucking much that it hurt, but I'm not the same, and neither are you. You want me to rip the creatures that did this to tiny pieces and eat their souls? That I can do, and I'll relish every second of it. But mourning her loss? I don't feel the earth-shattering sadness I should. Maybe Hades can bring her back?"

"She isn't like you," Hades's deep voice emitted as he appeared before me, his violet eyes moving between us and my mother's corpse. "Her sacrifice wasn't pure; it was to protect herself, not Kendra. She cannot be brought back as you were, her soul is already gone. When I brought you two back, you wanted to come back. You were just hovering between life and death, reaching for Nyx and her power to bring you back. Your mother made a choice, and where she is now, it's so much better than what we face. You should have known the angels were here for the child, Lucian. When have those selfish, self-serving pricks ever stepped out to help without having alternative motives?" He spat onto the steps, as if it was vile on his tongue.

"I was busy hunting for something that's been lost a long time. Something that can hold the devil himself," Lucian stated as he stood up and stared down Hades.

"And the warehouse?" Hades asked as he pushed his

thick, midnight hair out of his face.

"It was a trap, one meant to kill us," I admitted.

"And yet you didn't die?" he countered.

"No, we had Erie with us to dismantle any wards, but the moment she began to search them for a way to bring them down, it triggered a failsafe in the wards, and gargoyles awoke to attack us."

"Gargoyles?" he shivered. "Nasty pricks, those little buggers."

"Buggers?" I frowned. "They meant to rip us apart."

"I'm sure they did, but that shouldn't have stopped you. Lucian, you fancy a trip to an angel warehouse? I could use a workout."

"Lena?" he asked, watching as I slid my gaze back to my mother and then to Joshua.

"I'm staying," I uttered as I slid my fingers back to Joshua's and held his hand. "My family needs me more than you do. Kendra is still lost."

"Gods, they took her?" Hades huffed. "The fucking hell did you guys do? Leave those bloody bastards alone here while you went off to search for shit?"

"They're archangels; they're supposed to protect people."

"That's your first mistake, Lena. They serve no one but their own needs; they brought heaven to its knees *with* Lucifer."

I swallowed hard as I stared up at him. "They're working with him?"

"Those particular ones, yes," he nodded. "Raphael helped kill a few others, Diana included, you met her briefly, I believe. There's only one being who could kill an archangel minus current company and a shadow who seems to have gone missing, and that's Luc. I'm sorry, but you fuckers got played. And it looks like it cost you an entire coven's worth of witches."

I stared out across the funeral pyres that were being built and realized it had cost us greatly. Assuming they'd been on our side had lowered our guard, and we'd rushed at the chance to bring Lucifer to heel, and in doing so, we'd lost most of the coven, and a few humans in the process.

"They came for the witches," I uttered thickly. "They wanted them out of play, why?"

"They have ancient ones who need new bodies, and the only way they can transfer souls is to have ones who match them in magic and power. My guess, they needed vessels to transfer into. A Sarah suit would indeed be something they'd want, and need."

I stared at Hades and then opened my mouth and closed it. My teeth gritted as anger shot through me, unfurling my wings to deadly tips as I rose and faced him.

"The warehouse can wait; to transfer would take a magical point of the leyline. They're in Metaline Falls. At the house. At our house. It's where the leyline meets and dumps power into the Inland Northwest. Once they removed it from this Guild, it's where it began to push up through the ground. Lucian…" I growled, but he smiled, watching me with pride as I reached for him. "Take me home." I shivered as memories seemed to slither into my mind, my heart clenched as I considered the last time I'd been home.

For Kendra, I'd go back.

For Grandma, I'd go back.

To get revenge, I'd go back.

"Lena, the last time you were there…" Joshua argued.

"I slit my fucking throat. This time, I'm going to slit theirs."

CHAPTER
thirty-three

You are not a drop in the ocean. You are the entire ocean in a drop. ~*Rumi*

Lucian

She's darkening, deeper

into the form she'd become. Her eyes leak tears, and yet she doesn't feel the death as she would have if she'd housed a soul. Empty and cold, devoid of the emotions she should feel for the loss of her parent.

Joshua watches her, his stare unnerving and condemning and yet the rest who she claimed were soulless aren't entirely so. They house more of their soul than she does, she who has none of what she once held, and something Hades slipped into her as if she was a fucking cocktail he was creating.

It's not that I don't enjoy knowing that she cannot find release or pleasure with others, but that she doesn't mourn the loss of her loved one. She should be screaming, tearing the world apart with her loss, but instead, she's calm, empty.

I watched her pile wood beneath the corpse with a cold detachment that is driving me bugfuck crazy. I wanted to hear her screams, the denial that her mother was lost, and yet she didn't rally the pain; no, she clung to the cold rage that slithered through what she had become, and begged to bathe in the blood of those who took from her.

Fury: a mythical being who seeks justice for those too weak to claim it…How ironic that my girl would seek to right the wrong done to her, even though she herself ended her life. She no longer fears death because, in her own way, she's become it.

She'd become a winged warrior who craves chaos and blood in payment for those who took from her. It's a small miracle that she doesn't crave my blood for what I had done, for the game she was forced to play as I fought to protect this world from the responsibility I'd fucked up. I'd done this to her, my game with Katarina as I struggled to free her took the only being I craved more than life from me.

She faltered next to the shrouded body of her mother as Alden approached, his eyes rimmed red from the loss. He searched her face, scouring it for any sign she felt the loss, and then she wiped away the single black tear that slipped free.

"You will be okay," he stated, his grey eyes watching her as she stepped away from him, letting him touch the corpse of the woman he'd briefly found love with. "Fiona knew what the cost was to protect her children; she knew she'd pay with her life eventually."

"You loved her," she stated, her hand fisted at her side as she watched him with a detached sentiment.

"I did," he admitted, his silver hair sparkling beneath the moons iridescent glow. His flesh is red, rimmed with the glow of the immortal blood he'd consumed to heal as he had. He'd woken up pissed, assuming they'd made him immortal against his wishes, but then calmed once he had figured it out. Most people would kill for immortality and yet he'd come enraged when he'd assumed they'd changed him into a vampire.

"You need to back the fuck off," Joshua snarled, his eyes alight with the need to fight.

"I loved her," Alden snapped, holding his ground as the Fae sidled closer to the old man who had yet to release his hold on Fiona, as if he could will her back to life.

Personal experience told me otherwise, and yet I moved, closing the distance between Lena and myself as Joshua prepared to fight anyone stupid enough to touch his mother.

"Enough," she uttered thickly, her eyes slowly moving from Alden to Joshua. "She loved him too, Joshua. You can't fight him because he loved her, so thank him. Thank him for being there when I died, and holding her through the pain because I remember wishing one person would hold me when news of your death reached us. I had no one, no one to hold me and tell me it would be alright."

"I loved her," he argued.

"No one is questioning that," she replied sharply. "No one doubts you loved her. I sense her loss, even though I cannot feel the pain. There's a place that is…voided. As if her leaving has left a hole, and yet while I may not feel it, I understand it should hurt. I sense you feel it on a different level, and I wish you didn't."

"He retained pieces of his soul," Hades admitted as he stared at Joshua. "That's how he found you, knew you as he had in life. You, on the other hand, had no soul to save. You know what you should feel because you've retained your mind, but the soul is where we feel loss when it comes, and without one, you only know what you should feel. You just can't feel it because it isn't the soul you house's loss, but you're aware of it. Inside, you feel something missing, like something was stolen from you. Use that to find the ones who remain, Lena. You know how to find them and when the time comes, you'll save them."

"Shouldn't we go now?" she asked, her voice low but even as she squared her shoulders, no longer letting them droop with the loss she'd felt guilty at not mourning.

"No, it takes time to prepare to transfer souls into a body, and right now they're expecting you to show up with an army at your back. Right now Lucifer is holding your sister, telling her all of the horrible things that will happen to her when she births the antichrist into existence. She's safe, or as safe as she can be considering he sees you when he looks at her. You...pissed him off pretty good, Fury. Not many can say they've crushed the skull of a fallen angel and lived through it. Luckily, he wants you alive to use against us."

"Us?" I snapped coldly.

"Us, Lucian," he nodded as the words left his lips. "He's aware of why she is alive, and who brought her back to you. More than that, he's aware she cannot be killed easily, but that she can be killed. That is actually why I am here. There's a blade, one forged in the river of the Gods that can kill her. We need to find it and destroy it before he does."

"You think he'd kill her? He wants me to suffer because unlike him, I am not bound to Hell, or trapped there. I'm free to walk the earth."

"He isn't bound there anymore. Magdalena freed him when she entered Hell knowingly, remember? I do believe you spanked that perky ass for doing it. Then you impregnated her as the eclipse played out. Now I'm here to help clean up your mess again. The other Gods have been awakened, and while you may not die, Lucian, there are other things, worse things than death."

"They can try, but they will fail as they always have," I grunted, watching as he nodded but turned those violet eyes onto Lena, who snapped her fingers as flames leapt to the several funeral pyres around us. She silently stepped closer to me, her hand skimming against mine as if she wanted or needed comfort and then her words replayed through my mind.

She'd never had anyone to comfort her as she'd dealt with Joshua's death, alone. No, only the darkness she'd let in, the darkness she'd let me glimpse in the blood ritual had comforted her, and even though she'd died, it had remained inside her, like a viper waiting to strike.

Her face was bathed in the firelight, caramel-colored hair as she watched the flames lick her mother's remains. Embers from the shroud floated in the air, revealing the calm, petite face that looked so much like Lena's that my stomach tightened. I wondered if she'd have come back if they'd chosen to burn her ashes, to try to force the other side to accept her soulless body. Her fingers curled through mine, pulling my arm closer as she leaned against me for comfort.

"I have you, little one."

"I know," she answered as she continued to watch until the flames burned the flesh, filling the area with the intoxicating, obnoxious odor. Still, she remained as others dispersed. I tighten my arm around her, pulling her into my embrace as the Fae, Alden and a few others remained. "And we're returned to the ashes for which we were born, to the witches who called us into this marvelous storm.

I send you back to whence you came, I free you now in this eternal flame." The flames leapt, sending nothing but ashes into the sky with her words. She'd whispered a spell, one that released the souls of the dead, to speed their process to the other side.

"Only high priestesses can do such a thing," Joshua marveled as he stared at her with wide eyes and his mouth hanging over. "You're…you're not even a witch!"

"I'm…more," she muttered silently, her eyes watching as the ashes seemed to be sucked into the heavens above. Power, raw, uncut, unchecked power buzzed at my side as she continued watching her mother's ashes as they returned to where her soul had been born.

I held her closer yet, unable to get close enough to reassure she was real, that she was still the innocent girl who'd lipped off at me, and had grabbed my dick with a naiveté that had been addictive to watch. Those eyes lifted, holding mine as a subtle smile played across her full lips.

"I'm…tired," she admitted, even though she didn't crave sleep. She didn't have a soul that needed rest or to recover. Only a craving for what she desired and what she needed: revenge. "I'm hungry."

"You don't eat," Hades said with a lopsided grin. "You need to fuck. Let out the Fury that is trapped within."

"I have let her out."

"No, you've let her taste a sample of this world, but you're strong, and you hold her on a leash. Let her out to dance with Lucian, and then to feed on the blood of the angels tomorrow morning. She can't hurt him; she's bound by laws older than space and time to protect him. Let her out to feed, to show you what she needs to live."

"I'm bound to protect him?" she snorted. "He's

fucked."

"He enjoys being fucked," Hades chuckled. "Trust me, let her out and see what it's like to embrace what you've become. No more holding back, it's time you learned your limits, and who is whispering to you when you think no one else notices. You have two faces now, Lena. One is yours, the other is who you are to become. If you think you're powerful now with only this version of yourself, know this, you're weak. Once you can let her out, let her spread those wings without fear of hurting others, she will teach you what you have truly become."

"And if I lose myself when I let her out?" she asked softly.

"Then we will be right here to help you find yourself again. That emptiness you feel, that craving for more? That's her, trying to feel her way into your world. Trying to merge herself with you to become one. I've let you stumble enough, little she-cat, now spread those wings and embrace what you truly are. You're a fucking butterfly, fly free."

I swallowed hard as I stared at the composure on her face, the steel spine that spanned straighter as she tilted her head as she stared at Hades. I'd felt her magic growing and then slipping away, and yet I'd no idea she was the one pushing it away.

"Lena, we should…sleep," I offered, knowing she knew I had no intention of sleeping. "Hades, find that blade. Spyder is hunting the archangels, aware of where they may be hiding. The others are setting up a perimeter around their estate as we speak. Hellhounds have been unleashed, but we know they won't attack him. Not willingly, let's give them some incentive to do so. Everyone else should rest because tomorrow, tomorrow we unleash our own brand of hell onto the archangels and the devil himself."

"Lucian," she whispered as she turned, curling her delicate frame against my body, seeming so small in the clearing with the ashes still floating into the sky. "Take me to the club, where I can't hurt anyone."

"How did you know it was rebuilt?" I asked, and she smiled the most wicked smile I'd ever seen grace her lips.

"You have your ways, and I have mine." She shrugged as she lifted on her toes, pushing her mouth against mine. "Take me away where I can be free, where I don't have to fear hurting others. Where I can fucking own you," she added and a growl resonated from deep in my chest at her open challenge.

"You think you can own me? You can try, but not even letting her out to play will help you from me, little Fury."

"Prove it," she whispered huskily.

CHAPTER thirty-four

We cannot learn without pain. ~*Aristotle*

Lena

"You're going to wreck the club, aren't you?" he asked as I paced in the bar area, noting the new wards and structure. It was built to be comfortable, and yet to withstand an assault. He'd built us a sanctuary in case we'd needed one, but all the witches were either dying or dead now.

It was vacant, empty, not a single other person was inside the club as I took in the newly rebuilt place with a critical eye. Lucian had gone all-out, pulling no stops into the luxury that was his club.

Lights flickered on above us, and I spun in a circle, taking it all in. Above our heads were strobe lights, flickering as music began to play through multiple speakers. The song was quick and fast paced had my body itching to move to it. However, the plasma screens that lit up with gyrating bodies that seemed oblivious to us watching them didn't miss a beat as they fucked on a crowded dancefloor right as the person filmed it.

"Live?" I asked as I stepped closer, feeling a pull to the screen as the couples moved, dancing as their bodies connected and matched the beat of the light.

"No, previously recorded from another club right before it was attacked," he admitted.

"He's targeting you," I mused, hating that he was, in fact, the target of Lucifer's rage. Considering everything that continued to happen around us, it was surprising that it was tossed aside.

"He blames me for her death, and a few others he played with," he shrugged as he watched me closely, as if he feared I'd change my mind. "I created a room for you, would you like to see it?" he asked, his eyes turning to liquid pools of blue fire as a smile danced wickedly on his mouth.

"I'm guessing it was made with pleasure in mind?" I wasn't going to lie, the man knew how to fuck, how to destroy a girl's will and take a wrecking ball to her senses.

"Among other things," he said softly as he reached me and pulled me into his arms. "I burned this place to the ground because that beautiful smile of yours fucking haunted me. When I rebuilt it, I did so with your pleasure, and your needs in mind."

"You didn't have to do that," I pointed out. "Throwing a fit and burning this place, your club, to the ground was rather brash and wrong of you. But I do like the new look." And I did, it was done in shades of blue that matched my eyes, silvers for the dress I'd worn when I'd first kissed him, and the pictures that covered the walls were of me, things I'd done inside this club with him. Yet you wouldn't know it was me unless you had been there, been a part of it.

On the far wall was a picture of the dimples on my

back, his hands touching my hips as he'd fucked me, which made my panties wet with the memory. Next to it was my body on a bed, with his men around us as Spyder held me, his hands covering my breasts as my hair pooled around them. The dark head between my legs, biting the inside of my thigh was Lucian. Blood oozed from my shoulder, and yet in this lighting, it could have been anyone or anything happening. On the wall over the sex club's entrance was a picture of me in Lucian's lap and yet it faced outwards, an image of everyone watching us with their faces perfectly marked by memory and I smirked, remembering exactly how they'd watched us, how they had looked as he'd taken me with his fingers.

"You approve," he said, not a question.

"I do like that no one else would know they're of me," I admitted. "Except you," my tone lowered, thickened as I turned to stare up into his midnight depths. "You had these made before I died, didn't you?"

"I had them taken as they happened," he agreed, his hands slipping into mine as he started us into the next room.

"Because that isn't creepy at all," I mumbled as he chuckled.

The next room was hands-down fucking erotic, not because of the round alcoves for lovers, but because an image of me riding him had been painted on the ceiling. His tattooed arms held my waist, and my head had been thrown back in the throes of passion. The glass was tampered, lining the bar along the edge of the wall. I moved towards it, slipping behind it as I pulled down a bottle of scotch, his preferred brand and age.

"You missed me," I laughed, the sound deadened and yet the light in my eyes seemed to grow as I stared at him. "You put pictures of me up wherever you'd thought of me. Which means, you thought of me everywhere," I muttered thickly as I filled both goblets to the top, tipping it back to chugged it in an un-ladylike move.

"Someone people leave a hole when they leave so big and so painful that it never stops aching," he uttered as he drank his, mirroring my action before he pushed the glass towards me. "When Katarina died repeatedly it simply sucked. I felt like you do now, empty and missing something. I ached, but I didn't know why."

I swallowed as my eyes dropped to the glasses as I filled them. It hurt, straight up fucking hurt like someone had just punched me in the gut. Where was the fucking numbness at? How could I feel everything about him and yet not the death of my mother? He reached over the bar and lifted my chin.

"When you died, I wanted to destroy the entire world. I wanted to set it on fire and watch them all burn to death, to feel a sliver of the pain I felt at losing you. I wasn't created to love, to care if something happened to someone I liked, and through the years I've watched thousands, and millions of people being slaughtered and never once had I even fucking flinched, until you. Something inside of you makes me need to be better, to be more for you. That first kiss, I wanted to break your pretty little neck because I felt it, this pull to you. I wanted to fucking destroy you, but first I wanted to see what you were, or why you pulled me to you. Nothing before you had ever kept my interest. You did, I needed to know why. And then you grabbed my dick and told me to go have pretty babies. So yes, I painted your image everywhere and anywhere I saw you because I couldn't get your pretty eyes or smile out of my head, and even though you'd died, you drove me insane."

"Good," I smirked as I pushed his glass across the bar. "I missed you too, asshole."

"You left me, Lena. You fucking died."

"Semantics," I frowned as I stared up into his eyes. "You're more than me, so I had to become more to stay with you. I wasn't enough, not strong enough, not stable enough, not brave enough to face the world you live in. Now I am a part of it. I lost a baby, and yeah, I'm pissed about it. I'm changed, but becoming this thing, it meant changing who I was to be who I needed to be. I'd accepted the darkness, so taking the next logical step was figuring out how to wield it, how to make it what I needed it to be. Did it suck? Hell yeah, but I'm here and you're here, and while we may be losing, we have not lost everything," I whispered hoarsely as I lifted tear-filled eyes to his. "My mom died," I uttered as something pulsed through me. Pain? "I hate that you make me feel shit."

"You need to feel it, to let her go."

"I let her go the moment I slit my throat, Lucian. I let them all go except you, and maybe I did let you go. I never intended to come back here, to make my existence known, but things happened, and then I was drawn to the Guild, or something in it. I'm guessing it was you, even though I really didn't want it to be."

"Good," he tossed back as he touched my hand and we materialized in a darkened room. This room was dangerous. A large cross sat against a wall with shelves of toys next to it. A bench sat beside it, which looked like a sawhorse with an oval cushion on top of it. In the middle of the room was a bed with cotton sheets, and lengths of lace that hung from the large, metal frame that mirrored a cage. It had a door that led into the bed, and I turned, tossing Lucian a curious look over my shoulder.

"What the fuck is the bed caged for?" I asked hesitantly, and yet my voice came out heated. I blinked as I tried to figure out whose voice it was, that sultry tone that slid over my flesh.

"You, because I'd cage you in a heartbeat to protect you," he said sharply.

On the wall were pictures of me in all types of poses, as if he'd always been watching me. From the moment I arrived home, to the moment I'd left his club to sacrifice my life to save them all. I wondered if he had some of those somewhere as well.

"You were always watching me," I stated as I followed his gaze to the pictures as he nodded.

"Minus in the cabin with your brother, and the moment you left this club to do…to do what you thought you had to do to save us."

"Our son was meant to destroy you, to destroy everything I loved," I admitted as I watched him carefully. "Your seal would have driven him until he either succeeded or killed you. I saw it play out, seen my lifeline end in the sands and in the bones. I died no matter what scenario we ran or tried. He died as well, probably at your hands. So I chose to go out in my way, not theirs. I know you think there was another way, but if there had been, I'd have taken it."

"You could have fucking warned me."

"No, Lucian. I couldn't because you'd have locked me up and this, this world would have paid the price for whatever it was between us."

"No one likes a fucking martyr, Lena." He snorted; his eyes dared me to argue.

"And I'm not, a selfish bitch who knew I was coming back. I knew if I made that sacrifice, that I'd come back in one way or another, but you? You'd suffer for forcing me to play a game I never asked to join. I won, I won even though it cost me more than either of you selfish assholes were willing to give. Neither one of you ever sacrificed your life to end it; that was the cost."

"Your life never should have ended; you shouldn't have been the one to die. It should have been me."

"You weren't born with a monster in your soul," I pointed out.

"I don't have a soul," he countered, and I blinked at him. "You're not the only one who was created, Lena. Now, on your knees, so I can show you what that pretty mouth is for. I'm done talking, let's play."

CHAPTER
thirty-five

Our existence is but a brief crack of light between two eternities of darkness. ~*Vladimir Nabokov*

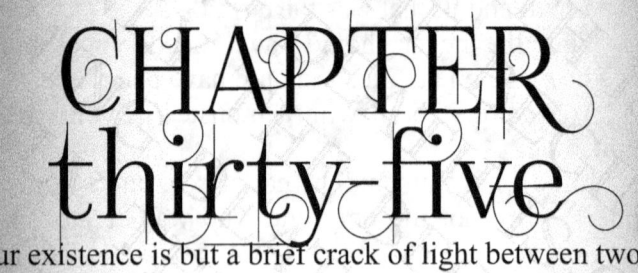

I grinned at him, starting to lower to the floor as he'd asked, but the moment my knees brushed the floor, power ripped through the room. I bowed my body, arching it as I screamed as absolute pleasure tore through me. He watched, his eyes alight with wickedness as he gazed at my body which was alight with every nerve ending being touched at once.

Moaning, unable to get words or even thoughts to register, he watched me, never stepping closer. His fingers moved and my clothes were ripped from my body, shredded in the heavy weight of his power as he fed me the full force of it. I felt my body being yanked forward, my ass in the air, exposed as something pushed into my core, filling me until I cried out as pain lingered, and my body clenched violently around it.

"Come on, little Fury, let's see what you got," he purred thickly, his fingers moving deftly to slowly unbutton the shirt he wore. I wanted to rip his clothes off, to ruin the suit he'd worn, but nothing happened. I screamed in frustration as the movement in my body grew faster, harder, his fire blue eyes knowingly anticipating exactly what he was doing to me. "Nothing? I thought you'd at least put up a fight. Pity," he shrugged as he shook out of the shirt and tossed it aside. "This next one is going to sting a bit," he chuckled, and then something pushed into my ass and I exploded, my body a trembling, quivering mess of nerves that fired on every thrust as the magic took turns exiting and entering my body.

"Son of a bitch," I snapped crossly as it lessened, slowly without stopping. I tried to stand but my knees shook too hard to even manage that simple task, and then my body was up, floating as he watched it. My legs spread wide as he stepped closer, pushing his fingers through the wet mess he'd created.

"I didn't have a mother," he uttered against my ear as his mouth lowered, biting the hard tip of one nipple and then the other as his teeth scraped against the sensitive flesh. His hand slapped my pussy, and I cried out, and then again as I was dropped to my knees and my hair was pulled, forcing my head back to stare up at him as he undid the buttons to the suit pants he wore. Magic rippled around us, and they vanished as he reached down to grab his heavy cock, pushing it against my lips. "Suck, show me what that mouth is good for other than arguing with me."

I sent my tongue down his silken cock, slowly drawing circles on the sensitive edge of it until he hissed. The moment my lips wrapped around him, the magical hold on my hair sent it down my throat and threatened to choke me unless I adapted. Then it started using me like I was his to do whatever he wished with. The fullness increased and my eyes watered against the sensation of his too-large cock buried in my tight throat as the overwhelming sensation of being fucked and too full shot through me.

My entire body went taut as the orgasm ripped through me without warning. He smiled down, and his thumb stroked my cheek as his gaze consumed mine, holding it hostage as he watched me sucking his cock. His magic filled the room, a palpable living thing that threatened to consume us both.

"Lucian…"

"Let her out to play with me, Lena. She's hungry and I'm fucking hard. Stop being a selfish bitch and let me see what you're hiding."

"I don't know how!" I growled as the magic started up again, violently until every part of me ached, every inch of my body was covered in sweat. My wings uncurled, pushing from my spine as he watched me, his cock taunting me as his magic used, consumed, and fucked me until orgasm after orgasm held me prisoner. I couldn't think, couldn't move, and if I died…well, it wasn't the worst way to go out.

I rode it, the magic and the orgasms. I accepted it until something inside of me lifted its head, peering out of my eyes to see what was causing us pain and pleasure. He smirked back, only it wasn't friendly at all. It was wild, untamed, and I shivered violently as the magic got stronger. He was inside of me, I realized, the sweat that dripped from his brow, his body covered in a fine sheen of sweat that drenched him in the most seductive way possible.

He was fucking me every way possible, all at once with a single thought of his dirty fucking mind. He felt it. He'd done it before, only I'd thought it was something else the second time…but it had been him. My ass ached, my pussy was one big sore muscle that clenched, and tightened around him and yet he just watched me come again and again.

Electric blue wings unfurled from his back and lightning moved in his vision as it pulsed through me, making my body hum with the sheer force of it. His wings mirrored mine, his body was covered in pulsing blue runes that seemed to glow from within, and when he opened his teeth, the blunt white ones ground together as he continuing taunting me.

"You're weak." His voice filled my ears, echoing off my head as he spoke to me through my mind. "Katarina would have played with me, she'd have…"

Power exploded from my body as I rose to my feet, staring at him. "Finish it."

"There she is," he smirked as he watched my claws extend as my wings grew larger, shadowing against the wall as I stared at him in loathing and anger.

"Finish it," I repeated, and he shook his head.

"She'd have played with me. She'd have let her monster out to have fun."

I attacked, slamming my fist against nose as he picked me up and threw me across the room. I sensed his move before he made it, slamming against him as I shoved him into the wall, pinning his body between my wings as I hissed with razor-sharp teeth against his lips.

"I hate you."

"No you don't," he crooned as his tongue came out to lick my bottom lip. "Let her out, Lena. I can handle her, and you. You can't hurt me, and neither can she."

"Fuck that," I snapped crossly, throwing him across

the room before I turned and sauntered towards him. He smiled, letting that magic back at me tenfold. I dropped to my knees and then bucked my hips to adjust to the fullness.

His finger traced my wings, showing me how sensitive they were in my current position. He showed no fear for the deadly talons that they exposed, nor did he stop the magic as he settled between my legs behind me. His hand slowly pushed up my spine, and then he entered me, hard, without warning.

I screamed as he used me, his magic never stopping as he took me from behind, filling my body past its boundaries as he fucked and claimed ownership. His hand clapped against my ass, and then magic started pulling on my nipples, pinching them as tight as any clamp I could have imagined. Something sucked against my clitoris, and everything went black.

I went dark.

"I see that wild thing in your eyes," he uttered. "That monster lurking in the darkness," he crooned, his magic never stopping as he continued using my body in an assault that forced me to give up control.

I was riding in the backseat of my body. My arms moved, attacked him as my hands flipped him over as I stood, staring down at his body as if he was my fucking dinner and dessert. Emptiness. Anger. Blood. Passion. Sex. I craved nothing but that. I cried out a warning, but no sound escaped my lips, not anything but a haughty laugh that sent Lucian's mouth contorting into a deadly smile.

"She's...human," it stated from my lips.

"She's mine."

"You're ours," it purred, and then she moved to him,

straddling his waist as he shook his head, pushing her away easily.

"She's mine, and you will let her out once you've finished feeding, understand?"

"And if not?" she asked, her eyes surveying him like he was utter perfection. "She isn't strong enough to hold us both yet."

"Then help her," he argued as he strode closer staring down at her. "She's newly born, you're not. You're recycled through the ages, Fury. She holds three of you in her, three. No other woman has ever been strong enough to bear that burden and survive it. She is. So you will teach her, because she needs you. We all do. Your power is hers to call upon, so teach her how to wield it or go back to your eternal slumber, forever. I will take Nyx's heed to be sure you can never be awoken again."

I flinched, she flinched, and it was awkward.

"She's aware of what you threaten her mother with," she hissed. "She sees you now, what you will us to see."

"I let her see it before you took control. That girl? I will destroy this entire world to protect. She's mine. She is everything good in this world and so much fucking more. And Nyx isn't her mother, her mother was just sent to the otherworld on a funeral pyre she erected and set blaze to."

Sadness filled me and then something was touching me inside my body. Hands held me, cradling me as if they offered comfort and yet didn't really know how to do so. I felt the loss; my body trembled as all the emotions I hadn't felt hit me at once. And just as quickly as they'd come, they were gone.

"She has experienced much and yet she is stronger because of it. Weird; normally mortals snap or break into worthless piles of shit when they feel too much."

"You'll also give her back her emotions, her pleasure to feel other men. You will give her back everything Hades took, except her mortality and then you'll help her heal from within. You will teach her how to wield the power of the three Furies. She's going to set this world on fire, and she needs you to show her how. So stop being selfish bitches and do what you were awoken to do, save her."

"We're awoken to protect you from her, and what she holds within her," she hissed. "If you're opened, this world and every other world will die. You will kill them all. Ahh," she said as I perked my ears and shivered. "She doesn't know what she fucks, or the beast who rides her for pleasure, does she?"

"No, and if you tell her I will pull you from her body and show you why the Gods tremble in my presence." She shivered and just like that, she was gone. "There's my girl."

"You didn't need her to feed her, you wanted to threaten her," I accused harshly.

"Ready?" he asked, and then I was pushed against the wall by invisible hands, and he was there, pushing inside my body as he lifted my legs and then wrapped his hand around my throat, peering into my eyes. "I am the beast, the monster that kills and destroys other monsters, Lena. I am judge, jury, and executioner to immortals. So fuck me like you hate me because I'm about to do the same to you."

He bit into my shoulder, and blood dripped from it as I exploded around his cock and teeth, feeling every inch of his power as he let it out to play. Mine clashed against his, a mindless thing that tossed him away from me as I swayed my hips towards him as he lifted on his elbows to watch me. I'd knocked him to the floor, and then I straddled him as my mouth kissed my way from his navel to his lips, where I claimed and conquered.

He turned me over, pushing my legs apart as he fucked me without pretending to be mortal. His body moved faster than I could see, and I was forced to hold on or get lost trying to see his flesh, and then I exploded, lights blinking behind my eyes and the room was bathed in darkness, the only light was from his eyes, his wings, and the runes that covered his flesh. He tensed, rocking against me as yet another orgasm slowly took hold, claiming me in an endless pleasure hold that refused to release me.

"You're mine, from now until the end of time. Not your silly fucking mortal time, but mine. Even when this world ends and we move to the next, you're mine. Say it."

"I've always been yours since the first moment your lips touched mine, Lucian," I said huskily. "Now move, because I'm not done with you yet."

"Good, because someone else is here to sever the bond because he needs to let you go," he rumbled thickly as Spyder stepped from the shadows, watching me as I stared back, panic and something else ripping through me as I swallowed hard.

CHAPTER
thirty-six

She's my kitty, and I'm about to make her purr, and then, then I'll release her and never look back. She's a wildcat, one who can only be tamed if she allows it. *~Spyder*

"Kitty, are you ready to purr for me?" Spyder's thick voice entered the room as he stepped from the shadows, staring at me as his eyes slowly slid over my naked, red flesh. Lucian had left me sore, and yet here was Spyder, needing to sever the bond, which I knew had been building. It had gotten to the point where I felt him to the very marrow in my bones, which meant he'd felt us too. "If you don't want this, if you don't want me, tell me now." His gaze dipped to my naked sex, feasting on the nakedness he found waiting, willing. "You don't want me, tell me, and I carry this. I'll carry it to the end with me. This fucking craving for you is too much. It's consuming me, and I know you feel it too."

"What…what do you mean?" I uttered thickly, my body heating under his heavy stare.

"The bond that tethers us together, it needs to be severed and this, this is the only fucking way we can figure out how to mute it, or sever it completely. It followed you through death, into this new form. Remember Portland? That fucking need that almost consumed us? It's tenfold for me. It's never-fucking-ending, and as much as I wish it otherwise, nothing we have found has lessened it."

"So how do we end it?" I asked carefully, already knowing why he'd be here in this room with us.

His dark gaze followed my frown, watching every emotion that flowed through me as I stared at him. "I need you to trust us, to see if this will end it, or sever it. If it doesn't, and it cements it, then it will at least be muted. I'm going insane with the need to have you, to be with you, and that shit doesn't fucking work for me. You get me? I feel it every time you fuck him, and you don't need me anymore. You are immortal, and Luc can't touch you now. Yet I still suffer for what we did, and no matter what I do, no matter how much I fucking drink before you fuck Lucian, I feel it. You don't need me, and I can't keep craving you. It's not fair to any of us that we crave something that we no longer need."

I swallowed hard as I stared at him as a strange pang started in my chest. Let him go? Could I? He deserved to be happy without having to feel me fucking another man; it was selfish to keep him with me. The things I'd felt in that fucking boutique were things he continued to feel every time I was with Lucian. Because he'd tried to protect me, he hurt.

"Tell me what to do, tell me how to sever it."

"We have to give it what it wants, but instead of you drinking our blood, we will drink yours."

"That's it?" I asked carefully as I turned to look at Lucian who showed no emotion as he watched me. He stepped away from me as the candles ignited inside the room. The cage around the bed vanished, and he smiled sadly as he watched me.

I turned, staring at Spyder as he lifted his shirt, revealing rows of hard, sinewy muscle that rippled as he moved. His hair brushed against his shoulders, dusting the tops as he watched me. He dropped it to the floor, staring at me as his hands went to the buckle of his pants, asking a silent question.

"You'll be with me tonight, Kitty. Tonight we share you, just this once. Then, if it works, we won't feel this thing between us, or I won't. You seem immune, and I need that, I crave that numbness where you're concerned. I can't stand this shit, it's like being punched in the fucking nuts every time you two fuck, and this is the only way to fix it. I mean, you'll still want to fuck me, because you're you and I'm fucking hot and one hell of a catch, but it won't be this brutal."

"I have to let you fuck me to erase the need you feel?" I bit my tongue as it slipped from my lips.

"We'll take it as it goes," he announced. "If we can reach the end without you having to let me into that pretty naked pussy, we will forgo it, unless you want it. Lucian doesn't like sharing, but he made this deal to protect you from Lucifer, who is no longer a threat as he was. You're stronger, able to withstand his assault from the other realms. I tire of daydreaming about you riding my cock, and even when I'm not dreaming of it, I'm thinking of it. Everything inside of me screams to take you, to end this endless torture I feel every moment of every day."

"And you're okay with this?" I asked Lucian who watched me through liquid pools of lust that carried no anger or judgment.

"If this gets his mind on the fucking job at hand, and

you stop slipping your pretty blue eyes in his direction with that lust in them, then yes. I'm willing to let this play out to end it. He did this for me, to protect you. It is no longer needed, and he suffers when you are with me. He's done what was asked of him; now it's time to sever the bond, and I'm a selfish prick, I don't like sharing you, but that's what is happening when we fuck, Lena. He's with us, and it isn't a choice any of us make, it's just how the magic worked."

"I understand," I whispered thickly as I turned back to Spyder, finding his sleek, muscled body bare of anything hindering my view. Spyder naked was something to behold, like the Gods themselves had created the magical perfection that was him. His tattoos slithered, pulsing with a tempo that made my heart stop and stutter before it matched the heady beat of his siren's song. "This is… not something I'd ever do again," I admitted. "Just this once, to let you go," I squeaked as I dropped my gaze to his generous, thick cock.

"The idea is that this breaks the need we feel since it isn't us who want it, it's the magic that connects us. We're bonded; this should sever it, releasing us from its hold."

I nodded, shivering as Lucian stepped closer with a goblet that he sat beside the bed and tilted his head to stare at Spyder who slowly stepped closer, his hand reaching out to pull me closer. His dark head bowed as he watched Lucian, even as he curled my naked form against his. My wings curled in, hugging my spine as they disappeared as he dropped his lips against mine, brushing them ever so softly as he explored them.

"Can't say I don't plan to enjoy this," he uttered before his teeth pulled against my bottom lip, tasting me. His teeth released my lip as his tongue pushed into my mouth, claiming mine as a growl ripped from his lungs. Magic danced in the room as he slowly walked me back to the bed. Once there, he released my mouth long enough to pick me up and push me onto the bed, staring down at my naked sex as if it was his salvation.

His hand slid between my leg, leisurely exploring it as his mouth kissed the inside of my thigh, slowly, exploring my flesh as he climbed my body to claim my lips hard, no mercy granted as his tongue delved between mine, consuming me as if he was fucking starving and I was the air he needed to breathe.

Spyder's hands captured mine; pushing them against the bed as his mouth sent me into the unknown, fear slowly kicking my mind as his kiss devoured me. His body against mine was a potent aphrodisiac, sending any fear away the moment it grazed mine. His cock rested between my legs, scraping my flesh with its heavy weight as his tongue took what it wanted from me.

He pulled away, lifting himself up to stare down at me, down to where our bodies could join and yet he didn't move to make it happen. Instead, he lifted me, pulling me towards his massive frame as he traded placed with me. He leaned me against his chest, facing Lucian, who watched me through heavy, lust-filled eyes as he produced a knife and set it on the bed before crawling to join us.

Yet he didn't; he sat beside me, watching as Spyder tested my breasts before his hand slipped between my legs, finding me wet and aching to be filled. His fingers pushed my sex apart, slipping into the welcoming heat as a moan slipped from my lips. My eyes held Lucian's, knowing he was doing this because he wanted me to himself, and we both knew Spyder had given enough, and if this freed him, it was worth it.

I knew if we went too far, we'd cross a line and it wasn't something I'd allow to happen. Neither would they, which was why I knew I was safe with them. They were more than just best friends, whatever the fuck they were, they were ancient. They'd done this with other girls, and yet this was different for them. I was different from them.

Lucian lowered his mouth as if he'd sensed my worry and clamped onto my clitoris, sucking it into his mouth as Spyder pushed his fingers deeper, adding another until I was stretched and he growled against my ear. His cock rubbed my ass as Lucian used my hips to rock my body onto the digits Spyder wielded until I was moaning as the crescendo of release took hold, sending me over the edge as Spyder growled against my ear.

"Gods, kitty, you make the most delicious fucking noises."

"My turn," Lucian growled, moving his mouth between my legs to suck the arousal from my flesh before Spyder released his hold, moving his hands to part my legs for Lucian's kiss as he fucked my flesh with his mouth.

It was erotic, being with them both and yet something inside of me didn't want this, didn't want him to be in my naked sense, and as I peered down at Lucian, his eyes watched me even as the orgasm ripped through me, Spyder holding me through it as Lucian continued. He didn't stop sucking against my flesh until the tremors eased and he rose, rubbing his cock against my belly as he kissed me, erasing Spyder from my mind as he took control, took me back with a subtle reminder of who I belonged to.

I felt him enter me, and I screamed as I slid down his cock, and then my nails dug against his arms as Spyder kissed my back, neck, and shoulders as Lucian kissed the other. I knew it was coming, knew the pain that would only ache until it was replaced by magic, and then pleasure.

Teeth sank into each shoulder, and then the slurping sounded in the room as their heartbeats echoed in my ear. Spyder's hand drifted around, rubbing my clit as Lucian pounded my flesh until I was screaming and coming as they continued to suck blood from the bites they'd taken in each shoulder.

The room was filled with the intoxicating scent of magic, sex, and blood as Lucian continued to take and give. Spyder's touch sent me over the edge, careening for the cliff and then they flipped me over without warning. Lucian entered me from behind, and the moment I opened my mouth to scream, I opened my eyes to see what touched my cheek, I found Spyder there, waiting, his eyes begging permission as he watched me.

My hand gripped his cock, unable to wrap around it and then I leaned over, kissing the silken tip before my tongue brushed against it. Lucian's hands gripped my hair, holding me there as I decided my next step.

Let him go…

Sex, blood magic came at a hefty price, and they were willing to let me escape it even though he had paid it to protect me. I lifted my eyes to his and then took him into my mouth, pushing against him as Lucian held me there, telling me he was okay with it as long as it didn't happen again. He was willing to let this play out to release Spyder from the weird threesome we had going.

Spyder pushed against my throat, and I opened for him, using Lucian to push me further until the room exploded in magic and the tether of the bond released a tiny bit, and then more… I sucked harder, working his cock as he fucked my mouth even as the orgasm from Lucian worked harder, using me and my mindlessness to force him into the barrel of my throat. I knew what it took to let him go, and for him, for my friend, I'd do this.

I felt him tense, felt the bond clenching and then releasing. I felt him coming apart, as I came apart for Lucian, and then he pulled me up, taking me from Lucian as something ancient peered through Spyder's darkened gaze.

"You're one in a million, kitty, but you're not my one in a million. Thank you, thank you for letting me go," he growled before his mouth crushed against mine and then his forehead rested against mine as he stared into my eyes. "You fucking hurt him, I'll be the first to find you, and I will kill you. Do you understand? You're his hard limit, his fucking endgame. You're not mine. Fuck with him, and you'll wish he was there to protect you from me, because unlike him, I don't have mercy. I fuck to destroy." His hands cradled my face before he lowered his mouth to mine, kissing me. "In the morning, you won't ever think of this again."

"Did it work?" I asked, and he smiled sadly as he withdrew from the bed, leaving me on my knees with Lucian holding me up as we watched him.

"We won't know for a while," Lucian answered behind me, and I turned, staring at him. The door closed and I swallowed hard. "He couldn't force it. You doing what you did, it may have lessened it, but what the bond demanded, you couldn't give him, and that's okay. It's enough for us. You did well, but he'd never force you to do something you didn't want to do. Now get over here, because watching you with him turned me on. It was unexpectedly…erotic."

"You have never shared?" I asked, leaning back as I spread my legs for his greedy gaze.

"Share women?" he chuckled. "All the time before I met you, but you, you're not other women, Lena. You're not something I relish sharing, and he needed it to let you go. Even if the bond remains, it will not hurt him as it had, since you gave him release. If it remains, he'll feel you, but not on the same level. As the bond grew, it strengthened, demanding he claim you, and you helping him find some semblance of release has loosened that pull."

"He should be free of me, Lucian. I don't…I never wanted him like that. I wanted you, only you."

"And so you shall," he growled as he lifted my legs, slamming home into my body as with both exploded together. Fire burned through us, and my spine arched as I screamed as pain and anguish ripped me apart. He pulled back, his teeth clenched as he stared down at our bodies where they were joined and then back up into my panic-stricken gaze. "Fucking Furies," he snarled. "You had no right!"

"What?" I demanded.

"You just fucking claimed me," he snapped.

"I claimed you a long time ago, Lucian," I pointed out crossly as I sat up, staring down at the matching glyphs that covered my hip and his. They were strikingly beautiful, curling lines that swirled from our hips to where our bodies were still joined.

"They didn't claim me, you did. As in, you can never touch another living creature for pleasure, or we both die. We're now mated in the ways of the Gods."

"Fuck," I uttered breathlessly as the pain continued, my body bathed in sweat from earlier and anew as something inside of me reached for him. As if we were fusing into one being, able to sense the other without trying.

"Fuck is right," he snapped as he started moving.

"Scream for me," he demanded as he leaned down, kissing my neck as he sucked the quick beating pulse between his teeth as I exploded around him, my body clenching against his.

CHAPTER
thirty-seven

When I am silent, I have thunder hidden inside. ~*Rumi*

Fires bathed the mountains as we slowly approached the house, the night a mixture of flames and chaos as demons converged to the location of their dark master. We remained in the shadows, watching, observing as they danced naked, screaming and celebrating the coming arrival of the antichrist as they referred to the innocent life of my niece.

As if the birth of his child would signify the ending of this world, while bringing in a new one, and hell, maybe they were right. Perhaps if we failed, we didn't deserve to be here. Life was precious, her tiny little life was precious, and yet the archangels who paced alongside the demons seemed to be uncaring that she, a tiny little being, was being celebrated as bringing about the end of days.

"Kendra," I whispered, sending it through the bond with everything I had in me, all the strength from ignoring it since I'd come back from my death. I felt her stir, her

mind grasping onto the fact that I was here, with her. I'd never leave her alone, ever. *"Fight him,"* I instructed. *"I'm coming for you."*

"You won't make it; you need to stay away from here. It's a trap." Her voice was filled with emotion, pain etching and pushing through the bond even though she tried to hide it from me.

Her contractions were fast, violent as her body arched and then sagged as each one hit harder than the last. She was tied to one of the beds from inside the house that they'd brought out for her. Her mouth was filled with cloth, preventing her from screaming too loudly as the demon peered down, dragging the sharp edge of a knife over her cheekbone, yet it didn't pierce her flesh.

"You're going to die, whore," it crooned gently, *pushing a hand against her swollen middle as if it could force the babe from her body. She screeched as pain erupted and I winced as it slithered through the bond, threatening to take me to the ground as I struggled to remain with her.*

"Ignore it," I uttered as sweat beaded against my brow. *"It fears hurting you, which means Lucifer is near."*

"He knows I will die when I give birth," she informed tensely, *her tone a mixture of resignation for her situation and pain for what her child would surely endure at the hands of her father. "You need to go, get as far away from here as you can. He doesn't want her or me, he wants you. He wants to punish you for what you did to him. He showed you his true self, his insecurities, and you hurt him for it."*

"Kendra, we are coming, just hold on. Please? Please hold on for me," I begged and then she did the last thing I expected; she whispered a goodbye.

"I love you, and I'll always love you, Lena. I know you were afraid of hurting me, I felt it. I let you have your space, and I wish I hadn't. I wish I'd hugged you one last time, held you and told you how much losing you hurt me. I know what you are about to go through and you need to know that you're not alone. You've never been alone. You're my sister, my soul. My womb mate and my best friend. Life wasn't supposed to be like this, but you will survive this. It's going to hurt, and it's going to tear you apart for a while, but you will get back up. You were always the strong one. You will raise my daughter, and you'll tell her about me, won't you? You will be a good mom, Lena. You can't let him keep my daughter. She will need help that you can provide. You'll teach her how to love, how to live. I can go if I know that she will be loved. I'm okay with dying to bring her life, but I need to know you will save her, that you will fight for her. You think you're darkness, but you're not. You're the light that shines in this dark world, a bright star that refuses to dim your light for anyone or anything. Teach Makenna that, teach her how to be good. I love you; I love you both so much that it hurts."

"Don't you fucking give up on me."

I waited, searching the bond and then withdrawing from my mind as I stared into midnight eyes.

"We're out of time," I announced as I stepped from the shadows, staring out over the chaos that was ensuing. "She's giving up."

"We need more time, Erie is finding us a way into the wards," Lucian uttered as he watched me. "Tell her to hold on."

"She pushed me out," I admitted. I exhaled as I stared at Joshua, knowing he felt it too. Our bloodline was dying out, becoming a thing of the past. I swallowed hard as I turned, searching the faces of those who had come to help, and then sucked my lip between my teeth as I considered our next move.

Lucifer wouldn't allow anyone else into the warded area, except me. He also had acquired a dagger which could end my life, for real. But if everyone here fought, they could die as well. Wouldn't it be better to give him what he wanted, what he craved?

"Don't you even think it," Spyder snapped, his eyes holding mine as I struggled to figure out how to save everyone. "He will kill you for what you did."

"And if I die, and she survives, it would be worth it."

"She doesn't have to die," Vlad acknowledged.

"She won't accept immortality, neither will my grandmother. That's my people out there! They're dying, the witches are already feeding off the weaker of the coven they took, and the moment they're strong enough, my grandmother will become nothing more than a vessel to them! Give me another option, anything," I growled as the hopelessness swelled through me.

"They can't," Hades crooned as he stepped into the shadows, staring at us. "We can't fight him because we're bound by rules and laws that prevent us from intervening. Unless Lucifer touches someone who isn't meant to die, we can't intervene in his affairs. Not without giving something in return for meddling."

"What the hell does that mean? You're a God?" I asked, directing my question to Lucian who shook his head, his eyes watching mine before he replied.

"No, I'm not. Neither are my men, but we are bound by similar laws to not intervene in the affairs of mortals."

"So then we go in, and we save our family alone," I

argued as I stared at Joshua who nodded.

"I'm okay with that," he acknowledged.

"I'm not bound by their laws, no Fae is," Zahruk announced softly, his lip twisting into a dark smile.

"So who do we have then?" I asked.

"I can help, but I cannot intervene against mortals," Synthia said, and Ryder shook his head. "I can help her, and I will without being the one to end a life or change the outcome to one. Those are the rules I have to abide by."

"Synthia, the laws aren't swayed, and by going in with Lena, you will be changing the outcome."

"No, no she won't be. Kendra will die, that much we know. How she dies is different," I mused as I stared at her. "It's not changing the outcome of a life if we are taking one away from the father. I'm going in there to save my niece, not from death, but from becoming evil."

"And you're so sure she isn't evil?" Hades questioned.

"Children are not born evil or wrong, they're turned into that somewhere in life. If we can get her out, protect her from him, we can sway which side she chooses to be on." Joshua nodded, his matching blue eyes sharp as grief filtered through.

I wasn't an idiot; I knew Kendra was dying. I could feel her slipping further away from the bond as time moved, passing as the demons continued their endless chanting. I didn't need these creatures or Gods to fight Lucifer for me; I just needed them to get me close enough so I could fight him.

"You mentioned glamour; can you make yourself look like me?" I asked and watched her platinum head move up and down before a smile played across her lips. As I watched, she changed, becoming the mirror image of my reflection. "Good, now give me your face."

Once we'd switched looks, I stepped next to Lucian and touched him, leaning in close enough that he inhaled and then frowned.

"You smell like a Goddess," he mused as his brow line creased and he lifted his eyes to Ryder's, who smirked. "It's almost foolproof, and yet he may note the way you talk or walk. It's not worth the fucking chance."

"It's not your choice to make," I pointed out. "It's mine, and that's my family in there, Lucian. I won't let them die for nothing. You can't ask me to stand here and watch it play out. Not after everything I've been through."

"That doesn't mean I have to fucking like it."

"No, but it means you will help me. You can't fuck with what is happening, but you can kill demons that had their time here. You can take them out because, in the grand scheme of things, they don't belong here. Correct?"

"And Synthia, what is she supposed to do?" he asked as he watched me with worry in his inky depths, something I'd never seen in his eyes before.

"She's going to make sure that when that dagger is used, it isn't used on me. Lucifer can attack her, and she'll be immune to it. Get it from him, and then destroy it."

"You make it sound so simple," he growled as he pulled me in close and kissed me until my world teetered around me and I hung onto him as worry flooded my senses. This had to work because there was no backup plan. This was it, this Hail Mary we were throwing up as we went in to save my niece and maybe my grandmother, and then, then I'd hold my sister until she took her last breath on this earth and left me to pass onto the next.

CHAPTER
thirty-eight

I do not suffer from insanity, I enjoy every minute of it.
~Edgar Allen Poe

I stepped up to Synthia as we pushed through the horde of demons, the men fighting their way through them until we toed the wards that separated us from my family. Erie continued working, her hair slick with sweat as she followed us as the men protected her.

Kendra's pain-filled scream tore through the night, shaking the confidence I held as I stared at her, tied to a bed with her legs apart as her body jackknifed. Blood covered the sheets she had been laid upon, and Lucifer stood beside the bed, watching us as we ripped the demons around the warded circle apart.

The barrier itself was shaped in a circle, and on the ground was painted the symbol of the pentagram. Added protection against us getting inside? Probably. I turned my head, taking in the coven members who had been tied to chairs, some staring at the ground with vacant eyes as the death haze coated them, and others seemed mindless as they waited for death.

Four of the highest ranking coven members had been stood up, their hands tied to an ancient tree that sat in the middle of the yard, strung up with tiny slits cut into their flesh, draining pools of their blood into the earth they stood on.

Power erupted, and I turned my head, watching as Spyder's body disappeared, becoming a shadow as he moved around it, pushing through the demons which seemed to drop their human host suit the moment his darkness touched them. Lucian watched us, his eyes blue liquid as souls slithered around his armor.

I didn't dare reach for the bond to my sister, not when I felt her slipping further and further away. She alone could give away that I wasn't Synthia. I watched Lucifer as he moved towards Synthia, who tilted her head and spoke with my voice.

"Let her go, you don't need her," she urged, and he snorted.

"You had a chance to join me," he rebuked.

The wards slithered as he pulled her into them, his magic blasting her to the ground as she sagged, and I winced. If she could disturb the ground, we could get inside. I could get to my sister. Her hand dragged over it, and I pushed into them, forcing my magic to meet his head-on until I felt my wings starting to uncoil from my spine.

Not yet. I pushed them back, using every lesson Lucian had taught as I struggled to remain under the glamour Synthia continued to throw over me. He pulled out a dagger, tossing it into the air as he stared down at her, uncaring that I was trying to push through the wards because he didn't think she could intervene. Only it wasn't her who was about to burst through them. I added more power as he watched her.

"You should have taken me up on my offer, Lena. You could have been in her life; all you had to do was give in to what you wanted, what you craved when I touched you. Yet you played me. Now you've lost your chance to be in her life, to watch as she brings down the gates of heaven to Hell, and unseats the old God to become the new one."

"And let me guess, you'll rule this world with her? Through her? Didn't you try this before?" Synthia scoffed as she eyed me, taking in the progress I made as I fought the magic to reach Kendra, who was screaming as she cradled her stomach.

"She can't help you," he chuckled. "She can't even intervene to save you. Gods are fickle fuckers, and yet they stick to the rules because they tend to attach themselves to creatures, and if they break them, they lose what they love most. So no, she won't help you."

I burst through the wards and sagged as the magic hit me, hard. It was spelled inside the circle? I coughed up bile, and blood exploded from my lungs as I threw it up. Lucifer tilted his head as if it was wrong, and then stared down at Synthia who still wore my face.

"Interesting, since it isn't spelled against Gods, only…"

Synthia lunged, ripping the knife from his hands before she spun, throwing it to Lucian, who caught it and the moment he did, it vanished from his hands, and only a thick cloud of dust remained. I was up, moving towards Lucifer, who smiled.

"You didn't think I wouldn't plan to lose, did you, Lena?" he smirked as I lunged, catching nothing but air.

I looked around at the demon's that covered the ground, finding no sign of Lucifer as I turned in a full circle. "I knew you'd come, and I knew you wouldn't be stupid enough to rush right in. Though, I did leave you a parting gift."

I stared at him as his body misted and then reappeared across the grass, next to Lucian who reached out, his hand going through the image Lucifer projected. I swallowed hard as I moved to the bed, finding Kendra watching me with a sadness that wrecked me.

Her hair was slick with sweat, her body lying in a pool of blood that seemed to continue flowing from her. I sat beside her, cutting her free as I shook my head.

"Stay with me, please, please stay with me," I begged as I pulled her to me. Her hands clung to me, her body shivering as it went into shock. I felt the wards being lowered as Erie cried out, even as demons tried to attack her, only for a large male to step out at the last minute, sending power rippling through the area. "Stay with me, stay with me," I chanted as I rocked her in my arms as she held onto me.

"You have to find him, you have to save her," she pleaded as I shook my head. "He has my daughter, Lena. Promise me, promise me you'll find her and keep her safe."

"We will find her, you and I will find her," I promised.

"Not us, you. I'm dying," she cried as her strength flowed from her as surely as the blood that left her system.

I watched Vlad as he sat beside her, slowly opening his wrist and then before she could protest, he pushed her mouth against it. I watched, knowing she'd hate me for forcing this choice, for forcing her to stay with me and yet she shook her head as she smiled.

"My soul is leaving," she uttered. "It's protected. You have to let me go."

"Bullshit, you need to stay with me and fight," I pleaded softly as black tears trailed from my eyes. "I need you. I need you to fight this."

"I can't, he promised to make the pain end if I agreed to his terms. He warned me that you would fight him."

"Who?" I demanded.

"Death, he told me you'd find her, but that I had to go. He told me my time is finished, and I would know peace. I'm okay with dying, Lena. Because I know you will continue living, you'll protect my daughter for the monster who sired her."

"But you're a momma," I argued. "Kendra, let us save you so you can be her mother!"

"She has a mother," she said gently as she touched my cheek. "You will be her mother. You'll teach her everything. You have a second chance to be a mom, Lena. I'd have died, either way, even if I'd chosen to stay with her, he'd have figured out a way to have taken me. So I made a deal, my soul is safe from anything trying to turn me. My daughter is immortal, she's like you. Like you and Joshua, which means you can find her and save her, and you can tell her about me. Tell her how much I loved her, how much I gave to be sure she could live."

"Dammit, Kendra, you can't do this to me!" I snapped as I watched her flesh grow pale, the blood continually flowing from her.

"I love you, Lena. You're going to get through this. You're the strongest person I know. Find her, find them and make him pay for what he has done to us."

"That's sweet," Lucifer's voice sounded from beside me. I turned, staring up at where he watched with a squirming baby in his arms.

"Give her back before you ruin her!" I demanded, unwilling to let Kendra go from where I held her, cradled in my arms.

"Lena, she isn't healing." Vlad's words forced my eyes to his silver ones and then down at Kendra, who stared up at Lucifer.

"I'm going to find you, and I'm going to destroy you. I don't care if it ends the fucking world, so long as you can never hurt another living soul!" I snapped, and the squirming baby began to mewl.

"She looks like you, you know," he said, ignoring my words. "She has her mother's eyes, and nose. She's beautiful."

"And yet you will ruin her?" I uttered hoarsely. "Bring her to me, and walk away. Let me love her."

"You'd love something that has a piece of me in it?" he asked, lifting his electric gaze to mine.

"I could," I nodded. "I do, I do love her already, Lucifer. Bring her to me."

"No, no, she's mine. You want her? Come to me. Come to me, and we will raise her together, and eventually, I'll forgive your betrayal."

"I'm coming for you," I snapped, and then he smiled sadly.

"I'm counting on it, but then the witches are aware of you and are connected now. You lost, Lena. I told you that I'd win, that I'd rule the world and all you had to do was be at my side. You chose badly, she is mine," he said as he cradled the babe as if she was the most precious thing in the world. "I'm sorry about your sister; it was never my intent to end her life."

"You will pay for this!"

"No, he won't," my grandmother's voice sent my hair rising against mine my spine as I ripped my eyes from Lucifer to where she stood, her eyes glowing red as she watched me.

"Do it," I said to Lucian who stood behind her. I watched in silence as his blade came crashing down, severing her head from her shoulders where she'd stood. A scream bubbled up in my chest as Lucifer clucked his tongue.

"One down, only three more to go," his eyes roamed over my face before a coldness entered his stare. "I'll see you soon, my queen."

He disappeared, and with him, my sister's child.

"She isn't coming back," Vlad said, his arm still wide open as Kendra's head rolled in my arms, pressing against my chest as I held onto her.

"Lucian," Adam's voice pulled my eyes to his as he watched me. "I'm calling in my debt."

"Now?" Lucian growled.

"She's spelled to release her soul, and yet she's a vessel. A perfect vessel," he stated carefully as he watched me. "She'll be able to track her daughter, even if it isn't her soul in the body. I did what you asked of me to save the woman you loved, now save mine."

"Lena, they're...dead. Our bloodline is dead," Joshua stated, and I lifted my eyes to his as something snapped inside my head. "There are no more Fitzgerald witches, the entire line is gone."

"We have to remove it from the world," I uttered as I stared into my sister's unseeing gaze as Adam stepped closer as if he intended to take her. I growled at him, but I'd heard him. If I wanted to track my niece, I needed my sister's blood. I needed it alive.

"I'll make sure she remains safe until we need it," he offered, and I watched Lucian as he reached for her.

"What are you doing?" I demanded.

"Upholding my end of a bargain I made to save your life."

CHAPTER
thirty-nine

Hope is a waking dream. ~*Aristotle*

Life wasn't easy; it wasn't something you could win. You went through the motions, the wins, the losses, the hardships, and the difficulties that forged you into what you would become. You would get knocked down, and I had. It wasn't about getting knocked down; it was about getting back up and being stronger, smarter than I had been when the world shifted from beneath me. You could either stay down, or you got back up. You could either let it forge you into something colder, smaller, or you grew from what you endured. I had endured, I'd sacrificed, and I'd gotten back up because, for me, it was the only option I could see.

I would rise, and I would take down the things that had knocked the world out from beneath my feet. I'd carve my name into this world, and I'd find my place among the immortals who had become friends and family.

You couldn't win every fight you entered, which was

a lesson I'd learned the hard way. I'd lost my family, all in a very short time and yet I had managed to remain on my feet. I mourned, I ached for them, and yet I wouldn't bow to the pain. I wouldn't forget who had caused the pain, either.

I watched Joshua exit the manor house, tossing an empty can of gasoline into it as he walked towards me. I didn't flinch when he withdrew his lighter and set the house ablaze as we stood together, shoulder to shoulder watching the last remnants of our bloodline vanish into the blaze he'd set.

Life was tricky. Grandpa once said that you couldn't dwell on the past, because you lived in the future. It was the past for a reason: you were already in the future. I'd done what the darkness had whispered to me: I'd eradicated myself, finding a new creature that had lived inside of me. One who welcomed both the light and the darkness, and was stronger for housing both of them.

"Who will bless it?" Joshua asked, and I shrugged as I continued to watch the house we'd shared and lived in as it crumbled against the night as flames licked the wood. Windows shattered, and I smiled as memories of another lifetime played in my mind.

"I will if you'll allow me to," Alden said, and I turned, eyeing the man who had fought to protect my coven. He was covered in bruises, battered from being fed off of by monsters the archangels had allowed into the Guild, and yet he stood beside us as we said our final goodbye to our bloodline.

"Thank you, Alden. Please, you loved her as we had, maybe even more at the end."

"Just because you didn't feel it, doesn't mean you didn't love her. She loved you both, but she was terrified of admitting it, afraid that if she dared to love you, she'd lose herself and you in the end. So she gave you space to come to her, to choose your path."

"Honestly, it doesn't matter now. She's gone; they're all gone because we failed them."

"Not all of them; Kendra's daughter is out there, and she needs you to save her, to find her and protect her. She left you a note, Kendra did. I saved it for you in case she didn't survive this. She wrote it a week ago, knowing she'd never survive the labor."

I took the note and stepped back from him, watching as he used holy water to bless the house, to release the souls that it contained if any had been trapped, and then it began to burn. Long into the night after the others had left and only a few of the flames remained did I exhale the pain that threatened to consume me.

The Furies held it locked into a part of me that I didn't want to touch, didn't want to open. Not yet, not until I could actually face what had happened, and grieve my losses properly.

I opened the letter and stared at the words, my throat tightening as I read her last wishes.

Lena, I know it's you reading this. Who else would receive my last wishes? Funny how life works, how everything turned out, isn't it? If you're reading this, then I'm gone. We knew one of us would eventually die, but I kinda figured it would be much later.

So here's the thing. If she survived this, if she's out there and you're holding her, kiss her and tell her she was worth it. Tell her I loved her; that I tried to stay with her but that life isn't about choices, it's about living in the now, living the best life possible. I lived, and while there's a ton of shit I'd have done differently, or went back and changed, I lived.

You're a mom now, her mom. Raise her as we were raised, to love and to fight for what we believe is right. Don't fuck her up because I'll haunt your ass, and shit. Raise her to be like you, not like me. She needs to be stronger, smarter, prepared for what will come after her. She will never be safe with him hunting for her, so protect her as I know you will.

I love you, Lena, I hated you for leaving me, and now here I am, leaving you. Life's about losses, about moving forward, and you taught me that. Keep me alive with you, hold me and carry me in your heart as this world continues to burn around us, and keep Mom and Grandma safe, they need you. This world needs you because, in the darkness, you are the light that fights for us. Even though you think you're dark and scary, you're you. You can't eradicate yourself, it cannot be done, not even if you were technically remade. I saw you watching me, the way your eyes followed me around the Guild. That was you, you wanted me to see you, and yet it terrified you to let us in. Don't do that shit, Lena. Let them in.

You are my moon to my sun, and I your stars in the darkness, but really, it was always you who shined the brightest. You are good. You are everything this world needs, and now more than ever, we need you to fight them when we cannot. So fight, and protect Makenna. Makenna Sarah Fitzgerald needs you. I love you, I love you so much, and Joshua too. Fight for us, fight for this world, it's worth it.

I folded the letter and pushed it into my pocket as I turned to stare at Lucian, who moved closer to where I stood.

"I have to get her daughter back," I uttered thickly as

I stared at Lucian.

"We will," he replied, his eyes moving to the immobile form that slumbered beside the Fae. Her body was vacant of a soul, lifeless. Kendra's soul had passed on to be reborn, leaving the horrors of this world. I didn't feel her, couldn't touch the shell that she'd become even though her heartbeat continued, she had died. "We have her DNA, her scent to track her daughter. We will find her, Lena."

"And you're so sure of that, how?" I demanded, sensing the others as they began sifting out, heading back to the Guild to protect it. Lucian pulled me into his arms, his mouth hovering against my ear as he whispered into it. My eyes widened, my body trembled at the impossibility of his words as I shook my head. "That's impossible!"

"Scared?" he chuckled as he watched me process what he'd just said, what he was…

"That's not possible! That would mean you…you're… *No*."

"Eternal? Endless? The things that Gods fear? What, Lena?" he uttered thickly as he watched me pulling away from his embrace. "You won't leave me. I told you before, you're mine. I am a monster, one even the Gods fear, especially the ones who know what I am. Scared now, little one?"

"That can't be, you can't be!" I whispered, horrified as the world shifted out from beneath me.

~Lucian~

Three days later.

"It's done," Death stated firmly.

"It is, the Fitzgerald line is ended, they're no more."

"You really think she will forgive what you have

done?" he asked.

"I think when she figures it out, it won't matter. She will know what and why I have done this. Her line was marked for death the moment she escaped death. I merely sped the process for you, for him."

"And all this for him?" he countered. His greenish blue eyes scanned my face as I smirked, watching him for any fucking weakness. "You told her you couldn't fight Death, and yet you are the only one who could."

"He is everything. And we had a deal, and going back on it wasn't an option. I wouldn't fight you for her because I had already sacrificed them to bring him back," I uttered as I stared down into matching midnight eyes that stared back with no fear. My hand moved, touching the baby-soft hand as fingers curled around my finger. "Your mother misses you, little one," I murmured, watching ancient eyes as they smiled up at me. "She is good, too good for us. You will love her; she is so easy to love."

"He doesn't understand what you're saying. And really, Lucian, do you think she'll love you once she figures out that his life cost her the lives of her family?"

"He is everything to her, and I was the only one who could save him from you and those vile bitches you sent to rip him from her womb."

"They meant her no harm, and she made the deal. She sacrificed him to save you."

"And you knew she would end her life and yet you forgot to mention it to me. You should go before I decide to give you a final ending, Death."

He swallowed hard as his gaze dropped to my son. "He will end this world. He was born of what you are, and what she was. He is the Harbinger of Doom, Lucian. The Gods will seek to destroy him."

"Then I'll kill them all." I lifted my son, his new body feeble and yet the strength in his eyes was akin to his mother's, a force of nature that could indeed wreck and destroy this world. "A wise woman once told me that evil is created, forged in the fires of what life forces them to endure. He will be raised by that woman, and she won't allow him to become a monster. She's pure of heart, and beautiful fucking chaos, and she's his mother."

"And Lucifer's daughter?" he returned, his chaotic eyes watching as I cradled my son.

"Lucifer has no daughter, she will be mine. Lena will destroy him, and then we will raise them together. I will give Lena the world; she's earned it. I have played the games with the Gods long enough. If they want to continue existing, they'll leave us alone. Or…they will go to war, and *I* will win. I will bring this world to its knees for her, and further if I am pushed. Makenna is her blood, so we will get her back, even at the cost of destroying this world."

-The End For Now-

About the Author

Amelia lives in the great Pacific Northwest with her family. When not writing, she can be found on her author page, hanging out with fans, or dreaming up new twisting plots. She's an avid reader of everything Paranormal Romance and Urban Fantasy.

Stalker links! Want to keep up on what I am doing? Follow me below and watch for author updates.

Facebook: www.facebook.com/authorameliahutchins
Website: http://amelia-hutchins.com
Amazon: www.amazon.com/Amelia-Hutchins/e/
B00D5OASEG
Goodreads: www.goodreads.com/author/show/7092218.
Amelia_Hutchins
Twitter: https://twitter.com/ameliaauthor
Pinterest: www.pinterest.com/ameliahutchins
Instagram: www.instagram.com/author.amelia.hutchins/
Facebook Author Group: https://goo.gl/BqpCVK